Bluebells and Tin Hats

Pamela Cartlidge

For my sisters

Christine, Susan and Lesley

Chapter One

April 1933

"Pass me the spanner." Harry demanded authoritatively. His oil smeared hand was already outstretched in readiness.

Louisa quickly did as she was told. She gazed at her brother in admiration as he wielded the spanner around the nuts to reposition the pedal on her bicycle. After a few minutes, Harry straightened up and with a bent arm pushed back his thick brown hair from his forehead and surveyed his work. He wheeled the bicycle around the yard, then he swivelled the pedals to test them. Satisfied with his task he handed the machine back to his sister with a warning grin.

"Quick. Try it out before they get back!" he urged her. Harry's grin broadened and his blue eyes twinkled as he watched Louisa leap on to the saddle. She gingerly placed one foot on the repaired pedal and tested it for reliability. Immediately assured that the pedal was safely repaired, she pushed herself forward and away from the garden shed. Her confidence in the machine now restored, she pedalled along the gable end of their terraced home towards the lane. "It works Harry!" She called over her shoulder. "Thanks."

"Look where you are going, and be careful." Harry called after her. Louisa stopped alongside the gate of their small front garden and stood on one leg, letting the machine rest against her hip. She took just a few seconds to turn around to acknowledge her brother's warning with a wave of her hand. Then, smiling gleefully to herself she pedalled furiously down the lane and round the corner towards the bluebell wood. She soon reached the dirt track that went through the wood. It was well worn by the miners who trod it several times a day on their way to work and on their way home again from the coal mine. The colliery pit head lay on the opposite edge of the wood in the neighbouring village of Gresford. Sometimes when Louisa cycled down the path she would pass some of the workers on their homeward journey, their eye lashes blackened with soot and their unwashed skin pale grey. She knew quite a few of the colliers, most of them were in their thirties, but several of the younger ones were only two years older than herself. They had left school at fourteen to work down the pit. Louisa shuddered. She would hate to have to go down a mining shaft, not even for a few minutes. The thought of working without natural light for a whole twelve hour shift appalled her. She admired those who did it, but she knew she could never work underground where even day time was like perpetual night. She gazed around her. There was no-one in sight at this hour, as the men from the early morning shift would have arrived home by now. They would have already passed their colleagues going the opposite direction on their own way down to the pit head to work the next shift.

The late afternoon sun glimmered through the trees, and the scent of the honeysuckle in the hedgerow wafted in the warm afternoon air. Louisa breathed in the delicate fragrance and sighed with pleasure. She loved the wild flowers and being in the woods. It made her feel free. Ever since Mr. Fern, her

4

Father's employer had given her this old bicycle she had felt as if she had been given her independence. Her mother did not approve of her riding the bicycle. She told her it was unladylike. She often regaled her with comments such as "It's about time you behaved more ladylike, instead of cycling up and down the countryside with your skirt tucked up and your hair flying about like that. What will people think? You are fourteen now and as soon as a position comes up in service you will have to look more respectable! They won't take you on if you look like a scarecrow!"

Fortunately Louisa's two older brothers Harry and Arthur always defended her on these occasions. Their mother, a quietly spoken woman, though resolute nevertheless, always took more notice of the opinions of her sons, rather than those of Louisa. So on the occasions when they jumped to her defence, she would make an exasperated sigh and then turn away from her daughter with a vexed expression on her face. Then, for a little while at least, nothing else would be said and Louisa would continue to roam the countryside on her bicycle.

Louisa's father would say nothing and kept his own opinions to himself. William was a gentle and fair minded sort of man, and it was rare that he would disagree with his wife. Being a farm worker and loving to work outside in the fresh air with the shire horses, he shared his daughter's love of the freedom of being in the countryside. He tactfully stayed out of any potential quarrel with his wife and his daughter. He had been delighted when his employer Mr. Fern had given his headstrong daughter the bicycle, and felt he had to accept some of the consequences. For now though, whenever his wife became exasperated with their daughter's demeanour he wisely kept his own counsel. He knew that sooner or later, he would have to give his wife some support when they faced together the unpleasant task of sending Louisa away to work.

Louisa hated the idea of going into service. She didn't want to go away from home like some of her friends from school had done. Her friend Betty wrote to her now and again and Louisa knew she was very unhappy working in Kent. It was a long way away from Wrexham, but Betty was the oldest of six girls and her parents couldn't afford to keep her at home any longer. Louisa felt that as her two older brothers were working locally on Mr Fern's farm as well as her father, why should she have to work away from home? She accepted that she had to contribute to the household but she desperately didn't want to go as far away as Kent to work like poor Betty.

She dreamed of being a dressmaker. She was good at sewing and had a flair for designing clothes. She also thought of becoming a nurse. When she had broached the possibility of nursing to her mother she had been told her she was too young to work in a hospital. She had fobbed her off by telling her that she needed to be eighteen before she could enter a nursing college and in any case she needed a higher education to be admitted as a trainee. When Louisa had suggested she stay on at school to get a higher education certificate than the one she had, she was told she would be better off trying to get a job and to earn some money. The family couldn't afford for her to stay on at school any longer than necessary. Louisa was disappointed to get such a reaction from her mother. She had done well at school, was an avid reader and her teachers had encouraged her to be ambitious. She sighed. Surely there was something else she could do. She had heard that some women were now working in factories and others were learning to be secretaries, but her mother had been adamant that going into service was the best course. As regards dressmaking, her mother had said that there was no money in it, and she would be working long hours for little return.

The path through the woods narrowed and it was difficult to keep her balance on the bicycle, so she dismounted and leaned the bicycle against the kissing gate. She walked through the gate and strolled along the path to her favourite spot. Strands of honeysuckle had weaved themselves across the trees intermingling several times to create an archway of yellow and pink flowers. And as she looked through the loosely woven network of shiny green leaves above her head, splinters of the pale blue sky met her gaze. Standing underneath the bowers the heavy scent was intoxicating. Louisa breathed it all in ecstatically and sighed as she thought about her future. Everything was still undecided and it made her uneasy. She knew she would miss her cycle rides if she had to work away from home. More importantly, she didn't want to be a servant. Surely she thought, in this day and age there was something else she could do besides being a servant to the landed gentry! She would miss her family and she would certainly miss little Dorothy her sister. With a heavy heart she walked back to the kissing gate and aggressively pulled at her bicycle to turn it round. One of the handlebars had got stuck in the holly growing through the gate. She put her hand carefully around the handlebar and wrenched it free but not without catching her finger on a holly leaf. Blood spurted out which worsened her mood, and angrily she sucked her finger to stop the blood flowing. After a few seconds the bleeding stopped and she mounted her bicycle again to ride the short distance home.

Soon she emerged from the woodland path and on to the lane which ran past South View cottage. South View cottage was on the corner of the lane owned by Mrs. Gittins who offered bed and breakfast in her two guest rooms. Not many people stayed there. After all who would want to come and stay in a small sleepy village like 'Pandy' thought Louisa. She smiled ruefully as she acknowledged that no-one would really except of course herself. She took a deep breath and exhaled in an attempt to push her dismal thoughts away from her. When things went wrong for her, she had the knack of being able to put on a cheerful face and hope for something good to happen.

As she cycled down the lane towards her home she wondered if she would manage to arrive home before her parents and Dorothy. It was market day today. The first Monday in every month Mr. Fern took animals to the beast market where they were sold on to other farmers for either breeding or for meat. William also went and drove the cattle along the lanes from Stansty into Wrexham towards Smithfield. More often than not, Louisa's mother Mary Ellen would get a bus to Wrexham on these Mondays to do some shopping. And when she had finished shopping she would get the bus back and get off near Dorothy's school so that she could help her carry the heavy bags home.

Whilst her mother went shopping in the town, Louisa was left at home to clean up the kitchen, and to make all the beds. This arrangement had been in place ever since Louisa had left school a couple of months earlier soon after her fourteenth birthday. Young as she was and though she loved to roam the countryside, Louisa took her duties seriously. She had set about doing all her tasks in the house efficiently so that she would have more time to go cycling. So that afternoon she had wheeled her bicycle out of the shed ready to set off, and that was when the pedal had fallen off. It was fortuitous that her brother had called to see if she was alright. Harry had found her staring in dismay at the contraption with the dirty pedal in her hand. Fortunately Harry was good at fixing things, and he knew how important it was to Louisa to have her independence. He liked to keep an eye on her and he often called at home on market days to make sure she was coping on her own. He had recently bought a motorcycle and was very proud of it. The machine gave him the kind of mobility he had never dreamed of before and he often gave his brother Arthur as well as Louisa and Dorothy rides on the pillion.

When Louisa arrived at the side entrance of their end of terraced house, she saw Dorothy emerge from the garden with a bowl of blackcurrants and redcurrants. There was a heavy yield of soft fruit that year. Dorothy stopped by the garden shed when she saw Louisa put her bicycle away.

"Oh there you are." Dorothy smiled at her sister." Have you been far?"

"Just as far as the bluebell wood."

The sisters walked into the house together. Despite the four years difference in their age their similar features were striking and they could easily have passed themselves off as twins. Both had dark hair and large brown eyes etched into creamy white complexions. Having just returned home from school Dorothy's hair was in a much tidier condition than Louisa's, and Mary Ellen lost no time in making a comment about it. In the kitchen their mother was unpacking groceries. Both girls rushed to help her.

"Where have you been Louisa?" her mother asked, "as if I didn't know. On that bicycle again judging by the state of your hair. Go and tidy yourself up and help me butter some bread for teatime."

Louisa went to the small room at the side of the kitchen where there was a large sink and she washed her hands and combed her hair. As she dried her hands on the towel she noticed that a small sack of potatoes had been put just behind the door. There was scarcely any space to move really, as the room was not much bigger than a walk in cupboard. In front of a small window was a huge white enamel sink that was used for washing vegetables or meat. It also served the whole household for washing themselves.

Mary Ellen Edwards was a slender woman of forty years. A practical and efficient wife and mother, her plain-speaking and down-to-earth demeanour was borne out of necessity. At the age of twelve, unfortunate circumstances had handed her the responsibility of looking after her dying mother and her seven siblings. Whilst still grieving the death of her mother, one of Mary Ellen's sisters, Matilda had died at the age of six. These two deaths so close to each other, had

10

compounded Mary Ellen's grief and it had affected her deeply for many years. Even now if she ever spoke of her sister and her mother, unshed tears would film over her eyes. However, there had been no time to mourn, her father had needed to go to work and depended on her to run the household. She often talked about Matilda who apparently had been beautiful but frail and had died of consumption. Whenever Matilda's name was mentioned, it always brought an expression of tenderness tinged with sadness to Mary Ellen's face.

Louisa often wondered how her aunt Matilda would have developed if she had lived. In her imagination, she visualised Matilda to resemble her mother's youngest living sister Nancy. Louisa was fond of Nancy who had recently got married, and now lived in Ellesmere near a lake. They had visited Nancy and her new husband Alf last summer and had stayed with her for a few days. Louisa recalled how warm the weather had been, and how all the family had enjoyed cooling off in the lake. Each day they had routinely walked from the cottage and down the lane to the water's edge with a picnic. It was here they spent some happy hours swimming and enjoying the refreshingly cool water. During these few, pleasant days snatched from her otherwise busy life, Mary Ellen too was able to relax. By the same token her children were pleased to witness the tender side of their mother which was frequently hidden underneath her cool, capable demeanour. Throughout their short stay in Ellesmere, she frequently told them how fortunate they were to get a holiday. This was only because Alf was the gamekeeper for a wealthy and generous land owner. Alf too, considered himself lucky to get such a good job and with a large tied house. This, plus the fact that Alf's employer allowed him and his family access to the parkland and lake, was greatly appreciated by them all.

Aunt Nancy loved living in the tied capacious cottage. She had managed to furnish it, by renovating and polishing up old pieces that she had either scrounged from friends or family or managed to buy cheaply from second hand shops. She seemed to have a natural artistic flair for refurbishing, and she had managed to create a warm and inviting atmosphere. She was also very high spirited as well as very generous, and her nieces and nephews were very fond of her. Mary Ellen was very fond of her youngest sister too, after all, she had helped to raise her and there was a bond of mutual trust between them.

Having such a good role model in her mother, Louisa too was adept at her household duties and quickly buttered the bread. She made ham sandwiches for herself, her mother and ten year old Dorothy. They sat down together at the large kitchen table and ate their meal. After Louisa and Dorothy had helped clear things away Mary Ellen addressed Louisa softly and showed her a letter she had received. The contents shattered Louisa's day completely. As Mary Ellen read out the letter, she heard her mother tell her the dreaded news.

"There is a position for you in Wallasey. They need a housemaid." She glanced at her daughter's indignant face and expecting a protest, quickly rushed on. "It's a good opportunity. Harry can take you to the station on Thursday. Someone will meet you the other end and take you to Patterson house."

"But I don't want to go." Louisa started to say.

"It's a job Louisa. An excellent offer. These opportunities don't come very easily." She said this gently. She knew her daughter was distressed about leaving home, and she herself had some misgivings about sending her away, but she felt she was doing the best for her daughter.

"It's so far away Wallasey. Can't I wait for something nearer home?"

Mary Ellen sighed. "You could be waiting forever. These positions don't come so easily nowadays."

"What if I don't like it?"

Mary Ellen looked at her daughter kindly. "All I ask is that you try it. You might like it and not want to come home ever again."

"Oh don't say that. I will always want to come home."

Louisa's mother softened a little and said. "Just give it a go. That's all I ask."

Louisa wasn't convinced but she knew it was no use arguing. Notions of running away drifted in and out of her head. She knew none of these ideas were practical, and she had very little of her own money to live on. So reluctantly she agreed to try out her new role as housemaid. She bargained with her mother that she would try hard to make it work on the understanding that she could come home if she felt very unhappy. Worn down by Louisa's persistent haggling and aided and abetted by her brothers, Mary Ellen finally agreed and Louisa felt a little relieved, though not much. She dreaded Thursday coming, and spent most of the next few days cycling around Pandy. She gazed at all her favourite places, trying to imprint into her memory every scene, every swathe of flowers in bloom and every grassy lea. She hoped that she would be able to recall these memories vividly when she was homesick, because she knew she would miss them all very much.

Early Thursday morning, Harry took Louisa on his motorcycle to Chester train station. Louisa felt safe when she was with her brother and didn't want to let him go when they finally arrived at the ticket office. He stood by her whilst she bought her train ticket and he carried her small suitcase to the platform. When the train arrived Harry hugged her and wished her luck. He was distressed to see his little sister go, and he handed her a handkerchief to wipe away her tears which were now running freely down her hot cheeks. She held on to her brother as long as she could, finding comfort in his strong arms around her. For his own part, Harry was at a loss of why his sister had to go away into service. He had tried to change his mother's mind but eventually conceded that his mother was only trying to do her best for Louisa. At twenty years of age he was a self-confident man, strong, reliable and independent. He always tried to reason things out and was patient when dealing with people. His brother on the other hand was less patient. Though just as reliable and capable as Harry in many things, Arthur was less amenable to negotiating, and usually followed a slightly aggressive route to achieve the things he wanted. He had argued with his mother about sending his sister away but she had been unyielding, and Arthur too, had had to reluctantly concede. Louisa adored them both. Tearfully she listened to what Harry was saying to her.

"Remember what Mother said. Just try it, and try to be cheerful. You are good at that." He smiled encouragingly at her, hiding his worry.

Through her tears she nodded and said she would try. So she said goodbye to Harry and waved to him as the train pulled out, taking her towards another phase of her life. She sat in a compartment that seated eight people. Two of the seats were not occupied, but both of them were near the door. Being unable to get a window seat made her feel even more melancholy. She felt that not only was she going to somewhere she didn't want to go, but that she was being denied the opportunity to look through the window to say goodbye to everything familiar. She sat still as she felt the train lurch forward, replicating the sinking feeling of anxiety in her stomach. After half an hour or so she noticed that her fellow travellers were taking out packages of sandwiches to eat, so having nothing better to do herself she opened the package that her mother had given her. She wasn't really hungry, but as a special treat her mother had made her a blackcurrant tart. Half-heartedly Louisa bit into it and felt the bitter sweet taste of the blackcurrants. For the rest of the journey she could taste the semi sour fruit on her tongue, and the flavour seemed to mix itself up with her churning insides. When she arrived at Wallasey the first thing she did was to look for a Ladies cloakroom, where she wretched up the contents of her stomach. She swore she would never eat blackcurrants ever again. Once she had cleaned herself up, she went out of the station and looked anxiously around her for the person who would be collecting her. She expected to see a horse and cart somewhere but there wasn't one. Nearby a young man wearing a checked tweed coat and a flat cap was standing with a large card in his hand that advertised Patterson House. As Louisa approached him, she guessed his age to be about eighteen or nineteen. He had a thin dark moustache and kept playing with it with one of his fingers. Idly allowing her imagination to take over her anxiety for a few minutes, Louisa thought that the young man's gesture was as if he was checking to see if it was still there. Nervously she approached him and asked him if he was waiting for someone.

"Are you Louisa Edwards? The young man returned quickly. Louisa nodded. She was suddenly dumbstruck.

"Come on, we need to hurry there's a lot to do." He grabbed her small suitcase and she followed him up the road that ran alongside the railway station wall. She looked around for a horse and carriage but he led her to a motor car. "My name is Jack," he said as he swung her case in to the vehicle. "Get inside here." He opened the door and somewhat astonished that she had been greeted by someone in a motor car she got inside.

"You are lucky that we are driving in this motor car. There is such a panic on that the boss told me to bring you in this. The horse would have been too slow." He flashed her a grin. "Have you been in one of these before?"

"No never." Louisa said. She was impressed with the speed and the luxurious fittings of the vehicle. Is it difficult to drive?"

"Dead easy." Jack answered cockily. "Mind you the boss don't like it. He wanted it, but won't drive the thing, nor his wife. Usually I drive him around to work and that kind of thing."

"The boss is The Marquess of Borrowton isn't it?" Louisa asked.

"Yeah that's right. You will meet him and the Marchioness soon enough tonight. We don't call them that though, we refer to them as Lord and Lady Borrowton or the Borrowers when they aren't listening."

"What's the panic you were talking about?" Louisa inquired. She was beginning to feel nauseous again.

"Dinner party tonight. Cook's in a flap. Violet has gone and she is short staffed. That's why I have to get you to the house pretty sharpish."

"Who is Violet?"

"Cook's assistant. She was a good cook, but got a better job closer to home apparently. Didn't give much notice either, just two days. Working for a Duke now, or so she says. Mrs. Barlow is in a flap. She was relying on Violet to do the puddings. Violet's replacement doesn't start until next week. Looks like Doris will have to do until then, and you will have to replace Doris. Trouble is, you were supposed to replace Mabel. She walked out on us last week without any notice at all."

Louisa gulped. She wasn't expecting to start work straight away. She had naively thought she would be allowed to settle in to her room until the next day. But that wasn't to be. Jack had been told to get Louisa to the kitchen as soon as possible and he drove the car through the main gates of the drive towards the mansion. As they got closer to the main door, Jack swung the vehicle towards the side entrance where

17

he turned off the engine. He leaped out quickly and opened the passenger door for Louisa. At the same time he seized her suitcase and then disappeared down a flight of stone steps. He turned his head to indicate Louisa should follow.

A chaotic scene greeted Louisa. In the very large kitchen, sacks of vegetables were scattered in various places under the table. At one end of the table a servant was whisking eggs in a bowl and standing beside her another servant was peeling potatoes. At the opposite end of the table there was a very bulky, sour faced woman fashioning a rack of meat to what Louisa guessed would eventually be a coronet of lamb. This woman looked up when Jack and Louisa entered the kitchen. She nodded to Jack who told Louisa to take her coat off and wash her hands. He put her suitcase beside a box of apples and left her to it.

Without stopping what she was doing the sour faced woman who Louisa later discovered was Mrs. Barlow the cook shouted instructions to Louisa. "When you have finished washing your hands, put on that apron hanging up by the tap and come and help Olive here to peel these potatoes. Then when you have done that you can start on the carrots."

Sensing an atmosphere of intense frenzy and that this woman was not someone to argue with, Louisa quickly did as she was told. She managed to grab a tumbler she saw at the side of the sink and poured in some water from the tap. She drank it thirstily before she made her way towards the end of the table. Her stomach was still a bit queasy but the water helped a little. The maid Doris who was whisking eggs made space for her next to Olive, and Louisa started peeling potatoes. After she and Olive had done the carrots, they were

18

told to chop onions. Amidst the tears produced from the onion skins, she managed to find out from Olive, that the dinner party that night was for eighteen people and that there would be six courses. When she saw the menu Louisa was flabbergasted. She had never seen so much food and so many dishes. Not even at the farm where Mr Fern occasionally had dinner parties had she seen so many dishes of food. The Borrowton's style of living was far above that of Mr. Fern's modest entertaining habits.

Once or twice when Mr. and Mrs. Fern had been entertaining guests, they had been short staffed, and they had asked Mary Ellen to help. They knew she was a good cook and house keeper, so when Mary Ellen had agreed to help, she had taken Louisa to assist her in the kitchen. The food had been plentiful, but the dishes were nowhere near as elaborate as the menu Mrs Barlow was commanded to carry out.

All afternoon they worked hard to prepare the food with scarcely a break. When Cook was satisfied that she could do no more preparation or cooking until the guests arrived, she told Olive to put the kettle on and make them all some tea. Louisa was glad to sit down and relished the cup of tea handed to her. Olive passed her a dry biscuit which she welcomed gratefully. The biscuit helped to eradicate the horrible taste of blackcurrants still lingering in her mouth. She wondered when she would be able to go to her room and unpack her things.

The staff had scarcely finished their break when the first guests arrived. Wilfred the butler and Jack now dressed as a houseman were despatched to greet the guests and take them platters of canapes and glasses of sherry. Again all the staff were set to work with Mrs. Barlow bellowing orders to everyone. Many hours later, after the last dish had been served Mrs. Barlow sank in a chair and wiped her face. She told Louisa, Doris and Olive to sit down for five minutes. She then told them what they had to do next. She pointed to the piles of dirty dishes, plates and crockery that Doris and Jack had brought back from the previous courses and were filling up the sink and large metal bowls at the side. Larger dishes were stacked on the floor at the side of the sink.

"You can both start washing all these up with that crystal soap and make sure you get every bit of grease off."

Louisa was exhausted, but determined to do her bit, she followed Olive to the sink where they started to clean the dishes. They were about half way through, when Doris and Jack brought in the remainder from the final course. Louisa felt like crying when she saw the rest of the dishes but gallantly continued cleaning them. Just when she thought everything had been washed, dried and put away, and she could go to her room to rest, Mrs Barlow came behind her to issue more instructions. "You and Olive can scrub the kitchen table now and then sweep and scrub the floor."

"I'm glad you don't have dinner parties every night." Louisa whispered to Olive.

"What's that? Did I hear you complaining Louisa Edwards?" Mrs Barlow shouted across the room.

"No Mrs Barlow, I was just saying…"

"I know what you were saying. Just get on with it. The sooner you finish the floor the sooner you can get to bed. Don't forget I want you down here at half past six in the morning to start cleaning the fireplaces."

Eventually at ten thirty Olive showed Louisa to her room. She helped her with her suitcase to walk up four flights of stairs to the attic rooms. "You will be sharing with me now that Doris has moved in to Violet's room. She will be sharing with the new kitchen maid when she starts next week."

Louisa threw herself on her bed and closed her eyes. She was too tired to get undressed. "Don't we get any free time?"

"Not much." Olive said. "There's always something happening here, visitors and dinner parties and things. And Mrs. Barlow will always find you something to do."

"So If I start at half past six in the morning what time will I be finished?" Louisa asked innocently.

Olive laughed, tired though she was. "You don't finish until Mrs. Barlow tells you, and usually it's about half past nine or much later – just like tonight."

Louisa sat up in bed and opened her eyes in despair. "But that's not fair."

Olive shrugged. "Life isn't fair for the likes of us. Sometimes it's a bit better, if Lord and Lady Borrowton are invited to dinner elsewhere, and that does happen from time to time. Even Mrs. Barlow enjoys a bit of free time when they go out for dinner. It means we can finish about seven o clock then." She sat down on her narrow bed. There was scarcely any space between her bed and Louisa's. "In many ways we are lucky. I know someone who works like us in a family with two teenage children. And the children are very demanding. Horrible beasts they are. Poor Betty has to be at their beck and call and often doesn't get to bed until eleven o clock at night. She's always glad when they go away to boarding school. Things are better for her then."

At the mention of Olive's friend Betty, Louisa began to think of the letter she received from her own friend Betty. Meanwhile Olive handed Louisa a few clothes she had brought upstairs with her. "These are your working clothes for the kitchen, and this is what you wear if you are serving on the guests or the family." She pointed to a grey cotton dress and a white overall, and a black dress with a white frilly apron.

Still lying fully clothed on her bed, she spoke to Olive through half closed eyes. "We're just skivvies."

Her companion agreed. "You'll get used to it."

Louisa doubted it very much.

Chapter Two

Olive woke Louisa up at six o clock the following morning.
Louisa felt exhausted and was dreading having to black lead
the grate and polish the hearth. Olive had brought a jug of
water in a large, ceramic bowl and placed it at the side of
Louisa's bed. Yawning considerably, Louisa watched her
companion plait her auburn hair and then fasten it tightly to
the back of her head before placing on her cap with some
clips. Reluctantly getting out of bed, Louisa poured some of
the water in the bowl and began her own toilette. There was
not much space in the tiny room to move around, but
eventually she was washed and dressed and had tied back her
long dark hair. She twisted her hair under her cap so it did
not hang over her face. Louisa was determined not to make
her mother ashamed of her. She followed Olive downstairs
who showed her what to do. Olive helped her to begin with
but soon left Louisa to continue alone as she had other duties
of her own to do. She gave Louisa instructions what she
should do next, this involved lighting the fire in the kitchen
range. When Olive returned, she helped Louisa light the fire
and explained that from now on she was to fill the kettle to
make morning tea for the rest of the staff. They usually
emerged for breakfast at seven thirty. Then they all had tea
and breakfast together. Louisa helped her carry large jugs and
buckets of water from the tap in the kitchen to the range.

"You will have to do this yourself next week." Olive told her. "I will be switching duties with Doris. Don't take the kettle to the tap it will be too heavy to lift. It will be easier if you put the kettle on first and then bring buckets of water to fill the kettle bit by bit. You will just have to make sure you don't spill it on the fire."

Louisa sighed. "I thought we would have another pair of hands on Monday when the new girl starts."

Olive shrugged. "The new girl will be cook's assistant. Doris will only help in the kitchen when my lady allows her. Doris is going to be Lady Borrowton's personal maid. That's what Violet used to do. In between helping in the kitchen that is."

"So that's why Doris kept disappearing from the kitchen yesterday." Louisa exclaimed.

Olive nodded. "Yes she did the work of three yesterday."

"Why don't they get more servants?" Louisa asked.

Olive laughed. "That's a good question. Come on I will show you where we keep the dusters and polish to clean the brass and silver."

It seemed to Louisa that she spent all day scrubbing and cleaning floors, polishing surfaces and peeling vegetables. Then when all the meals were served, she had all the dishes to wash and the table to scrub before she went to bed. On her second night she and Olive managed to get to their room at eight o clock as the Borrowtons were dining out.

Though it was still light outside Louisa was too tired to explore the grounds. She declined Olive's invitation to take a walk in the garden at the back of the house. She thought it would be better to save her energy for the next day. She looked forward to Sunday when it would be her day off.

However on Sunday morning, Olive woke her at six o clock as usual and informed her that Mrs. Barlow was too short staffed to allow Louisa a day off and in any case as she had only been working a few days she was not entitled to a day off.

Louisa was extremely indignant and deeply disappointed upon receiving this information and was in two minds about walking out of the house and finding a way of getting home. However Olive managed to calm her down and assured her that she would definitely have a day off next week. Louisa, heartened by Olive's encouragement felt that if Olive could put up with such poor working conditions then so could she. So she got out of bed and resolutely performed her tasks. She was glad that Olive kept an eye on her and admired that girl's cheerfulness. She put it down to the fact that, as from the following week, Olive would be able to have an extra hour in bed whilst Louisa had to do everything else by herself. She dreaded it.

On Monday, Violet's replacement arrived. Her name was Nora. She was a little older than Olive and Louisa, and had worked in a stately house in Cornwall working herself up from scullery maid to kitchen maid and then Cook's assistant. As soon as she arrived Mrs. Barlow took Nora to see Lady Borrowton where they discussed the week's menu.

"Here we go again." Olive said. "That will upset Mrs. Barlow, she likes to be with Lady Borrowton on her own to discuss the menus. It makes her feel important." Olive rolled her eyes, and Doris grinned.

"Maybe it's because she's new." Suggested Louisa.

Doris nodded her head. "Lady Borrowton randomly asks to see new people coming to work here. If she likes the look of them they stay, if she doesn't they go."

"She didn't ask to see me."

Doris grinned. "Consider yourself lucky, I say."

Inwardly, Louisa thought that maybe if she had been introduced to Lady Borrowton and she hadn't liked the look of her, Louisa would have been given the perfect excuse to return home.

Eventually Cook and Nora emerged from Lady Borrowton's meeting and Cook informed everybody of the staff changes. Doris was to be Lady Borrowton's personal maid and housemaid. She would also give help in the kitchen when Mrs. Barlow needed another pair of hands, but only on special occasions. Nora would be Mrs. Barlow's assistant, Olive was to remain as kitchen maid and help Doris in the house, and Louisa was to continue as scullery maid.

"It looks like Nora is staying, so her face fits." Olive whispered. "At least we will have another pair of hands. Apparently she is a good cook."

"So much for me being a housemaid then." Louisa sighed indignantly. "They got me here under false pretences."

Olive sighed too. "Yes, they have decided not to replace Mabel. It seems every time someone leaves they decide not to replace them and we have to work harder. It's only because Mrs. Barlow insisted she needed an assistant that we got Nora. I don't think Lady Borrowton realises how difficult it is to get staff to stay."

However, even with Nora, work did not get easier for Louisa, if anything, things got harder. She no longer had Olive to help her scrub floors or black lead the grate which she detested more than anything. There was always a mountain of dishes to be cleaned; things to be scrubbed; and brass or silver to be polished. Louisa didn't think she would make it until the following Sunday. But eventually that day arrived and she stayed in bed until eight o clock. She went down to the staff kitchen for some breakfast, and then for the first time in ten days she stepped outside in to the fresh air. She walked around the back of the house towards the driveway.

Although it had only been ten days earlier that Jack had driven her down this very driveway it seemed to her as if it was much longer. At the end of the driveway she walked down the lane towards the village. She saw a lot of people going into St. Nicholas's church, but she did not feel like praying. Now she was out in the open air she felt that being inside a church would be too claustrophobic. Instead she sat on the village bench by the cross roads and stared miserably down the road. She was bitterly homesick and tears dropped on to her red scrubbed hands. Eventually, she took out her book and began to read. For a little while she was able to escape the drudgery of her work and immersed herself in her book, reading with compassion about a family who had lost their home. As she read she became conscious of the congregation in the nearby church singing her mother's favourite hymns, and Louisa began to cry again.

This time she couldn't hold back the tears and she gave vent to her feelings. She felt a bit better after her weeping, and continued to walk around the village. However she scarcely took any notice of her surroundings.

Later that day she wrote a letter to her mother and father, and then a letter to her friend Betty. She tried to remain positive in her letters, even when she described all her chores. She thought her mother would be interested in the furnishings and crockery in the house. She also described the dinner party and that there would be another one very soon. Once they were finished, she went out again to post her letters and returned back to Patterson house ready for the next day.

On Monday Mrs. Barlow announced that there would be another Dinner Party on Wednesday evening and that everyone should pull their weight. "This is very important for the Marquess." Mrs. Barlow informed them sternly and with some pride. She loved using the title of Marquess and Marchioness. "We have to make a good impression."

"We can't work harder than we are." Louisa complained bitterly to Olive. "Who is coming?"

"The Lord and Lady Wilmslow. Apparently he is involved in some family dispute. His grandfather has died and left him some land, but two of his cousins reckon they should each inherit part of it." Olive informed her. "The Marquess has been approached for his advice and assistance. Apparently he experienced a similar situation several years ago when he inherited this place."

Louisa was impressed. "How did you find that out?"

"Doris told me." Olive said smirking. "Doris overheard my lady talking about it to my lord when she went up to dress her this morning."

"Can't she dress herself?" Louisa asked. Olive burst out laughing. Despite herself Louisa laughed too.

Wiping the tears from her eyes from laughter, Olive said "the upper classes seem to think that just because we are servants, we don't have feelings or aspirations. Nor do they think we don't gossip. Sometimes I think that they think we are deaf."

Louisa nodded her agreement. "I would like to see the marchioness on *her* hands and knees scrubbing the floors."

Olive began to laugh again, but managed to stifle her laughter when Mrs. Barlow stepped out of the larder and glared at the both of them. "Have you two not got enough to do besides larking about?"

Apparently Wednesday night's dinner party was a huge success. Lord Wilmslow had been impressed with the knowledge and advice he had gleaned from Lord Borrowton. They had talked for several hours after their meal and had also consumed several glasses of brandy. So it was late before all the guests had departed. This meant that the servants had a late night too.

Despite all the extra hard work, scrubbing and cleaning and clearing away every utensil Cook had used the night before, there was still more hard work the following morning. Mrs. Barlow decided that Louisa should scrub all the floor tiles in the entrance hall. She said that they looked grubby due to the amount of guests walking in and out the night before. Louisa couldn't see any dirt herself and thought a brush up would be enough. This was not good enough for Mrs. Barlow and so Louisa had to get down on her hands and knees to start scrubbing. She was still doing this at half past ten, when she heard a commotion in the kitchen. Mrs. Barlow was arguing with someone - a man. The man's voice seemed familiar to Louisa. She remained kneeling down though she stopped scrubbing to listen. The male's voice came to her ears again. "I have driven all this way to see my sister and I am going to see her. Surely you can spare five minutes."

Mrs. Barlow replied harshly. "Her day off was Sunday, you should have come then."

"My day off is today, so it wasn't convenient."

"And it's not convenient for me today." Mrs Barlow's voice boomed. "Hey come back here. You can't go in there."

"I told you I am going to see my sister. Where is she?"

Suddenly Arthur appeared in the main reception hall. He stopped suddenly when he saw Louisa on her knees with a bucket of water and crystal suds. She got up with a cry of delight when she saw Arthur. In one quick movement he had lifted her up from the floor and swung her around. She put her arms around him in delight. As she glanced over her shoulder, she saw the angry expression of Mrs. Barlow and the bemused expressions of Olive and then Nora who had followed cook to see the 'intruder'.

When Arthur put Louisa down again he grasped her hands and she winced. "What's wrong?" he asked then saw her reddened sore hands. "My God, look at these, after only two weeks." He turned around on Mrs. Barlow. "What have you done to my sister? She is nothing more than a skivvy." Cook stared at Arthur open mouthed. For once she was stuck for words. Arthur turned to Louisa. "Pack your bags you are coming home with me."

Much though Louisa wanted to go home, her conscientiousness momentarily overtook her. Too tired to grasp the fact that she had an opportunity to escape, her mental reasoning left her and she became trapped in her own exhaustion. "But Arthur, I have to finish scrubbing this floor."

But Arthur would not take no for an answer. "Louisa go and pack now. You are not staying here any longer. She can finish it." He pointed at Mrs. Barlow who had now found her voice and glared at Arthur.

"How dare you speak to me like that! Get out of this house this instant and take that idle chit of a girl with you."

Finally Louisa came to her senses and pushing past Mrs. Barlow and Nora, she ran quickly through the kitchen and up the stairs two at a time to get her things. She could hear Arthur shouting at cook and was relieved that both Borrowtons were out. However she still worried that Lady Borrowton might return from her calls to witness the disturbance that Arthur was causing. She hurriedly packed her few things together and was soon ready to leave.

By the time Louisa had started to climb down the final staircase leading on to the kitchen, Cook had returned to the kitchen along with Nora. Doris had also appeared along with Wilfred the butler. Wilfred had been in the wine cellar and had returned to the kitchen wondering what the commotion was about. He was now standing close to the range glaring at Arthur. When Louisa reappeared at the bottom of the staff staircase with her small suitcase, her heart missed a beat as she saw her beloved brother in the kitchen. He was standing near the steps that led to the building's entrance hall, and was defiantly returning the glares he was receiving from Wilfred and Mrs. Barlow. The tiny window above his shoulder allowed some light to blaze through his dark wavy hair. This brilliance matched the intensity that flamed through Arthur's fierce, piercing blue eyes which seemed to bore unflinchingly into first Wilfred's stern countenance and then the harsh face of the cook's.

As she gazed in admiration at her brother, Louisa was reminded of her father, the resemblance was quite striking. She gulped as a wave of homesickness engulfed her. Uncomfortable under Arthur's glowering stance, Wilfred turned his glare on Louisa. "So you have decided to desert us Louisa." He spoke calmly, almost resignedly. He was getting used to the household staff coming and going so frequently.

"Where's Olive?" Louisa asked frantically. She couldn't leave without saying goodbye to Olive.

"She's finishing your chores for you." Mrs Barlow replied through tight lips. She was standing with arms crossed and still glowering at Arthur. For his part he stood up straight and fearlessly scowled back at Mrs Barlow. In response to Mrs. Barlow's words, Louisa risked a fleeting look at Arthur and relayed an urgent message to him with her eyes. He caught her glance, and gestured with his own eyes that he understood what she wanted to do. Without a word, he tugged her suitcase from her hands as she ran past him towards the stone steps. Feeling her confidence return, Louisa dashed up the steps from the kitchen and returned to the hallway to find Olive on her knees scrubbing the floor.

"Oh Olive, I'm so sorry you have to do this."

Olive used the back of her hand to return a wisp of her auburn curls under her cap and managed a brave smile. "I'm getting used to this. People are coming and going all the time these days. Times are changing I suppose."

32

"I will miss you." Louisa said honestly.

"I wish I had a brother like yours. Good looking isn't he?" Olive smiled and blushed as she turned round to see Arthur standing behind them both. "Take care."

Arthur still holding the suitcase with one hand, grabbed Louisa's arm with the other. Then with little hesitation, he guided his sister across the hallway. As they walked towards the door, they both took care to avoid the washed bits of floor. Gently pushing Louisa in front of him Arthur wrenched open the door, and ushered Louisa out. Then with a wink at Olive, he pulled the door behind him with a resolute slam.

In the driveway was a motorcycle. Arthur's new purchase. "I bought it yesterday and I drove up here today to visit you and show it to you. I didn't think I would be taking you back home." He chuckled and although Louisa was feeling overwhelmed she began to grin. Arthur produced some string out of his pocket and fastened the case to the back of the pillion seat. He then revved up the motorcycle and motioned Louisa to get on the back. They drove down the drive just as Jack drove up the drive in the Borrowton's sleek motor car with Lady Borrowton sitting at the back. Jack stared at Louisa then Arthur. His gaze took in the suitcase and he tooted the horn. Lady Borrowton gazed in front of her totally aloof. Louisa smiled to herself thinking that her departure might mean that Lady Borrowton would have to learn to dress herself.

During the journey home, Louisa began to worry what her mother would say when she saw her arrive with Arthur. She needn't have worried. Her mother took one look at her daughter's appearance and her sore hands, and accepted that Arthur's decision to bring his sister home was the right one.

"Go upstairs and rest, and we will talk later." she said to Louisa. For her own part that is all Louisa wanted to do. She eagerly went upstairs to the room she shared with Dorothy, hoping that in her absence her mother had not discarded her old bed. With relief she entered the room to see that everything was more or less the same. Despite her exhaustion, she found enough energy to leap on to her old bed where she fell asleep straight away. Two hours later Dorothy arrived home from school. As soon as she was told of Louisa's return, she ignored her Mother's warning not to disturb her, and excitedly burst into the bedroom to say hello to her sister. Louisa was only too pleased to see her sister. They hugged each other and Dorothy laughed when Louisa had told her what had happened.

"I've missed you Louie, I hope you don't have to go away again." Louisa sighed and hoped so too.

A few days later, Mary Ellen informed Louisa that she had found her a new job. Louisa became alarmed at hearing those words and was confused when she caught her mother smothering a smile.

"Mr. Fern has found you something to do, though there will be little money in it." She gave Louisa a crafty look. "It will involve riding your bicycle. Arthur has cleaned it up for you and checked the tyres and brakes."

Louisa, perplexed at her mother's countenance gazed intently at Mary Ellen somewhat intrigued. She caught her mother struggling to maintain a serious face. Slowly Louisa realised that her mother was not joking and she began to

34

relax. Mary Ellen was pleased to see her daughter smile again, but knew she had to explain that this was only a part time, temporary job. She would earn very little money and that she would have to be prepared to get a better job. She informed her daughter that she had written to three places to inquire on her behalf if they needed any servants. As anxiety crept over Louisa's face again, her mother tried to reassure her.

"Don't worry. These vacancies are nearer home, so if you are successful, you should be able to visit us regularly. And in my letters I have been explicit that you are looking for a house maid or ladies maid position and not a scullery maid."

Louisa relaxed a little, but felt guilty that other people such as Olive and Doris were not so lucky. She wished she could help them in some way.

The next day Louisa rode her bicycle up to Mr. Fern's farm. She had been told to arrive for nine o clock. Her father and her two brothers had left for work much earlier than that. Her father had to bridle and harness the shire horses and her two brothers Harry and Arthur were on hand to do whatever else needed to be done on the farm. Two other young men worked on the farm as well as Harry and Arthur. There was always some task or other to do and the hours were long. She felt guilty that she had complained about the long hours she had had to work at Patterson House, but both her brothers reassured her that there was no comparison.

"We get plenty of rest time in between jobs." Harry had assured her. "We get plenty of food and Mr. Fern doesn't ask us to do what he wouldn't do himself."

Arthur had agreed. "And in the winter there is less to do. Though there is less money too." He shrugged.

"That is one drawback." Harry said, but we do get paid by the hour in the summer so it sort of compensates."

"Not a lot though." Arthur grumbled.

At the farm Louisa met Mrs. Fern who had just come out of the chicken coop. She beckoned Louisa to follow her into the shed at the side of the coop. She placed the eggs on a straw tray and asked Louisa to count them into lots of half a dozen. Louisa did so quickly. Meanwhile Mrs. Fern prepared ten paper bags and wrote on the bags the names and addresses of various people who lived in the neighbourhood.

"Five and a half dozen plus three over." Louisa stated.

"Fine, now put half a dozen in each of these bags very carefully." Mrs Fern said.

Louisa obeyed and Mrs. Fen took three bags outside to see if they would fit in the basket on Louisa's bicycle. They fitted easily and Mrs. Fern packed some straw around each bag. Then placing more straw on top she placed another three bags of eggs. She then handed a list of names and addresses to Louisa. "I want you to deliver these eggs to these people. Do you think you can do that without breaking them?"

"Yes of course." Louisa beamed at her. She eagerly took the list and got on her bicycle.

"I have put them in order, so the ones on the top will be delivered first. When you have finished you can come back to get the rest. I will leave them here for you." She pointed to the box with the rest of the eggs.

Louisa set off gingerly at first and stopped every few minutes to make sure the eggs were not broken. They all seemed intact, and after two hours she had delivered all of the first round. When she got back for the next round, she found a glass of lemonade waiting for her with a note from Mrs. Fern to help herself and to return again in two days. She drank the juice thirstily, packed up the eggs and went on her second delivery round.

When she got home later that day, her mother was in the kitchen preparing a meal. Dorothy was helping her.

"I can see by the look on your face that you have had a good day." Her mother remarked as she put a pot of tea on the table. "Go and wash your hands and come and eat with us."

The arrangement of delivering eggs two days a week suited Louisa. The rest of the time she helped her mother about the house and whenever she could she manged to read her books. However she always made a point of accompanying Dorothy on her walk to school every morning. It was nice to chat to her sister. The age difference of four years sometimes didn't matter. They would talk about books and the latest fashion, both of them were avid readers and could also sew and knit very well. They also liked to design clothes for themselves, though they didn't have the money to buy the necessary materials. Sometimes they were able to alter the clothes they already owned to try to create their designs.

One afternoon a month later, Louisa's bicycle skidded on some mud in the road on her way home from the farm. Without warning, she fell and slithered into both the mud and some loose stones. In exasperation she kicked the bicycle to the side of the road and limped the rest of the way home. After an examination by the doctor, it appeared she had broken her wrist. Though she was no longer able to deliver eggs, nor be of much use to anyone in the house, the accident did bring some personal compensation for Louisa. This was in the form of valuable free time. She was now able to indulge herself in reading her favourite books. Being able to walk to the bluebell wood with a book under her arm was something she relished. An added bonus was, that it enabled her to stay out of her mother's way.

As summer faded to August, Arthur seemed to be getting restless. Then one day he announced he was going to finish at the farm and was going to work as a mechanic in a garage in Wrexham. Since buying his motorcycle he had become obsessed with engines. He spent all his spare time reading about engines and taking apart his own motorcycle. He would often be outside in the late summer light tinkering with the engine whilst humming tunes to himself that he had heard on the wireless. Usually, Harry would be with him, and most evenings Louisa went out to chat with them.

One particularly warm evening Louisa sat on the back door step watching her brothers tinkering with spare parts as usual. The night before, the wireless had broadcasted a variety of songs and the one title that Arthur seemed to have in his head was "*Lazy Bones*." They all hummed it as Arthur fiddled with spanners and screwdrivers. When it got too dark to see they went inside where their parents were listening to a news bulletin about Germany. It seemed that Adolf Hitler had banned political parties in Germany and that from now on there would only be the Nazi party.

"That means there will be no democracy now." Harry said grimly. "They won't be able to get rid of Hitler now unless there is a civil war in Germany."

"Well that isn't going to happen." Arthur said. He pushed away a lock of his dark hair from his forehead with the back of his hand and left a trail of oil on his face. "He's broken up the unions and destroyed any group or society that could possibly dare to defy him. Bit by bit he's taken away all the tools ordinary people could use to organise themselves to overthrow him."

Harry nodded. "It's going to get worse. How much do you bet that the next thing he does will be to try to take control of the army? The man is a maniac. I have a bad feeling it will affect the rest of Europe."

"Surely he couldn't take control of the army." Louisa said. She was alarmed at Harry's words and looked from one brother to the other. They both looked angry and she felt uneasy about their anger.

"Let's talk about something more cheerful," she said, then added, "Is Dot coming on Sunday?"

A smile slowly edged across Harry's face. "Yes." He looked secretive. "We've got a surprise for you."

"Oh what?" Louisa asked him. She looked from one brother to the other. Arthur shrugged.

"You will have to wait and see." Harry grinned.

Louisa couldn't wait for Sunday. She loved surprises, but she was impatient to know what the secret was about. No matter how she tried to get more information out of Harry he wouldn't tell her anything else. In any case she looked forward to seeing Dot. She regularly visited them on Sundays. Harry and Dot had known each other since they were both in school and were what most people referred to as childhood sweethearts.

Harry brought Dot on his motorcycle for Sunday afternoon for tea. When they arrived, Dot stood in front of the mirror that hung over the sideboard to comb through her dark brown hair that had got tangled on the motorbike. She then adjusted her clothing on her slim figure, before joining all the family gathered around the table. When they were all seated, Harry announced that he and Dot were going to get married.

Harry had told William and Mary Ellen earlier about the engagement. Louisa noticed that neither of them looked surprised when he formally made the announcement at the tea table. However even they were surprised when Harry produced a bottle of malt whisky and a bottle of sherry.

"You are pushing the boat out aren't you?" Arthur said with a grin.

Harry laughed. "Well if I can't celebrate an important step in my life with some kind of a toast, then when can I? Life is too short not to observe such an occasion. I've been saving for these." He smiled at Dot then added. "Mind you I will have to save like mad now for the wedding."

"So will I." Dot said. "I intend to carry on working after we are married. If I can."

"Good for you." Mary Ellen said approvingly. "Will they let you?"

Dot shrugged. "I can only ask."

Louisa was surprised her mother supported Dot's intention to continue working after her marriage. Later though when she had time to analyse things, she realised that her mother's work ethic would naturally support women continuing to work after they got married.

"To Harry and Dot." William said and they all raised their glasses. Even little Dorothy was allowed a sip of sherry diluted with a little lemonade.

The wedding was to be in November and Louisa and Dorothy were to be bridesmaids. Dot had two sister's Iris and Margaret, and they too would also be bridesmaids.

A few days after Harry's announcement, Louisa returned to hospital so that the hardened plaster could be removed from Louisa's wrist. It was a relief to be able to use her left arm again, but with the relief came the dread of being sent away again to work. And as feared, a week later, Mary Ellen informed Louisa that she had been to the employment agency in Wrexham and they had found her a place as a kitchen maid in nearby Broughton Hall.

Chapter Three

As far as Louisa was concerned, the only good thing about going to work at Broughton Hall was the location. It was only three miles away from home. Two short bus journeys took her there one fine Monday morning in September. She was greeted by the cook Mrs. Henderson who took Louisa to a small sitting room at the side of the enormous kitchen. "This is the staff sitting room." She was informed.

"We usually sit here in the evenings about half past eight when everything has been done. We have a rota so that if Mr. Thompson or Mrs. Thompson needs something then one of us will sort it out. It is very rare though fortunately for us. They both dine out a lot in the evening, and tend to entertain at the week-ends. When they have dinner parties, I expect everyone here to pull together to make it a success." She smiled at Louisa who was staring at her open mouthed. She couldn't believe how friendly the cook was. Mrs Henderson glanced at the large clock on the wall. It struck ten o clock. "There is just time to show you your room before everyone gathers in the kitchen for morning coffee. You will meet Mrs. Smedley the housekeeper tomorrow. She isn't here today. It's her day off." She got up and beckoned Louisa to follow her. As if in a dream, Louisa followed the very tall, sprightly woman to the end of the kitchen to a staircase which led up four flights to reach the top of the house. She was guided along a narrow corridor and into a very large room with two beds. "You will be sharing with Ivy. I believe she sleeps in that bed nearest the window. Leave your stuff here for now and then come back down to meet the staff and I will give you your uniform."

Once Louisa had met all the staff and had drunk her coffee she was put to work in the kitchen. The atmosphere was much friendlier in this kitchen and Louisa felt sure that she was going to be much happier than at Patterson house. It was still hard work, and cook had high standards, but she was realistic about what could be done in a day without making her staff exhausted or resentful. No-one had left employment for years. Louisa was replacing someone who had left to look after her sick father. Her name was Doreen and everyone had said what a wonderful person she had been, and that they would all miss her.

Later that evening when Louisa went up to her room to unpack her clothes, Ivy followed her and sat on her own bed to chat to Louisa. She told her she had three sisters and three brothers. The brothers had joined the army, one of her sisters Grace was married with two small children and the other two, Rose and Daisy, were in service in different houses in Manchester.

"Rose seems to work harder than us." Ivy said. "I get letters from her now and again and she is always complaining about scrubbing floors and scrubbing vegetables. It's not so bad here. I've worked in worse places. The Thompsons seem reasonable people for toffs. Mr. Thompson's family go back generations round these parts. Apparently they were in to all sorts of industry like coal mining and lead. Mrs. Thompson used to be one of the Clayton's who also owned mines. So no scrubbing floors for the likes of them."

Louisa shuddered. She remembered too well how she spent most of her time on her knees scrubbing at any whim of the cook.

"When Doreen went off to look after her father, I asked Rose to come down here and work in Doreen's, oops – I mean your place."

Louisa was taken aback at this information. She looked at her squarely wondering whether she should be concerned. Part of her half wished that she no longer had a job so that she could look for something more interesting. The other part of her didn't want to let down her mother.

Ivy laughed. "Don't worry. I asked Mrs. Henderson and she was fine about it, but Rose wouldn't come. She's got herself a boyfriend up there. He's one of the servants and obviously worth the pain. Daisy wanted to stay in Manchester, so then Mrs. Henderson decided on you." She rolled off her bed and fished in her handbag and produced a packet of cigarettes.

"Do you smoke?" She offered her the packet.

Louisa shook her head. "No thanks."

"Have you tried?"

Louisa shook her head. "No, but my brothers have. They said it was like chewing coal. They also said that if I started to smoke I would never have any money." She grinned. "But I might try it one day just to see what it is like."

Ivy passed her lit cigarette to Louisa. "Here try it." Before she could stop her the cigarette was pushed between Louisa's lips and she gasped at the taste of the tobacco. She took it out quickly.

"That's horrible. If that's what it is like I won't bother."

44

Ivy laughed again. She pulled a hairpin out of her hair and let her blonde curls fall down over her shoulders. "Very wise. What are your brothers like? Are they available? Not that I am looking for a boyfriend." She attempted a nonchalant expression but couldn't hold it and a mischievous smile slowly spread across her face.

Louisa grinned. She told her about Harry's coming wedding and Arthur's new job as an apprentice mechanic.

"So what's your bridesmaid dress going to be like?" Ivy asked.

"Dot wants us to have blue satin dresses with a sweetheart neckline and puff sleeves."

"Sounds a bit like that stuff you see film stars wear in the films."

Louisa grinned. "Yes she likes all that film star stuff. She and Harry go to the cinema a lot when they can. She's probably been influenced by films. There's one called '*She done him wrong*' Dot often talks about that."

"Oh yes. I know that one. I haven't seen it but I heard the review on the wireless." She walked to an old wooden table by the window and switched on the enormous wireless that had been placed on it. "Let's see if there is any music on." She turned the dial but all she got was a squeaky noise. The noise was piercing and Louisa put her hands over her ears. Ivy gave up and switched it off.

"Sometimes the reception is better than other days. It depends on what time of night it is and whether the neighbours are trying to tune in too. This one isn't as good as the one in the servant's kitchen. The trouble is cook doesn't like having it on, she says it is a distraction. Maybe

45

we can try later and we can have a bit of a boogie if the music is on. It's got a horn so we can both hear it, not like those old battery and accumulator things with headsets. Sometimes it's depressing stuff about Hitler and Germany." She lay back on the bed and sighed.

The thought of dancing in their bedroom amused Louisa. It would never have been allowed at Patterson House. She looked around the room she shared with Ivy. It was twice the size of the room she had shared with Olive. And to have a wireless too was a bonus, even if it didn't work very well! Louisa had no misconceptions about the wireless though. She reckoned her employers had bought a new, smaller version and had dumped the old one in their room. She was used to her brothers talking about modern wirelesses. Apparently there was a shop in Chester that had started selling them. Arthur had often cycled to that shop to get parts for his and Louisa's bicycle, and had become friendly with the owner who had started to branch out from bicycles and was now selling wirelesses. She wondered if her employers had bought one of the new more sophisticated wirelesses that Arthur kept talking about. She glanced at the one that Ivy had been fiddling with. She knew that if you moved the knobs too far, the receiver would act more like a transmitter and interfere with any receiver in the area. She thought she would have a go at working the knobs in the next couple of days, and see if she could find some music for Ivy. She felt fairly confident she could do it. She had watched her brothers and father doing it, and their wireless was even older than this one. Arthur said he was going to save up to buy a new modern version as a surprise for their parents.

Getting into bed much later, Louisa smiled to herself in the dark. She knew she was going to be happy in Broughton House, but she reminded herself she didn't want to be a servant for ever, and as soon as she could she would get a better job.

The next day Mrs. Henderson introduced her to Mrs. Smedley the housekeeper. She welcomed Louisa to the household and told her that her day off would be every Thursday. She was also informed that she was free to take Thursday off that same week.

So three days later, overjoyed, at the prospect of seeing her family again so soon after starting work, Louisa got an early bus to Wrexham bus station. The bus stop was very close to Broughton Hall and so she had little difficulty getting to the bus stop. It was a long walk down the drive to the road but she managed it within ten minutes if she walked briskly. In the town centre, she excitedly waited for the next bus to take her home to Pandy. She arrived just after nine thirty and found her mother in the back parlour swamped with yards of blue satin. Her mother's sewing machine was set up at the window and her Mother who looked up when Louisa walked into the house, had pins in her mouth so couldn't speak.

Louisa smiled a greeting to her mother and went into the small scullery to fill the kettle. She carried it through to the kitchen and put it on the range. "Tea mum?" Louisa popped her head around the door and her mother nodded. Eventually she used up the supply of pins in her mouth and was able to address her daughter. "You look happy. I take it things are alright at Broughton hall?"

"Oh yes." She picked up the pattern for the bridesmaids. There were three versions on the cover. "Which one is mine?"

Mary Ellen pointed to the one in the centre with puff sleeves. "I've already cut it out. Dot was able to get enough for both of you. It was the end of the roll from the market stall and she got it a bit cheaper. It's got creased at the end, but I think we can manage. You are so thin and Dorothy is little so there is just enough for the main part, if we use some contrasting material for the sleeves. If you can start to take the paper off, I can use it again to cut out Dorothy's. I will have to adjust it for size."

Carefully Louisa removed the tissue paper pattern from the material, making stiches to mark where the darts and seams should be. Meanwhile Mary Ellen finished pinning together the selvedge of each piece of fabric ready to lay out the pattern again for the second dress.

"I suppose Dot is making her own wedding dress." Louisa said, as she watched her mother pinning the pattern on to the satin.

Mary Ellen shook her head. "No. Mrs. Ferguson has given her a white silk dress which apparently Dot is ecstatic about."

"That's kind of her." Louisa enthused.

"She is being recognised for her good work. Mrs. Ferguson will miss Dot when she leaves St. Peter's Manor and goes to start her new job in Greene and Madisons. She's done a lot of alterations to Mrs. Ferguson's dresses and probably saved her a lot of money. Not forgetting all the mending she has done on her other clothes. Mind you, Dot was lucky to get that position as personal maid in Rossett. Not too far away from home. Just like yourself." Mary Ellen gave Louisa one of her rare smiles, but Louisa chose to ignore it. She was thinking about whether working at the same store as Dot would be better than being in service. She knew that Dot thought the move for her was better. For a while she put the matter out of her head.

"Has Harry and Dot made plans where they are going to live when they get married?" Louisa asked. She started to tack the darts on her bridesmaid dress and carefully laid it on the opposite end of the table from her mother.

"Dot's Grandfather has said they can move in with him. He has said they can have the back parlour for their own and he will live in the kitchen. He's got a nice comfortable arm chair which he can put by the range. They will have to make sure there is plenty of firewood and coal to make two fires when Harry comes home in the evening."

"That's lucky." Louisa said. "I suppose Dot will cook for all of them though."

Mary Ellen got up to move to the sewing machine. "Yes I expect so. Dot will have to organise her time whilst she is working and at least her Grandfather can help, he will be glad of the company."

Louisa and her mother sewed all day, and by the time her sister came home from school, both bridesmaid dresses were at a stage when they could be tried on for the first fitting. Whilst Louisa continued to adjust her sister's dress, her mother made some soup and cut up some bread for the three of them for their tea. Dorothy went in to the garden to look for some late raspberries.

Much later when the rest of the family were home, Arthur took Louisa back to Broughton Hall. He grinned when she got off the motorcycle. "It's funny I'm taking you back to work rather than kidnapping you."

She grinned back. "Yes it is." She looked up towards her bedroom window and saw Ivy peering through the lace curtains. Louisa couldn't help thinking that Ivy was probably interested in Arthur. She kissed her brother goodbye and went in to the house. She couldn't help feeling smug that both her two brothers were very good looking. She felt very proud of them.

Louisa spent every subsequent Thursday with her mother and Dorothy sewing until finally all the bridesmaid dresses were finished. Her mother had also helped Dot finish the other two dresses for her two sisters. Fortunately Dot's cousins had been bridesmaids before and had worn similar coloured bridesmaid dresses. The two cousins had donated the dresses to Dot for her own bridesmaids. So all they had to do was alter them to fit Dot's sisters. By the time the wedding came along, Mary Ellen told everyone that she was fed up of seeing blue satin.

The wedding was to be on a Friday and Louisa had arranged to change her day off so that she could attend. Everything went according to plan, and after the small reception in the church hall, they waved the newlyweds away. Harry had saved up some money to take himself and his new wife for a week end in Blackpool.

Eventually it was time for everyone to go home, and once again Arthur took Louisa back to Broughton House. This time, when Louisa got off the motorcycle, Ivy came running out of the house. She had a lot of make up on Louisa noticed, and she only had eyes for Arthur.

"Hello Louisa" she gushed. Louisa stared at her in amazement. She didn't normally speak like that. "Did the wedding go off alright?" She sidled up to the motorcycle.

"Yes it was marvellous." Louisa replied frowning in bewilderment at Ivy's demeanour.

"This must be your unmarried brother Arthur." Ivy said. She held her hand out to Arthur. "Pleased to meet you."

"Arthur this is Ivy." Louisa said awkwardly.

Arthur grinned and held out his hand. "Good to meet you Ivy." He waved to Louisa and revved up his motorcycle then rode off.

"Short and sweet." Ivy pouted. "Has your brother got a girlfriend?"

Louisa stared at Ivy in amazement then laughed. "No, not yet, but I have a feeling it won't be long before he does."

As Louisa became more settled in to her new lifestyle, her relationship with her mother changed. Mary Ellen began to treat her daughter as an equal. Louisa enjoyed helping her mother on her Thursdays off, and as the run up to Christmas became closer, it became a very busy time for everyone. Two weeks before Christmas, Arthur announced he was bringing a young woman home to meet the family. This was to be on a Sunday, the week before Christmas Eve. Louisa was disappointed that she would be unable to meet the young woman whose name was Megan. However her mother said she would tell her all about Megan the following Thursday. So when Louisa's day to visit arrived, they sat in the parlour with Dorothy to chat and to drink tea with the mince pies that

Mary Ellen had made that morning. It seemed to Louisa that she was surrounded by mince pies both at home and at Broughton Hall. Mrs. Henderson and Charlotte her assistant produced them by the dozen. They had been baking seasonal food all week and the mixed aromas of cinnamon and apple perpetually wafted from the kitchen.

"Megan is a lovely girl. She seems a little frail though, she is very pale and thin. She needs to build herself up a bit I reckon. It would be good if you can meet her on Christmas day. I don't suppose you can get some time off on Christmas day can you?" her mother looked at her hopefully.

Louisa shook her head. "I wish I could but it will be chaotic."

Her mother looked at her thoughtfully. "How about if Harry or Arthur came for you at nine o clock and brought you back here for half an hour, then took you back?"

It seemed like a good plan, though Louisa wasn't sure if Mrs. Henderson would allow it. So when Arthur took her back that evening, she asked him to wait until she had spoken to Mrs. Henderson. As usual, upon hearing the motor cycle engine, Ivy came flying out of the house to talk to Arthur. She had never given up on him, even though Louisa had told her that Arthur was only interested in Megan. Louisa left them talking whilst she went in search of Mrs. Henderson. Cook said it was unlikely the Thompsons would need the staff once they had eaten their meal on Christmas day, but she was unable to promise. She agreed to let Louisa go for an hour if Arthur picked her up at nine o clock, then brought her back at ten o clock. However, Mrs. Henderson warned her, that if the Thompson's family needed all the staff then her plans would have to change. Louisa ran out to tell Arthur this information. He was still chatting to Ivy. He looked bored, and as soon as Louisa had imparted her news he revved up the engine and disappeared. Ivy looked disappointed and Louisa shrugged. She couldn't wait to meet Megan.

The few days before Christmas Eve the kitchen seemed to be perpetually in use.

The Thompsons did a lot of entertaining and everyone was kept busy. Delivery boys brought sides of ham and two turkeys, a large leg of lamb; as well as boxes of vegetables and potatoes. As fast as eggs and sugar and flour arrived they were whisked up by Charlotte and Mrs Henderson. Between them they produced all sorts of cakes and pastries.

When Christmas Eve finally arrived, things got even more hectic. Mrs. Henderson issued orders to everyone, and all the staff jumped to it. Though it was hard work, there was an excited buzz in the air. Mrs. Thompson's sister and her husband were staying in the house as well as the Thompson's two young sons who were home from boarding school. They kept running up and down the house playing Christmas carols on their clarinets. They played their musical instruments proficiently and the staff within earshot enjoyed listening as they worked. The music helped to create a festive atmosphere.

When the evening meal was over and everything cleared away all the staff sat in their tiny sitting room to drink some cocoa before going to bed. They were gathered together an hour later than usual. Everyone was exhausted.

"Well at least everything is prepared for tomorrow." Mrs Henderson declared. "The family and all the guests will be going to church in the morning for the eleven o clock service. Afterwards they have invited a few friends as well as the Vicar and his wife to the house for sherry and canapes. This means that Christmas lunch will be served later than usual at half past two. I think it would be better if we all had a small snack ourselves at half past twelve since it is Christmas day."
Everyone looked up surprised at this announcement from cook. Usually the staff ate their meal after they had served their employers.
"I will make some extra sausage rolls and canapes for us." Cook declared. "This will keep us going, because we probably won't get our Christmas meal until much later. Then we can have a rest for a few hours. Believe me, after a later than usual breakfast; and then the sausage rolls; canapes and mince pies with the sherry, they won't want to eat again until much later. I have discussed this with Mrs. Thompson and she agrees."
Ivy grinned. "Yes the vicar usually stays until about two o clock anyway. He's rather partial to cook's sausage rolls and mince pies, and whatever else is going."
Cook glanced at Louisa and Ivy. "You two will have to make sure that the platters of food are replenished, so you may have to take it in turns so you can get something to eat." She gave them a wink before saying, "we need to make sure they are not hungry! Robert can also help you." She turned towards Robert the footman who was slumped across a chair next to Dora the scullery maid. Robert was also Mr. Thompson's personal manservant and was given to

gossiping. He had very dark hair and small blue eyes. Louisa always felt that his eyes seemed to pierce into her every time he tried to tell her a joke. Unfortunately the jokes were never very funny though Robert always found them amusing and even laughed when he related them.

Thomas the butler came into the sitting room, and informed them all that they could all go to bed as they wouldn't be needed again until morning. Everyone let out a sigh of relief and started to prepare themselves to go up the staff stairway to their respective rooms. Louisa was tired and was worrying if she would be able to go home the next day. She was looking forward to meeting Megan. If the Thompsons were having a late lunch, wouldn't that mean they would have a late evening meal and she would be needed in the kitchen? Ivy tried to reassure her.

"I've got a feeling we will have the evening off." Ivy said. "I'm sure that's what happened last year. Cook prepared lots of cold meats, pies and salads, cakes and trifles and they were left on the sideboards for the family to help themselves. The children and their parents either read books or played lots of board games on the tables. There were jigsaws everywhere and books and games all over the place. No visitors or extra guests other than Mrs. Thompson's sister and brother in-law. It was just one day when the Thompsons relaxed and so we all did too. Mind you, there was a lot of washing up and tidying to do the next day."

"I hope you are right." Louisa whispered before falling into a deep sleep. The washing up would be worth it.

On Christmas morning after an extra hour in bed all the staff set to work to carry out Mrs. Henderson's plan. She and Ivy served platter after platter of food to the guests and all the while Louisa worried whether she would be able to get to Pandy for an hour that evening. Ivy did her best to try to reassure her and it turned out that Ivy was right. At seven o clock all the staff were told that they could have the rest of the evening off and so Louisa was able to rest a little and freshen up before waiting for her brother to arrive. At nine o clock that evening, Louisa was ready at the back door when Harry turned up on his motorcycle. He brought her a scarf to put around her neck as it was bitterly cold outside.

"Make sure it's secure inside your coat. We don't want it getting tangled up in the wheels." Louisa did as she was told and her face beaming with pleasure got on the motorcycle behind her brother, and he drove the short journey to their parents' home in Pandy.

All her family were sitting around the fire in the back parlour when Louisa arrived with Harry. There wasn't room for everyone to sit down around the blazing fire, so Dorothy got up from the small sofa so that Louisa could sit down between Dot and Megan. Arthur sat on the arm of the sofa next to Megan and was holding her hand. Harry and Dorothy sat on the floor, each of them flanking the fireplace. Meanwhile William and Mary Ellen sat on the two arm chairs.

It was warm in the small room, and as well as the heat from the glowing coal fire, there emanated from the company a relaxed feeling of wellbeing. This genial atmosphere caught at Louisa's emotions. She felt very happy to be with her family even it were to be just for a short time. Arthur gently touched her arm and introduced her to Megan who turned towards Louisa and smiled. "I'm pleased to meet you

Louisa. I have heard so much about you from Arthur. Do you like your new job?"

Megan seemed very thin compared to Louisa yet she was very slim herself. Megan's long, auburn, wavy hair framed a pretty yet pale, sculptured face. Her full red lips and big blue eyes reminded Louisa of a doll she used to have. She was very friendly and obviously adored Arthur. There was nothing about Megan to dislike.

Mary Ellen got up and poured small glasses of sherry. "We've been waiting for you Louisa as she handed her a glass. "Merry Christmas."

They all cheered Merry Christmas and began to exchange gifts. Amidst the cries of delight from everyone who opened their parcels, sparks from the fire jumped out singeing the rug. Everyone had to move quickly from the fireplace as William hastily stamped out the singed corners of the rug. He glanced at Mary Ellen who shrugged. "Another Christmas, another singe." Everyone laughed. Just then Harry informed them all that he was leaving the farm, and that he was going to work as a painter and decorator. Harry had already confided this news to William and Mary Ellen, and of course Dot. So upon imparting the news to his siblings, they were immediately surprised and delighted for Harry. It seemed like a good opportunity, as it meant he would be working less hours, yet still earning the same amount of money.

Soon Louisa had to go and she followed Arthur outside to his prized machine. She was laden with gifts of hand knitted scarves, mittens, hats and slippers. Mary Ellen took them from her and wrapped them all up in a piece of brown wrapping paper and string. She also tucked in two bars of nutty chocolate as an extra gift. She kissed her daughter goodbye and Arthur revved up and drove off towards Wrexham.

As usual Ivy was in the window upstairs in Broughton Hall. She pushed the lace curtains aside and waved as she saw Louisa and her brother arrive. She didn't come down though. Probably because it is too cold Louisa thought. She shivered as she watched Arthur turn his motorcycle around. "So you like Megan then?" he said with a broad grin on his face.

"Yes of course."

"I think I'm going to marry her."

"Oh wonderful." Louisa gave her brother a hug. "When? Does mother know and father?"

He shook his head. "No, not yet. And I don't want to get married too soon like Harry. I want to save some money to buy a place. There's no room for us all at home, and I don't want to start married life living with Megan's family."

"Is it a big family?"

Arthur shook his head. "No, but it is a very small cottage. She has an older sister who is getting married next year, and a younger brother. Her Grandmother also lives with them and of course her parents."

"It sounds a bit cramped."

"Exactly. I don't want to have to make do. I've had enough of that. And I'm determined not to buy things on the *never never*." He kissed her forehead and she waved to him as he drove away.

The following Thursday morning, Louisa sat in her Mother's parlour drinking coffee with her mother. "I suppose Arthur has told you that he is going to get engaged to Megan."

Louisa nodded, "but he wants to save up first for a house."

Her mother nodded. "I'm glad he wants to wait, but it could take years. Still he is only eighteen."

"Well he knows what he wants and he is determined to do it." Louisa said. "And he is doing well at Clark's garage. I wouldn't be surprised that before long he has his own workshop."

"You are growing up Louisa and becoming very wise. Working at Broughton Hall suits you." She got up to take the dishes to the scullery and patted her daughter's head. Louisa followed her into the small scullery. She was about to tell her mother that she didn't intend staying at Broughton Hall forever. Working as a servant may suit her for now, but she wanted to do something more meaningful with her life. She wanted time of her own.

Before she could speak, her mother began to ask her questions about Broughton Hall.

"What are the plans for New year's Eve at Broughton Hall?" Her mother asked. She loved to hear the gossip relating to the house and Louisa was glad to give it to her.

"Mr. and Mrs. Thompson want to give a late night dinner at nine o clock, then serve drinks and canapes at midnight. Cook isn't very happy about it."

"I'm not surprised. It will make it a long day for her and for all of you."

"Cook said we should all rest for an hour during the afternoon, but there is always something to be done." Louisa decided not to tell her mother about her plans for the future just yet. It could wait for now.

It turned out that cook had come up with a plan to help everyone keep going on New Year's Eve. She had spoken to Mrs. Thompson who fortunately wasn't an unreasonable woman. They had agreed that cook should organise a rota, so that everyone could rest for an hour each during the afternoon.

It was four o clock in the afternoon when Louisa got her rest and she gladly crept up the staff stairs to her room and lay down on her bed. Outside it was already pitch black. She had switched on Ivy's wireless with the intention of listening to some music, however once she was comfortable lying down she very quickly drifted asleep. Ivy shook her awake at five o clock and she hastily washed her hands and face to go back down again.

"Some of the guests have arrived already," said Ivy as she threw herself on her bed. "They will be wanting refreshments no doubt. Robert has taken them some tea and fancies, but those nobs will probably want more. They always do."

Ivy was right and as soon as Louisa got down to the kitchen, cook shoved a platter of titbits in to her hands for her to take to the drawing room. She spent ten minutes circling the room ensuring the guests were able to help themselves from the platter. When the platter was empty she returned to the kitchen to see Robert go in with another platter. "Not another one" Louisa whispered. "Surely they won't want more."

"Don't you believe it. These toffs eat like gannets."

The rest of the evening flew by quickly. At midnight those members of staff who happened to be in the kitchen linked hands and sang 'auld lang syne'. Unfortunately for Robert and Thomas they were both serving the guests with drinks and couldn't join them. However Mr. Thompson told Thomas to take a bottle of sparkling wine to the servants' quarters to share it out with the staff. When Thomas produced the bottle, they all agreed it would be better to clear away the dishes and tidy up first. So it was nearly two o clock in the morning when Thomas opened the bottle. Louisa felt too sleepy to drink hers, but urged by Ivy she managed to drink the gassy drink.

Unused to drinking alcohol, and especially at such a late hour resulted in making all the staff bleary eyed the next day. This, coupled with the fact that they had all worked so hard with very little rest the day before, had rendered them all sickly-looking. Through her yawns Louisa managed to laugh, and commented that it was just as well that New Year's Eve was only once a year. Fortunately the Thompsons and their guests didn't stir until eleven o clock that morning and the servants sat in their own lounge for an hour drinking coffee and making plans for 1934.

"Who made any resolutions?" Dora asked everyone. She was a very quiet person normally and didn't usually start conversations. Her complexion was paler than usual and wisps of dark hair fell from under her cap accentuating the whiteness of her skin.

"I make the same resolution every year but it never happens" said Ivy.

"What's that?" Robert asked, "as if I didn't know it. Get rich, or marry a rich man." He laughed and so did Ivy. Charlotte and Mrs Henderson laughed too but neither of them contributed to the conversation.

Louisa wondered what the next year would bring for herself. She would be fifteen in April. She wondered about making plans for her own future but couldn't make up her mind what she wanted to do. More than anything she had wanted to stay on at school and get a better education. She hadn't given up on her education. However, for now she was content where she was, though she wished she had more free time to study. She felt sure that if she had more time to read as many books as she could, her new knowledge would lead her to a better future. She resolved to try to read more whenever she could. Next year, she told herself, will be the start of something new.

Chapter Four

1934

Things settled down into a routine during the first two months of the New Year. The weather was bitterly cold and in February there was a lot of snow which made it impossible for Louisa to get home. She spent two consecutive Thursdays in the room she shared with Ivy at Broughton Hall. Having no heating in the room, she found herself wearing several sweaters to keep warm. To cheer herself up she read books, listened to Ivy's wireless or tried to do some sewing, though her fingers were too cold. She liked thumbing through the magazines that Mrs. Thompson left lying around. She loved looking at the fashion pages and tried to copy some of the designs, usually with very good results. When her fingers were too numb to do anything constructive, she went down to the servants' kitchen to warm up by the big fire, taking care not to get in anyone's way. She did this several times throughout the day before returning upstairs to either resume her sewing, or to sit on her bed to read books and listen to music. She soon learned many of the songs she heard on the wireless and often hummed one or the other as she went about her chores.

At the end of February the roads had been cleared sufficiently for buses to get through, though very slowly. So it was lunch time one Thursday in early March, when Louisa managed to get to Pandy. Mary Ellen had made some vegetable soup and Louisa was grateful to be served a portion. The short journey had chilled her and the meal warmed her up.

After she had helped her mother to wash up the dishes she helped her make a treacle tart for tea time. She stayed to sample a piece with Dorothy, when she came home from school, just when the weather turned bad again. Dorothy complained that almost as soon as she had eaten her tart Louisa was pulling on her coat ready to leave.

"We've hardly seen you lately Louie," she said as she wiped some treacle off her face with the back of her hand.

"I know, but I can't risk staying any longer, in case the roads get bad again. I am going to get a bus back to Wrexham, whilst they are still running."

She wondered how her brothers were coping with their motorcycles in such bad weather. Her poor father was having to walk through the snow to get to work.

By the end of March, the weather turned milder and so Louisa was able to continue her weekly visits to see her parents and Dorothy. She saw little of her brothers until her birthday in April. Harry was enjoying married life and Arthur spent a lot of his free time with Megan going to the cinema or visiting her family.

Louisa's fifteenth birthday was on a Wednesday, so she had to wait until the next day to receive any presents from her family. It was a nice surprise to see them all there in the late evening. Arthur and Harry eventually began discussing the news and inevitably about Adolf Hitler. For once William didn't join in with their conversation about Germany. He told his sons to shut up and be more cheerful for Louisa's birthday. Arthur shrugged and then disappeared upstairs and then came down again with a bottle of sherry. He handed a glass each to everyone to toast Louisa's birthday. Megan only sipped hers and left most of it. She had a bit of a cough which she couldn't get rid of. It had lingered with her since New Year's Eve she said. Megan worked as a laundry maid at Alynsedge Hall in Gresford. She often complained about the steam getting on her chest and that sometimes the room where she worked was so thick with steam she could hardly breathe. Alynsedge Hall was owned by Mr. Benson who was a share holder in one of the many coal mines across North Wales. Mr Thompson of Broughton Hall also had shares in some of the coal mines. Louisa was never quite sure which ones, as there were so many,

At the end of April, Megan's cough worsened, and was unable to continue working. She stayed in bed for several days, then on the fifth of May she died.

Arthur was devastated, and as the weeks rolled by, Louisa felt that her brother would never get over Megan's death. The sparkle seemed to have gone out of his eyes and he rarely smiled for months. It was a depressing time for all the family.

Throughout the summer, Louisa visited home regularly on her Thursdays. Her relationship with her mother improved each time and Mary Ellen loved to hear about the people Louisa worked with at Broughton Hall. So whilst she cheerfully helped her mother with her daily chores she always looked forward to the evenings when she could see her brother and her father. Very often Harry would call for half an hour on his way home. They always listened to the wireless and then they would discuss the news. The subject was usually Hitler.

"This so called German socialist party, ought to start doing socialist things in Germany." Harry commented one evening. Arthur agreed. "Yes why don't they do what they were elected to do instead of persecuting innocent people?"

William smoked his pipe and nodded his agreement with his sons. "The trouble is the original socialist party in Germany, is now considerably weaker. And any activity by those leaders brave enough to do anything are being persecuted too! There will be more bloodshed you mark my words. This man is evil. He will try to take over the army next. It's just a matter of time. At the moment he is just testing the water to see what the reaction will be from the big bosses in Germany."

As the summer passed into autumn news from Germany was more alarming. It was also reported that a prominent figure in Germany – Ernst Rohm had been removed from office and shot by Hitler too. When news about this filtered through, Louisa felt that the atmosphere all around her was changing. Her father especially was noticeably withdrawn almost as if he was expecting war to break out. He remembered too vividly the Great War, and how his wife's brother had been killed at the battle of the Somme in 1915. Mary Ellen too recalled how distressing that event had been. That particular evening in late September Louisa had returned to Broughton Hall in a very subdued state of mind. The events that quickly unfolded did nothing to cheer her up.

At four thirty the following morning on the twenty second of September, Ivy shook Louisa awake. There were tears in her eyes. "Louisa get up there's been a terrible explosion."

Louisa looked at Ivy's tear stained face, and fear gripped her stomach. "Where? What's happened? She yawned and sat up in bed.

"At the pit in Gresford."

"What? Oh no." Louisa was wide awake now, and got out of bed quickly, though she didn't know what she was going to do to help. She knew many people who worked at Gresford colliery. "Has there been anyone injured?"

"We don't know yet but everyone is expecting the worst. Robert has a brother working there, and Dora's father and brother work there too. Cook has told Dora she can go and find out what she can. She is so worried she can't work anyway. Mr. Thompson has been there since three o clock this morning when a messenger came to the house. Thomas the butler let him in to the house and then he told Robert what had happened. He agreed to let him go to Gresford too. He went on his push bike, but Dora will have to wait until the buses start. It's too far to walk."

Louisa got ready to go downstairs. She was shaking with emotion. She felt lucky that none of her family worked down the pit, but many of her mother and father's neighbours did. She had played with the sons of the neighbours when they were children. She knew that at least four of those sons worked at Gresford colliery. When she got to the kitchen Dora was crying inconsolably, she had no means of transport and was shaking so baldy she couldn't think properly. Louisa tried to calm her, but neither she nor anyone else

67

could say anything to help her. Eventually she went outside, but came back into the kitchen five minutes later with George one of the meat delivery boys who brought more news about the explosion. This made Dora worse, and George offered to give Dora a lift to the pit head where hundreds of people were already gathering waiting for news.

Apparently six people had managed to escape but they didn't know if there were any more survivors. George was worried too, and his usual cheerful face was masked in anxiety. He had an uncle working at the pit, and his mother and aunt were anxiously waiting for news.

"They have managed to bring up seven bodies so far." He said. "Let's hope there are more people alive. There were over two hundred and fifty working that shift last night in the Dennis shaft. It's one of the deepest shafts in the Denbighshire coalfield you know. And my Uncle Tom said that there's a lot of gas down there. I hope to god they are not all dead."

Dora began to tremble and cry again. "Come on Dora," George said. "Let's go and see what else we can find out."

Silently Louisa, Ivy, and Cook got on with their duties as best they could. At mid-morning Thomas came in to say that Mr. Thompson had sent a message to Mrs. Thompson that the pit was still burning and that three men from the rescue team were dead. They too had been miners, in a neighboring colliery in Llay.

Mr. Thompson had part shares in ownership in a colliery and knew most of the share holders of all the other pits in the area including the one at Gresford. He was aware that news of this explosion would travel far and wide and that workers from other pits including those where he had shares would want to come and help. He had already been informed that the local fire fighters were finding it difficult to fight off the fire. Within a few hours of the first explosion, there had been another, and the rescuers were finding it more and more difficult to reach the men they knew were trapped behind the fire.

Fear was mounting amongst the rescuers, most of them miners themselves, felt that many of them would have been overcome by the fumes, and would have died of carbon monoxide poisoning. When another explosion came a few hours later, some rescuers feared the worst. They said that if there had been any survivors from the first blast, who were trying to get out, they may well have been killed by the subsequent blast. Nevertheless, other miners worked flat out to try to rescue their colleagues. Throughout the day messengers called at Broughton house to give them more news. In Gresford, there continued to be a steady flow of anxious volunteers from other pits in the surrounding area. Meanwhile, large crowds of other miners who had not worked that particular shift and relatives of all ages, gathered forlornly in silence to stand at the pit head. All of them desperately waiting for news, dreading to hear the worst.

Mr. Thompson returned to Broughton Hall late on Saturday night only to change his clothes and get something to eat. After a few hours rest he returned to Gresford, this time taking Thomas with him. Before he left he came in to the kitchen and asked Cook if anyone had relatives working at the mine.

Mrs. Henderson replied. "Dora, Robert and Charlotte. Both Dora and Robert have already gone to the pit head sir. Today is Charlotte's day off. I know her father works at Gresford colliery." She wiped her eyes with the corner of her apron. Mr. Thompson's face was grim. He said no more and then left the house.

It was a heavy heart that Louisa went to bed that night. She felt as helpless as all those relatives standing at the pit head waiting for news. By the end of the next day, rescuers were still fighting the fire but were unable to make any progress. Despite the pouring rain, relatives and other miners continued waiting for news. Hoping against hope that they would find some men alive, mothers, wives and children braved the weather and stoically stood. However it was hopeless. It was deemed that all two hundred and fifty miners were dead and it was too dangerous to try to bring the bodies back to the surface. A decision was made to seal off the fire by capping both the burning Dennis shaft and the Martin shaft. Hours later, another explosion occurred and blew off one of the seals. Tragically the debris from this secondary explosion hit and killed one of the workers who was working above ground.

On Monday morning Mrs. Thompson came into the kitchen with her housekeeper Mrs. Smedley and asked Cook to bring her staff into her parlour. She explained that Dora, Charlotte and Robert had lost members of their families and that they would not be working for the rest of that week. She sighed as she addressed them.

"This is a terrible tragedy and it has been felt across the whole of Wrexham. As you know my husband Mr.

Thompson has shares in other coal mines in the area and so will be extremely busy for the next few weeks trying to help the owners of Gresford to sort out the mess. In the meantime we will be short staffed. Mrs. Henderson and Mrs. Smedley, I want you to re-organise the remaining staff so that we can carry on as normal in the best way we can. For my part, whilst my husband is pre occupied I will take my meals on a tray, and we can revise the week's menu to make simpler meals. I have cancelled the two dinner parties planned for this week too."

When they all trooped out of Mrs. Thompson's parlour, cook sat with Ivy and Louisa to discuss how they would get all the chores done. "There's just the five of us, so I can manage to prepare the meals myself." She said. "You two divide the cleaning between yourselves, and then help me wash up and scrub the kitchen. I must ask you both to give up your day off this week."

Both Louisa and Ivy agreed without hesitation.

Amidst all the sorrow of the mining disaster, Arthur arrived at Broughton Hall with a message for Louisa. She was pleased to see him. He told her that their mother's young sister Nancy was coming to visit for a few days. She was hoping that she might see Louisa.

Arthur smiled wearily at his sister, and Louisa thought how desperately tired he looked. He hugged his sister before continuing.

"I suppose you know about the disaster at the pit?"

Louisa nodded.

"Working for someone who has shares in coal mines, you couldn't fail to know." He said bitterly. He looked so angry

71

and tired that Louisa looked over her shoulder in case Ivy or Cook could hear him. She beckoned to him to go outside in the yard so that they could talk more freely.

"All for nine shillings a day. Did you know that those six miners who managed to escape have had their wages docked because they didn't work a full shift? It's scandalous. And there are still hundreds of wives and children waiting at the pit head. They have been there for days now standing helplessly even in the rain. They are still thinking all those dead workers are coming back, but they never will. They are in their graves a mile underground."

"Have you been helping with the rescue team?" Louisa asked him gently.

Arthur nodded. "Yes and Harry and Father. We've been working nonstop then Harry had to go because Dot wasn't feeling very well. We all assumed you wouldn't be coming home this week."

Louisa sighed. "Dora, Robert and Charlotte have lost relatives, so we are short staffed. I suppose I will be able to come home next week after the funerals."

"You can't have funerals without bodies." Arthur said grimly. "Two hundred and sixty five men have lost their lives and we have only eleven corpses. I don't think we will be able to get the rest of the bodies out. The public support has been wonderful, people have come from all over the place to help, but we can't get down the shaft because it is too dangerous." He wiped his face with the back of his hand.

Louisa could see that he was very emotional and she hugged her brother. After a couple of minutes he got back on his motorcycle and she waved him goodbye.

A week later, Dora, Robert and Charlotte returned to work. All three of them looking desperately sad. They went about their duties quietly and no-one talked about the mining disaster. Mr. Thompson continued to spend most of his time at the colliery. Meanwhile his wife along with the wives of other coal mine share holders, took it in turn to visit the one hundred and sixty four widows. Some women had suffered not only the loss of their husband but also a son, some of them two sons. Louisa discovered much later that four hundred children had lost their fathers and some had lost brothers too. She knew that aside from lost siblings and fathers, that there would also be lost uncles, cousins and nephews.

When Louisa arrived in Pandy on Thursday there were four such widows in her mother's kitchen drinking tea. Louisa smiled and offered her condolences to them. Through her tears one of them – Margaret Davies - tried to smile. "I hear you are enjoying your new job. You are at Broughton Hall aren't you?"

Louisa faltered, she wasn't sure how the widows felt about her working for a man who was in the coal mining business.

"Yes I like it much better than I thought I would." She replied guardedly. She glanced at her mother who got up and told the little group that she needed to send Louisa on an errand. She gesticulated for Louisa to follow her outside and across the back yard to the garden shed.

"I have a surprise and a favour to ask you." Mary Ellen said. She opened the door of the shed and Louisa saw her bicycle now repaired after her fall on it the previous summer. "Harry has finally managed to fix it for you. The pedal was in a very bad state and he needed to weld it."

"He has also done something to the handlebars." Louisa examined it delightedly.

"We thought it would make it easier for you to come back and to from Broughton Hall, though Arthur will still take you back when it gets too dark in the winter." She watched as her daughter wheeled the bike out on to the yard.

"As you can see everyone is very sad at the moment, and I'm trying to help these families through their loss. Not that I can do much to take away their pain except make endless cups of tea. The point is I can't spare the time to help Dot. Harry said that she's had a very bad dose of flu and is still off work." She sighed and wiped a tear from her eye with a handkerchief. "So I thought you could ride over to see how she is and see what you can do to help." She smiled when she saw the expression of delight on Louisa's face.

"Of course. I would love to go."

"I never thought I would be pleased to see you on that bike again, I must admit." Her mother said, but it will be useful today at least." She hurried in to the house and then came back with a package. "Take this treacle tart for Dot, it's her favourite." She managed a smile for her daughter.

It was only a mile to Rhosrobin where Dot and Harry lived, and the road was flat, so it took Louisa just ten minutes to get there. Her route took her past the entrance to Bluebell lane and she glanced to her right as she levelled with it. Not so far away was the colliery and she could see the smoke and smell the fumes from the burning shaft. It was completely closed now, both the Dennis shaft which would probably never open again and the Martyn shaft closed for safety reasons. There would soon be an inquiry in to it all. Meanwhile a lot of men were out of work. She knew this from what Thomas had told cook, and cook had told the rest of the servants.

Dot and Harry's cottage was the middle one of a terrace called Aber Gwilym. The front door opened out on to a lane, and there was nowhere Louisa could safely leave her bike. She wheeled it around to the back and left it in the back yard leaning against the wash house. Dot herself opened the door and she hugged Louisa when she saw her.

"You look better than I expected." Louisa said to her sister-in law.

"I feel better today thank goodness." Dot coughed. "I just can't get rid of this cough." She ushered Louisa into the small parlour. Dot's grandfather was asleep in the arm chair.

"Let me make some tea." Grandad is quite deaf and out for the count. He's been sitting in here with me since last week. When Harry comes home in the evening he goes and sits in the other room. Everyone has been fussing over me."

Louisa followed Dot into the small kitchen. "I thought your mother would be here." Louisa said as she watched Dot fill the kettle and light the gas ring to boil it.

"She was here this morning, but since the trouble at the pit she's been helping out with some of the bereaved families. She's started a collection for money. It's terrible isn't it?"

Louisa nodded. "So very sad."

The kettle boiled and Dot poured the hot water onto the tea in the tea-pot and then put a tea cosy over it. She got some cups and saucers out of the cupboard. "I'm afraid I have no cake or biscuits to offer you."

Louisa laughed and produced the treacle tart. "Mother sent this. I'm quite pleased that I got it here in one piece."

Dot's eyes lit up. "I love it." She cut two pieces and put them on plates. She gestured to Louisa to sit down at the small kitchen table to drink their tea.

"We're so lucky that we don't have relatives working in the mines." Dot said. "I'm glad that Harry decided to do an apprenticeship as a painter and decorator." She bit into her treacle tart. "Your Mother makes the best treacle tarts."

"Arthur told me that he and Harry tried to rescue the men."

Dot nodded her head. "Yes, but the fire was too great, and there were more explosions after the first big one. It was amazing how many people came to help. As well as the wives and mothers waiting for news, a huge amount of miners stood waiting as well. They were the ones who were on a different shift. And there were also all those other miners from the Martyn shaft. According to Harry there were another two hundred and fifty miners who all got out of the Martyn shaft when they heard about the Dennis shaft." She shook her head as if trying to shake away the terrible explosion. "People came from the nearby pits in Hafod and Bersham as well as Llay to help. Some people even came from further afield and some came from as far as Liverpool."

"Liverpool!"

"Yes. It's wonderful isn't it? It was reported in the *Liverpool Echo*. So nice to know that people care. Your Arthur is very angry you know. I've never seen him so angry and sad all at once since Megan's death. Harry has lost some friends too, and he is very upset. I suppose this explosion has just brought back Arthur's grief over Megan."

"Megan was very frail." Louisa said remembering how Megan always seemed to be waiflike despite being very cheerful.

"Yes she was." Dot agreed. "But Arthur is still very bitter about losing her. He loved her very much you know. He thinks she was worked to death." Dot coughed and reached for her handkerchief.

Dot glanced at Louisa's concerned expression before she continued. "Besides we know how hard it can be working in service, don't we? I'm so glad I got out and have much better working hours at Greene and Madisons."

Louisa sighed. "I know it was hard for Megan. The conditions for me in Broughton Hall are much better. I must admit though, it would be nice to have more time of my own instead of having to be at the beck and call of the Thompsons. Poor Arthur. He doesn't seem to be the same anymore." She got up and took the cups and saucers to the sink to wash despite Dot's protests. "Is there anything else I can do for you before I go? I could make you some soup if you like." Dot shook her head. "I have some soup here I can warm up later, my mother brought it round last night. You go home now and have lunch with your mother."

"Will you thank Harry for me for fixing my bike?"

Dot smiled. "I will. It has come in handy already hasn't it?" She hugged her sister in law. "It was nice to see you. Thank you for coming, and thank your mother for the treacle tart."

Louisa glanced at the sleeping old man who hadn't stirred all the time she was there and then waved goodbye to Dot. She cycled back to Pandy thinking that she knew so many people who in some way were bereaved due to the Gresford explosion, yet she and her own family had somehow managed to avoid that particular tragedy.

Her mother was alone in the kitchen when she got back. She was making some sandwiches and some vegetable soup for herself and Louisa. When it was ready she put some aside for Dorothy for when she arrived home from school. Meanwhile she had another big pot of soup cooking on the stove. Louisa glanced at the fire place. It was ready to light, but her mother had not lit it. She caught her glance.

"I'm saving the coal. There might be a shortage." She sighed. "Who knows what will happen in the future. Both pits closed, men out of work, so many dead. I'm making soup for Margaret and the other three widows who were here this morning. It's the least I can do." She wiped her eyes and sat down at the table with Louisa.

They ate their meal in silence, and after she had helped her Mother to clear away, Louisa showed her mother the cardigan that she was knitting but was having difficulty with following the instructions to decrease for the neck. Her mother took it off her and explained how to do it.

Dorothy arrived home at four o clock looking very subdued, and Louisa reflected how the tragedy had affected everyone in the village even those children who had not lost relatives. School friends had lost relatives, teachers had lost relatives and the upsetting news marked a grim period for all of them at school too.

At half past seven Arthur arrived home. He had with him a friend who he introduced as Fred. As soon as Louisa saw

Fred she felt her heart fluttering and couldn't stop staring at the man. He was very tall with dark brown hair, and twinkling, brown eyes. Louisa thought he was the most handsome man she had ever seen.

When he spoke he had a funny accent and she thought he might be foreign. However Arthur explained that he was from Liverpool.

"Liverpool!" exclaimed Louisa for the second time that day. "Dot said that there were people here from Liverpool. Did you all come together?" asked Louisa.

Fred turned his attention on Louisa and smiled. "No, I came by myself, but I know there are other scousers here besides me."

"Scousers?" Louisa repeated. "What are they?"

Arthur and Fred exchanged glances and Arthur laughed. "Some people from Liverpool call themselves scousers. Fred does anyway. Didn't you know?" Arthur said. Louisa shook her head and gave Fred a friendly smile.

Mary Ellen got up and tapped Louisa's shoulder. "Come and give me a hand to make these men some supper. Your father will be home soon."

"So where are you staying?" Louisa asked Fred after her father had arrived and the three men had been fed.

"In the bed and breakfast place around the corner." Frederick answered. He smiled at Louisa and she felt her heart miss a beat.

"The white cottage?" Dorothy asked excitedly.

Fred nodded his head. "It's a bit crowded though. A lot of people wanting to stay local so they can help at the pit."

"I bet Mrs. Gittins is happy." Louisa said. "Hardly anyone stays in Pandy and now the place is bursting at the seams."

"Some people do well out of other people's tragedies." Fred commented and then turned his attention to Arthur.

Louisa felt she had been heartless. "I didn't mean that Mrs. Gittins doesn't care. I'm sure she does, it's just that it's rare to know that her guest house is full."

Fred turned to look at Louisa again and she felt her insides melting. He smiled. "I understand."

Very soon Arthur offered to take Louisa home as she had no lights on her bike and it was now getting quite dark. He promised he would get some lamps for her before the following Thursday. She could pay him back then. Though he pointed out that she probably wouldn't want to cycle home in the dark anyway.

When she got back to her room, she threw herself on her bed and began to think about the events of the day. She didn't want to go down to the servant's parlour because she felt the atmosphere may be too gloomy. She had witnessed a lot of heart breaking grief that day, and whilst she wholeheartedly sympathised with the bereaved, she wanted to be alone with her own thoughts. Meeting Fred had had a great impact on her emotions and she couldn't wait to tell Ivy.

It wasn't long before Ivy came upstairs with two mugs of cocoa. "Did you have a good day?" she asked.

Louisa told her about the widows that her Mother was helping and that she went to see Dot. Her face was glowing and she burst out, "Arthur brought someone from Liverpool home to have supper with us."

"Who is he?" Ivy asked. "And what is he doing in Wrexham?"

"He came to help the rescue team. He read about it in the *Liverpool Echo* and came to help. Now he is helping to seal the mine. His family are builders and he thought he might be able to use his skill with the sealing of the mines."

"What's he like? Is he seeing someone?" Ivy asked. She was always interested in available men."

Louisa smiled dreamily. "He's tall, dark and handsome." Ivy groaned at the cliché.

"I don't know if he has a girlfriend though."

"I think you fancy him don't you?" Ivy grinned. "When will you see him again?"

Louisa shrugged. "I don't know, but hopefully next Thursday. He's staying in the guest house in Pandy. He said that the work in the pit could take a few months."

"If he's helping, that means he won't be paid. So he may not stay." Ivy said.

Louisa stared at Ivy somewhat crestfallen. "I didn't think of that."

"Looking by your face I think you are smitten. What are you going to do?" Ivy grinned.

"I will try to find out from Arthur." Louisa announced. She believed Ivy was right. She was smitten already with this stranger from Liverpool.

Chapter Five

The following Thursday Louisa set off more eagerly than usual to Pandy. She arrived at half past ten to find her mother baking in the kitchen. She was making food to hand out to some of the widows. "Giving food is all I can do." Her mother said. "I hear that the Lord Mayor of Wrexham is starting a fund for the widows and children. I just hope there will be enough money to go round because there's also a thousand miners out of work now that the colliery is closed completely." She sighed. "God knows what the future will bring. Put the kettle on will you and make us some tea. You will have to use the gas ring. I haven't lit the fire yet."

Just as Louisa poured tea there was a knock on the door and Dot arrived. She had caught the bus from Wrexham and walked to the house from the Smithy. It was her first time in weeks that she had walked so far. She looked a bit flushed but otherwise quite healthy. Louisa pulled out a chair for her and helped her to take off her coat. Mary Ellen looked at her and was satisfied she looked well. "You had a bad bout of flu, you can't be too careful."

Dot shrugged. "How are things at Broughton Hall?" she asked Louisa.

"It's very quiet. We hardly see the Thompsons, Dora doesn't want to talk about her loss and neither does Charlotte. Robert keeps talking about the football match that his brother had wanted to go to. Apparently he had changed his shift so that he could have the afternoon off, and instead he was killed. Robert keeps saying "if only Steven had not changed his shift."

Dot nodded sympathetically. "Yes, Harry told me that quite a few miners did a double shift so that they could go to the match. But some of them wanted to take their children to the fair. So sad."

"How is Harry? I haven't seen him for a while." Louisa asked.

"Well you will see him later, because he is coming here to fetch me home. He's going to have a half day from work."

"So you can go back on his motorbike?"

"Yes. He has been asked to work on a house near our street. He's painting the outside of it. So he is going to drive over here later to take me back. He also knows you will be here, so he thought he could have a few minutes to see you too."

Harry arrived at three o clock and Louisa made another pot of tea, whilst Mary Ellen picked up her knitting.

"By the way Louisa, Arthur has put some lamps on your bike so you can ride in the dark," said Harry. "Are you sure you want to do that though?"

Louisa glanced at her mother who was frowning.

"I will tonight to see how I go on. At least I will have it ready at Broughton Hall, if I need it."

"If you intend to ride it tonight you had better go earlier than usual before it gets too dark. The nights are drawing in now." Mary Ellen commented.

Louisa's heart sank. She wanted to stay to see if Arthur brought Fred home with him. She didn't trust herself to talk about him, in case her mother got suspicious. She was saved from that though by the arrival of Dorothy who at four o clock came in from school. She sat down to chat whilst she drank a glass of milk. She looked a bit more cheerful Louisa thought absently as she listened to her sister chatter.

"It's nice we'll all be together again when Arthur and Father come home," she said. "Is that Fred coming for supper again? He talks awfully funny." She tried to imitate Fred's accent and they all laughed.

Mary Ellen shook her head. "No I believe he's gone back to Liverpool."

"Oh no what a shame. Is he coming back?" Dorothy asked.

"You will have to ask Arthur. He knows more than I do." Her mother returned.

"Have you met him Dot?" Dorothy asked.

Dot smiled. "No, but I have heard a lot about him from Harry. He seems a nice man. He was one of the first people outside Wrexham to come to help when he read about it in the newspapers."

Louisa was now torn between waiting to hear what her brother had to say about Fred, and leaving early so that she could cycle back to Broughton Hall in relative daylight. She wasn't too worried about cycling in the dark, but she hadn't done it before, and hadn't cycled to Broughton Hall before either. She convinced herself it would be easy, so she decided to wait to hear what her brother had to say.

At six o clock Mary Ellen lit the fire and started to make supper. Dot and Louisa helped her whilst Dorothy sat at the kitchen table and showed Harry her school books. Arthur arrived home at half past six and William arrived a few minutes behind him. Already light was falling, and when

William opened the door a chilly draught wafted in to the small kitchen.

The first thing Arthur said to Louisa was to tell her about the lamps on her bicycle.

"Thank you, Harry has told me that you have put them on for me. How much do I owe you?"

"Not much. Tuppence."

Louisa opened her purse and handed her brother the money.

"Are you sure you don't want me to take you back?" He asked.

"Quite sure." Louisa was aware that everyone was staring at her. "I'll be fine."

They sat down to eat and Louisa was glad when Dorothy asked if Fred was coming back from Liverpool.

Arthur nodded. "Yes. He's gone back to Liverpool to get the rest of his things. The company that has been appointed to seal the mine have offered him a contract. He's a qualified and experienced brickie. So he's going to live in Pandy. At least for a few months anyway. That's how he makes his living apparently, working from one building contract to another. The one in Liverpool was coming to an end anyway, so his brother will finish things off for him."

Louisa's heart quickened and she held her head down concentrating on eating her sausages and mashed potatoes.

"There's going to be an inquiry soon." Her father said.

"So they should." Arthur said grimly. "Two hundred and sixty five men dead and eighteen hundred men without work. Someone should answer for that. The people who employ you Louisa should be very worried. They are very involved with the mining business."

85

"Don't forget there is more than one owner. I believe there are four." Harry said. "And it is not just our Louisa who works for a mine owner, but so does Father. Remember Mr. Fern is only the manager of the farm and not the owner. He has nothing to do with the colliery. It just happens that Mr. Lawrence owns the farm and also has shares in the colliery."

"I don't think Mr. Thompson has shares in Gresford pit." Louisa stated. "He has some shares in a mine but I don't think it is Gresford.

William who had been listening intently to his sons and daughter was unhappy at how the conversation was developing and decided to intervene. "Well let's wait to hear the results of the inquiry," he said. "There's nothing we can do about it."

"I've heard that a lot of the miners have managed to get work in Bersham and Llay." Harry said. "Hafod and Southsea are taking some too."

"Well that's a start." Mary Ellen said cheerfully. She tried to change the subject. "Does anyone want some blackberry and apple pie and custard?"

At nine o clock Louisa got ready to leave. She tucked her skirt beneath her to sit on the bicycle, and then waved goodbye to all her family who gathered at the door to see her go. The journey didn't take her long and by half past nine she was lying on her bed waiting for Ivy to bring her cocoa.

"Well, was Fred there?" Ivy asked her excitedly.

Louisa shook her head and shrugged, then explained things to Ivy.

"Better luck next week then." Ivy said. "Now do you want to hear my news?

86

"Yes of course. What's happened?" Louisa turned to look at Ivy's beaming face.

"I'm leaving. I'm going to secretarial school to learn to be a secretary. I've been saving hard these last few years and now I have enough to pay for a course. No more scrubbing floors, peeling vegetables and dressing madam for me."

"But when are you going to do this? And where?" Louisa was flabbergasted. She was also distressed to lose someone she considered to be a friend. They had become quite close over the last year.

"I'm going back to Manchester. My Mum said I could stay with her until I qualify. She reckons it's a good investment. I'm bound to get a better paid job, then my sister Daisy is going to do it too. That boyfriend of hers - George his name is - has already done it and has got himself a good job. He is working in an office in a rubber factory in Patricroft."

"Patricroft?! Louisa wrinkled her nose. "Where's that?"

Ivy smiled. "It's in Manchester. There's more work going on there than here. Despite the recession George has still managed to get work. He is encouraging Daisy to do it too! I just wish our Rose would think of it too. She is really unhappy in her job. She has finished with her boyfriend now so maybe she will think about moving!"

"So when are you going?" Louisa asked. She sat on the edge of the bed and began to take out the hairpins from her hair.

"After Christmas. I want to give Cook plenty of time to replace me." She sat down on her bed to face Louisa cupping her mug of cocoa in her hands smiling. "The course starts in January. I've had confirmation today. I'm a good speller, always was good at that in school so I won't have problems with the shorthand. I can't wait to leave and get a job in an office. No more being a servant for me. After my course, it will be 'take a letter Miss Dawson'." She laughed, and Louisa laughed with her too. She was genuinely pleased for her friend and hoped she would realise her ambitions.

In the darkness Louisa lay awake wondering about her own future. She didn't want to spend all her life as a servant either, but she didn't really know what she should do. After her first bad experience working in Service she felt much happier. She concluded that for now she should be content with her lot, at least for a little while longer. Arthur and Harry had both warned her that if the owners of Gresford colliery were prosecuted, there could be repercussions and Mr. Thompson may be caught up in the backlash. Things could get unpleasant especially if nearly two thousand miners became redundant. If the mine was closed there would be cut backs everywhere and she might lose her own job as a consequence.

Louisa felt the miners were brave to go to another pit after what had happened in the Dennis shaft. Knowing how claustrophobic she would feel if she had to work down a mine, she had to admit she was lucky to have the job she had. Sometimes though, she felt she should be doing something more interesting with her life. She had very little free time, so she couldn't even volunteer to help in charity work because of the hours she worked.

The following morning, Louisa walked in to the kitchen for her breakfast and was surprised to hear Dora talking to Robert of the coming inquiry about the explosion. It was the first time Dora had referred to it, and Louisa wondered whether both Dora and Robert were coming to terms with their bereavements.

"I'm told that Sir Stafford Cripps is going to represent the Miners." Dora confided in Robert.

He nodded his agreement. "Yes the North Wales Miners Association are going to brief him. There have been rumours flying around for months that the pit was prone to firedamp and that there was a high level of gas. My dad knew it too, he often mentioned it to me. The owners were told but, my dad said they totally disregarded the warnings, and as far as he could see, they did nothing to try to make the place safer for the men. All they seem to care about is profit. They also encouraged double shifts, to keep the mine working twenty four hours a day. So when miners asked to double up so that they could have time off to go to the race course in Wrexham to watch the football match, they weren't going to stop them. That's why there were so many men working there that Saturday night." Robert's voice was bitter, and Louisa glanced at him warily. Ivy came and stood beside her and they exchanged worried glances whilst Robert finished talking.

"If it was dangerous why didn't the miners tell the managers or the supervisor's?" Ivy asked innocently.

Robert wheeled on her angrily. "They did, but nothing was done. All through September they have been working non-stop. I bet that's why there was an explosion. Too much gas, and too much jack hammering. That's what my dad told me. It would only take a spark to start things off, just like this." Robert smacked both his hands together as if to demonstrate the effect of gas being ignited by a spark. Ivy, Louisa and Dora jumped nervously at the sound.

At that point Thomas walked in followed by a downcast Charlotte, and all of them fell silent. Louisa helped herself to a cup of tea whilst Thomas walked towards the sink to wash his hands. Robert turned quickly towards Dora to put a finger to his lips. Daring to glance at Louisa and Ivy he sent them the same signal. Robert's eyes were still brightly intense with anger. They fell about their duties as normal, and for the rest of the week Robert and Dora whispered to themselves in private whenever they could.

On Wednesday cook told them that Charlotte had handed in her notice and would be leaving the following week. Charlotte's mother was struggling to cope with the loss of her husband and she had decided to go and live with her sister in Wolverhampton. Charlotte was going with her. Charlotte's aunt Maud had told them that she would probably get a well-paid job at the huge textile factory that was not far away from her home. She was hoping that her mother would also get some sewing work. Her aunt Maud seemed to think that sewing machinists would be in demand. The factory's policy was not to employ married women but Charlotte was optimistic that they would make an exception for her mother now she was a widow. She wouldn't have a problem herself, and her wages would be far more than she was getting as a kitchen maid. The three of them should manage well enough to live together.

"I wonder who will be going next." Ivy whispered to Louisa when they were alone in the kitchen.

"More importantly – will we get a replacement for Charlotte?" Louisa replied. She was beginning to feel unsettled again.

When Thursday came, Louisa cycled across to Pandy and arrived in the middle of the morning. Her mother was mending shirts and Louisa sat beside her to help sew on a missing button from one of the cuffs. After they had finished their work her mother boiled some milk and made some coffee and asked Louisa for the latest gossip from Broughton Hall. Her mother listened sadly when she told her about Charlotte, Dora and Robert. "God bless them." She said wiping tears from her eyes. Louisa finished her gossip by telling her mother about Ivy's plans for the future then asked her mother what she thought about Louisa doing something similar.

"I think you should stay where you are for now. We don't know what is going to happen yet. It could take months and months before we get an outcome about the explosion." She looked up at her daughter's face. "Cheer up, all this coming and going has made you restless I know, wait until things settle down before you start thinking about your future. Anyway I thought you wanted to train to be a nurse, and you are still not old enough yet." She got up and put down her mending, then went into the front parlour. She emerged a few seconds later holding an appliance that Louisa had only ever seen at Broughton Hall. "Look what Arthur's bought for me. It's a vacuum cleaner for cleaning carpets." She laughed. "Pity I've only got one carpet to clean."

"That's very generous of him." Louisa smiled.

"Aye he is generous. He's got too much money if you ask me."

"We've got one at Broughton Hall. It makes life easier for me and Ivy though, especially the stairs. Mrs Smedley was given one by the Thompsons to try out about two months ago. They said that if Mrs. Smedley was pleased with it, that we could keep it. And I'm pleased to say that we did."

At lunch time, Dot arrived and chatted with Louisa whilst she got on with her embroidery.

"Arthur is going to the Majestic cinema tonight to see a film with Fred, do you want to go too? He's asked me to ask you." Mary Ellen said this as she looked up from her sewing to glance at her daughter.

Louisa was surprised and pleased. "Yes, I would like to, but will there be time to have supper and get to the 'Majestic'?"

"They are going to get changed at work and go straight to the cinema. Apparently they will get a snack from the snack bar and will meet you there at seven o clock." Her mother replied.

Louisa looked down at her clothes. She had dressed sensibly because she was cycling and hadn't expected to be going out. Still it was a nice invitation and a chance to see Fred.

Her mother looked at her softly. "You will do like that, it's dark in the cinema anyway." She chuckled.

"What film will they see?" Dot asked.

"I forgot to ask." Mary Ellen confessed.

Louisa set off at six thirty and eagerly cycled to the Majestic cinema which was on the outskirts of the town. She arrived at ten minutes to seven and saw Arthur standing in the doorway with a crowd of other people. He gave her a hug.

"I'm glad you could make it. Otherwise I would have had to sell your ticket. I bought it for you because there was a queue, and I thought you would miss the beginning of the film."

"Thanks. How much do I owe you?"

"It's four pennies. You can pay me later. Let's join Fred and Beryl quickly or we won't get seats together." He led the way quickly towards the entrance to the theatre where Fred was standing arm in arm with a woman. Louisa's heart sank. She hadn't realised that Fred already had a girlfriend. She was pretty too with long red hair hanging down her back. Arthur introduced them and they found a set of four seats half way down the aisle.

Despite being disappointed about not getting much chance to speak to Fred, Louisa enjoyed the film and managed to concentrate on the story rather than think about him. During the interval the two men went to buy ice creams and Louisa had opportunity to talk to Beryl. It turned out she was from Liverpool and had arrived yesterday to see Fred.

Louisa didn't know what to think about that. "So are you staying at the same lodgings as Fred then?" Inwardly she felt indignant that Beryl could be so forward. Then she began to wonder whether they may be engaged and she quickly looked at Beryl's finger to see if there was a ring. There wasn't.

Beryl laughed. "No, I wish I was though. I'm in a B & B in Wrexham, I have to go back to Liverpool tomorrow, I can't afford more than two nights. I just wanted to surprise Fred."

"It was a surprise too." Fred said as he gently stepped over Louisa and Beryl's feet to sit next to Beryl again. He handed her an ice-cream, then Arthur sat down next to Louisa and handed her an ice cream too.

"What do you think of the film?" Arthur said to everyone as he licked his ice cream.

"The camera work showing the height of the giants is good. You get the idea that they are gigantic compared to everyone else on the ground." Fred volunteered this as he glanced at first Arthur then the two women.

Arthur nodded and continued to lick his ice cream.

"It's a bit frightening though." Beryl said and clutched Fred's free arm possessively. Beryl's hold on Fred's arm seemed to convey a declaration of ownership and Louisa's heart sank. It seemed quite obvious to her that Beryl wanted Louisa to know that Fred belonged to her. In Louisa's opinion the film wasn't frightening at all. If anything she would have said that the film content was poignant because the four giants had lost their way back to their secret kingdom and ordinary people were afraid of them instead of trying to help. She felt that Beryl pretended to be afraid so that she could clutch Fred's arm. She hid her disappointment by concentrating on her ice cream. She was glad when the lights went down again and the second half of the film continued. The concluding part of the film was very gripping and Louisa managed to forget Beryl and Fred as she watched the actors trying to guide the giants to the secret pathway that led to their homeland.

When the film was over they all casually walked out of the cinema and Louisa settled up her debts with Arthur. She gave him four pence for the ticket and then asked him how much she owed for the ice cream.

"Fred bought the ice creams. It's his treat to celebrate getting a permanent contract of work."

Louisa turned towards Fred to thank him and he winked at her. "My pleasure. I hope you enjoyed it – and the film."

"Yes thanks. I did." She turned to go.

"Where did you leave your bike?" Arthur asked her. "We will walk you to it just to make sure no-one has pinched it."

All four of them walked down Regent Street, then turned into Duke Street where Louisa had tied her bicycle to some railings under the archway.

"Couldn't you find anywhere closer?" Arthur asked smiling at his sister.

"I thought it would be safer away from the cinema. And besides I thought it might rain so the roof of this arcade would keep it dry."

"Good thinking. As it happens our motorbikes aren't far away. They are behind the library in Queen's Square."

Louisa smiled and started to untie the string on the railings when Fred put his hand on her shoulder. Louisa trembled at his touch. "Do you have to go back straight away Louisa?" He looked at Arthur as he spoke. "Just thought it would be nice to go for a pint in that pub over there."

Arthur gazed at his sister thoughtfully. She held his gaze. She had never been to a pub before. The one that Fred was pointing to had a thatched roof and was called the "Horse and Jockey". It was a pub she knew her mother and Father went to occasionally on a Saturday lunch time, if they had been shopping. They enjoyed the pub's steak and kidney pies.

"What do you want to do Louisa? Just a quick one?" Arthur suggested.

Louisa hesitated and then agreed.

Inside the crowded pub Arthur ordered two pints of lager and two half pints of shandy. He handed the half pints to first Louisa and then Beryl as they stood together. The pub was filling up quickly, and Louisa recognised some people she had seen seated in the cinema. Arthur gently pushed Louisa towards a small window where there was a table and two stools. Fred indicated to the women to sit down to drink their beverages. It was getting quite noisy in the pub and as Fred and Arthur were talking about work and car engines, Louisa was forced to make conversation with Beryl.

"How long have you be going out with Fred?" Louisa asked innocently. She was interested very much and couldn't understand why she felt immensely jealous. But she felt she had to find out about the relationship as much as she could.

"A couple of months on and off." Beryl replied casually. "It's a bit difficult when he's here and I'm in Liverpool."

Louisa nodded her head in agreement. "I suppose so."

"What about you? Have you got a boyfriend somewhere?" Beryl asked her. She took a cigarette out of her bag and offered one to Louisa, who declined the offer.

"No boyfriend. Don't smoke, but you like shandy, is that it?" Beryl blew smoke in the air and stared at Louisa. She smiled at Louisa though her eyes were cold, and Louisa thought she detected a condescending tone. "What do you usually do in your spare time?" Beryl asked.

"I read a lot, and visit my family, help around the house, that sort of thing you know." She took a gulp of her drink and glanced at Arthur to see if he had finished his pint. Both he and Fred had drunk about half of their drinks. She turned towards her companion again and tried to be civil. "What do you do in Liverpool?"

"I go dancing a lot and to the cinema a lot if I can afford it. I've got a few pals to go out with." She took another drag of her cigarette and then added, "If we're broke by mid-week we go round to each other's houses and chat or dance to the music on the wireless. Irene and I live quite close so we take it in turns to listen to music on the wireless. At least until my Mam or Irene's Mam tells us to shut up."

"So don't you work?" Louisa asked. Despite her jealousy, she was fascinated at this description of Beryl's life.

"Of course I do. But not in service like you do. I live at home and go to work every day at John Lewis'. I see Irene after work in the evenings."

"What's John Lewis?" Louisa asked.

"It's a big department store. Haven't you heard of it?" Beryl stared at her companion incredulously.

Fred must have heard Beryl, and suddenly said. "Louisa hasn't been to Liverpool and there isn't a John Lewis around here Beryl, so she wouldn't know would she?"

Beryl shrugged, and Louisa was delighted that Fred had stuck up for her. At this point, Arthur asked him what he thought of the local Lager.

"It's a good lager. I normally prefer ale, but this is a very strong lager."

Arthur agreed. "Yes it is quite strong. The brewery was set up by two Germans. Apparently it's like German lager."

"Get away." Fred said, then taking another swig, drained his glass. Arthur finished his drink too and asked the girls if they were ready to go. They again escorted Louisa back to her tied up bicycle. Beryl and Louisa were silent whilst the two men discussed the forthcoming inquiry about the mining explosion.

The inquiry had opened on the twenty fifth October and Sir Stafford Cripps had cited many causes of the explosion. Just as Robert had suggested, Sir Stafford Cripps was looking at management responsibility towards safety procedures. He wanted to examine whether there had been adequate safety measures in place. During the inquiry he had also suggested that there was a history of bad working practices in general, and that there was poor ventilation in the pit. Louisa remembered that Robert had told her that Sir Stafford Cripps was representing the miners.

"I reckon the most likely cause was an explosion caused by a build-up of gas, probably methane." Fred was saying. "This could have been ignited easily enough by a spark from a metal tool."

"I think you are right, but how can you prove it?" Arthur agreed. Let's hope that Sir Henry Walker will get to the bottom of it."

"He's the chief Inspector of Mines isn't he? Louisa said. "Do you think he will get the Dennis shaft re-opened?

Arthur shook his head. "I doubt it. What do you think Fred?"

"I think it might be too dangerous, it's hard to know how much gas is still there."

All this time Beryl had leaned against the wall under the archway looking bored. She lit another cigarette and scowled at Fred. "Are you taking me home or what?"

With that, Louisa untied her bicycle and got ready to leave. Arthur warned Louisa to be careful on her way home. She waved goodbye to everyone as they watched her cycle along Regent Street in the direction of Broughton Hall.

Ivy was still awake when Louisa crept in. She had never arrived back at Broughton Hall so late before and Robert had looked at her in surprise when he opened the door for her. She had tiptoed upstairs to her shared room trying not to wake up the rest of the household. When she had gingerly opened the bedroom door that she shared with Ivy she had discovered her reading a library book.

Ever since she had made her mind up to go to secretarial school, Ivy had been spending every spare minute reading novels. After she had finished a book she loaned it to Louisa, so that she could read it too. This was a good arrangement for Louisa, because it meant she could use most of her days off to go to Pandy instead of to the library. It limited her choice of books because she had to depend on Ivy's selection from the library, but generally the girls enjoyed reading the same novels. Both girls wanted to stretch their minds, and Ivy wanted to improve her spelling. She spent most of her spare time at the library in Wrexham. Ivy spent so much time there that she had become friendly with one of the librarians who worked there. She seemed to have taken Ivy under her wing. Both Ivy and Louisa admired the woman as it was unusual to see a qualified female librarian working in Wrexham Library.

"How did it go with Fred?" Ivy whispered in the half light. Louisa told her all that had happened and how she had met Beryl.

"Did Fred seem ecstatic to see her?"

Louisa thought about this before answering. "I don't know. He spent a lot of time talking to Arthur."

"Hmm. It won't last." Ivy pronounced knowingly.

Despite herself, Louisa laughed. "How do you know that?"

"I've got a feeling that's all." Ivy returned. She waited for Louisa to get into bed and then switched off the bedside lamp which they shared on the small table between the single beds. It was a luxury both of them treasured. Neither of them had ever had electric bedside lamps in their bedrooms at home.

Chapter Six

The following week was Dorothy's birthday and Louisa had bought her sister a new purse. She wrapped it up carefully and put it in the basket in front of her bike, before setting off for Pandy. Whilst Louisa and her mother waited for the rest of the family to join them later, she helped her with her mending and hung out some clothes to dry. Though it was the middle of November it was a dry sunny day despite it being quite cold. Mary Ellen hoped that the mid-day sun would dry the working clothes she had washed that day. As she pegged out the clothes Louisa hoped that Fred would accompany Arthur that evening to eat with the family.

After a light lunch, Mary Ellen slipped out to see some of her widowed neighbours. She had taken with her some jars of homemade blackberry and apple jam and some loaves of bread. Finding herself with some free time to herself, Louisa pulled out her book from her bag and began to read until her sister arrived home from school. All the time she was reading she felt her stomach knotting itself in hopeful expectation of a visit from Fred. She had never experienced this feeling before and found it difficult to overcome.

Two hours later, Dorothy ran in to the house to hug her sister just as Mary Ellen returned. Louisa handed her sister the present she had bought her and was rewarded with a cry of delight.

"Thank you Louisa it's lovely." She opened the purse and found a silver three pence that Louisa had slipped in for luck. "And a threepenny bit too. Oh thank you."

Dot arrived soon afterwards, straight from work and she also handed Dorothy a present. This gift was also received with a delighted whoop of joy. She immediately pulled on the red woollen mittens and scarf which Dot had knitted herself.

"I'm glad you like them and that they fit you."

When all the family were seated around the table for supper that evening, Louisa was disappointed to see that Fred had not accompanied Arthur. Meanwhile, Mary Ellen presented a Victoria sandwich cake she had made as a surprise for Dorothy. They all began to sing Happy Birthday, and just as Louisa managed to settle down the turmoil in her stomach, a knock on the door bringing Fred on the doorstep set it fluttering again. He had popped in to say happy birthday to Dorothy.

"Just in time for the birthday cake" Mary Ellen welcomed him with a smile."

Meanwhile William was listening to the wireless and told everyone to be quiet because it had just been announced that there was growing concern about Hitler's increasing air force. The news presenter also informed the silent listeners that Sir Winston Churchill had warned the government that if war was declared on Britain that it would not be just by land or by sea but the country could be attacked by dropping bombs from the air. William shook his head in disbelief.

"Let's hope we don't have another war. It was bad enough the last one. We lost too many men and women then."

Arthur agreed. "Hitler wasn't around then either, or at least he didn't have a position of power. The man is mad and I reckon he means to declare war on Britain. Why else would he build up the air force and the army and get all this power? The British government must be worried even if they aren't saying anything. Churchill is only reiterating what Baldwin said earlier this year. Do you remember? He said that if Germany build up their air force then they will bomb us from the air. How can you stop that? For all we know they are building war ships too."

"After the Great war wasn't there a treaty that Germany shouldn't build any more battle ships?" Harry commented.

William nodded his head in agreement. "However I don't trust Adolf Hitler. For all we know he could be building other ships in secret."

Fred agreed. "He is very devious. His persistent persecution of innocent people is disgusting."

William got up and switched off the wireless. "I've heard enough of Germany for one night."

"Do you fancy a game of chess Dad?" Dorothy asked.

William nodded and so Dorothy brought the chess board out and they settled down to a game.

"Do you play chess Fred?" Arthur asked.

Fred nodded. "Yes quite a bit, my brothers and I used to play a lot." He gazed enthusiastically at the chess board whilst Dorothy and William set up the pieces. Meanwhile Louisa started to get ready to leave. Fred smiled at her as she put on her coat, and Louisa felt a lump in her throat and looked away. "Are you leaving now?" he asked her.

Unable to trust herself to speak, Louisa nodded. Fortunately Harry came to her rescue. "We will walk with you as far as the fields.

"Where's your motorbike tonight Harry?" Louisa asked.

"I thought it would be a nice change to walk over, it's a fine night and not too cold if you wrap up warm." Instead of leaving them at the stile, Louisa decided to walk with them over the field and Harry held open the field gate so that she could push her bicycle through after Dot. Louisa told them about Ivy's plans to do a secretarial course and she was wondering what she should do with the rest of her life.

"What do you fancy doing?" Harry asked.

"I thought you wanted to be a nurse" Dot said.

I've always thought that's what I wanted to do, but I'm not sure now." Louisa said. "Mother said I needed to get a better education first, but how can I do that if I am working. I like the idea of getting a better education, but if I have to wait for years and years before I can train, maybe nursing isn't such a good idea."

"They might pay you to train. You might have to go away to training college though. Would you mind going away from home again?" Dot asked her.

"I'm not sure." Louisa said. "I suppose if it was to do something I wanted to do, it would be alright. I'm just not sure what I want."

"Why don't you write to the War Memorial in Wrexham, or that new hospital that's just been opened?" Harry suggested. That MP Lloyd George opened it not long ago. It's going to be called the Maelor Hospital."

"Maybe I will." Louisa answered. "But mother thinks I still might not be old enough."

"Well you need to think properly what you do want and then you can work towards achieving your goal." Harry said.

"At least I know I don't want to work in service all my life. I think I mentioned nursing to mother because I needed to suggest something as an alternative to working in service."

In the dim light, Louisa could see that Harry was grinning. "Good, I'm glad to hear it. You can do better than that. What you need is some time to think. Don't do anything rash."

Presently they came to the end of the fields on the outskirts of Rhosrobin. After manoeuvring the field gates to get on to the road they parted company and Louisa cycled back to Broughton Hall. The last part of the road was edged by tall dark trees and there was scarcely any light, she was glad Arthur had bought such a strong lamplight for her bike.

As usual Ivy was reading a book when Louisa got into their shared room.

"Any developments with Fred?" she asked.

Louisa shrugged. "No but he was there, talking about Germany with my dad and brothers again."

"Did Dorothy like the purse?"

"Yes she did thanks. Do you want some cocoa?"

Louisa took off her coat and slipped downstairs to make some cocoa for herself and Ivy. Her mind was jumbled up with thoughts of Fred, interspersed with the comments her father had said about Hitler. Surely there won't be another war she told herself. Why would Hitler want to start another war? She took the cocoa upstairs and got undressed and

105

slipped into bed to drink it. Ivy continued to read, only looking up now and again to sip her hot drink. Somewhat soothed and warmed by the beverage, Louisa lay on her pillow, and closed her eyes. Her thoughts now shifted to mull over the advice Harry had given her, and then what Dot had said about the new hospital. She decided she would wait until after Christmas before embarking on anything new.

At the end of November, Louisa cycled across to Pandy to find her mother listening to the wireless whilst she did some ironing. It was the wedding of Prince George the duke of Kent to Princess Marina of Greece and Denmark. As the details were being broadcasted, Mary Ellen listened whilst she put the iron in and out of the fire. She liked to listen to the wireless as she pressed the sheets she had washed and dried the day before. Louisa smiled at her mother's excitement and then bustled around the house trying to make herself useful. She herself wasn't so interested in royal weddings, though she loved to hear the descriptions of the dresses. Based on what she had heard, she loved to imagine what the clothes would look like and she would sketch designs on pieces of paper. Ivy often saw them and told Louisa she should be an artist. But Louisa only laughed and said she would rather design and make the clothes.

When her father and Arthur arrived later with Fred in his wake they were all surprised to see that Fred had brought cakes and chocolates for them all. "Are you celebrating the royal wedding?" Louisa asked incredulously.

Fred shook his head sheepishly. "It's my birthday."

They all laughed and sat round the table to eat the lamb casserole that Mary Ellen and Louisa had made between them.

"Did you have many nice presents?" Louisa asked Fred.

"My sister Mary sent me some socks and Cecelia sent me some fags."

"What about Beryl?" Louisa asked as casually as she could.

"She sent me a card, but I will probably see her at the weekend when I go to Liverpool." He caught Arthur's eye and they exchanged a look that Louisa couldn't interpret.

"So will you be having another birthday on Saturday with your family?" Dorothy asked.

Fred shrugged. "Maybe."

"Will you see your brothers?" Dorothy asked.

"Yes probably."

How many have you got?"

"I've got six brothers."

"Six!" Dorothy squealed. That's a lot of brothers. Do they all live in Liverpool?"

He nodded.

"What are their names?" Dorothy wanted to know.

Obligingly, Fred relayed all the names of his brothers. "James, Robert, Alfred, Thomas, John and Edward."

"Are any of them married?" Dorothy persisted. She was fascinated by this information. Louisa was too, and was happy for Dorothy to ask all the questions.

"Three of them are married and so is one of my sisters. Her husband is Irish."

"So do you have just the two sisters? The ones who sent you presents?" Louisa ventured to ask.

Fred turned to look at her as he answered her question, and she felt an unsteady wobbly feeling in her stomach whilst under his gaze. She swallowed hard to compose herself.

"Yes. Cecelia and Mary."

Whilst Dorothy digested this information, the conversation then returned to the royal wedding. Louisa got the impression that Fred was not very interested in the royal wedding, nor in the royal family. She helped herself to a piece of his birthday cake and tried some of his chocolates, then reluctantly pulled on her coat to go back to Broughton hall. She was pleased when both Arthur and Fred walked her to the end of the road. Fred went into his bed and breakfast place at South view cottage on the corner of the lane and called goodnight as she pedalled home. Then Arthur turned back to walk the hundred yards back home.

As she cycled along the lanes, Louisa kept thinking about Fred and Beryl in Liverpool.

When she told Ivy about Fred going to Liverpool, her response was that maybe Fred was just going to see his family and not just Beryl.

"Maybe he doesn't want to see her again." Ivy suggested.

Louisa was not convinced. She told herself that Fred would never think of her romantically and she decided that the best thing she could do was to forget him and move on with her life. She still had Christmas to look forward to, and she had plenty of things to think about over the next three weeks.

Chapter Seven

Two weeks before Christmas, Ivy found Louisa sitting on her bed surrounded by two huge bags of assorted sweets and caramels. On the floor at her feet she had placed her sewing bag which was overflowing with pieces of felt and embroidery silks. Fascinated Ivy sat on her bed facing Louisa and asked her what she was doing.

"I'm making Christmas bags of sweets for the children who lost their fathers in the Gresford explosion." She put a piece of sewing thread between her teeth to break it off. Bending down she showed Ivy some of the green felt bags she had already finished. Each one had been embroidered with either a robin or a reindeer and she had made some white French knots around them to represent snow.

"They are beautiful!" Ivy exclaimed. "Can I help you?!

"Are you any good at sewing?" Louisa said doubtfully. She had never seen Ivy mend anything.

"No, but I could fill the bags for you" she replied pleadingly. Louisa nodded. "Thanks. Do you think you can manage to tie them up with a bow with these ribbons?" She showed Ivy what she wanted and they worked together for an hour until they had made seven pretty bags of sweets.

"I need to make another thirteen before next week!" Louisa yawned. "I should just about manage it before I take them home."

"I will help you." Ivy said. "Do you know who you are going to give them to?"

Louisa nodded. There are eight children belonging to the neighbours where my parents live and the rest I am going to give to Dorothy to take to school for her classmates."

"That's very kind of you Louisa, you are so thoughtful."

Louisa sighed. "It's the least I can do. My mother and other neighbours have been giving food and there have been a few jumble sales to raise money."

"Yes I saw some street collectors in town when I went to the library, I put some coins in. It all helps."

Christmas Day that year was to fall on a Tuesday, so the Thursday beforehand Louisa cycled excitedly across to Pandy. It was a mild day, in fact the weather had been mild all that month and they had scarcely seen any snow. This was good because she had arranged to see a film with Arthur and Fred.

It seemed that Ivy was right after all and that Fred had finished with Beryl. The previous Thursday whilst sitting at the table with her family, Mary Ellen had asked after Fred as she hadn't seen him for a while. Arthur had informed her that Fred had started working different shifts and that he was going to come round on Saturday. They were both going to go to the football match together. Unable to stop herself, Louisa had asked Arthur, if Fred was going to ask Beryl to come down to Pandy for Christmas. Arthur had shaken his head and shrugged before explaining, "He didn't invite her down last time she was here. She just turned up. Fred's been trying to shake her off for ages but she doesn't seem to get the message."

Ellen looked at her son in surprise. "That's not a very nice thing to say."

Louisa felt ecstatic but tried not to show it. Apparently Beryl had been visiting Fred's mother regularly to try to get information about him. The last time Fred was in Liverpool he had gone to see Beryl and told her that he had never been interested in her and that he didn't want her to just turn up in Pandy totally uninvited.

"How did she find out where he was living?" Mary Ellen had asked him as she handed him a bowl of stew.

"His mother told her. She didn't know that Fred had been trying to get away from her for months. Beryl gave Fred's mother the impression that they were a couple in love. They went out together once during the summer and Beryl seemed to think they are a couple and of course they are not."

"Is Fred going to go back to Liverpool for Christmas?" Mary Ellen asked as she sat down to eat. Arthur shrugged. "I don't know. He hasn't told me his plans."

And now, so close to Christmas, the three of them were going to celebrate Christmas with a film. Louisa was looking forward to this because she doubted very much she would be able to get any time off on Christmas day. She remembered sadly the previous year when she had excitedly looked forward to meeting Megan. So much had happened since then.

Her mother was sewing together the pieces of knitting she had made for a cardigan for Dorothy. As she sat sewing

Louisa proudly produced her own knitting and her mother congratulated her on the green fleck cardigan she had finished knitting for herself. Louisa was pleased. It wasn't often that she got praise from her mother.

"Have they got a replacement for Charlotte yet?" Mary Ellen asked.

Louisa nodded. "Yes. Her name is Hilda. She is from Summerhill. Sadly her brother was killed in the explosion. He was only fourteen. Her father worked there too but he was on a different shift and was at home when it happened."

Mary Ellen shook her head as if to shake away all the grief. "This Christmas is going to be very hard for all those families."

"Apparently the relief fund has raised half a million pounds." Said Louisa.

"Yes but it won't go far with thousands of mouths to feed, and there has been no work since it happened. Some people are starving."

"I suppose we should consider ourselves lucky." Louisa said. Her mother nodded in agreement. "I've been reading in the *Wrexham Leader* about the inquiry, the matter is still unresolved. It seems Sir Henry has adjourned the inquiry for now. They still seem to think they can get evidence from the Dennis shaft."

"I didn't think they would be able to get any more evidence unless they go down and it's too dangerous isn't it? Fred is still working at the colliery to seal it off." Louisa replied.

Her mother shrugged. "Who knows? Your father is getting agitated because some of the farm workers are grumbling about Mr. Lawrence. It doesn't help that our neighbours keep saying Mr. Lawrence should have done more to prevent the explosion. He has been good to your father so it is difficult for him to take sides."

"Well you can't blame the miners surely. Mr. Lawrence is one of the shareholders." Louisa said simply. "They are looking for someone to take responsibility for what happened. I know it must be difficult for father though. After all it's Mr. Fern who manages the farm on behalf of Mr. Lawrence. Mr. Fern is a good manager too."

Louisa would have liked to discuss the matter of who managed the safety of the miners on behalf of the owners of the mine, but knew she was treading on thin ground. Both her mother and father were extremely loyal. She also knew that Mr. Lawrence had a high regard for her father because he had a special way of dealing with the shire horses.

Her mother shook her head unhappily and made no further comment. Louisa didn't pursue the topic. She didn't want to upset her parents. Instead she showed her mother the Christmas bags of sweets for the children and her mother exclaimed over them in delight.

"Dot's mother has been helping to raise funds. Did you know that the people in Hereford have donated apples for the families? It's wonderful the national support. Even donations of dried fish from Grimsby has been sent."

For a little while the inquiry was not mentioned and when Arthur and her father arrived for supper, neither of them mentioned it either. When they had finished their meal Fred arrived at the house and asked how they would all travel to the cinema. Arthur suggested that Louisa rode pillion with him and Fred would follow on his motorbike. He would then take her back to Broughton Hall and would pick her up the following Thursday after Christmas so that she could ride her bike on her return to work. Louisa agreed at once. It would make a nice change and she rarely got chance to use the bike during the week anyway.

"What film are you going to see?" Dorothy asked. "I wish I could come."

"When the pantomime starts next week I will take you there." Mary Ellen promised. You can't go with them now you need to go to bed."

"Anyway the film they are going to see is not suitable for you." William added.

"What is it?" Dorothy persisted.

"*The Last Baron of San Picardy.*" Arthur said. You wouldn't like it."

"I bet I would." Dorothy said. "I would also like to see '*The knowledge of Mrs. Burns.*' I heard on the wireless that it is a good film."

Fred laughed indulgently at Dorothy. "Yes I heard that too. There's also a new comedy out about a haunted castle, I think you might like that when it comes around."

"Don't encourage her Fred. She listens to the wireless too much. I'm not sure about Mrs. Burns knowledge, but Dorothy knows too much of the wrong thing." Mary Ellen said. Her voice was stern but she was smiling at Dorothy. "You three go and enjoy yourselves."

At the cinema Louisa sat between Arthur and Fred and she felt quite excited that at last she was sitting next to Fred. He didn't seem to notice her though and both he and Arthur's eyes were glued to the screen. During the interval Fred went

114

to get ice creams and Arthur asked Louisa if she was enjoying the film.

"Yes, it's good, but it's not exactly like the book though is it?" Louisa said.

"I don't know. I haven't read the book. I keep meaning too though. Is there a copy at home?"

"No, I have it at Broughton Hall, I've been reading it at night time. It's good. Do you want to borrow it? I think its Harry's actually."

"What's Harry's?" Fred asked as he sat down and handed out the ice creams.

"The book about this film." Arthur said. Louisa has been reading it and she reckons the film is not like the book."

"It never is." Fred replied. "They just take the basic idea and then make the film different. The success of the film depends on how good the film director is, and of course the cast."

"Have you read the book?" Louisa asked.

Fred nodded. "Ages ago though."

Just then the lights went out and they licked their ice creams in darkness as the film continued. On the way out of the cinema Louisa asked Fred if he was going home to Liverpool for Christmas.

He shook his head. "No, I'm going to stay here. I've been offered overtime. Besides your mother has just invited me to Christmas supper so I will be with your family instead of my own." His eyes twinkled, and Louisa wished that she could be home on that day, but she knew she wouldn't be able to get time off.

"Do you think they would let you go for an hour or two if I came for you and brought you back? They did last year." Arthur asked. He tried to hide his unhappiness as he spoke, though Louisa could see that he was still hurting inside remembering Megan.

Louisa shook her head. "I don't think so, but I will ask. I'm not sure what Cook has arranged with the Thompsons. She just told us all not to expect time off. It all depends on how much entertaining they do this year, what with the explosion at Gresford and everything."

"They would do well to remember that a lot of families won't be able to celebrate Christmas this year." Arthur said grimly. Louisa nodded glumly.

"I'll just turn up at seven o clock and see what we can wangle with that cook of yours." Arthur decided. They walked back to their motorcycles and Fred said goodbye to them both. "Hopefully see you Christmas Louisa" he said.

Arthur said the same when he dropped Louisa off at Broughton Hall. "I'll see you anyway if even for a few minutes, but with a bit of luck that cook of yours will let you have a couple of hours."

Louisa smiled. Arthur had a way of getting his own way. Maybe he would be able to charm Mrs. Henderson.

When Louisa crept into the small bedroom she shared with Ivy, the little lamp was still on and Ivy was still reading her book *"Little women."* She looked up and smiled at Louisa as she hurriedly got undressed and slipped into bed. "How was the film?"

"It was good."

"Did you see Fred?"

116

"Yes, he was there with us. He bought the ice creams. My mum and dad have invited him to Christmas supper and I won't be there." She sighed. "Arthur is going to come and ask cook if I can have some time off. He is going to use his charm on her." She closed her eyes and giggled as she remembered how Arthur had rescued her from the clutches of another cook eighteen months earlier.

Ivy closed her book and put out the light. "You might be in luck. Mrs Henderson told us today that the Thompsons have decided to go away for Christmas to spend time with the mistress's sister in Lincoln. Apparently she is married to an earl. So Mrs Henderson said that as long as we do our usual chores on Christmas day, and that as we haven't got to be waiting on the Thompsons, we can all have a few hours off."

Louisa opened her eyes wide, and in the darkness of the room her heart skipped a beat. "Are you sure?"

"Yes very sure. We have to make sure everything is done though, she's going to sort out some kind of rota with us tomorrow."

It seemed that when it came to sorting out the rota, the rest of the staff preferred time off earlier during the day rather than later, so when Louisa asked if she could go at seven o clock everyone agreed. Ivy wasn't going anywhere and neither was Dora. She said it was too upsetting to go home and in any case it was too far to walk to Acton so she was going to stay and read a book. Hilda decided to walk to Summerhill to see her mother for an hour in the afternoon and Robert said that he was going to see his mother in Hightown. He just hoped that his bicycle didn't fall apart as it was getting old. He wanted to spend as much time as possible with his mother

117

and young sister. Louisa was sorry that she couldn't offer him her bike as it was in Pandy but offered to work an extra hour for him so that he could stay longer with his mother.

"Thanks Louisa. I really appreciate it. It means I can spend more time with my mum. She has been worrying about this inquiry. Everybody thought it would be straightforward and the owners would be blamed, but what with some of the miners too frightened to give statements in case they lose their jobs, and those solicitors suggesting that the miners were to blame, it is very distressing for her. You know that the owners have refused permission for anyone to enter the closed-off pit. They say it is dangerous, but some people think it looks as if the owners are deliberately covering things up."

Soon after lunch he set off and Louisa thought it was nice to see him smile again. She knew he had been worrying about his mother. In the shadow of the tragedy of the explosion, Robert's mother and many other widows would find it difficult to cope over the Christmas period. Their loved ones would be missed. There was also the issue of money. There had been a huge fund set up for the bereaved, and people from all over Britain had given generously. Louisa herself had contributed and she had heard that it had raised over half a million pounds. She didn't know how the money was allocated to all the bereaved but she had heard that it didn't compensate for a regular income. And it certainly didn't compensate for the loss of loved ones. She felt she couldn't agree with Robert's suggestions that the owners were trying to cover things up. She believed that it was too dangerous to go down the Dennis shaft looking for evidence. However she did feel that surely the owners must share some responsibility for the explosion. But she didn't want to discuss this with Robert and upset him further. When Arthur arrived on his motorcycle Louisa was ready and waiting in the doorway as he drove up to the kitchen door. A couple of minutes before seven she had hurriedly run upstairs and slipped out of her uniform to get changed. She ran out to her brother and he guessed from her smile that he did not have to beg the cook to let his sister have time off. He wasted no time and he drove quickly back to Pandy.

When they both opened the back kitchen door, they found Mary Ellen, Dot and Dorothy making turkey sandwiches. They all looked up when they saw the door open and they beamed with pleasure when they saw Louisa.

"Merry Christmas Louisa."   Dorothy ran in to her arms. "I'm glad you could make it."

Louisa slipped her coat off and washed her hands and happily helped the female members of the family prepare supper. She found a tray in the pantry and laid it with the home made chutneys and pickled red cabbage and eggs that Mary Ellen had made the previous September. When they had prepared everything, they took it all into the front parlour. William was sitting in his favourite chair next to the fire place. In the opposite chair sat Arthur. On the small cottage sofa were Harry and Fred. Both of them got up when the women arrived and Dot and Louisa sat down on the sofa after putting the trays and plates of food on the little table between them. Dorothy squeezed between them, and then Arthur got up for his mother to sit in the other arm chair. The three young men then leaned against the sideboard as they helped themselves to food.

"So how did you manage to get time off Louisa?" Fred asked between bites of a sausage roll. Louisa swallowed her sandwich quickly to be able to answer. After she had explained the situation at Broughton Hall, Arthur couldn't help but comment that he thought it was just as well that the Thompsons had gone to celebrate Christmas out of Wrexham. "They are probably enjoying themselves whilst a hundred and sixty odd widows and their fatherless children here in Wrexham are having a miserable time."

Louisa said nothing. She had torn loyalties. She felt very sorry for the bereaved families of the miners, and she adored her brother. But the Thompsons had been good to her, and she was reasonably content working at Broughton Hall.

Dot tried to change the subject. "You must give me the recipe for this chutney mother, it is lovely." Everyone else agreed it was good

"Shall we sing some Christmas carols?" Dorothy said excitedly. And before anyone could answer she started to sing "The first Noel." Soon everyone joined in and Louisa relaxed and felt happy to be with her family. Out of the corner of her eye she could see that Fred was enjoying himself too.

At nine o clock Arthur drove Louisa back to Broughton Hall. The kitchen lights were still on downstairs and Louisa peered in and to her surprise found most of the staff sitting around the huge table eating mince pies and drinking cocoa. At least everyone except Mrs. Henderson who appeared to have a large glass of sherry in her hand. "Merry Christmas Louisa, did you have a good time with your family?"

Louisa nodded. "Yes thank you." She sat down next to Ivy who whispered to her "I think she is drunk. She's been drinking sherry since you left, and she told everybody to take it easy and come and sit here with her."

"What does Thomas say?" Louisa whispered back. She shook her head when Ivy passed her a mince pie.

"He said that she deserves a drink. It's been a difficult year for her, what with the trouble at Gresford and staff coming and going." Ivy sighed before continuing, "And of course I'm not helping with the situation as I will be leaving in two days."

"I'm going to miss you." Louisa said. She and Ivy had become good friends. The last three months had been difficult for everyone, especially for those who had lost people at the coal mine. She acknowledged that it must have been difficult for Mrs. Henderson too who worked as hard as the rest of the staff. But everyone had pulled their weight in the household. Furthermore, a special bond amongst the staff between those who had lost family members in the tragedy and those that hadn't, had emerged from the wreckage. Louisa got up and made her cocoa. Her movement appeared to signal to the small group that they should go to bed and get some rest.

As they all trooped up the servants staircase, they saw that Mrs. Henderson was beginning to go to sleep in her chair. She didn't look very comfortable and Louisa feared she may fall. However, just as Louisa thought she would rush down the stairs again to help her, Thomas entered the kitchen and he gently shook the sleeping woman. He helped her up and escorted her to the door to her private rooms behind the kitchen. Louisa had only ever been in there once and she had noticed how warm it was. She supposed it was because cook's room backed on to the great fireplace in the huge kitchen.

Two days later Louisa tearfully waved goodbye to Ivy as she set off on her new career. She promised to write to Louisa to let her know how she was getting on. "You must let me know how things progress with Fred." She whispered to Louisa as her parting shot.

Her replacement would arrive the next day. Mrs. Henderson had said that it was just as well the Thompson's were away, so they wouldn't be rushed off their feet like they usually were over the festive period.

Almost as soon as Ivy had left Broughton hall for good, Dora moved in with Louisa. The new girl would share Dora's old room with Hilda, which was a smaller attic room adjacent to Louisa's. There was just room for two narrow beds and a small bedside table with a candelabra. Electricity had not been put into that small room, but as Dora had pointed out, it did have a tiny window to look out. When Dora moved her possessions into the room she would share with Louisa, she said that she felt she was now moving in to a place of luxury.

Meanwhile, Louisa felt sorry for Anne who arrived one cold morning with a very small holdall. Dora took her up to the small attic room, and she reported to Louisa later that the new girl was quite cheerful. She had confided that in her last place of employment she had been expected to share a bed with the parlour maid! At least now she had her own bed and could store her few things under the bed in the large trunk which the Thompsons had provided for both her and Hilda. There were two hooks on the back of the door where Hilda and Anne could hang up their uniforms and their coats. So it seemed that for a while the servants were satisfied with their accommodation.

Anne took up her duties very quickly and often commented that it was heaven working in Broughton Hall after some of the places she had worked. Louisa guessed that Anne's past working experience was similar to her own, but she had not had a brother like Arthur to rescue her. Louisa realised that she was luckier than most of her fellow servants, but she still felt that she could do something more fulfilling than being a housemaid.

Chapter Eight

1935

In the New Year the Thompsons returned and the household resumed its normal activity. Mr. Thompson still spent long hours away from the home, either at meetings with his solicitor or at the office at the pit head in Gresford. With regard to running his estate he delegated that to his estate manager Mr. Garston. Meanwhile, Mrs. Thompson continued to visit and be visited by the various local gentry and it seemed that Mrs Henderson was perpetually making afternoon teas. It was left to either Louisa, Dora, Hilda, Anne or Robert to fetch and take the never ending supply of sandwiches and cakes every day. Despite this constant stream of afternoon tea parties, the Thompsons's demands on the staff had reduced. There were fewer dinner parties, and apart from solicitors and mine owners visiting the house from time to time, to talk to Mr Thompson, whereupon he and his wife would require simple suppers, the household staff became less and less busy. Louisa began to wonder if any of them would be made redundant.

One Thursday afternoon on the twenty eighth February Louisa sat sewing with her mother waiting for her father to arrive home from work. This was to be his official birthday because William was born on a leap year. Louisa had bought ingredients to make him a cake and her mother had graciously allowed her to make it in her kitchen.

When all the family had arrived and they had eaten their supper Louisa brought the cake from the kitchen and cut huge pieces for everyone.

Fred, who was now a regular visitor at Pandy commented on how lovely and moist the cake was and Louisa blushed at the compliment.

"We ought to go to the cinema again soon," he said through a mouthful of cake. *"The Scarlet Pimpernel* is going to be coming out soon."

"Good idea." Arthur said. "I will get a copy of the *Wrexham Leader* to see if it is advertised when it is coming to the cinemas."

"It should be a good film." Harry agreed. I wouldn't mind seeing it myself when it gets to Wrexham. What about you Dot?"

"Yes I would love too when it gets here."

"Well we don't know when that will be yet though." Arthur commented and then switched the wireless on as if it would tell him there and then. The wireless made a whining noise, and he fiddled with the knobs trying to get a signal. "That's funny, I can't get a signal. It's not usually like this."

"Probably the Germans trying to interfere with our radio waves." Harry commented half joking.

"That wouldn't surprise me" Fred said. "They're increasing their army and navy and air force. What's to stop them trying to improve air waves so they can spy on the rest of Europe?"

William stared at Fred. "Is that really possible?"

Fred shrugged. "The way new developments in communications are going I shouldn't wonder. They would try to use radio waves to mark our position so that they could bomb us." He stopped talking when he caught the look of fright on the women's faces.

However Arthur continued where Fred left off. "There is every possibility of the Germans carrying out air raids on Britain and dropping bombs on us. I bet our government must be preparing for a possible threat."

Harry chipped in. "And the threat of invasion by air and sea must be on their minds too. If they can use radio detection through radio waves then the possibilities are enormous."

William frowned at Arthur as he struggled with the knobs on the wireless. "Well I don't know much about radio waves but aren't you supposed to have a powerful transmitter?"

Fred and Harry shrugged just as Arthur shouted "yes at last." And the sounds of *Limehouse Blues* suddenly filled the room. "That's more like it." William commented.

Louisa got up to go. "I have to go Father." She dropped a kiss on his forehead.

William squeezed her hand. "Mind as you go. Thank you for the cake. See you next week."

Mary Ellen and Dorothy accompanied Louisa to the door and watched her cycle down the road towards Broughton Hall.

The next day Louisa received a letter from Ivy. She had settled in to her secretarial course and was enjoying life. She asked how Louisa was getting on with Fred. When she saw the question, Louisa asked herself exactly the same thing. Whilst he continued to be friendly towards her, she felt it was more of a sisterly relationship rather than anything else. Still she comforted herself, he finished with Beryl and he hasn't got another girlfriend. This comforting thought was to be short lived though. Two weeks later she was told that Fred had gone to Liverpool to look for work as his contract at the pit would soon finish. The sealing of the Dennis shaft was nearly complete and he was unsure if he would be needed much longer.

"So won't we see him again?" Dorothy wailed.

Arthur chuckled. "Yes he is coming back. He will be here for at least another month. He wanted to visit his mother whilst he was in Liverpool, she hasn't been very well. So he thought he would scout around for work whilst he is there."

"What's wrong with his mother?" Louisa asked.

"He didn't say. I think she is delicate."

The following week Fred returned and at supper Dorothy asked him if his mother was better.

"Yes she is much better. My sister Mary is looking after her and my other sister Cecelia has returned from Ireland to help her."

"What about your father. Is he there?" Louisa asked.

A sad expression veiled Fred's face for a few seconds then lifted again as he spoke. "My step father is at home too."

Louisa got the impression that he didn't want to talk about his step father, so she changed the subject. "Did you manage to get out and see your brothers?"

Fred grinned. "Yes I went with my brother John to see a film with his girlfriend Hazel and her friend Daisy."

Louisa's heart sank when she heard this, especially when Arthur started asking questions about Daisy.

"She's coming here on Saturday to see me, so you will meet her then." He grinned at Arthur. "Perhaps we can go to the dance at the church hall. You could ask that Iris you were talking to the other day."

Mary Ellen who had been listening to the conversation whilst she was knitting bootees for her next door neighbour's baby looked up at that in surprise. "Who is Iris?"

Both men sniggered and Louisa felt sick. Dorothy was grinning looking first from Fred to Arthur in bewilderment.

"Someone who works in the teashop where I sometimes go when I am in work." Arthur confessed.

Mary Ellen smiled. Her eyes twinkled and Louisa was pleased that Arthur was at last getting over Megan. But she was annoyed with Fred. All the way home she pedaled her cycle furiously. She resented deeply that Fred was seeing another woman. And she was jealous that the woman Daisy was actually coming to see Fred on Saturday and she, Louisa wouldn't even be around to see her.

The following Thursday Louisa decided not to stay for supper. She told her mother that she had a headache and was going back to Broughton Hall to lie down. Secretly she was planning on trying to make Fred miss her. The Thursday after that she cycled late in the afternoon to see Dot and Harry. She told her mother she would have supper there, then go straight back to Broughton hall. The problem with this was that she missed seeing her father. So when the next Thursday came around she resolved to stay later so that she could see him. If Fred was there then so be it she decided. She was not going to let her feelings for him stop her from seeing her father.

As usual her mother was in the kitchen when Louisa arrived. She was washing sheets and was ready to put them through the mangle. Louisa helped her to lay them flat so that they would go through the rollers evenly. The mangle was old and unreliable. Once the sheets were hung outside on the line her mother filled a kettle to put on the range to make some tea. They sat down on the cottage chairs by the range and ate some toasted fruit bread that Mary Ellen had made the day before.

"Any news from Broughton Hall?" Mary Ellen asked munching her toast.

Louisa shook her head. "No not really. Dora has brightened up a bit though she still misses her dad. Robert is still very bitter, and Hilda and Anne have settled in o.k. We hardly see the Thompsons so we are not very busy. As long as the house is clean and the meals are on time they don't seem to bother."

"Doesn't she get lots of ladies calling on her?"

Louisa nodded. "She used to, though not so many now. It seems to have tailed off. Mrs. Thompson prefers to call on others rather than be called on. Cook makes lots of little fancies just in case, but we usually end up eating them in the staff kitchen." Louisa laughed. "I suppose I should be grateful, but sometimes I just wonder what I am doing with my life."

Her mother looked at her sharply. "There are plenty of other people who would gladly swap places with you. It sounds like you haven't got enough to do. If you like you can sew some buttons on your father's shirt. He's lost two of them now." Louisa did as she was asked and when she had finished that chore she helped her mother with the rest of the washing. Despite late March it was a sunny day and her mother was taking advantage to get as much washing dried as possible.

When William arrived later for supper, both Arthur and Fred arrived at the same time. Louisa said hello to both of them but scarcely said anything else. Dorothy was looking forward to Easter and was making a bonnet for the occasion. Louisa busied herself with helping her. Meanwhile Arthur and Fred commented on the lengthening of the days as spring was in full flow.

"I read somewhere that there is going to be a new marking in the roads called Katz eyes. That should make it easier for us

129

driving at night." Fred said. He glanced at Louisa but she did not say anything.

"Don't you think so Louisa?" Arthur pursued.

Louisa looked up from her sewing. "Yes I suppose it will help." She looked back at her sewing again.

"What's up with you? You are very quiet tonight?" Arthur asked. "Are they giving you hell at Broughton Hall? Do I need to rescue you again?"

Despite herself Louisa smiled and shook her head meanwhile Arthur turned to Fred. "Somebody ought to give hell to those managers involved with all the collieries."

Fred nodded his head in agreement. "Yes there is still a lot of bitterness at Gresford. The inquiry is taking ages. That Sir Henry Walker the chief Inspector of the mines is chairing the inquiry and he is saying that the evidence of what happened is still in the mine."

William grunted. "Well that stands to reason, and if they can't get down there because of the gas they will never get any concrete evidence."

"But Father, the miners have been saying for months, long before the explosion that there was inadequate fire-fighting equipment and water precautions. No one was listening." Arthur said heatedly. "I knew a lot of the men who worked down there. I've lost some good friends. Surely the statements from the miners is all the evidence they need. I remember Ralph Roberts telling me about the poor working conditions. He was on the rescue team."

"Some of the solicitors who are defending the owners of the mine are trying to say that the miner's themselves should shoulder the blame. The colliers I am working with at the pit are livid. They reckon the owners are trying to pass the buck." Fred added.

Arthur snorted. "Well that doesn't surprise me. They only think about the profit, they don't want to know about the men working down there in terrible conditions. Surely the share holders, must have been aware of the problem." Arthur was getting angry again.

William glared at his son. "The share holders employ managers to oversee the pit. You can't blame them if they weren't informed."

Arthur opened his mouth again to argue, but he caught his mother's frowning expression and he changed his tack. "Well if I owned a business I would want to know what was going on and would be monitoring my managers very closely." This statement was met with silence. Arthur then focused on Fred who was putting his coat on ready to go. "Well, you will be best out of it soon old mate won't you?"

Fred nodded whilst Arthur continued. "Fred's going to be working in Wrexham next week in his new job."

At this news Louisa's heart sank. Would she never see him again?

"Has the work in the Dennis shaft finished then? William asked. He spit a bit of tobacco out of the side of his mouth in to the fire.

"Yes more or less. They are hoping to open up the rest of the mine soon." Fred watched him as William tried to light his pipe.

"Does that mean we won't see you again?" Dorothy said.

"I'm sure you will." Fred said. "Maybe at the weekends. I haven't got new lodgings yet so I won't be far away."

Arthur agreed. "Yes you won't have to work every day of the week now the Dennis shaft is sealed. You can have Saturday afternoons off to go to the football match with me and still have Sundays off."

Fred looked at Louisa as he got up towards the door. "Maybe I will see you at the cinema soon Louisa. There are some good films coming out soon."

Louisa could hardly trust herself to speak. She managed to say, "Yes that will be nice."

As soon as Fred had gone, Louisa got up and put on her coat, scarf and hat. "I suppose I had better go to, but I can't find my gloves."

Her mother handed them to her. Mary Ellen had taken them off the sideboard where Louisa had left them and had put them on the shelf above the range to warm. She pulled them on and said goodbye to her family before getting on her bicycle. She switched on her lights and she thought about the Katz eyes that Fred said would make cycling in the dark easier. She sighed heavily whilst she worried about when she would see him again and if he was still seeing that Daisy woman.

Chapter Nine

When Louisa got back, Dora who had seen her put the cycle away in the shed at the back of the kitchen had thoughtfully made some cocoa for them both. She came up the stairs behind her with two mugs of the hot beverage. Now that Ivy had gone and they shared a room they had become quite friendly and shared each other's confidences. When both girls were in their beds sipping cocoa with the bedside lamp on, something they still both regarded as a luxury, they chatted about the day's events. Dora announced that she was going to work in the Brewery in Wrexham and that she would be leaving Broughton Hall the following week.

This was quite a blow to Louisa. Everything seemed to be changing. "But aren't you happy here Dora?"

Dora shrugged. "I suppose they have been kind to me here, but I can't help thinking that I am a traitor working here after what happened at Gresford." She stifled a sob. "So at least I won't have anything to do with collieries, and I will be able to live with my mum and get to work easily."

She looked across at Louisa. "My mum is hoping that Sir Stafford Cripps will win the case and she will get some compensation." She sniffed as she held back her tears. "Thanks for being so kind to me Louisa. I don't know how I would have coped without you. I miss my father and brother so much."

Lying down in the dark Louisa began to wonder what would happen next. She fretted about seeing Fred again, and Dora's intention to leave unsettled her.

When she saw her mother again the following week, she noticed her mother was unusually cheerful and Louisa could tell that she was bursting to tell her something. All day she hummed and looked as if she had a secret. It was only when Dorothy came home from school that Mary Ellen decided to tell them. "It seems you two are going to be aunts in a few months."

Both girls looked at each other puzzled, then realisation dawned on both of them. "Do you mean Dot and Harry are having a baby?" Louisa exclaimed excitedly.

Mary Ellen nodded, a grin spreading across her face. "Yes, you are going to be an aunt." Her mother confirmed. "Dot is expecting." Her mother beamed and her smile was so infectious that Louisa smiled too. Dorothy started to jump up and down "hurrah, I'm going to be an auntie."

"When is it due? She asked.

"October."

Louisa sat down as her mother got her work basket out and showed her the wool she had already bought to make a christening layette for the baby.

"Won't Dot's mother want to knit something like this?" Louisa ventured to ask fingering the soft white wool.

Mary sniffed. "Her knitting is not as good as mine. She can make the cake."

Louisa hid a smile, she knew her mother was very competitive when it came to knitting and sewing.

Later when Louisa related the information to Dora they both smiled at Mary Ellen's insistence that her knitting was better than Dot's mother. When Louisa saw Dot again it was on Louisa's sixteenth birthday in April and Dot happily confirmed that her mother had conceded that her knitting was not as good as Mary Ellen's. Indeed when Mary Ellen had proudly shown them both the progress she was making with the layette, Dot and Louisa admired the technique that Mary Ellen had used. Dot had caught the bus to Pandy purposefully that day to see Louisa and to give her a blue silk head scarf for her birthday.

"I hope you like it. I saw it in the hat shop near the bus station last week and I thought it would be ideal for you for the spring when you are riding your bike."

"It's lovely and I do like the bluebell edging." Louisa enthused. "A bit more classy than Dorothy's Easter bonnet." They both laughed just as Dorothy came bursting in to the kitchen. She was wearing the said bonnet and flung her arms first around Louisa then Dot.

"I've just seen Emily Gittins in the street." Dorothy sat at the table and drank the milk her mother provided for her. "She told me that Fred is moving out of his lodgings on Saturday and going to live in town near his work. He's working on a building site. She said she is going to miss him."

"I bet she is." Mary Ellen said and bit her lip as if regretting what she had said. Dorothy continued to drink her milk and got up to get a book she had left on the sideboard. With her back turned Mary Ellen winked at Louisa and Dot as if to say something about Emily Gittins that she didn't want Dorothy to hear.

Much later when Dorothy had gone outside to talk to a school friend who lived two houses away down the terrace, Mary Ellen explained that she had heard that Emily Gittins was making herself a fool chasing after Fred. "I think that's

135

why he is moving out of Emily's boarding house. Poor chap, from what I can gather this is the third time in as many years that he has had to find lodgings, twice in Liverpool and again here. Let's hope he has found somewhere better on the Holt Road. It isn't far from where the building firm's office is situated so I suppose it will be convenient for him."

When Arthur, Harry and William had arrived, they all sat down to supper and Louisa blew out the sixteen candles on her birthday cake that her mother had made. She was just cutting slices for everyone when there was a knock on the door. Dorothy rushed to answer it. "Fred. What are you doing here?"

He had a bunch of flowers in his hand. "I have brought these for Louisa. It's a special birthday isn't it? Sorry I am so late, I've been sorting a few things out."

Seeing him standing in the doorway clutching the flowers, Louisa's heart leaped. He looked so handsome. She got up to welcome him and took the flowers. "That's nice of you. How did you know?"

Dorothy told me last Sunday when I was here last. He sat down and thanked Louisa for the piece of cake she handed him.

"We hear you are moving lodgings." Mary Ellen said. She was unable to keep the news to herself.

"Yes I have found two rooms in a house on the Holt Road in Wrexham. The house belongs to my new boss. I will be sharing with two other men who work with me. It's quite a big and very old house but it has been modernised. It has a bathroom upstairs. It's like some of the smaller versions we are building on the housing estate."

136

"Indoor bathroom!" Dorothy said. "Can we have one Father?"

"Yes tomorrow." He replied shaking his head at the same time.

"I wouldn't mind buying one of those houses that you are building when I have saved some money." Arthur said.

Mary Ellen looked at her son sharply. "Whatever for? Are you getting married to that Iris you have been seeing? Oh Arthur you could have told me, I haven't even met her yet."

"Mother hold on. I haven't seen Iris for ages have I Fred? I only went out with her twice the same time as Fred went out with Daisy. I'm not seeing anybody at the moment thank you. And Daisy went back to Liverpool. I don't think she was impressed with Wrexham was she Fred?" Arthur winked at Fred in an attempt to take the spotlight off himself."

"Fred chuckled. "I think you are right. Daisy only came down from Liverpool a couple of times, and I only saw her once when I went back to see my Mother and the kiddies. She likes the bright lights that girl. We didn't really get along very well. But she insisted she wanted to come to see me in Wrexham."

"You seem to have a lot of women chasing after you Fred." Mary Ellen commented.

Fred shrugged. "Not the right ones though unfortunately." He glanced at Louisa and she felt her heart leap.

Meanwhile Dorothy was indignant about Fred's reference to his siblings.

"Kiddies!" Dorothy said. "How old are they?"

Fred shrugged. "Edward is fifteen and Mary is thirteen."

"But that's not kiddies." Dorothy exclaimed. "I'm twelve and I'm not a kiddie."

Everybody laughed including Fred. "I know, I just call them that because I keep thinking they are kiddies, but you are right they are growing up fast." He got up. "I have to go. Enjoy the rest of your birthday Louisa."

"Fred! Before you go will I see you on Saturday afternoon for the match?" Arthur called. He got up to walk to the door to talk to Fred. The family heard them talking and Fred whispered that he needed to spend the Easter week end with the family. Arthur returned to the kitchen table and muttered something about Fred's mother wanting him to celebrate Easter with her.

Louisa couldn't help smiling to herself all the way as she cycled back to Broughton hall. The flowers were carefully arranged in her basket along with her other birthday gifts, and she couldn't wait to put them in water in her room. Hilda, who was now sharing the room with her after Dora's departure helped her to find a suitable vase, and they put the pink carnations on the windowsill so that they could both admire them.

"I think he must like you a lot if he remembered to bring you flowers." Hilda said. She had become Louisa's new confidante now that she had lost Ivy and Dora.

"Yes but not enough to ask me out though." Louisa sighed.

"Give him time. He has probably got a lot on his mind what with a new job, new lodgings and his family in Liverpool. Anyway maybe he has been waiting until you are sixteen. He is a lot older than you isn't he? Plus he is your brother's friend, maybe he doesn't want to rock the boat."

Hilda seemed quite wise about these things. She was two years older than Louisa and came from a big family just like Fred's. Her words seemed sensible and gave Louisa new hope. Every morning she looked at the flowers on the window and they cheered her up. She was quite sad when two weeks later she had to throw them out.

At the beginning of May, Dora's replacement called Peggy arrived and she was shown into the tiny room to share with Anne. The day Peggy arrived which was a Monday, Robert told them that he was leaving Broughton Hall and was going to work in the Majestic Cinema and Theatre in Regent Street and had given the Thompsons one week's notice.

"I'll be sorry to see you go." Louisa said. She realised with a pang that all the original staff she had first met when she started working at Thompsons had now left. Only Mrs. Henderson the Cook and Thomas the Butler remained. Mrs. Smedley was still there too but she hardly saw her.

"After Dora went, I felt I owed it to my family to go too." Robert said.

"Because of the Gresford pit explosion?" Louisa said sympathetically.

Robert nodded. There were tears in his eyes, but also a determined expression on his face.

"The Majestic looks good now it's been refurbished from the outside and the inside." Louisa commented. "What will you be doing there?"

"I will be in the box office for both the theatre and the cinema side, and we will be taking bookings on the telephone. I will have to help in the café bar as well, but it will be better than working here. I will be able to live with my mother and cycle to work every day now that my bicycle has been repaired."

"Maybe I will see you when I come to the cinema again." Louisa said and was rewarded with a rare smile from Robert.

A few days later when Louisa got to Pandy there was little news of Fred and Louisa hoped that he had settled into his lodging. Meanwhile the news on the wireless was dominated by King George's Silver Jubilee. Then the following week they heard of the death of T E Lawrence who had been killed in a motorbike accident. This sparked conversation about the film *'Lawrence of Arabia'*.

"That was a very good film." Arthur enthused after he had switched off the wireless.

"Have you seen any others lately? You usually go with Fred don't you? Louisa asked.

"As a matter of fact I had planned to go next week with Fred. Do you want to meet us there? It's either *'Alice Adams'* at the Majestic, or *'Thirty Nine Steps'* at the Hippodrome."

Louisa's heart quickened. "I don't mind. Which do you prefer?

"Well Fred prefers *'Alice Adams'*. I prefer *'Thirty Nine Steps.'* but I don't really mind which, so we both agreed you should decide."

"Does Fred know I am coming then?" Louisa asked innocently. Arthur nodded and stared strangely at his sister. "Does it matter?"

"No, no. of course not. I think I prefer *Alice Adams* at the Majestic. It's not too far for me to cycle back then."

"Alright. I will tell him on Saturday at the match. And we will see you outside the Majestic next Thursday."

Louisa was excited when she chained her cycle to the drainpipe at the side of the cinema in Regent Street. She knew she was ten minutes early. Her mother couldn't understand why she was so edgy, and Louisa couldn't explain.

When she saw Arthur ride up on his motor cycle she ran to meet him and then saw that the person riding pillion was a girl. "Hello Louisa, this is Gladys. I think you might know her?" He grinned cheekily at her and so did Gladys. The girls knew one another because Gladys lived in the street parallel to their own street. Their back garden backed onto Mary Ellen's and William's garden. "We're keeping it a secret for now." Arthur said a big grin on his face, so don't tell them at home yet will you?"

"No of course not. If you don't want me to say anything, I won't." Louisa replied. She hoped that Fred wasn't bringing a girl too. However two minutes later Fred parked his motorcycle behind Arthur's and no one slid off the back of his vehicle. When it was their turn at the kiosk to pay for their tickets, Louisa recognised Robert behind the window of the kiosk. He smiled at Louisa and asked how she was. She returned her smile and asked him if he was happy in his new job.

He nodded. "Yes I like it very much, it's a dream come true."

When they got into the auditorium Arthur asked Louisa how she knew Robert and she explained that he used to work with her as the footman in Broughton hall.

"Good for him that he's managed to get out of service." Arthur said and they settled down to watch the film. During

141

the interval both men got up to get ice creams and the girls chatted for a few minutes. "How long have you been seeing Arthur?" Louisa asked.

"About a month. I see him twice a week." Gladys smiled. "How about you and Fred, how long have you been together?"

Louisa laughed. "We aren't really a couple, we are just friends."

"Oh excuse me, I thought he was your boyfriend." She hesitated, "but looking at your face you wish he was."

"I don't think he is interested in me that way." Louisa answered. She turned her head quickly in case the men came back and overheard her talking.

"Well try telling him. Give him a sign. He's a good looking man, don't lose him without a fight." Gladys advised hurriedly. She could see both men heading back with the ice creams. Louisa followed her gaze just in time to see her brother and Fred walk along their row to regain their seats. Licking her ice cream in the dark, Louisa found it difficult to concentrate on the film. She kept thinking about what Gladys said. So without thinking what she was doing she let herself lean towards Fred so that their shoulders were touching. She was gratified that he didn't move away, but was unsure if he had noticed, because he seemed to be concentrating hard on the film. She could feel her heart pumping excitedly and she wondered at herself being so forward.

Later when her companions watched Louisa retrieve her bicycle they made an agreement that they should all do it again soon. Louisa nodded her head in acquiescence but inwardly worried about who would be the woman sitting at the side of Fred next time. She sighed when she got into the kitchen at Broughton hall, she had enjoyed the film but was wondering if she ought to forget Fred. She went to bed with a heavy heart.

At nine thirty the next evening just as all the household staff were having their cocoa in the kitchen before going upstairs to bed, they heard the roar of a motorbike coming up to the back of the house. Louisa immediately thought it would be Arthur and was frantic in case there was something wrong at home. Dot's baby wasn't due for four months yet so she wondered what it could be. Mrs. Henderson opened the door and then called to Louisa to come to the door. It was still quite light and warm outside and she stepped into the yard to see a man standing by his motorbike. Her heart leaped into her mouth. "Fred." She gasped.

"Hello Louisa. I'm sorry to startle you. I know it's late. It's just that I thought you might like to come to a dance with me a week on Saturday. Do you think you could change your day off with somebody?" He looked down at the ground nervously then looked up at her again. "That's if you want to come."

Louisa stared at him astonished and excited at the same time. She had dreamed of this and now she was tongue tied. She tried to speak but started to choke.

"Are you alright?" Fred asked anxiously.

"Yes. Yes. I'm fine." Louisa replied. "I would love to go dancing, but I will have to check with the others first." She looked worried. "How can I let you know?"

"Tell Arthur on Thursday and he will tell me on Saturday at the match." He got back on his motorcycle and rode away leaving Louisa speechless.

The only way Louisa could get a Saturday night off was if the Thompsons were not entertaining, because usually it was all hands on deck. If they were not entertaining then that privilege fell to the Cook Mrs. Henderson or her assistant – Hilda. So there were two hurdles for Louisa to get over and as she closed the door to go back inside she was pessimistic about her chances of getting any Saturday off. However when she turned round she saw the household staff including cook with her arms folded all staring at Louisa. Staring and smiling. Even cook was smiling at her.

"Before you ask, the answer is No and Yes." Cook said. Louisa gaped at her unable to take in what she was saying.

"Mrs. Smedley has told me that there won't be any entertaining a week on Saturday, but as it happens there will be this week end – both days, so you can have your following Saturday off. As you know that is when I have my day off, but as I was not planning anything special, I will take your Thursday. But tell that young man of yours he is not to do this again. Is that clear?"

"Yes cook. Thank you cook." Louisa was in a dream world. Her mind reeled as she recollected what cook had said "that young man of yours". She practically sailed up the stairs to bed and Hilda laughed at her. "You look as if you are in a trance." She said.

"I feel it." Louisa said and threw herself on the bed. She began to giggle. Then she stopped. "What am I going to wear?"

The week end was extremely busy. One of the busiest since the Gresford explosion had occurred nine months earlier. Three of Mr. Thompsons's guests were solicitors. Louisa didn't recognise any of them. However she knew that Mr. Thompson had shares in other collieries in North Wales and so she assumed that in the light of the inquiry at Gresford, he would want to talk to his business associates. She had seen many visitors come and go over the previous few weeks. She wondered if they were from the same office of the solicitor Mr. Shawcross. She had read that Mr. Shawcross was representing the colliery owners into the inquiry over the explosion. Mr. Thompson's other guests were in varying degrees connected to the coal mining industry.

The solicitors stayed overnight on Saturday and Sunday, and they resumed their talks on Monday with two other solicitors who arrived with their assistants. Along with an already demanding group of eminent man, these new arrivals who stayed all day, kept all the household staff extremely busy. Despite the extra demands, Mrs. Smedley who was a very capable housekeeper and Mrs. Henderson the equally capable cook, dealt with everything efficiently. Their expertise in directing and delegating work calmly and orderly ensured that the rest of the staff were calm too. So although very tired by Monday evening, all the household staff had not felt agitated or stressed because they had pulled together as a good team.

When the last guest had gone sometime after lunch on Tuesday, Mrs. Smedley came into the kitchen and congratulated Mrs. Henderson on her menus and the efficient manner in which everything had been executed. She told

145

them that the mistress Mrs. Thompson was very pleased with their efforts.

Over lunch which was quite a feast as Mrs. Henderson and the housekeeper had made sure there was plenty of food in case the solicitors decided to stay for another day, the staff chatted about the previous evening. Sidney who had replaced Robert was the first one to speak. This was his first job working in service and he was trying to learn what was required of him. "Those toffs know how to eat don't they?" he said. "And drink. I've never seen so much food and wine and brandy all at once."

"As long as they are happy." Mrs. Henderson replied sternly. "And at least we get fed well too. I've known some stingy households in my time I can tell you."

"Did anyone manage to find out what they were talking about?" Hilda asked timidly. "I think it might have been about how to represent the masters at the trial from what bit I overheard when I was serving the puddings." She said.

"I think they are trying to say that the manager didn't keep the records up to date, but I'm not sure what records they were referring to." Louisa offered. She had heard this when she had gone in to the vast dining room to help clear the second course dishes.

Whatever else had been heard no-one else was willing to say and so they got on with their duties.

On Wednesday twelfth of June news came to them about another mining accident. This time it was in Barnsley in Yorkshire. Nineteen miners had been killed.

"This ought to be a message to all owners of coal mines." Arthur said the next day when he heard about it. He was

146

furious and started ranting on about employee welfare rights. In the end William told him to be quiet and to change the subject. At which point Harry added more gloom to the supper table by saying that it was worrying that the British government were planning to triple the United Kingdom's air force. "This is because Baldwin is fearful that Hitler is increasing his own air force."

"Are they preparing for war?" Dot asked anxiously. She patted her stomach protectively of her unborn child.

"Of course they are." Arthur said. "The writing is on the wall."

"I'm sure the Prime Minister is just taking precautions." William said to Dot and glared at Arthur. "Can we talk about something more cheerful now?"

"Well I've got some news." Harry said. "It seems that Fred, Arthur and I won't have to take a driving test. The new law about driving tests says that because we have been driving motorcycles before April 1934, that we are exempt." Harry concluded trying his best to please his father by diverting his brother from talking about the government.

"That's good news isn't it?" William looked at his sons. Then he gazed at his eldest daughter. "Good job Louisa hasn't got a motorcycle."

"Heaven forbid." Mary Ellen said. Meanwhile Louisa glared indignantly at her father and her brothers. "I'm sure I could pass the test if I put my mind to it. By the way I won't be here next Thursday, I've had to swap my day off so I will be here on Saturday instead."

"That's nice to have Saturday." Said Dot. Perhaps you can come over and see me before you cycle back."

"Can I come?" Dorothy asked. Louisa began to panic she didn't want to involve her sister with her date with Fred.

Fortunately Arthur came to the rescue. "I thought you wanted to go and see the matinee of *Thirty Nine Steps*?"

"Oh Yes I do. Are you going to take me? Can I go mother?"

"Is it suitable?" Mary Ellen asked doubtfully.

"Yes!" Said Harry and Arthur together.

"Why don't you come too Louisa?" asked Dorothy.

"No thanks. I will go and see Dot and have a chat with her." Louisa was grateful that her brothers had helped her out of a delicate situation. However she was a little suspicious that they were both keen to get Dorothy to the cinema without her. She wondered how much they knew about her date with Fred. She glanced at Dot whose expression gave nothing away. Meanwhile Dorothy didn't pursue her notion of accompanying Louisa to visit Dot now she knew that she was being taken to the cinema by her brother.

Before Louisa went outside to get her bicycle she caught Arthur's eye and he followed her outside. "I didn't know you were keen on Fred, why didn't you say something before? I know he likes you a lot."

Hearing this from her brother, made Louisa's heart unexpectedly thump wildly against her chest. "I was waiting for him to say something." Louisa said. She tried to appear casual though she was secretly pleased to hear Arthur say that Fred liked her.

"So you were able to get next Saturday off?"

She nodded.

"Fred said that if you like, he will pick you up from Harry's at half past six. He thought you might not want mum and dad to know just yet. Is that o.k?"

Louisa nodded again smiling.

"He also said that if you leave your bike at Harry's he will take you back to Broughton Hall after the dance. You'll have to get the bus back here the following week though, or walk."

So Fred seems to have thought of everything, Louisa thought.

"Alright. Thanks. Will you be going with Gladys?"

"Do you want me to come?" He asked kindly. "Or do you want Fred all to yourself?"

Louisa suddenly felt overwhelmed. "It would be nice if you were there."

Arthur patted his sister's head. "o.k. I will be there for your first date."

They both grinned. "See you a week on Saturday."

Chapter Ten

The days seemed to drag by for Louisa. She tortured herself either by worrying that Fred might change his mind or wondering what she would wear. She had only one good quality cotton dress which was nice but not really a dance dress. The only other dress that she felt would be suitable with some adjustment was the one she had worn as a bridesmaid for Harry and Dot. On the Friday night before the dance she took it out of the bag she had brought with her from home on a previous visit and shook it out before placing it on the bed. Hilda looked at it with her and suggested taking out the sleeves and shortening the length. Louisa agreed.

"I'm pretty good with a needle and thread, I will help you if you like." Hilda offered.

"Thanks. I am pretty good too, but I haven't got a lot of time."

Hilda took hold of one sleeve and Louisa took the other and carefully they unpicked the sleeves from the dress. After they had cut twelve inches off the bottom of the dress, Hilda neatened the raw armholes whilst Louisa made a new hem. It was nearly midnight before they had finished but when Louisa tried on the adjusted garment they both agreed it looked good for purpose.

"Thanks Hilda. I'm going to make you tired for work tomorrow whilst I can have an extra hour in bed."

"It's worth it." Hilda said yawning. "And at least we won't be so busy here this week-end, now that the Thompsons have gone away." She lay back on her bed and watched Louisa pick up the discarded scraps of material and idly folded them in her fingers.

"I could try to make a cape with this, but not tonight though. I will have to make do with my cardigan." She yawned too.

The next morning Louisa laid the dress carefully in her basket and cycled directly to Harry and Dot's house. Dot was surprised to see her so early, but understood once she had explained that she wanted the dress to hang up so that it didn't get creased. Another reason was that she didn't want her mother to know.

"Don't worry I will press it for you and hang it up ready. Do you want to borrow my little white lace shrug to go over it? You will be cold on the back of Fred's motorcycle."

"Thanks. I was going to put my cardigan over it and then take it off later, but the shrug will look better. I will wear the cardigan like a jacket. I'm glad it's not raining though." She giggled excitedly.

"I'll put all of them ready for you. See you later."

So by the time Louisa got to her parent's house it was mid-morning and her mother was making coffee. Or at least she would have done if the milk pan hadn't boiled over and the milk spilt into the fire.

"Drat!" her mother said. Louisa smiled. She couldn't count how many times her mother had done that.

"So you are using the coal fire again now to heat the milk." Louisa commented as she kissed her mother good morning. It seemed strange to be at home on a Saturday morning with Dorothy sitting at the table reading her book.

"Yes her mother replied. "Now they have re-opened the Martyn pit I daresay there will be coal again, and in any case

151

we have got plenty in the coal shed. We won't have to hit into the big block yet." She smiled. "But if you want some coffee you will have to go and get some milk from the dairy shop."

"I'll come with you." Dorothy said. Together they walked down the road to the shop. Whilst Louisa was paying for her purchase Dorothy stayed outside and stared at the notices that was in the window. One advertised the church summer fete in Garden Village. Dorothy's eyes seemed to be glued to it. Meanwhile another notice caught Louisa's eye and she exclaimed excitedly to Dorothy.

"Look!" She said, pointing to the advert. "It seems the dairy is advertising for a shop assistant."

"Are you thinking of applying?" Dorothy turned to her sister. "It would be good if you could get the job, then you can come home again?"

They both stared at the advert. "It's not a bad idea." Louisa said. "I think I will."

Louisa read the advertisement again then glancing at her sister she shrugged. "Why not?" She left Dorothy outside again, and she returned into the shop, then tried to catch the eye of Jenny one of the shop assistants who had just served her. Louisa knew her slightly. She lived two streets away near the Chester road. Her father had been killed in the colliery explosion.

There were quite a few people in the shop and Louisa felt a little self-conscious. She whispered to Jenny that she was interested in the situation vacant. The young woman got her notebook out and wrote Louisa's name down on it. "We have had three people asking about this. Mr. Griffiths has

152

told me to say that he will write to everyone at the end of the week and invite those interested for an interview."

Louisa bit her lip. "I am working at the moment, do you think if I get an interview it will be on a Thursday?" she asked anxiously. Jenny replied that he would get her to telephone to make arrangements. The job doesn't start until next month you know. It's because I am getting married and leaving the area with my husband. He is joining the army and I am going with him. She blushed. "So there is plenty of time really. Don't you like your job at the moment?"

"Oh yes I like my job, but I don't get much time off you see, so that's why I need to know if the interview will be on a Thursday. That's the day I have off. Today is unusual I just had to swop with someone."

Violet smiled. "Well if you do get the job you will get a lot more time off than Thursday. We close on Saturday afternoons and all day Sunday. We have Wednesday afternoons off too on a rota. And I'm usually finished in here by six o clock at night. Mind you we start early."

Louisa was flushed with excitement when she went outside to join Dorothy. "What did she say?" Dorothy demanded to know. Louisa explained and finished up by saying. "If I do get offered the job, I might accept but it would depend on the wages. It might be less than I am getting now. We will just have to wait and see."

They both giggled all the way back home imaging all the things they could do if Louisa was working closer to home. Dorothy was pleased that she had a secret, because Louisa had made her promise not to say anything to anyone just in case she didn't get the job.

153

Arthur arrived home from work at one thirty and after a quick wash he had lunch with his sisters and Mother, then took Dorothy to the cinema as promised. Louisa helped her mother with the dishes and then set of excitedly to see Dot. She reminded her mother that it would be twelve days before she could come back to Pandy again.

As good as her word Dot had pressed the dress and hung it up. She had also fished out a dark blue velvet bolero top with sequins on which complemented the colour of the dress.

"I take it you still haven't told your mother that you are going on a date with Fred?" Dot asked.

Louisa shook her head. "I thought it best not to just in case it goes badly and it spoils things for everybody. I don't want people taking sides if we don't get on."

"Very wise. Best to tread carefully to begin with."

At half past six Fred arrived at Dot and Harry's house. By this time Harry had arrived and he invited Fred in for a few minutes. "Look after my sister for me won't you Fred?" Harry said grinning at both of them.

"Of course I will." Fred replied.

"So where are you taking her? Where is the dance? Harry asked.

"It's in the Miner's Institute in Grosvenor Road. Arthur is coming too."

"With Gladys?" Dot asked.

Fred and Louisa stared at Dot. "How did you know?" Louisa said.

Dot laughed. "Gladys is telling everybody. So it won't be long before your mum and dad know."

When Fred parked the motor bike in the space behind the Institute, he helped Louisa off so that she didn't catch her dress in the wheel. Louisa was pleased that he had taken care of her. When she had straightened her dress, they saw Arthur drive up and park his motor bike and he helped Gladys down. They made their way towards them. "Well the news is out." Arthur called as he put his arm around Gladys. She laughed up into his face.

"What news?" Fred and Louisa asked.

"Mother and father know about us." He bent down and kissed Gladys on the cheek. "But you needn't worry, you two are still a secret. I don't know who has been spreading the gossip though."

Neither Louisa nor Fred enlightened them, and as Arthur seemed cheerful, Louisa felt she would not bother to tell Arthur that Gladys had gossiped. She worried that Gladys may have gossiped about herself and Fred, but felt that there was little she could do about it now.

Fred proved to be a good dancer and Louisa enjoyed every minute of that evening. There was a lively band playing and they danced most of the evening. It was quite warm in the hall and she didn't need to wear her bolero and it was good to feel free to put her arms around Fred. She didn't want the evening to end. However soon after midnight the music stopped and they had to leave.

After saying goodbye to her brother and Gladys, Fred took her back to Broughton Hall and kissed her goodnight. It happened so suddenly and so naturally that Louisa couldn't believe it. She watched him drive away, but not before they had arranged a second date. Then she skipped light heartedly into the house. She had explained to Fred earlier about the Thursday arrangement with cook, and so they agreed to meet at the Majestic again in two weeks' time. They would watch whatever film that happened to be showing. Sidney was in the kitchen making a hot drink and opened the door for her so that she noiselessly slipped into the house. When she went in to her shared room with Hilda at midnight she felt as if she was dancing on air. She quietly undressed and got into bed so as not to wake her companion, and surprisingly she fell asleep as soon as she had settled her head on the pillow.

Louisa was scarcely out of bed the next day before Hilda bombarded her with questions. Between washing and dressing Louisa told her everything about the night before and how Fred had asked her out again on her next Thursday off. Satisfied with all the information Hilda followed Louisa downstairs both of them smiling. It seemed that both girls were smiling all through the next week. Then on the last Friday morning of June the postman delivered to Broughton Hall three letters for Louisa. One was from the dairy asking her to contact Mr. Griffiths to arrange an interview. The second was from Ivy who had written to tell Louisa that she had passed her preliminary exams and was now working in a typing pool in the general office of an aircraft manufacturer in Manchester. She sounded very excited and said she was earning a lot of money. She also wrote to say that she now had a boyfriend but didn't want to marry him because she wanted to get on with her career.

Ivy also told Louisa that her other sister Rose had now finished work as a scullery maid and had moved further north to Chesterfield. She had been offered a much better job in a factory packaging bandages and dressings for wounds. Her new boss was the supervisor called Muriel and they were getting on very well. Ivy concluded her letter by asking how Louisa was getting on with Fred. Louisa folded the letter and smiled. She couldn't wait to be able to write back to tell Ivy all her news.

When she opened the third letter she saw it was from Olive. This letter was very depressing. Olive had worked so hard in Wallasey, and was always cheerful, despite the way she was treated by Mrs. Barlow. She had been allowed one afternoon off to go to her mother's funeral, and when she had returned to work she had been so upset she was unable to carry out her duties. She had had an argument with Mrs. Barlow and then walked out never to return. She had returned to the rooms where her mother had lived and was now using her savings to pay the rent.

"Good for you." Louisa thought. Then read on. It seemed Olive had been ill and very depressed for two weeks and had been unable to look for work. When she did try, Mrs Barlow had not given her a good reference which had put prospective employers off. Though she didn't ask for anything, Louisa had a feeling that Olive needed help. It put a damper on the morning as Louisa did not know what she could do for her friend. Inwardly she cursed Mrs. Barlow.

Whilst the rest of the household were having their lunch, Louisa ran outside and down the drive to the main road where she managed to catch a bus to the town centre. She knew that the Crosville bus would run past the post office where there was a public telephone box. Gasping for breath she dialled the number and pressed the button for the money to register when she heard a voice on the other end. She explained who she was and was put through to Mr. Griffiths who agreed to interview her the following Thursday at half past two. Sighing with relief, Louisa managed to get another bus as far as the main road and she ran back quickly along the half mile drive to Broughton Hall.

Louisa arrived in the kitchen just as Mrs. Smedley the housekeeper walked into the kitchen. The household staff had just finished their lunch and were getting up ready to do their chores, but Mrs. Smedley told them all to sit down again. She glanced at Louisa's flushed face as she came through the door. Cook also gave Louisa a quizzical look as she tucked her hair back under her cap.

When everyone was seated Mrs. Smedley informed them that a Mr. Roger Thompson the older brother of Mr. Thompson was coming to stay at Broughton Hall for a short time. He was an invalid after having been wounded in the Great War where he had lost one of his legs. This would mean that he would need some special care and consideration. He was bringing a personal assistant with him whose name was Albert Hanley.

"I hope all of you will do your best to make both Mr. Thompson and Albert welcome." Mrs. Smedley finished. She turned to go but stopped when cook asked her when the new people would be arriving.

"Monday afternoon I believe." The housekeeper informed her and then left the kitchen. As soon as she had gone, the staff began to speculate on the new arrivals. Louisa was glad that they had forgotten that she had gone missing for half an hour. She told herself that it wasn't their business anyway.

If she chose not to sit and eat with them, that was her business and nobody else's.

Hilda and Louisa had been tasked to make the rooms ready for the new arrivals. When the guests arrived as expected after lunch on Monday, all their luggage was taken up by Sidney and Thomas to the allocated rooms. Cook then arranged for Peggy to take a tray of afternoon tea and cakes to be taken in to the drawing room. When she returned to the kitchen she brought Albert with her and she introduced him to the rest of the staff who were all drinking cups of tea. Mrs. Henderson poured Albert a cup of tea and he sat down at the table and thanked her.

"So how are we going to get him up the stairs?" Sidney asked bluntly.

Albert laughed. "He can probably manage by himself. He has been doing that for years now. With the aid of a stick of course."

Everyone gaped at him incredulously.

"He has had an artificial leg for several years, and manages quite well. He just needs me to take it off and strap it back on again." He sipped his tea. "Of course there are other things I help him with. He is a barrister you know and he still does legal work. I sort out documents for him. I'm not idle."

"No of course not." Everyone chorused. Just then the drawing room bell rang and Thomas went to respond. He returned to the kitchen quickly and told everyone that they were to go to the drawing room to meet Mr. Roger Thompson. The man himself got up to greet them and though he leaned heavily on his stick, he still managed to

159

shake hands with everyone and appeared to be much more amiable than his younger brother.

Sidney commented upon that and Albert replied "I think the war took the airs and graces out of him. He's lucky to be alive. He was in the trenches with the rest of the soldiers you know."

Sidney was very impressed with this information and warmed to Albert. From then on they became good friends and Sidney was only too happy to answer Roger Thompson's bell if Albert was not around. Sidney's father had been killed in the trenches and his mother had brought him up with the help of her own parents.

When Thursday arrived Louisa had to get a bus to her sister-in law's house to retrieve her bike. She spent just a few minutes with Dot and her grandfather and after explaining about the interview retrieved her bicycle. She was so nervous she nearly fell of her bike when she rode to Pandy. She had made sure she had a clean blouse and skirt to wear for her interview and kept checking it was alright in the basket. Consequently she frequently lost concentration and wobbled the bike. To add to her agitated state, she was worrying about telling her mother about the interview, and was also worrying irrationally about whether her mother had found out about herself and Fred.

As the morning wore on, Mary Ellen could see that her daughter was agitated over something, and in the end she asked her outright what was troubling her. Louisa, who by this time was so wound up told her mother that she had an interview at the dairy. To her surprise her mother burst out laughing. "Is that all? I thought something dreadful had

160

happened. Are you going to get changed? You can't go looking like that."

Louisa nodded numbly, relieved that some of her troubles were off her chest. She went upstairs to change into her skirt and blouse and then set off down the road. She was pleased that her mother called "Good luck."

Mr. Griffiths seemed to ask Louisa numerous questions during the interview. He took notes as Louisa described her duties, and the duties she had had previously in Wallasey.

"But you haven't served in a shop before or done any stock taking?" He asked her.

"No. I'm afraid not. Though I did help in the farm shop at Stansty. And I was very good at arithmetic at school, so I could soon learn to do the accounts."

Mr. Griffiths closed his notebook. "Well those are all the questions I have. Do you have any for me?"

Louisa looked startled. "No, I don't think so."

Mr. Griffiths laughed. "You are the sixth girl I have seen today, and none of them have got any experience either. Yet they all asked me the same question. Do you know what that was Miss Edwards?"

Louisa shook her head.

"The wages. They all wanted to know the wages. Don't you want to know what the wages are?"

"Yes of course."

"Do you want the job?"

Louisa thought that was a daft question but she answered "Yes of course."

161

"Well the job is yours if you think thirty five shillings is enough to tempt you. I will give you another two and six after a month's training if I think you are any good."

"Oh. Thank you Mr. Griffiths." Louisa managed to gulp out the words. "When should I start?"

Mr. Griffiths looked at his file in front of him. Jenny is leaving the end of July to get married. If you could start the day before so she can show you the ropes that would be good. He looked at the calendar on the wall. Let's see today is the sixth. You can start on the twenty eighth of July. He closed his book. Anything else?

Louisa shook her head. "No, thank you. Thank you very much. See you on the twenty eighth of July.

Her mother hugged her when she told her the news. "Well done. I'm impressed. Let's have a pot of tea and some treacle tart to celebrate." She filled the kettle and for once put it on the gas stove instead of on the open fire. Louisa couldn't stop smiling. Later she helped her mother to peel potatoes for suppertime. "Don't you think you should get changed out of those nice clothes" her mother advised. "It would be a shame to get them dirty."

"I think I will leave them on. I'm going to see a film later. I will put this pinny on." She took one of the pinafores off the hook from behind the door of the small scullery.

"I suppose you are meeting Fred and Arthur with that Gladys." Her mother said grimly. Louisa looked at her in surprise. "Don't you like Gladys?

"Of course I like her. It's just that…why didn't Arthur tell me he was going out with Gladys instead of me hearing it from her mother. I felt a fool."

"Maybe he wanted to make sure how he felt before saying anything. It took him ages to get over Megan."

Mary Ellen sighed. "Yes, I know. She was such a sweet little thing. She reminded me of my sister who died when she was only seven." She looked misty eyed, and Louisa felt a pang of guilt. She knew that Gladys couldn't keep a secret. She didn't want to risk Gladys's mother telling Mary Ellen about herself and Fred. So she took a deep breath and said, "Mother when I go to the cinema tonight I'm going with Fred. He's asked me out." She blushed as her mother whirled round. She stared at her daughter then slowly a grin broke out on her face. "Well I'm glad you told me. He's a nice boy. At least I will have something to tell Mrs. Taylor next time I see her."

Fortunately William took the news about Louisa and Fred very well too. He also congratulated her on the new job. "So we will be seeing a bit more of you soon. I'm glad."

"And I am glad too." Dorothy said. I've missed you."

Louisa was just getting on her bicycle when Arthur arrived home. "Off to see Fred?" He grinned.

She nodded. "Are you seeing Gladys tonight?" He shook his head. "No I am seeing her on Saturday. Did you enjoy the dance last week? It seems a shame that the dances are usually Fridays and Saturdays and you can't get to them."

"I will soon though." She told him about the new job which would enable her to have more freedom.

"Well done. Good for you. I'm glad you won't be working for that lot anymore. See you next week. Tell Fred I will see him Saturday at the match."

Fred was waiting outside the Majestic Cinema when Louisa arrived. He helped her to chain her bike next to his motorbike, and then holding her hand led her to the Majestic Cinema. It was a nice feeling to have her hand taken. It was even better when, seated in the theatre Fred put his arm across her shoulder and she rested her head on his shoulder. It was not until the interval that Louisa was able to tell Fred her news about the new job.

He looked surprised and pleased. "So when do you start?"

"In about three weeks." She smiled up at him. So we won't have to meet just on a Thursday."

"Does that mean you want to see me again?" Fred teased her. They both smiled. At the end of the film they strolled out of the cinema slowly hand in hand. Neither of them wanted to let go but knew they would have to.

"So what shall we do next Thursday?" He looked at the posters in the foyer. "There's a jazz band playing here next Thursday. Do you like Jazz?" Fred asked.

"Yes I do. That would make a nice change." She stood next to him and studied the poster. "It starts the same time as the films, so I can get here easily after seeing my family. By the way," she turned to him, I've told my Mother and Father that I am here with you." She studied his face. "Don't be alarmed. They seem quite pleased. I wanted you to know so that you are prepared when you next see them."

Fred's expression relaxed. "So they don't mind?"

Louisa shook her head. "And Arthur said he would see you at the match on Saturday. I think Harry is going too. So Dorothy said."

Fred kissed her goodnight and watched her cycle away before revving up his motorcycle and driving off in the opposite direction.

The next day Louisa told Mrs. Henderson that she would be giving up her position as housemaid. She said that she proposed to leave on Wednesday the twenty seventh of July so that she could settle again at home before starting her new job on the Friday.

Mrs. Henderson sighed. "It's getting harder and harder to get staff these days. At least you have given me a couple of weeks so that Mrs. Smedley can contact the agency."

"If you don't mind me suggesting something Mrs. Henderson, I do know someone in Wallasey who could replace me. She is having difficulty getting work at the moment, partly because she doesn't have a good reference. But if you like my work and trust my judgement I can recommend her to you. She's had some bad luck that's all."

Mrs. Henderson agreed to consider Olive and asked Louisa to write to her and invited her to Broughton Hall for an interview. Pleased to try to do anything to help her friend, Louisa wrote a letter to Olive that very night. She also wrote to Ivy to tell her about the developments with herself and Fred and that she too had a new job and more freedom.

The night before she was due to meet Fred, all the household staff sat in the kitchen to listen to the wireless before going to bed. They were all pleased to hear that in the next few weeks they would be able to buy paperback books. It was also announced that the novel 'The Seven Pillars of Wisdom' would be published.

165

Louisa commented upon this to Fred when she met him at The Majestic. "It will be cheaper to buy paperbacks rather than the hardback won't it? You will be able to buy more of your favourite '*The Saint*' novels." she teased him."

Fred grinned. "It would be if all the publisher's decide to print paperbacks. I think there is only one publishing house doing paperbacks at the moment and the series I like to read is published by somebody else."

"Perhaps in the future." Louisa smiled.

After the Jazz they arranged to meet again the following Thursday. "It will be my last Thursday off at Broughton hall." Louisa said.

"Will you be sad to go?"

"A little bit. But I think it's time for change."

They kissed each other goodnight and Louisa once again cycled back grinning from ear to ear.

Chapter Eleven

On Saturday Louisa received a reply to her letter from Olive. She wrote that she had been overwhelmed to hear from her and that she was looking forward to seeing her again. She had written to Mrs. Smedley separately and they had arranged to meet on Monday afternoon. When Olive arrived Louisa was making beds and dusting the bedrooms. Glancing through the window as she shook the pillows, she saw Olive walking up the driveway then disappearing behind the tall sycamore trees that lined the path leading to the back of the mansion. An hour later Louisa went down stairs to join the household staff for a cup of tea and was surprised to see Olive sitting at the table with everyone. She got up when she saw Louisa and flung her arms around her. There were tears in her eyes. She had lost a lot of weight and as she was dressed in mourning clothes looked very frail, but her face was cheerful enough.

"Louisa, it's good to see you again."

Before either of them could say anything else, Mrs. Henderson intervened. "Ah Louisa, I've been waiting for you." She turned to face the rest of the staff. "As you know, or maybe you don't," she paused and looked at Louisa, our housemaid Louisa is leaving us next week."

Everyone except Hilda gasped. Mrs. Smedley and Mrs. Henderson had asked Louisa not to mention it to the rest of the staff as she didn't want them to get unsettled again. Mrs. Henderson continued. "I have now decided to re-organise all the roles. So this is Olive who will be taking over Peggy's

167

duties. Olive will move in with Anne then Peggy can move in with Hilda."

Everyone began talking all at once, bombarding first Louisa with questions and then Olive. Eventually Olive said goodbye to everyone and went outside to walk the mile and a half down the road to the railway station. She would return on the same day that Louisa would be finishing.

Secretly pleased with herself that she had done something good for her friend, Louisa continued with the rest of her dusting. She was unperturbed that cook had said "be it on your head if Olive proves to be useless." She was confident that Olive would not be useless, and anyway Louisa wouldn't be there any more to face any recriminations.

When Olive arrived early on the allotted morning, Hilda showed Olive her room. Peggy had already moved her few things and installed them in the room she was now to share with Hilda. Louisa had stacked all her things by the door ready to take home. She didn't think she had many possessions, but she was surprised that she had filled two large shopping bags. She realised she would have to push her bicycle home as they were too heavy for her to cycle. At eleven o clock when Olive had settled into her room, Hilda brought her downstairs to meet the rest of the staff again and have their mid-morning cup of coffee. Louisa gave Olive her home address and told her to write to her as soon as she was settled. She also told her that if she was homesick she could come to visit her on her day off. It was still the height of summer and she would be able to get to Pandy easily on the bus. "Or possibly Arthur could bring you." Louisa suggested.

"You've been very kind to me." Olive said gratefully.

"I'm only too pleased to help. I don't know how I would have managed without you when I was in Wallasey. I don't know how you managed to put up with Mrs. Barlow for so long. I'm sure you will be happier here. Mrs. Henderson is fair minded and so is Mrs. Smedley. As long as you do your work everything will be fine."

At last, Louisa's shift at Broughton Hall came to an end. She said goodbye to everyone and at eight o clock opened the kitchen door to go out for the last time. She was surprised to see Fred standing outside with his motorbike. So was Arthur. Louisa smiled with pleasure. "What a surprise."

"We thought you may not be able to carry all your possessions on that bike, so we have come to collect the rest of your bits and pieces."

"How thoughtful of you both. I was going to tie everything on to the handlebars and put as much as possible in the basket then push the bike home."

Both young men took a heavy bag each from Louisa and put them in the luggage boxes at the rear of their motorcycles. Between them they shared out the contents of her basket which left Louisa with nothing to carry at all. She grinned. "Thanks. I will see you at home."

All her family except Harry and Dot were at home listening to the wireless when Louisa finally arrived home. She had ridden her bike as fast as she could but knew she would never be able to get home before the motorcyclists. All her belongings had been taken upstairs to the bedroom she would share again with Dorothy. Grinning she sat down next to Fred on the sofa and thanked her mother for the cup of tea she offered her. It seemed funny to be sitting next to Fred with all her family around her. "Welcome home Louisa." Dorothy smiled at her sister.

Jenny was waiting for Louisa when she arrived at seven thirty at the dairy shop on Friday. It had been a pleasure to walk down the road from home to get to work especially after an extra hour in bed. After she put on the white overall and cap that Jenny handed to her, she shadowed her all morning. The first thing she had to do was to try to remember the price of all the goods and where they were stacked on the shelves so that she could serve their customers efficiently.

"As soon as you remember all that, I will ask Winnie to show you how to manage the till. "Jenny said. "We also have to make sure everything is clean and tidy in the shop and in the store room. The milk and cheese and eggs are kept outside of the shop in the cold room, so we only bring in a small amount at a time. All the dry stuff like tea and tinned stuff is kept in the back." After half an hour Violet left Louisa in the store room by herself to try to memorise things. After she had been there an hour she was joined by Winnie the other shop assistant.

"Hello. I just thought I would pop in here to say welcome. I started at eight thirty today. Jenny and I take it in turns to have a later start in the mornings. I can do the same with you, if you like. I hope you enjoy it. The work isn't bad and you get to know the local gossip from all the customers." She winked. "It's amazing what you find out. Mr. Griffiths pops in every now and again. He spends most of his time in the dairy." She left Louisa to get on with familiarising herself with her new surroundings.

By the end of Saturday morning Louisa's head was buzzing with new information. When she went home later that afternoon she kept hearing the till ringing in her ears. After a bowl of soup and a sandwich with her mother and Dorothy, she helped Mary Ellen to do some household chores. Then having the luxury of a few hours to herself she read a book for a while before getting ready to go out with Fred later. He arrived at seven o clock to collect her to go to another dance. This time she didn't have to hide her dress from her mother and was pleased that she complimented her on the altered bridesmaid dress. She still had Dot's bolero jacket from the previous dance and was ready when Fred knocked on the door.

Every Saturday throughout the summer Fred collected Louisa on Saturday evenings and took her either to a dance or they went to see a film. By the end of August she knew she was falling in love with Fred. She hoped he felt the same way.

Just before the end of August Louisa received a message from Olive that she was settling down in Broughton Hall and would like to come and visit Louisa. After exchanging various letters Olive informed Louisa that she had negotiated with Mrs Henderson and Peggy that she could have Wednesday as her day off and that Peggy would have Thursday. They arranged that Olive would visit one Wednesday afternoon as it was half day closing at the dairy shop and Louisa would be at home. Normally, Louisa and Winnie were required to take it in turns to do some stock taking during Wednesday afternoons though in any case it was usually finished by four o clock.

That particular Wednesday when Olive planned to visit, Louisa was able to meet Olive at the 'smithy' bus stop and take her home to meet her mother. Mary Ellen had been baking and so both young women were greeted with tea and homemade scones. Almost as soon as they entered the kitchen, Dorothy, off school for the summer holidays, pounced on Olive eager to meet her sister's friend.

"Do you like working in Broughton Hall? Is it better than that place in Wallasey? Tell us about that horrible woman Mrs. Barlow." Dorothy bombarded Olive with questions. Between sips of tea and conspiratorial glances at Louisa she managed to answer the younger girl's questions.

When Arthur arrived he looked at Olive and said "I remember you. The last time I saw you, you were on your hands and knees scrubbing a floor with Louie."

Olive blushed. "I remember you too! I thought you were marvellous the way you stood up to Mrs. Barlow."

Arthur laughed loudly. His laughter was infectious and so they all spent an amusing half hour recalling all the terrible things Mrs. Barlow had done. To Louisa it seemed as if it had happened during another lifetime and not just two years ago.

Much later after they all had supper, Arthur offered to take Olive back to Broughton Hall. She looked nervously at him. "I haven't been on a motorcycle before, do I need to do anything."

Arthur grinned. "Just hang on tight and leave it all to me." Olive hugged Louisa goodbye and she waited at the end of the road until they were out of sight. Louisa was pleased that Olive had settled down in Broughton Hall, she certainly looked better than she had a month earlier.

As for herself, Louisa was now using her spare time to study dressmaking magazines and books she borrowed from the library. On Saturday afternoons when Fred was at a football match she would spend hours poring over the literature. It was still a novelty for her to have so much time to do the things she always wanted to do. Her skills in sewing and knitting were improving rapidly. She loved to experiment with colours and designs, sharing her ideas with Dorothy who was just as enthusiastic. Dorothy loved to draw too, though was not very interested in sewing.

Early in September Fred told Louisa that he was going to Liverpool for the week end to see his mother. She hadn't been very well again. He also wanted to see his sister Cecelia who had just given birth to a son. She had named him Neville. So that week end Louisa helped her mother around the house and managed to finish the back of a sweater she was knitting for Fred for his birthday at the end of November. She also finished knitting a matinee coat for Harry and Dot's new baby. She held it up for her mother to inspect who complimented her on the finished garment. Praise from her mother, who considered herself to be an excellent needlewoman was praise indeed.

When Fred called early the following Saturday afternoon, he found Louisa, Arthur and Dorothy listening avidly to the wireless. Mary Ellen was listening too and making blackberry and apple jam at the same time. The broadcaster announced that The Rich Citizenship Act in Germany had forbidden Jewish people to marry German nationals.

"The man is mad." Fred said as he sat down beside Louisa. She turned towards him and smiled her welcome.

"Why is nobody doing anything to stop it?" Arthur said. "It's going to get worse before it gets better. More and more Jewish people are fleeing the country. How many more indignities is he going to heap on to them?"

"It's not just Jewish people, it's even German people with Jewish ancestors he's persecuting." Louisa said passionately.

"Where are they all going to go?" Dorothy asked. "Will they be allowed to leave Germany?"

"Some of them are going to America or some are coming here to Britain. There are Jewish families in Liverpool." Fred said. "In fact my mother and step father rented rooms in a large house owned by a Jewish family in Islington. They lived next door and I used to run errands for them when I was a boy. There was a synagogue at the end of our street. It's still there and our Catholic church is virtually next door."

"Is that where your mother lives now?" Louisa asked curiously.

Fred shook his head. "Now that most of us have left home, they moved to somewhere smaller. There's only Mary, John and Edward living with Mother now."

"And your step father?" Louisa added. Fred nodded. Louisa got the impression Fred did not like talking about his step father.

"What was it like living in Islington?" Dorothy asked. "It must have been a big house for all of you to live in it."

Fred nodded. "It was. It was in a remarkable position as it was near the square. It was like the Hyde Park of London - it might still be, I'm not sure. But anyway all the politically minded used to gather there. You know, the Communists, Socialists and even a few fanatics who would have you believe that they knew everything and how the world should be run."

"I know the type." Arthur chipped in.

"Anyway over to the left of the square, on what they called 'Greenside' was a boys boxing club run by the Liverpool favourite boxer Ned Tarleton. Have you heard of him?" Fred looked at his little audience. Even Mary Ellen looked up from her jam making. She was interested in boxing and liked listening to it on the wireless. They all shook their heads. "Well anyway, this Ned Tarleton persuaded me into the ring, and used me as practice for other up and coming boxers."

"So can you box Fred?" Dorothy asked excitedly. Fred laughed. "I'm not much of a boxer but I know the moves." He pretended to punch Dorothy and she moved away quickly laughing. Louisa was very proud of Fred at that moment. "A man of many skills." She said.

"Perhaps all of you can use your skills and make some tea and butter those scones. I need to get this jam into the jars now." Mary Ellen said.

On October the fourteenth the long awaited birth of Harry and Dot's baby arrived. She had been taken to the maternity unit of the Maelor Hospital in Wrexham and Harry had waited outside all night waiting for news. As soon as the little boy had been born he had made sure that mother and baby were well and had raced home to tell his parents.

So when Louisa arrived home from work she found her mother making up a basket of food and blankets ready to take to Harry and Dot's home. "It's too expensive for Dot to stay in hospital, so I'm going to help her and her mother for the first few days until she gets into a routine. You will have to make sure everything is in order here and get something to eat for your father. Dorothy is coming with me to carry all these things."

So it was a few days later when Louisa was able to see her nephew for the first time. She had waited until Saturday afternoon to visit Dot and the baby. They had called him Gordon. Dot was very strong and was looking after the baby as if she had done it all her life. She allowed Louisa to hold the baby for a little while, and she gazed into his beautiful little face. Proudly she gave Dot the gift she had made herself and was pleased that her sister-in-law appeared to like the little knitted coat. "How is your romance with Fred?" She asked. "Still going strong?"

Louisa nodded. "It's good. We see each other about twice a week.

"Have you been to Liverpool yet to meet his family?" Dot asked.

"No not yet, but he promised he would take me some time in December to show me the Christmas lights." When Louisa returned home that Saturday afternoon she found her mother and father talking to a man she had never seen before. He was introduced as Robert Richards the current Labour Party Member of Parliament for Wrexham. He was seeking re-election. Before he could say anything, William told Louisa to go and sit in the front parlour. As she walked through she could hear her father speaking. "Louisa is not old enough to vote, and I hope when she is, she will be voting Liberal like the rest of the family. Good day to you sir."

In the parlour Louisa couldn't help smile, she knew that Fred would probably vote Labour if he could, but he wasn't old enough. He just missed the voting age by one month. She knew he was miffed about that but there was nothing he could do about it until the next General election. As it turned out on the fourteenth November, the Prime Minister Stanley Baldwin was returned to office at the head of a National Government. Meanwhile two weeks after the election it was confirmed that Clement Atlee had become the Leader of the Labour Party.

"Are you pleased about Clement Atlee?" Louisa asked Fred when she saw him a few days after the results had been announced. He shrugged. "Let's hope he turns out to be a good leader. Maybe Clement Atlee will be the Prime Minister soon. I don't think this National Government will make a difference to the unemployment figures."

"Well at least Robert Richards is the Labour MP for Wrexham, though my Father isn't very pleased with that."

At the end of November, it was Fred's birthday. Louisa presented him with the sweater she had made him. She also gave him the latest 'Saint' novel. "I hope you like it and that you haven't read the book yet." She said shyly.

He kissed her. "Thank you very much, I like both gifts very much. I haven't got this book, it was one I was going to get.

The pullover will keep me warm through the winter. It's getting colder now too."

The days were indeed getting colder and as November turned into December the skies became grey and often Louisa thought that a storm was brewing. She had got caught in showers a few times on the way home from work and the wind had blown her umbrella inside out.

On the first Wednesday in December, it was Louisa's turn to work during the afternoon to do some stock taking. She locked up everything at four o clock and put the keys safely in her bag. She felt proud that she had been given the responsibility to carry out this task. Outside the light was falling rapidly and there was a sharp chill in the air. She hurried home looking forward to a cup of warming tea. When she opened the back door into the kitchen she was surprised to find Olive sitting at the table with Mary Ellen. The young girl got up to greet her friend. "I have been chatting to your mother, and waited to see you before I go. It's very dark outside and I don't like walking from the town centre to Broughton Hall when it gets late. The next bus that goes near Broughton Hall is half past five so I should manage to catch it if I go now."

"Don't worry about that. Stay for supper and Arthur will take you home. He doesn't see Gladys on a Wednesday." Mary Ellen insisted. She got up from the table to look at a casserole she was cooking on the stove.

Olive hesitated and cast a nervous glance towards Louisa who reassured her. So the girl stayed awhile longer and she told them the latest gossip at Broughton Hall.

"Have they given away any more news on the colliery inquiry?" Arthur probed the girl when he arrived home an hour later. She shook her head. "All I know is what you know already. That it's dragging on and there are several versions of what happened. The solicitors and all the share holders have been to the house to discuss things with Mr. Thompson several times. Nobody wants to take the blame, though they are trying to say now that the firemen were to blame."

"That doesn't seem fair." Arthur said aggressively. Later he took Olive back to Broughton Hall and Louisa went up to the bedroom she shared with Dorothy and surveyed her wardrobe. She wasn't sure what clothes to wear to go to Liverpool with Fred the following Saturday.

"Are you going on the train or on the motorcycle?" Dorothy asked.

"Fred wants to show me the Mersey tunnel, so we will be going on the motorbike. But if the weather is bad we will go on the train. So I will have to put out two sets of clothes and see what happens. An idea occurred to her. Perhaps I could borrow one of Arthur's sweaters and put it over me when I am on the pillion to keep me warm then take it off when we get there."

"Good idea." Dorothy agreed.

The weather was dry but very cold and misty, so in the end they decided to go on the train to Liverpool. When they got off at Liverpool Exchange station they caught a bus to Salisbury Road in Everton, then walked a few hundred yards to Fred's family home. Once there, Louisa was introduced to

Fred's mother, and his sister Mary and brothers John and Edward.

Mrs. Barton had long red hair and though she was by now very frail, Louisa could see that she was a very attractive woman. Mary and Edward both had her features, and when they stood next to Fred she could see the similarities in all of them. Their Liverpool accent was very strong and it took a while to adjust to their voices. Many times she had to say "pardon" before she could understand what was being spoken to her.

Mary and Edward were very excited to meet her and chatted ten to the dozen bombarding her with questions. They all made her feel welcome and after several cups of strong tea Fred took Louisa back to Liverpool so they could see the Christmas lights. The famous department store John Lewis was still open and they wandered inside to look at the Christmas decorations. Louisa couldn't help thinking about Beryl when they walked into John Lewis, but she didn't see her anywhere. Later they went to a restaurant for a meal and then returned quite late to Everton. Everyone had gone to bed save Mrs. Barton, and after saying goodnight to her, Louisa tiptoed into Mary's bedroom. The girl was half awake and moved over in bed to make room for Louisa. Meanwhile, Fred was going to share with John and Edward.

On Sunday Louisa's head was reeling with so many names to remember. She had been taken from one house to another across Liverpool. This was so that she could meet more of Fred's several brothers and his other sister Cecelia. She held her little boy Neville for a little while, then she nursed the baby Margaret who was Robert's and his wife Margaret's

180

young baby. Eventually they were on the train back home to Wrexham again. Louisa was very tired but also happy to have met Fred's family. She also looked forward to the following April when she and Fred would return to Liverpool, to attend James and Anne's wedding.

James was the eldest of all Fred's siblings and from what Louisa could gather, he had been very protective of them all when they were little children. James had been fifteen when their father had been killed in the Great War. Fred had been barely two years of age and could not recall his father at all. His mother had given birth to John three months before their father was killed at Passchendaele in September 1917. Fred's mother Cecelia had re-married in 1921 and later gave birth to Edward then Mary. Apparently there had been another baby – Joseph but he had died in infancy.

Fred explained all this on the train journey home and Louisa listened fascinated by all the information she was gleaning. "Your mother is a remarkable woman to have got through all that." She finally commented.

"Yes she is. She has kept us all together. We're all very close despite my step father, but the least said about him the better." He said darkly. He pulled Louisa to him and she felt safe in his warm arms around her.

When Louisa finally got to her own bed on Sunday night and unpacked her few items, Dorothy demanded more information.

"Well they are all very nice. Mary is about a year older than you and Edward is a year older than her. John is two years more or less younger than Fred. They all want to come to Wales to see us, but they had better not all come at once, there's no room!" They both laughed. "Mother would have a fit." She switched off the light and got into bed. Before closing her eyes she said to her sister. "By the way Fred said that he would take us both to the cinema to see *A Christmas Carol*. Would you like to come?"

In the dark Louisa smiled at the anticipated enthusiastic reaction from Dorothy.

On Christmas day, the family were surprised that Arthur had been to Broughton Hall and brought Olive back for Christmas supper. Gladys who had just walked around from her parent's house almost collided into them in the doorway as they came into the front parlour. At once Louisa suspected that Gladys was jealous, though she didn't say anything. Mary Ellen greeted her with a glass of sherry and handed one to Olive. They both thanked her and Olive timidly sat on the arm of the chair next to Louisa. As there was little room for everyone to sit down by the fire Arthur remained standing and leaned against the sideboard. Fred got up to allow Gladys to sit down but Gladys stood next to Arthur and hooked her arm through his whilst all the time glaring at Olive. Meanwhile Louisa beckoned to Olive to take up Fred's place. Louisa felt that Olive was tense. She could sense an uneasy atmosphere that radiated from the hostile glances fired at Olive from Gladys. To hide her discomfort Olive gazed at the sleeping baby and commented to his parents that Gordon was a beautiful baby. Just then the baby woke up and began to cry and his adoring mother picked him up and put him on her knee. The little boy smiled happily and started to kick his legs out at his father. Harry got hold of his feet and tickled them tenderly.

"Plenty of strength in those feet, perhaps he will be a footballer one day." William joked as he watched his son and grandson.

They all laughed. Presently Mary Ellen handed the plate of mince pies around and Louisa got up to make another pot of tea.

When Olive said she had to go, Louisa went to fetch her coat and Arthur got ready to take Olive back to work. Gladys got her own coat and followed them outside with her arms folded grimly. Louisa went out in the cold night too and hugged Olive. "See you again soon."

Olive hugged her back. "Say thank you to your family, they have been very kind to me."

After they had gone, Gladys said she was going to walk back home to her parents' house. It was only a five minute walk. "Tell Arthur to come and see me tomorrow night." And she marched off.

Chapter Twelve

1936

The tension got worse between Arthur and Gladys on New Year's Eve. The four of them had gone to a dance at the church hall in Garden Village. All night Gladys had been on edge and when 1936 was chimed in she looked expectantly at Arthur as if he was to give her something. He kissed her and then they both left the hall. A few minutes later Fred and Louisa emerged from the hall to make their way to the cloakroom. Fred helped Louisa to get into her coat, and she shivered as she fastened the buttons. Fred put his arm around Louisa's shoulders and they began to walk out into the cold night air. Louisa felt warm and happy in Fred's embrace. But Fred took his arm away from Louisa when he saw Arthur and Gladys arguing on the pavement outside. He went as if to intervene, but Louisa pulled him back. "Don't Fred. Let them get on with it."

Reluctantly they both got on to Fred's motorcycle and they drove the two miles back to Pandy.

Fred waited for Arthur to return which wasn't long. He burst into the kitchen and told Louisa and Fred that he and Gladys had finished. He said no more but stormed upstairs only to be told off by William not to make too much noise.

Before he went to work the next day Arthur told his family that it was all over between him and Gladys. Both parents looked upset but made no comment to Louisa. For her part she didn't know what to think. Later that day when Louisa was walking home from work she saw Gladys getting off the bus. She was on her way home from Melia's grocery shop in Wrexham where she worked.

"I suppose Arthur has told you that it's all off between us." She said to Louisa.

Louisa nodded sympathetically. "Is there no chance you will make it up?"

Gladys pouted. "If he asks me to marry him I would consider it. I thought he was going to last night, but he didn't."

Louisa looked startled. "Has he mentioned marriage to you before?

Gladys shrugged. "Not in so many words, but he kept talking about the big house he was going to buy and all the things he was going to do. I just assumed he meant he was going to marry me. And as it was New Year's Eve, I just assumed that would be the perfect time to ask me." She pulled her cigarettes out of her bag and lit one as she walked up the street with Louisa. She took a drag before speaking again. Her expression was accusing and Louisa felt uncomfortable under her fierce gaze. "And now he is seeing that Olive friend of yours."

Louisa was taken aback. She felt she had been attacked. "He's not seeing her Gladys. He's just being kind. She's had a bad year, and she was good to me in Wallasey."

"Well he knows where I am if he wants me." Gladys stalked off, her heels clacking on the ground as she was followed by a billowing whiff of cigarette smoke.

After supper that night Arthur got up abruptly and declared he was going out.

"Do you think he is going to see Gladys?" Mary Ellen said anxiously.

"He doesn't usually see Gladys on a Wednesday." Dorothy said. She was still oblivious to the breakup of Arthur and Gladys. Mary Ellen didn't want Dorothy to know just yet in case things were mended. William grunted. "I don't know what's wrong with that lad at the moment." Louisa said nothing.

On Saturday afternoon Fred called around to the house and after a brief conversation with Louisa, he and Arthur went to a football match. Soon after they had gone, Gladys's mother Mrs. Taylor arrived. Mary Ellen told Louisa and Dorothy to leave the room so they could have a private conversation. The two girls obligingly put on their hats and coats and went for a walk to see Harry and Dot and the baby Gordon.

"Do you think they will get back together again?" Harry asked, as Dot brought in a tray with tea and fairy cakes she had baked that day.

By this time Dorothy had realised what was going on and said that she hoped so. Louisa was unsure. She didn't know what was going through Arthur's mind. She felt that her mother and Gladys's mother couldn't change the way the two of them felt about each other. She wondered what they were actually talking about.

When Arthur returned from the football match with Fred he seemed in a better mood. Later he accompanied both Louisa and Fred to the cinema. During the interval he told them that he had taken Olive out to see a film on Wednesday.

Louisa was astonished. "But what about Gladys?"

Arthur shrugged and tried to smile. "I wish I hadn't told her that I had taken Olive home after she visited us the first time. She was jealous of Olive. I was only being kind to her. She has to trust me, or things won't work between us."

"Well what does Olive think about this?" Louisa demanded. "I hope you aren't going to hurt her."

"Keep your hair on. There's nothing going on between us. She said she wanted to see a film and I offered to take her. I'm only being a friend. She doesn't go anywhere you know Fred. Louisa is the only friend she has. And she was good to Louisa in Wallasey."

Both Fred and Louisa stared at him. "So are you going to see her again?" Louisa asked.

186

Arthur nodded. "Yes, next Wednesday. She wants to see *Becky Sharp* but only if you two come too. Can you make it Fred? Louisa?"

With some misgiving on both Fred and Louisa's part they agreed to meet up the following Wednesday.

Olive was at once apologetic about being there and Louisa tried to put her at her ease. Though in some ways she felt she was being a traitor to Gladys. She didn't like being in such a difficult position. Her brother was very dear to her and she wanted to be loyal to Arthur, and so she tried to make Olive feel comfortable. "It's not your fault that Arthur and Gladys have split up."

Olive looked relieved. "I really think they will get back together again." Olive said. "Last Wednesday all he could talk about was Gladys." She sighed. "He's been very good to me. All of you have." She hesitated. "I don't want to cause problems for any of you. I like your brother very much, but I haven't been flirting with him. In any case he is not interested in me as a girlfriend. We get on very well together as friends, he is so easy to talk to and somehow I confided in him that I've fallen for Sidney." She blushed and looked away.

"Sidney Davies at Broughton hall?" Louisa said. Olive nodded. "He's very kind to me, and I think he cares for me, but he hasn't actually said anything. Oh this is so difficult. I don't know what to do."

Louisa grinned. "True love is hard sometimes. And if Sidney asks you out what can you do? His day off is Tuesdays isn't it?

Olive nodded. "Yes, but he has mentioned to me a couple of times that he could swap with Albert if he wanted. Albert can go any day he likes. Do you remember Albert?"

Louisa nodded. "Is he still there? I thought he would have left by now with the other Mr. Thompson."

"He's decided to stay until the spring, when the weather improves he says."

"It seems to me that Sidney is dropping hints to you and is waiting for you to say something."

Olive brightened. "Do you think so?"

Louisa nodded. "You will just have to let him know that you want to see a film or go dancing, and then see what he says. If he really can swap with Albert then put it to the test." Louisa couldn't help adding, "It worked with Arthur didn't it?"

"But I wasn't chasing after Arthur. I just mentioned it really. He suggested we went out. I think he wanted to make Gladys jealous on purpose." Olive protested. "I've made a mess of things haven't I?"

Louisa grimaced. She was torn between love for her brother and affection for her friend. "Did you tell Sidney you were going to see a film with Arthur?"

Olive nodded.

"Well you had better tell Sidney that he is my brother and that there is no romance involved. Then it's up to Sidney. What did Arthur say about Sidney?"

"He told me to tell Sidney how I felt about him, but I can't do that, it's too forward!"

Louisa laughed. "Well that sounds like my brother."

Just then both Arthur and Fred returned with ice-creams and they changed the conversation to discuss the film. Just before the lights went out Olive said to Arthur, "By the way, I overheard Mr. Thompson say this morning that Gresford colliery has started to produce coal again."

After the film, Arthur took Olive back to Broughton Hall and Louisa told Fred about her conversation with Olive.

"So it's purely platonic on both sides." Fred said with a grin. "What a mess."

It turned out that the mess was soon sorted out. The next evening Arthur went to see Gladys and returned with her a few hours later to tell the family that they were engaged to be married. Dorothy shrieked with excitement. "Can I be a bridesmaid?" Gladys smiled and said yes.

Two weeks later Louisa received a letter from Olive to say that she was going to the cinema with Sidney and she was very excited. Louisa wrote back to tell her that Arthur was engaged to Gladys. The wedding was to be in September.

Meanwhile Louisa started looking around all the expensive dress shops for ideas for an outfit. She couldn't afford the prices but was good at copying the designs. She had decided to make herself something for the wedding of Fred's brother James in Liverpool. She was hoping that she could wear the same outfit to both weddings, seeing that only Fred would see her in the outfit twice. The wedding was the weekend after Louisa's seventeenth birthday towards the end of April. They planned to go up to Liverpool to celebrate both events.

She finally decided on a fitted skirt and jacket. The jacket would be difficult to copy because of the elaborate collar but she felt she could manage it. She chose a heavy weight sky

189

blue crepe material from the haberdashery and fabric shop in Wrexham.

Whilst Louisa set upon designing her outfit, cutting and sewing the fabric, she listened to the wireless. Early in March she put down her scissors in disbelief as she heard some shocking news on the wireless that Hitler had re-taken the Rhineland. As the weeks went by the news from Germany got worse. In April the family were informed that Hitler had made Hermann Wilhelm Goering Commissioner of Raw materials. They were all gathered around the wireless one wet Saturday afternoon listening to the news. William shook his head as if to rid himself of evil thoughts. "This does not look good for Germany nor for the rest of Europe if I'm not mistaken. That man is dangerous. You know what this means don't you?" He glared at his family, his blue eyes fiercely bright with choked back anger.

His family nervously waited for him to enlighten them. William continued to glare, so Louisa ventured to suggest that raw materials might mean iron and steel for making machinery.

"Aeroplanes, tanks, ships!" exploded her father. "Goering was a fighter pilot in the Great war."

"Do you think there will be another war? Harry asked anxiously.

"I hope not." William answered sighing. He lit his pipe and stared gloomily into the fire.

On the twenty fifth April which was a Saturday, both Louisa and Fred had been given the day off from work so that they could travel to Liverpool for James and Anne's wedding.

Fred carefully laid his suit and Louisa's blue crepe skirt and jacket in his top box. Both had been wrapped separately in brown paper. They then drove all the way to Liverpool. When they went through the Queensway tunnel under the river Mersey, Louisa had expected it to be dark and was amazed that there were lights to lead the traffic through. In fact Louisa spent all week end being dazzled by the department stores in Liverpool, then the wedding and then by Fred's huge family. She had wondered if the wedding would be catholic but it seemed that unlike the rest of his siblings James was Church of England, so Louisa was familiar with the church service.

Afterwards at the reception in the church hall, Louisa chatted all day to various members of Fred's family and smiled as he danced with some of the younger children at the party. The celebrations went on all day and long into the night and it was well past midnight before everyone got to bed. Consequently when Louisa woke up at nine o clock on Sunday morning it was to a silent household. It seemed everyone had slept in that morning. She slipped out of bed and left Fred's young half-sister Mary sleeping, then tiptoed over Cecelia and little Neville who were sleeping on blankets on the floor. Carefully she dashed to the tiny washroom to freshen up and get dressed. When she returned to the bedroom Cecelia was sitting up and propped up against the wall with some cushions. She smiled at Louisa and whispered. "Are you alright girl?"

Louisa smiled and whispered back that she was. "Shall I go downstairs and put the kettle on?" Cecelia nodded. "Help yourself, I think I'll get in with Mary though for half an hour." She tucked up the little sleeping boy in to the blankets and then took Louisa's place in bed with her sister. The occupant moaned and turned over in bed totally oblivious.

Downstairs there seemed to be sleeping bodies everywhere and Louisa quietly opened the kitchen door to prevent disturbing them. She was surprised to see Mrs. Barton sitting in the rocking chair at the side of the range. She was nursing a cup of tea. She greeted Louisa with a friendly smile and then pointed to the teapot. "I've just made some tea. Do you want some toast? I will get Fred up now." She got up and Louisa heard her go upstairs and knock on Edward and John's bedroom. Soon Fred appeared downstairs followed by his brother Alfred.

"Did you sleep alright Louisa?" Fred asked. She nodded that she did and poured him a cup of tea.

"Is there any more tea in that pot wack?" Alfred asked his brother and Fred took the lid off to inspect it.

"Yes there's another brew there."

Alfred poured himself a drink and sat on one of the chairs at the table opposite Louisa.

"Where's Ellen?" Fred asked his brother. Louisa frowned trying to think who Ellen was then remembered she was Alfred's wife.

"She's sleeping at Bobby and Maggie's. She said she would share with Nancy, if Thomas would sleep downstairs on the sofa. The two little girls – Bobby's and Tommy's are with them too."

Alfred scratched his head and turned to Louisa. "We are such a big family. There's never enough room for all of us."

He began to cough and he pulled out his handkerchief to wipe his mouth. "Still it was a good do."

Fred's mother Cecelia buttered a plate of toast and put it on the table for them to help themselves. Much later Fred and Louisa spent the rest of the day visiting the rest of his siblings and then they set off to return to Wrexham. It was supper time when they got back, and after Fred had something to eat with Louisa's family he returned to his lodgings in Wrexham. They agreed to meet again on Wednesday evening.

At work, it was Louisa's turn to have the whole Wednesday afternoon off and she looked forward to having the rest of the day to herself. She was working on a dress that a neighbour had asked her to make. Her reputation as a competent dressmaker was beginning to spread and she was regularly getting orders to make clothes. The little money she earned from this work she saved in a special bank account. When Louisa arrived home she found Olive chatting to her mother. She got up to rush to Louisa when she saw her. "Don't worry I'm not staying. I just wanted to come and see you to apologise to you personally if I have caused any ill feeling. I have been thinking about it for months."

"Sit down Olive. There's no need to rush off." Louisa said kindly. She hung her jacket up on the kitchen door. "I told you Arthur and Gladys are happily engaged now and planning their wedding."

"I've already told her that." Mary Ellen said. "But I'm not going to suggest that Arthur takes you back to Broughton Hall in case Gladys gets upset again."

"No of course not." Olive said. "You have all been so good to me."

"Stay and have a cup of tea with me and then I will walk you to the bus stop." Louisa said. The girl agreed to do this and they exchanged news about their work. Olive was now seeing Sidney on a regular basis. Mr. Thompson senior was planning to move soon. He was going back to live in Cardiff and soon he would be taking Albert away.

"This will make it difficult for you to have time off with Sidney won't it? Because he won't be able to swap his day off with Albert." Louisa said.

Olive nodded miserably. She brightened up quickly. "But at least we see each other every day anyway, that's the important thing." Louisa agreed. She understood how Olive must be feeling, because the days she didn't see Fred she missed him terribly.

Chapter Thirteen

Throughout the summer Louisa and Fred saw each other on a regular basis. Sometimes they went to the cinema and at the weekends they would go dancing or take picnics to the nearby bluebell wood. One week end towards the end of July, Fred offered to take Louisa to Ellesmere to see her Aunt Nancy and her husband Alf. They both loved visiting the farm cottage near the lake and as it was a beautiful summer's day they went swimming in the lake. Later they dried off at Nancy's cottage and she made them high tea which they ate outside from a garden table. The three of them sat side by side basking in the sun on some deck chairs. Nancy had the wireless on in the kitchen and through the window they could hear the news being broadcasted. Recently there had been military risings in Barcelona and Madrid and it seemed the Republicans had managed to overcome the fascist rebels.

"It looks like the Republic in Spain is under threat." Fred observed, "and Hitler is supporting the military. I wonder why."

"I can't understand why he is trying to overthrow President Azana." Nancy said. "I don't trust that Hitler. He's already made himself head of the German military, he's up to no good if he is supporting the military and fascism in Spain."

"This could be the start of a civil war." Fred commented. "Is this just the beginning of Hitler's plan to invade Europe do you think?"

Both Nancy and Louisa grimaced at the thought.

"Let's not think about it, it's such a nice day." Nancy got up and went into the kitchen to bring some home grown strawberries from her garden. She dished them out fairly and poured some cream over the top. "Come on lets enjoy ourselves while we can."

Unfortunately for Spain things did get worse. The massacre of communists referred to in the media as 'Reds' caused ripples of fear and dread amongst all those people to whom Louisa spoke. The ripples were also felt across the rest of Europe if the newspapers were anything to go by, Louisa observed. She was very disturbed at these new developments.

Despite plans for his forthcoming wedding, Arthur still managed to find a passion to rage against Hitler and Franco. He confided in Fred that if it wasn't for the fact that he was getting married he would have enlisted himself to fight for the Republic. Fred was sympathetic but hated the thought of killing people. "Well at least the socialist French Prime Minister Blum is attempting to help the Republic. He's closed the borders between Spain and France which is preventing the enemy to bring in ammunition and troops."

"Yes and I heard that Stalin was supporting the Republic too." Louisa chipped in. She was taking a keen interest in what was going on in Spain. Eventually the conversation turned to the wedding which was to be the following week. Fred was going to be best man and Dorothy and Louisa were going to be bridesmaids. Dorothy was very excited and when the day arrived she couldn't wait to put on her special dress. Louisa had worked feverishly on making the dresses and had taken great care to make sure they would both fit perfectly.　Both dresses were a pale pink silk.　Gladys had decided to buy her dress from a bridal shop in Chester because she wanted no-one to see it except herself and her mother until the wedding day. The shop she had chosen was a very expensive shop, and it seemed that Gladys had been saving for years for her bridal gown and was determined to get the best she could afford.

Meanwhile, Louisa and her mother were kept busy the night before helping Mrs. Taylor to make trifles, and on the morning of the wedding were still helping Gladys's mother make sandwiches and sausage rolls for the reception at Garden Village Hall.

After the ceremony Arthur took Gladys away on his motorbike for a week end in Blackpool.　They would move in to their new home in Acton the following year when the houses were finished.　The company that Fred was working for were in the process of building the very same houses. Arthur had agreed to live with his mother-in-law for a year so that he could save up enough money to pay a deposit of twenty seven pounds on a new house.　He was determined to buy his own home.　Meanwhile he had set aside some money to be able to afford a week end honeymoon.

A few weeks later, Fred received a letter from his sister Cecelia to say that John was going to London to march with Oswald Mosley in East London.

Fred was very upset when he heard the news.　"What's got into him?　I can't believe it.　I'm going to have to go and talk some sense into him."

That very week end Fred went to Liverpool to talk to his brother.　When he returned on Sunday evening he called to see Louisa and she was relieved to see that he looked less distressed.

"He just got carried away with it all. He wanted some excitement and the idea of going to London with some of his mates appealed to him." Fred said. "He has no intention of going to Spain to fight for either side."

William nodded sympathetically. "That's how it was in the Great War. So many young men went looking for adventure, and they never returned."

Mary Ellen wiped a tear from her eye. "Like my brother. He was killed on the first day of the Somme. God bless him."

"That would be July nineteen sixteen. A year before my father was killed in nineteen seventeen. I was just a little toddler and John was only three months old. So neither of us can remember him." Fred said soberly.

"Do you think Cecelia and Robert remember him? They're a few years older than you." Louisa suggested.

Fred shrugged. "I don't know. They don't talk about it. Thomas and Alfred have mentioned him once or twice, but James remembers very well. However, my mother married again a few years later and it wasn't spoken of when she was around and especially never in front of her new husband John Barton."

"Talking of new husbands, it looks like the American woman Wallis Simpson will be getting a new one soon. She and King Edward seem to be in each other's company a lot." Mary Ellen said.

"Do you think she will be Queen Wallis?" Louisa asked. "I wonder what the government will have to say about that."

"We will have to wait and see." Commented Mary Ellen.

The family were soon to find out. On December eleventh the King abdicated so he could marry Mrs. Wallis Simpson. He made a speech to the nation and later it was announced that he would be known as His Royal Highness the Duke of Windsor.

"He must love her very much to give up being King." Louisa commented. "Not like Henry V111. I don't think he would have given up his kingdom for a woman."

In the same month of December, it was stated in the local papers that the two year long inquiry into the Gresford disaster had come to a close. Sir Henry Walker Her Majesty's Chief Inspector of Mines had made his final report. Investigators had looked at causes and circumstances of the explosion and had considered a range of angles. The list included management failures, lack of safety measures, poor ventilation and poor working practices. However it seemed that the general public would not hear the full details of the conclusion until the following year.

Meanwhile the words of a ballad describing the explosion was circulated quickly around the Wrexham area. Some people said that it had been written by one of the six survivors.

Chapter Fourteen

1937

In January 1937 Sir Walker's report was presented to Parliament at Westminster. He had written that it had been impossible to enter the Dennis shaft where the explosion had occurred. Therefore, to gather evidence to assess the cause and location of the explosion had made it an extremely challenging task.

"They never will get into the Dennis shaft again. I know for a fact after spending six months down the mine sealing it up." Fred said. He was reading the article in the *Wrexham Leader* that Arthur had angrily thrust before him one Saturday afternoon. They were all seated in Mary Ellen and William's kitchen. Gladys now visibly pregnant was sitting in one of the arm chairs by the fireside looking at knitting patterns that Mary Ellen had given her. Not that Gladys could knit. She was simply choosing patterns for Mary Ellen and Louisa to knit for her.

"I don't think they need to go down there anyway. It's common knowledge from the six survivors what happened. Poor working conditions and poor management. Presence of gas and lack of ventilation." Arthur said. "And the air was so thick with fumes from the blasting they could hardly breathe. For God's sake poor Alfred Jones told me that sometimes he was working almost stark naked it was so hot in there because there was no ventilation. No-one should have to work in those kind of conditions. And if that wasn't bad enough they were continually firing shots to loosen more coal. They were doing this, even when they knew there was gas about; well there was an accident waiting to happen!" He thumped the table hard and everyone jumped.

"Could you smell gas when you were down there Fred?" Louisa asked. She was relieved that his work down the pit was complete. He seemed to have settled down well at his new job working for a new building construction firm set up in Wrexham.

Fred nodded. "Occasionally I got a whiff, but not much, and once it was sealed the air was better. I'm glad I don't work there any more though."

"So am I." Louisa said. She smiled at Fred and he returned her smile with a grin. She loved him and cared deeply about his safety.

She hoped that he cared about her in the same way. As it happened, she did not have to wait much longer to find out.

At the end of March on Easter Sunday, Fred took Louisa out for a drive to Ellesmere. After he had parked his motorcycle near the mere, they walked hand in hand along the side of the mere, and Fred asked Louisa to marry him. He produced a diamond engagement ring from his pocket and went down on bended knee to ask her.

"Oh yes." Louisa squealed with joy and Fred put the ring on her finger and picked her up and swung her round and round till they were both dizzy with excitement. As they were so close to Nancy and Alf's house they called there to tell them their news and Nancy made them some tea. "I suppose I should offer you something stronger, but I'm afraid I haven't got anything. But congratulations anyway!" She smiled at her niece as she held out her hand to inspect the ring. "I wish you lots of joy and happiness."

The news was received with just the same enthusiasm in Pandy when they returned.

"So when are you going to have the wedding? Dorothy asked excitedly.

"We are thinking around October. This will give us enough time to save up for a deposit on a house. The company Fred is working for have bought a piece of land to build a new housing estate on the Chester Road in Garden Village." She took a deep breath before continuing, "and we are going to buy one when they're finished." Louisa explained. She was very excited at the prospect of having her own home with Fred.

"Will it have an indoor bathroom like Gladys and Arthur's?" Dorothy inquired.

"Yes. It will be wonderful." Louisa replied.

Fred agreed. "With a bit of luck the housing estate will be finished by then. We will have to get a solicitor to do all the legal side of the paperwork. I will have to ask Arthur which one he is going to use when he finalises his purchase."

William disappeared into the pantry for a few minutes then returned to the kitchen with a bottle of whisky and some small tumblers. Mary Ellen filled a jug with some water from the tap and whilst William poured out the spirit, Mary Ellen added some water to the drinks.

"Congratulations to you both. We couldn't have a better son-in-law." William said and Mary Ellen heartily agreed.

Later in their shared bedroom, Dorothy whispered in the dark to her sister. "Louisa have you given up the idea of becoming a nurse? You always said that when you are eighteen you would train to be a nurse?"

Louisa who was just about to drift off to sleep opened her eyes and turned to face her sister. She could just about see the outline of her head propped up on her bended arm.

"It's true I always said that, but you know something. Since I fell in love with Fred I haven't even thought about nursing. I suppose if I hadn't met Fred, I might have saved up to go to night school. Now that I have a better job and more time and more money I could probably do it. However, nursing was just a back up plan. I now have a responsible job and I get a bit of income from my sewing. In any case I think I would prefer to do something artistic rather than nursing." She turned over on her back.

"I think you have to be really dedicated to be a nurse." Dorothy said.

"I think you right. When I left school, I was so dead set about not being a servant and going into service, that I felt that nursing would be a better option. Mother was against my staying on at school so there wasn't much else I could do. I'm just thankful that I took the plunge and got the job at the dairy. I have more independence, and more free time. I'm also building up a good reputation with my sewing which though doesn't pay me a lot, provides a bit of extra pocket money. Besides that, I also have the man I love."

Dorothy giggled. "Fred is nice isn't he, and he adores you."

In the dark Louisa smiled. She felt very lucky.

"Maybe you could start your own business as a dressmaker. We could do it together. We could both design the clothes and you could sew. I'm not much good at sewing but I could cut things out."

"That would be nice." Louisa replied dreamily.

A few weeks later in the middle of April, Arthur gave Fred and Louisa a list of solicitors in Wrexham who specialised in conveyancing. "Most of these will be fine as far as I am aware." Arthur said. "A lot of them will be occupied with the court proceedings regarding Gresford pit. The explosion is keeping a lot of solicitors busy."

The hearings started on the twentieth of April at Wrexham County Petty Sessions Court. Over forty charges were made, most of them against the owners. Some charges were made against the manager. A few charges were made against officials employed by the company who were accused of breaking safety regulations. As the hearings continued many of the charges were either withdrawn by the miners or dismissed by the court. Rumours spread that some miners were afraid of appearing in court and were intimidated by the legal jargon.

In the end the court ruled that the manager was guilty of inadequate record-keeping. Apparently he was accused of not taking and recording measurements of air flow for at least two months before the explosion. The manager was fined £140 with £350 costs.

A week after the final hearing, Louisa received a letter from Olive. First of all she congratulated Louisa and Fred on their engagement, and then informed Louisa that she and Sidney were also engaged and that they were going to live in Cardiff. She explained that Mr. Thompson's brother was still living with them even though he had kept on his house and a part time housekeeper in Cardiff.   Olive thought that the only reason Mr. Thompson's brother had stayed in Wrexham so long was to give moral support during the court hearings of the Gresford explosion. Apparently he had been a successful barrister before the Great War. She had discovered that he had shares in the same coal mine as his brother, and also had an equal share of the estate left to them jointly by their father. Anyway it seems the part time housekeeper in Cardiff had resigned and Albert too had decided to leave working in service and had found work in Wrexham at the brewery. So the older Mr. Thompson who was returning to Cardiff had offered Olive and Sidney jobs in his home if they were willing to relocate to Cardiff.   Both of them had said yes though neither Mrs. Smedley nor Mrs. Thompson had been very pleased about it. The news had caused some ill feeling in the kitchen at Broughton Hall. Louisa wasn't surprised, but read on. Olive and Sidney were going to get married and their new employer had promised them rooms of their own in Cardiff. Olive guessed that he was desperate to get some staff straight away, and was willing to make some compromises. So Olive was to replace his housekeeper and Sidney was to replace Albert. Eventually they would want to find a place of their own and start a family, but until then, they thought the offer was too good to refuse. They hoped that there would be more opportunities for Sidney in Cardiff to get a better job in the future. Olive finished off her letter saying that the house was a very large one according to Albert and was situated near a lake in an area called Roath Park.

Louisa could sense her excitement in her letter and wished her well. When she showed Fred the letter he commented that, it would be a good temporary move and the sooner Olive and Sidney got out of working in service the better.

When she saw him a few days later towards the end of April he seemed very agitated about the news from Spain. As soon as he had sat down, Arthur arrived and they immediately began to discuss the German airstrikes on Guernica.

"That bombing raid sounds horrific. It seems it more or less flattened Guernica." Arthur said.

"Where is Guernica?" Louisa asked frowning, trying to picture a map of Spain in her head.

"It's Northern Spain – the Basque country." Fred replied. He sipped his tea and then said. "Hitler has a lot to answer for. I think he's testing out the reactions of the British government and at the same time using Spain as a practice ground for testing his armaments. He has all these new weapons and a new air force that has flattened a town and killed a lot of innocent people."

A few weeks later a letter arrived from Ivy. The contents of her letter reinforced Fred's views about getting out of working in service. She was happy working as a typist and so glad she had left working in service. She said she had more money and time to spend it. She went to dances and though she was never short of escorts, there was no-one really special in her life. "But, Louisa I wouldn't want it any other way. I don't want to get married and settle down yet. I want a few years of fun before I start looking for a husband and having babies. I know you and Fred are in love and I wish you well, but I've never met anyone to fall in love with." She signed her letter with a flourish with lots of x's and Louisa smiled. She seemed to have what she wanted.

As for babies, the following month in early July, Gladys gave birth to a baby boy. They called him Brian. Arthur was over the moon and was every inch the proud father. Each time Arthur and Harry got together, they amused Louisa by talking about their little sons. Though inevitably they discussed what was going on in Germany. One day Arthur said he was extremely worried about reports that said Hitler was building up his air force. "Can't this government see that Hitler is planning something sinister beyond building up his forces?"

Little Brian lay quietly on Arthur's knee, taking notice of everything around him. He was a contented baby and totally oblivious of his father's indignation. So was his cousin Gordon who was attempting to stand up with the support of his father.

Towards the end of August, the first phase of new houses that Fred was employed to build with his employer Roberts the builders, was ready to sell. Arthur and Gladys's house was also ready for them to move in. So all the family helped them to pack their things to transfer the small family to their new home on Cunliffe Road. Arthur was jubilant that at last he had got what he wanted though their possessions were meagre. "It's a beginning" he said.

At the same time Fred's mother became seriously ill and so Fred told Louisa that it would be better to postpone their wedding until his mother Cecelia recovered. Louisa was disappointed but she understood Fred's concerns. That weekend he went to Liverpool alone to see his mother.

Louisa spent the week end Fred was away, worrying about so many things. It didn't help that the news on the wireless was so depressing. General Franco seemed to be gaining ground over the Spanish Republic in various parts of Spain. Madrid had been heavily attacked by General Franco's artillery, as well as in the Northern town of Santander. It was also becoming patently clear that both the Italian and German fascist governments were aiding Franco. The Spanish Republic was suffering terrible losses and showed no sign of gaining the upper hand.

To add to the gloom she read about the rising conflict between Japan and China which eventually culminated in full scale war between those two countries.

"There is trouble brewing all over the world at the moment." William said with a sigh. He stood up and poked the fire with a vengeance, almost as if he was trying to stop all the violence. Mary Ellen agreed with him. She was sitting on an armchair knitting another matinee coat for Brian. Both Harry and Dot were sitting in the kitchen with them listening to the news. Despite it being August, it was a cold day and William had lit a fire for them all to sit around. Arthur and Gladys had just left to visit her parents and so the rest of the family gathered around the wireless.

"Do you think there will be another war Father?" Harry asked. He seemed to ask this question quite regularly now. Secretly he thought there would be but he wanted his father to disagree with him.

"I don't know but things are looking grim. We need to keep an eye on Hitler and Mussolini, maybe they are waiting to see the outcome of the war in Spain."

"That's what Fred said." Louisa commented.

"Let's change the subject." Mary Ellen said.

However, the subject of the civil war in Spain continued over the supper table when it was broadcasted on the wireless that Franco had overcome the Republicans in Gijon and had taken that town.

More bad news followed in November when Fred's mother died. The funeral was to be in Liverpool. On the day of the funeral Louisa accompanied Fred to the Yew Tree cemetery.

Inside the church Louisa was one again surrounded by Fred's many siblings and their wives. There were also several relatives from his step father's family in the congregation too. Later at the wake Louisa sat with Fred's eldest brother James and his wife Anne. James explained that his mother had been ill for a long time, and her condition had worsened during the previous three months.

"It's a shame she won't be here for your wedding. And of course you will have to put it off for a while now." Anne said sympathetically.

Louisa agreed but put on a brave face. "At least we have something to look forward to." She said.

Fred came and sat beside her. He had two small tumblers of whisky in his hand and handed one to Louisa. She sipped it and wrinkled her nose. Fred got up. "I will get some water to put in it. You will be able to drink it then." He returned very quickly with a jug of water and was accompanied by his two sisters Cecelia and Mary. The younger of the two – Mary looked very upset. Her eyes were red rimmed and Louisa couldn't help noticing that they seemed to accentuate the redness of Mary's lipstick. She was three years younger than Louisa and the youngest of all of Fred's siblings. She noticed that all Mary's brothers as well as Cecelia were very protective of her. Presently John arrived and before long the conversation turned to teasing John about his march in London with Oswald Mosley. He looked a bit shamefaced and said that he realised it was a mistake.

"Well even if you had joined the International Brigades to help the Republic I would still have been concerned." James said. "Though it would be a more honourable act, they are getting a raw deal, and the chances of you returning alive would be very thin."

"Things are looking bad for the Republicans in Northern Spain at the moment." Thomas commented. The others agreed. At this point Edward, who had been talking to his cousins joined them and Louisa could see the striking family resemblance. It was apparent even in Edward and Mary who were born after the second marriage of Fred's mother. Fred had been aged seven when his mother had remarried.

Eventually they said goodbye to everyone and got a taxi to Liverpool Exchange Station in Liverpool. Two of Fred's' older brothers Thomas and Robert accompanied them to the station. Both brothers lived not far from the city centre in Old Swan. They shook hands with Fred, kissed Louisa and then left them both on the platform.

Fred was very subdued as they waited for the train and Louisa in an effort to comfort him linked her arm in his. He squeezed her hand gratefully. The train was the last one to Wrexham and did not stop at the station in Pandy during the evenings. So when they got to Wrexham, Fred arranged for Louisa to be taken home by taxi, whilst he himself would walk to his lodgings in the town centre. "It's not far from here. It will only take me twenty minutes." He kissed her goodbye and they arranged to meet at the Empire Picture House a few days later. Arthur and Gladys were hoping to come too if they could persuade Gladys's mother to babysit. Harry and Dot were also joining them. Dot's mother was looking after Gordon. Fred wanted to see the film he had seen advertised in the *Wrexham Leader* as *Dead End*.

Whilst Louisa got ready to go to the cinema that evening Dorothy said that it wasn't fair that everybody was going out without her. She brightened up when she said that Fred and Louisa would take her to see a film as a Christmas treat. Dorothy's birthday had been in early November and she was now fourteen years of age.

Taking care to speak quietly to Louisa so that their mother couldn't hear, she pointed out to her sister, that she – Louisa - was working away from home and visiting cinemas when she herself was fourteen. Up to now Dorothy had resisted being sent away to work in service and had managed to get her own way. Mary Ellen said she should start looking for work after Christmas and Dorothy was scouring the newspapers for jobs because she was determined not to be a servant. "You have broken the mould Louisa and I am going to try to get a job like yours."

Louisa agreed with her sister and said she would help her. She was the youngest of the family and everyone had forgotten that she was growing up fast. At the cinema Louisa reminded her companions that Dorothy needed to be taken more seriously. They all agreed that they would take Dorothy with them next time they went out together.

211

When the family gathered together again just before Christmas, they heard the terrible news of the fall of the Spanish Republican army in Teruel.

"Franco's army have overpowered the Republican's in Northern Spain." Arthur commented. He put down the newspaper he was reading and waited for a response from either his brother or Fred. Both of them were reading different newspapers. Louisa had just entered the back parlour with a tray of tea and mince pies. She put it down on the sideboard. Before anyone could say anything she asked if that would mean that Franco would win.

"It's looking bad, and the cold weather isn't helping them." Harry said. Mussolini and Hitler's weaponry is far superior to the Spanish republic. Plus Teruel is more vulnerable to air strikes because it is a small town in the mountains. It's an easy target just like Guernica. And look what they did to that! Franco and Hitler between them!" He folded his newspaper in disgust.

Louisa poured some tea and handed the cups and saucers around as her mother and Dorothy entered the room with a plate of sandwiches. Mary Ellen quietly sat down by the fire opposite William who had been smoking his pipe and listening to the conversation about Spain. He made no comment other than to say it was all very worrying. He took a sandwich and munched it thoughtfully. "Where will it all end?" He said finally.

Fred took a sandwich and attempted to lighten the mood. "So which film are we going to see tonight? Snow White or Heidi?" He smiled at Dorothy when he said this and she laughed. "You know very well I don't want to see them."

They all laughed. "What do you want to see? You choose." Louisa asked kindly. She picked up Arthur's abandoned newspaper and looked at the adverts. "There's The *Squealer* on at the Majestic, *Girl on trial* at the Hippodrome and *The Rat* at the Empire." She put the paper down and sat on the arm of the sofa next to Fred.

"I reckon we should see *Girl on trial since* you are on trial with us Dorothy." Arthur teased her.

Dorothy tossed her head. "Well as it happens I would like to see it. It's a murder and suspense film."

"That's alright with me." Harry said. "I like those type of films."

"Well that's settled then." Said Dot who was sitting quietly next to Harry.

"How are you all going to get there?" Mary Ellen asked.

Arthur stood up and got his and Gladys's coats. "I can take four in my car, and Harry can take four in his. Fred can leave his motorcycle here." He turned to Fred unless you want to take Louie and then I can bring her back with Dorothy, so you can go straight home."

Fred looked at Louisa. "What shall we do?"

"I don't mind. Whatever is easy for you."

Fred hesitated for a minute then said. "Let's all go together and then I can come back with you all to get my motorbike."

On the way Harry asked Fred if he had thought about trading in his motorbike for a car. Arthur was able to get a discount from the place he was working at Clark's Garage, and had managed to get a good deal for Harry.

"I've been thinking about it, but I don't want to spend any more money just yet until I get enough money to buy a house for when Louisa and I get married."

In the backseat he held hands with Louisa and she smiled.

"Very wise." Dot commented. She felt lucky that though she and Harry were sharing a house with her grandfather, that she at least had some security. Harry had a good job as a painter and decorator and now they had a car they could take Gordon out to various places.

"So after Christmas you will be planning your wedding." Dot said.

"Yes but we are going to wait until next October. Fred's family are still in mourning." Louisa responded.

Chapter Fifteen
1938

In January lack of peace across the world was spreading and Louisa began to worry about how this would affect the United Kingdom. Everyone kept talking about a war being imminent and she dreaded the thought of what would happen to her beloved family. She tried to concentrate on her wedding plans and remain cheerful. Fred tried to allay her fears and often said that no matter what happened they would always love each other. They should try to be happy even if they only had a short time together. This made her cry and laugh at the same time.

"All this talk of war doesn't help though." Louisa told him one evening. "If this government thinks there is going to be a war, why doesn't it stop it instead of talking about taking precautions?"

"I think they are trying to see what happens in Spain." Fred tried to reassure her.

"And if the Spanish Republic falls to Franco and creates an alliance with Hitler and Mussolini, what then?"

He sighed. "I have to admit this country seems to be preparing for war, if you believe what is in the papers. New factories are being set up making weapons." He sighed.

"There's nothing we can do about it. We just have to be happy." He kissed her. "Try not to worry."

When Louisa was with Fred she felt better but she only saw him twice a week. Everyone she spoke to seemed to think that there would be a war. People at work, and people she bumped into in the street. After the usual greetings and talk of the weather, the inevitable conversation was whether there would be another war.

The headlines in most of the newspapers she read said that refugees were pouring into Britain, and the British Government were taking measures to stem the flow. Louisa felt that the reaction from the British government towards the German refugees entering the country was not very sympathetic. She was horrified that so many people had to leave their homes behind to escape persecution. She tried to follow what was going on in Germany as best as she could, listening to the news on the wireless during the odd hours that she could spare and scanning newspapers to get more news.

The more she read and heard the more she became convinced that war would inevitably happen across Western Europe. She visited the library on her days off and poured over maps so that she could get a better knowledge of Europe and in particular Spain and Germany. Then when she heard news that Hitler had virtually marched into Austria and seized that country she became indignant on behalf of Austria. The Nazis had taken complete control of Austria and declared it German territory.

"Well Hitler is from Austria, he probably feels it is his by right." Harry said sarcastically. He was sitting in the kitchen at Pandy one late Saturday afternoon. He had brought Gordon with him who was playing on the floor with a wooden toy train.

William who had only arrived home from work just an hour earlier, scratched his head. He was still in his working clothes and was looking very tired. "There doesn't seem to be much resistance from the Austrians," he said. "And what is worse there seems to be no objection from this country or France. But the Versailles treaty of 1919 forbade it after the Great War. I remember it well. It was to prevent Germany having too much power. The country was not allowed to develop an army, or increase its navy amongst other things in the Treaty. Yet Hitler seems to have total disregard for everything that was in the Treaty and is building up his forces right under our noses. Now he has made himself Germany's war minister." He shook his head sadly as he recalled the events of 1918.

Mary Ellen nodded in agreement. "I remember the Treaty too. Germany was blamed for all the damage across Europe and various government leaders demanded that Germany repaired the damage in some way. Yet some people said, and not without sympathy, that the country was so weak it couldn't possibly afford to pay compensation. They have obviously got money from somewhere though, how else could they begin to train an army? Why isn't the Prime Minister doing something about it? No doubt Hitler will start to persecute people in Austria too." She became quite indignant as she spoke and began to beat her cake batter extremely intensely.

"I suppose if Austria hasn't put up a fight, then Britain and France aren't going to cause trouble." Harry suggested.

"That will surely make him confident to invade other places like Czechoslovakia won't it?" Louisa commented. She looked up from laying the table for afternoon tea before Fred arrived. She wanted to make sure he had something to eat before they went out later. Harry nodded. "I shouldn't wonder." He reached for Gordon's coat from the back of his chair and helped his son into it. "I had better go and pick Dot up from town."

Louisa followed him to the little car outside and watched him put Gordon down on the passenger seat beside him. She kissed her little nephew goodbye. Harry started up the engine. "Enjoy the film tonight with Fred. Are Arthur and Gladys going with you?"

Louisa shook her head. "They can't get a baby sitter for Brian. Mother's doing something with the WI and Gladys's mother is also doing something. Our Dorothy is coming though."

Harry started the car up. "Ok see you next week." He was just about to drive off when a car parked in front of him. Harry got out of his car again grinning as he saw Fred swing out of a large shiny black convertible motor car. "Hello Fred, what do you have here?"

Fred grinned too. "It's not mine, it's the gaffer's. He said I could borrow it if I took him and his missus to Chester railway station. They have gone to London for the week end."

"Very nice." Harry said. He and Louisa walked around the car to admire it whilst Fred leaned against the garden gate. His face beamed as he watched them approve the lines of the vehicle. Eventually Harry got back in to his own car and left, and Fred accompanied Louisa into the house to find Mary Ellen pouring tea. "Hello Fred. Just in time come and sit down." Dorothy placed a plate of ham sandwiches on the table and Louisa lavished a great deal of butter on the scones her mother had made earlier.

Later, Louisa and Dorothy excitedly got in to the car as Fred drove them to the cinema. "What type of film are we going to see?" Dorothy asked.

"It's called *The detective agency.*" Louisa answered.

"You like detective films don't you Fred? And especially *The Saint.*" Dorothy teased. Both sisters exchanged knowing grins as they saw Fred trying to smother a smile and appear nonchalant.

One spring Saturday afternoon in late March, Louisa cycled across to Rhosrobin to see Harry and Dot. It seemed a lovely day yet the news about the Chinese and Japanese two week battle in Taierzhuang had dampened things for her. So many horrible things were happening to innocent people across the world, it made her feel helpless. She cycled round the back of Harry and Dot's home and called "hello" before she walked straight into the sitting room. She found them both sitting on the sofa playing with Gordon. Dot got up to make some tea and whispered to Louisa that she was worried about her grandfather. He had not been very well and was upstairs in bed. Louisa sat down on the sofa next to Harry whilst Dot went upstairs to take some tea for the old man.

"Have you called the doctor for Mr. Weaver? Louisa asked her brother.

"He insists he doesn't need a doctor." Harry returned. "I've tried to persuade him. I've told him if he is worrying about

219

the money I will gladly pay his fees, but he won't have it." He looked up as Dot came down the stairs. "How is he?"

Dot shrugged. "He seems about the same as yesterday. He's stubbornly refusing to let me call the doctor." She fetched the tray from the kitchen. "Have some tea Louisa, and try a piece of Victoria cake, I made it this morning." She handed the tea and cake on a small plate to Louisa and she cradled them on her lap. Gordon came and sat beside her and showed Louisa his wooden toy train engine. She put her tea and cake down on the small table beside her, so that she could examine it. She smiled down at her nephew as he pushed the toy on an imaginary railway line on the floor.

"It looks like your prediction of Hitler planning to take back the Sudetan from Czechoslovakia is right Louisa. I heard it just now on the wireless. It's a pity because although it was a made up country after the Great War, the economy seems to be flourishing. If Adolf Hitler gets his way it will break up a good democratic state."

"That man just likes breaking things. He's determined to cause trouble," declared Louisa.

"It's like as if he wants all Germans to be in one state. He can't accept that Germans live in other countries like Austria and Czechoslovakia." Observed Dot. "In fact some German people live here in Wrexham. I'm sure they are happy enough getting on with their lives without interference from him. I know a German family living in Bradley. And I think there is another one in Summerhill."

"I think you are right love." Harry responded with a shrug.

Louisa sipped her tea thoughtfully. "All this antagonism is making me feel uneasy, and it's quite obvious that our government is preparing for war. Fred keeps telling me not to worry about it, because there is nothing we can do even if there is a war. But that doesn't make me feel any better." She bit into her cake absently.

"He's right. We can't do anything to stop it, but I agree it is worrying." Harry smiled at her. "Where is he this afternoon? Are you not seeing him today?"

"He's working overtime, to save money for when we get married." Louisa returned her brother's smile. "The houses on Holt Road and Chester Road are nearly finished so we should be able to buy one soon. His boss is keen to get them done, because he has another project in mind on the other end of town in Acton. So there's plenty of work for him. I've been saving too. We have almost got enough for a deposit. I want to try to save a bit extra for our honeymoon and some furniture."

"You are lucky to be able to start married life in your own place. Not that we are not happy." Harry said quickly as he caught Dot's hurt look. "We've been fortunate too. We have our own things and space here, and Dot's grandfather is no trouble even though he's needing a bit of extra attention today. But we would have looked after him anyway even if we lived somewhere else. Dot's mother has been popping in to help, but I just wish he wasn't so stubborn about not calling for the doctor."

Dot put her hand on Harry's arm to reassure him, and in response he put his hand on hers. "I know what you mean. Some couples start married life with their in laws and it can be a bit cramped if there are siblings in the house too. Two of my brothers have that problem, and of course poor Arthur

221

is not having the start he wanted, so we are very lucky." She got up to go upstairs again to check on her grandfather.

"Those new houses that are being built by the company Fred is working for will have indoor lavatories and bathrooms won't they?" Harry asked.

Louisa nodded. "Yes it will be luxury not to go outside to the lav, especially in the winter. Arthur put a deposit on his almost as soon as they started building. It was amazing how they soon became sold. It will be good to move into our own house when Fred and I get married. It was lucky that he could put a deposit down so quickly and being a builder he knows the best plots. He said ours will have a nice little garden."

Harry nodded. "Good for him. Maybe I should start thinking on the same lines, but we are happy here. I will see the houses soon, probably before you, because Fred's company has asked the company I work for to do all the interior decorating." He laughed at Louisa's stunned face. "I know, it is a bit of a coincidence isn't it?"

"Does Fred know?" Louisa asked.

Harry's grin widened. Fred recommended us to his boss."

It was Louisa's turn to laugh. "That's just like Fred."

When Dot came down again, Louisa got up to go and fastened on her jacket. She looked about for her headscarf and bent down to pick it up from the floor. "How is your grandfather now?" She asked.

"He seems comfortable. He's sleeping. She kissed her sister in law goodbye. "See you soon." Louisa dropped a kiss on Gordon's head and then went to the back of the house to get her bike.

When she arrived home, she found Arthur with his son Brian on his knee. Gladys had gone shopping with her mother, and so Arthur had taken the opportunity to spend some time with his own mother. Dorothy was chopping rhubarb freshly picked from the garden. She was going to make a rhubarb pie under the supervision of Mary Ellen. When it was ready for the oven Louisa helped them clear away the mess on the kitchen table. This done, Mary Ellen as usual on a Saturday afternoon took out her embroidery and Dorothy played a game of patience with a pack of cards on the table. Louisa took the baby from Arthur and cradled him as his father stood up to stretch his legs. He looked at his watch. "What time is Fred coming?" he asked.

"About five o clock. He's working overtime again." Louisa answered as she rocked the baby.

Arthur groaned. "That's another hour yet. Gladys will probably be back by half past five."

"Did you need to speak to him about anything?" Louisa asked. She frowned. "Is there something wrong?"

"No of course not, I just thought I would have a chat that's all. Are you both going out later?"

"Yes we are going to the dance hall in Rossett. Why don't you and Gladys come with us?"

Arthur brightened. "If we can get a baby sitter, maybe we could."

"I can look after Brian." Dorothy offered. She loved looking after her nephew and she liked to make herself useful. Louisa suspected that Dorothy's offer was to distract their mother from sending her away to work in service. She had mentioned a few times lately that Dorothy should look for a better job. Dorothy had managed to get a job working at the new Stansty farm shop run by Mrs. Fern. The farm shop had thrived considerably since Louisa's spell of delivering eggs. The shop now sold fruit and vegetables as well as eggs though it didn't open every day. Dorothy's job was three days a week, and though she was now earning money, Mary Ellen thought she should be occupied for at least five days per week. So far though nothing had materialised and Dorothy was content to fill up her time with babysitting and helping her mother in the house.

Mary Ellen looked up as if to protest, then caught Louisa's eye and bent down again to concentrate on her embroidery. They both knew that Dorothy was capable of looking after the baby. However they also knew that since Brian had been born, Gladys's mother had resented Gladys and Arthur wanting to go out to enjoy themselves. She felt they should both be with the child. She loved her grandson but refused to take responsibility of taking care of him when his parents were out gallivanting as she called it. Mary Ellen didn't want Dorothy to cause any ill feeling. However Dorothy seemed to be immune from the disapproving glares she sometimes got from Mrs. Taylor, she had eyes only for her nephew.

Arthur looked so excited that his mother didn't have the heart to disappoint him. She conceded that he worked hard and deserved to have some excitement. "Do you want to bring Brian here, or do you want Dorothy to come to your place?" Mary Ellen asked him.

Before he could answer, Dorothy suggested she looked after Brian in his own home so that she could put him in his cot and watch him as he slept. "That means I can lie on your bed and read a book until you come home." She said. "I will come across later on Louie's bike."

"Well that seems settled." Mary Ellen smile. She was satisfied with that arrangement, and gently pushed her embroidery needle into her fabric.

When Fred arrived an hour later he seemed pleased with the arrangement too. Arthur and Fred spent some time chatting about football and both agreed they would go to the next Wrexham home game. Soon after half past five Gladys appeared and seemed delighted to have the opportunity to go dancing in Rossett. They arranged to go in Arthur's car. Arthur kept suggesting bargain cars to Fred, but Fred was adamant that he wanted to save his money towards his house first. So when they were all seated in Arthur's old but comfortable saloon car, and Arthur again broached the subject of cars for Fred, he again resisted. He did this with a smile. "I fully intend to buy a car in the future but not yet. Louisa and I are happy enough to get around on my motorbike, aren't we sweetheart?" He looked over his shoulder at Louisa who was sitting in the back with Gladys.

"Of course I am." She said in support. She enjoyed being in the car but also enjoyed being on the back of the motorbike with Fred and her arms around his waist. She always felt safe like that. It was also a feeling of freedom and yet safety at the same time. Just as she did when later they danced and Fred held her tightly in his arms.

They all agreed that the dance had been good and they promised to do something similar for Louisa's nineteenth birthday which was in a couple of weeks. Memories of the dance put Louisa in to high spirits each time she thought of

225

the previous weekend. However the nauseating news from Germany overshadowed her cheerfulness.

Hitler had passed a law that German employers were no longer allowed to employ Jewish employees. Louisa felt outraged over this and her disgust was shared with her family and friends. In the same month news came of civil unrest in Sudetan on the borderlands of Czechoslovakia. Rumours spread that Hitler had deliberately positioned an army all along the German Czech border with the intention of intimidating President Benes of Czechoslovakia. Whether the rumour was true or not, the result was that the President felt the need to mobilise his own army close to the same border.

Whilst the presence of Hitler's troops increasingly aggravated the Czech Republic, Hitler agreed to meet the Prime Minister, Neville Chamberlain to discuss the possibility of diffusing the antagonism. Eventually in July, it was reported that Hitler had promised Neville Chamberlain that he would not invade Czechoslovakia as long as he was given control of the Sudetenland. The news was received on the wireless one summer evening when the family were sitting down to supper. It was unknown for William Henry to raise his voice, but that evening he appeared to be incensed.

"What is the government thinking of?" He roared. "Can't he see that Adolf Hitler won't be satisfied until he gets back all the land that was taken from Germany under the Versailles Treaty? And to my mind, that means he wants Czechoslovakia! He's taken Austria, now he wants the Sudetenland back despite the Treaty of Versailles. He's

226

destroying that new country that was set up after the Great War – a Republic which if all accounts are true, is at the moment thriving."

"I always felt that the Prime Minister should have sent Hitler packing, and not agreed to discuss the matter any further with his cabinet." Mary Ellen said.

"What do you think will happen father?" Louisa asked. She had never seen her father so troubled.

"It depends on whether our government and the French government agree to this deal. If they do, then I think Hitler will eventually invade Czechoslovakia. Trouble is brewing and I don't like the way things are going. Surely if I can see it the British Government can see it. If he gets Sudetenland and it looks like he will, then I doubt Czechoslovakia will be safe. Then after that who knows what will happen may be he will invade Poland next?"

Discontent seemed to rumble on throughout August and by the beginning of September spasmodic riots occurred in various parts of the Sudetan, reputedly started by German nationals who were living there.

"It's like as if the riots are deliberate to try to dismantle Czechoslovakia." Fred commented one Saturday evening. They had decided to go for a walk along the bluebell path towards the river as it was a warm autumnal evening. "And if they are, it is because they are probably carrying out Hitler's orders."

"If Hitler gets his way and he is given control of Sudeten why would he want to dismantle the rest of Czechoslovakia?" Louisa ventured. She stopped half way through the kissing gate to turn to Fred.

"Because a dismantled country is easy to invade and take control. It would be one step more towards invading the rest of Europe."

"Do you think the Prime Minister and his cabinet are aware of that?"

Fred sighed. "I sincerely hope so. Who knows what kind of deals are being made behind closed doors? I don't have much faith in them I have to say." He followed her through the kissing gate and they made their way back to Pandy.

Louisa was disappointed when she discovered that Hitler had finally got his own way. She didn't believe Hitler's promise of peace in Europe. She became disillusioned with the British government when after a series of even more intensive rioting during the last ten days of September it culminated in Hitler getting Sudetenland.

When the decision to hand over the Sudetenland to Hitler was reported, William became incensed and Louisa was worried about how fearful he had become. "It seems to me that this decision has put the Czech government in a very vulnerable state now. I just hope I am wrong."

At the end of September Arthur and Gladys invited all the immediate family into their new home. It was a street conveniently situated off the Holt Road on the outskirts of Wrexham. It was a Sunday afternoon and Arthur looked extremely proud to show them their new purchases of furniture. Louisa was glad that he was happy. She was also excitedly looking forward to when she and Fred would move into their own home too.

Preparations moved on in October towards Louisa and Fred's wedding. Louisa was busy making her bridesmaids dresses, and her own dress of blue satin. She was very proud of her dress and tried it on and off many times before she was satisfied. Her mother helped her take it off when it was finally finished and hung it up for her in the wardrobe. "You've done an excellent job on this." She turned to see her daughter climb back into her grey skirt and blouse. "I just hope you don't lose any more weight, I can't believe you have a nineteen inch waist!"

Louisa laughed. "I won't."

A few days before the wedding all the females in the household were busy with making pies, cakes and trifles. As they baked and cooked, more food had to be prepared to feed the various guests who were arriving at intervals from all over the country. Fred's older brothers and their wives were being put up with Louisa's various family members around Wrexham. Where there were not enough beds, some blankets were found for the younger members to sleep on sofas or chairs.

Three of Mary Ellen's sisters and their husbands were coming from Oswestry. They were going to stay in the Pandy lodging house and the others had found bed and breakfast in Wrexham. It was fortunate that William's siblings lived locally in Highfield and Stansty and would not need somewhere to stay the night. William's sister Gertrude and her husband Frank lived in Bradley and they were going to provide accommodation for her own sister Fanny and for Mary Ellen's brother Alf. Dorothy was going to stay with Gladys's mother, and a friend of Gladys offered a room in her house in the village to create more space. The wedding was going to be a big family event. For Louisa it was both

229

exciting and overwhelming, she scarcely ever saw so many members of her family at any one time. Fred on the other hand took it all in his stride. He was used to seeing so many of his brothers and sisters and their friends gathered together, it didn't worry him one bit.

On the morning of the twenty ninth of October, Dorothy and Mary Ellen got ready to help Louisa into her wedding dress and to thread orange blossom in her hair. Together they went upstairs and giggled as they stepped over sleeping bodies on the floor in the parlour and some stretched out under blankets on the landing at the top of the stairs.

Louisa was already awake, her face radiant with excitement and nervousness. Dorothy was also excited as she put on her own bridesmaid dress. At twelve o clock William Henry brought around the horse and trap borrowed from Mr. Fern. It had been thoroughly scrubbed out and decorated with ribbons for the occasion. When it arrived Louisa put on her veil trimmed with orange organza. With one last look in the mirror, she glanced at her mother and Dorothy who smiled and nodded their approval before they went downstairs together.

William was downstairs nervously fingering his waistcoat at the same time as pacing up and down the parlour floor. All the sleeping bodies had already arisen and got themselves off to the church. When his wife and daughters arrived downstairs he shepherded them to the waiting horse and trap. Some of their neighbours had gathered at the garden gate and they wished Louisa good luck as she stepped out of the house. Finally the little party drove off to the Holy Trinity church in Gwersyllt, where Fred and Arthur his best man were waiting.

Louisa wanted the day to go on forever because she was so happy. At the reception in the church hall, she glowed when Fred got up to deliver his speech especially when he said "my wife Louisa." This was greeted with rounds of applause and then Fred's oldest brother James made a heart rending speech and wished his little brother and bride future happiness.

During Fred's childhood, James had taken on the role of the father that Fred and his younger siblings had never known. Louisa knew that Fred had always held his oldest brother in high esteem for helping their widowed mother to keep the family together. It must have been a difficult time for her to lose her husband in Passchendaele when he was so young. When their mother had re-married a few years later and had given birth to first Edward then Mary the strains on the family had increased. Fred would seldom talk about his step father but Louisa knew that he was a very strict man. Her conversations with Fred's brothers and sisters confirmed that fact. None of them wanted to talk about their step father. Even Mary and Edward looked nervous when John Barton's name was mentioned. He hadn't been invited to the wedding. James had been unable to bring his wife Anne with him as she was heavily pregnant and was not feeling very well. He left very soon after the wedding so that he could be with her. His brother Thomas and Nancy his wife also left with him.

After all the speeches had been heard and a toast to the bride and groom, someone put on some records on a gramophone and very soon the floor was covered with dancing couples.

231

Edward and Mary, the two youngest of Fred's siblings started everyone off. Edward pulled Dorothy out of her chair and they began to jive together whilst Mary soon found herself a partner with Louisa's cousin Dennis. When the bride and groom sat down out of breath they found themselves sitting next to Cecelia. "You look lovely girl. Happy days." She said to Louisa through a cloud of cigarette smoke. She grinned through the tobacco haze whilst fiddling with her box of cigarettes. Louisa had never seen her without a box of cigarettes.

"Thank you." Louisa smiled." Are you enjoying yourself?"

"Oh yes. Your mum and dad have done us proud. Such lovely home baked food. I bet you've all been busy to do all this."

"They have and I'm very grateful." Fred said. "It's been a wonderful day."

"And you have a nice new house to go to with all mod cons. An indoor lavatory and bathroom." Cecelia added. "You are both very lucky."

"You must come and visit us and stay with us when we are settled." Louisa said.

Cecelia grinned. "Oh I will, don't you worry. Jack and I will come with little Neville." She bounced the little boy on her knee before he got up and ran on to the dance floor to join his uncle Bobby. The man swung him up whilst he danced with his wife Maggie. Neville soon got tired of this and when Robert put him down he ran off to play with Gordon who was hiding under the tables playing with bottle tops. As the day came to a close Louisa looked around the room at all the happy smiling faces of her own and Fred's' relatives and felt that this was the happiest day of her life and that she would remember it forever.

Chapter Sixteen

1939

On Christmas Eve, just two months after the wedding, Louisa visited her doctor who confirmed that she was pregnant. Both Louisa and Fred were thrilled with the news which made Christmas that year an extra special time. They were excited about telling the family the news and waited until everyone had eaten their Christmas dinner. So when they were all gathered in the parlour in Pandy after having eaten their fill of the food Mary Ellen had prepared, Louisa proudly informed her family that she was expecting a baby. She and Fred were immediately smothered with kisses and handshakes and everyone started to talk excitedly about the coming birth. Dorothy handed out cups of tea and mince pies and laughingly said that she was going to be an aunt again. She announced that as she was working now, she would save up to buy the new baby some things.

As the months passed Dorothy took it upon herself to visit Louisa regularly in her new home to keep an eye on her. She was excited about being an aunt again and wanted to help her sister, though Louisa insisted she was fine. Between working and keeping the house clean and tidy, she kept busy sewing or knitting whilst she listened to the wireless. She now only worked part time at the dairy, and she was glad of the small income she was receiving from her sewing. Eventually she would have to give up work completely. Her employer was sympathetic about married women continuing to work, whilst they were healthy and able. However, he was not so well-disposed towards working, married women with young children. When Louisa had told him she was pregnant, he had been unsure at first, whether she should continue to work at all. Louisa had used all her negotiating skills to persuade him to let her continue to work, and eventually he had agreed to cut her days down to three days a week as long as she was healthy. She assured him she was very healthy for which she was very grateful. She was also grateful she could still earn some money before she gave up work completely. She knew it would be difficult to work and look after the baby and in any case Fred didn't want her to carry on working.

"Are you getting on alright at Mrs. Fern's?" Louisa asked Dorothy one Saturday afternoon in March. Dorothy had walked the two miles to visit her sister in her new home on Chester Road. They were sitting in the small bay window of the sitting room that looked out across the fields towards Acton Park. As they sipped their tea they watched several lorries drive past with bricks and cement for the building site on Holt Road. From the side window they could see all the way up to Garden Village and the construction site of what would be the new Acton Park hotel. Fred had told Louisa that plans had been approved for new homes to be constructed as well as the hotel. Fred had also commented that very soon they would not have such a clear view of the park. The new homes were to be built to the left of the new Acton Park hotel.

The road at the side of the Acton Park hotel site leading from the Chester Road was called Box lane and also looked out onto Acton Park. Louisa often wondered why it was called

Box lane, it seemed a strange name for a lane. Further down Chester road and towards the town centre was another large expanse of land that had been purchased for another housing development. Fred had been assured that there would be plenty of work for him as he was a skilled builder. Louisa was proud that Fred was such an esteemed employee and would be engaged to build the new houses.

Dorothy took a deep breath and offered a half smile as she replied to her sister's enquiry. "I am grateful for having a job at the farm shop. I was dreading the thought of having to go into service. But I don't want to stay at the farm long." She sipped her tea and glanced nervously over her tea cup at her sister who was eyeing her suspiciously. "I'm not going to meet many people at the farm, so I'm thinking of applying for a job in one of the department stores in Chester."

"Chester? Why Chester?" Louisa asked curiously. "How will you get there? On the bus I suppose or the train. She answered her own question."

Dorothy nodded. "Easy. There is a bus directly to the city centre from Wrexham. Or I could get the train from Pandy." Dorothy put down her cup and saucer and went to sit down on the cottage settee. "I haven't applied yet, but that's what I'm thinking. I want to see life first before settling down. I know I am lucky to have a job so close to home, but that's the problem. It's too close to home! Besides I want more money too!"

Louisa sighed as she sat down on the armchair facing her. "I understand what you mean. I didn't like being a servant, but I did get to see a different side of life. After visiting Liverpool with Fred, I can see that the world is so different in

236

the cities than it is here. Maybe if I hadn't fallen in love with him I might be as restless as you are." She patted her stomach. "But I am content at the moment. Besides even if I have a baby it doesn't mean I can't do other things or have a different life. I'm going to carry on working at the dairy until I can't bend anymore." She laughed. "Probably very soon!"

"So you aren't shocked then?" Dorothy asked her sister. There was some relief in her voice Louisa noticed. She realised that her sister wanted some excitement in her life, and the freedom to choose how she lived. She recalled how liberated she used to feel at the age of fourteen when she was riding her bicycle and roaming the country. Then there had been Fred who had shown her another world through films and visits to Liverpool. She acknowledged that before Fred came into her life, neither she nor Dorothy had been anywhere outside Wrexham except to Ellesmere to see their Aunt Nancy. They had made a few shopping excursions to Chester or visited family in Oswestry and that was all.

Several visits to Liverpool had widened Louisa's horizons, and she suspected that after she and Fred had taken Dorothy on one trip to Liverpool, they had contributed towards her restlessness. At the age of sixteen it was no wonder she was anxious to do something exciting with her life. Apart from the few cinema outings with herself and Fred or with their brothers, the extent of Dorothy's journeys had been few.

"No, I think it is an excellent idea. Why don't you get a copy of one of the Chester newspapers and have a look at the job advertisements."

Dorothy grinned and reached for her bag. "As a matter of fact I bought one from the newsagents before I came here. Let's have a look." She opened the newspapers excitedly at the Situations Vacant pages.

Louisa looked at her sister in amazement, then got up to look at the newspaper which Dorothy had spread over the table. "What exactly are you looking for? There seems to be a lot of adverts for typists and secretaries but you don't have any qualifications to do that. Do you want to train to be a typist?"

Dorothy shook her head. "No I just want a steady job and to meet different people, and besides Chester is a nice place to be."

"You will have to pay your bus fares though. So you need to make sure that the job has more money than you are getting now to cover the extra expense."

"I know I thought of that. I was hoping that the wages might be higher in the city. Anyway if I am working five days a week I will be paid more than I am getting now surely." She wrinkled her nose in despair. I can't see much. Most of the advertisements are for parlour maids and scullery maids."

Louisa shuddered. "That would be a step backwards. You don't want that. She looked over her sister's shoulder. "What's that in small type in the corner about Greene and Madisons?"

Dorothy read it out excitedly. *'Sales staff required at both Wrexham and Chester Stores. Good rates of pay for competent staff. Telephone for an interview.'* "That's more like what I'm looking for. I will do it now. She rummaged in her purse for some coins. "There's a phone box down the end of your street. I am going to telephone them now."

Louisa looked at her sister in astonishment and admiration. "Have you got enough pennies? Let me give you a few more just in case the pips go. Do you want me to come with you?"

Her sister took the extra pennies from her and looked ruefully at Louisa's swollen stomach. "Can you manage to walk down the road?"

"Of course I can. I'm not an invalid. Come on let's get our coats."

Both sisters were excited when Dorothy was invited to attend an interview the following week. Louisa was impressed that Dorothy was able to negotiate over the phone with the manager regarding the date of the interview. They agreed on Tuesday afternoon which was one of the days she didn't work at the farm shop.

"What do you think Mum and Dad will say?" Dorothy asked.

"As long as you are working and you are happy, I don't think they will mind at all. Let's face it they didn't mind sending me away when I was younger than you." There was some bitterness in Louisa's voice when she remembered how upset she was to have to go to live in Wallasey as a scullery maid.

"Mum cried after you had gone." Dorothy said. "So did I. Secretly, I think she was pleased that Arthur brought you back."

Louisa looked up startled. "Did she? I didn't know that."

"You weren't supposed to know. She always keeps her emotions to herself, as you are aware, but she does care about us. You know that surely."

"Yes I do really.   But I can't think what would have happened if Arthur hadn't come for me."

Dorothy laughed.   "You know very well what would have happened.   You would have walked out or started a riot." They both laughed.   "Anyway because of what happened to you, Mother is a bit wary of it happening to me.   So I have you to thank for that."

Louisa shrugged and kissed her sister goodbye and wished her good luck for her interview.   "I will see you next Saturday and let you know how I got on."

After Dorothy had left, Louisa switched on the wireless to listen to the news at tea time.   Once again her fears about war re-surfaced making her feel uneasy.   Neville Chamberlain was now saying that he had never trusted Hitler when they agreed over the matter of Sudetan.   And now he trusted him even less after he had marched his troops into Czechoslovakia earlier that month.   Louisa was livid when she heard that.   She had been suspicious of Hitler all along!

The Prime Minister now revealed to the interviewer that he felt Hitler had been lying to him at their meeting in Munich. So when Fred arrived home at six thirty he found his wife in an agitated state.   "I should have gone into politics," she greeted him and she told him what she had heard. "Apparently the Prime Minister has said that if Hitler invades Poland, then Britain will defend that country."

Fred tried his best to change the subject and cheer her up.   He had some news that he knew she would be pleased to hear. He had seen her brother Harry at the building site.   His brother in law had given him some good news.

"It seems that you are going to be an aunt again. Dot is expecting another baby."

"What?" Louisa laughed. "That's three of us pregnant all at the same time. When is she due?

"October, so Harry said." Fred patted Louisa's stomach fondly. "We ought to start thinking about names. How about Christine?"

"Hmm I quite like that, though I thought you may want to call it Cecelia after your mother if it is a girl, and perhaps Alfred after your father if it is a boy."

Fred shook his head. "No let's start our own tradition. Your Arthur told me that they are going to call their next one Maureen if it is a girl and Arthur if it is a boy."

"That's a bit confusing isn't it? Typical Arthur. I wonder what Gladys thinks about that." They both laughed. Fred kissed his wife. "What's for tea, I'm starving."

Over their meal Louisa told Fred about her sister's hopes to change her job.

"Do you think she has any chance of getting in at Greene and Madisons?" Fred asked.

"Well she seems determined, so let's hope she can convince them at the interview. At least she has a bit of experience working in the farm shop."

They were soon to find out about Dorothy's future employment. The following Saturday afternoon Louisa and Gladys were sitting in Louisa's small sitting room drinking tea when Dorothy came bursting in with smiles etching her face. She did not waste time telling them her good news.

Louisa hugged her sister. "Congratulations. When do you start?"

"I have given the farm a week's notice, so I start in a week's time on a Monday. I'm going to be in the Ladies fashion department." She sat down and poured herself a cup of tea from the tray, then helped herself to a wedge of Victoria cake that Louisa had made that morning.

"What did they say at the farm? I bet they were not too pleased, since you have only been there six months." Gladys asked.

Dorothy swallowed her cake before answering. "They were disappointed but to be fair both Mr. and Mrs. Fern were happy for me. They knew that sooner or later I would need to get something better. Mrs. Fern asked me to recommend someone else to replace me, but I can't think of anyone. Can either of you?" She took another bite of her cake. "This is gorgeous cake Louisa. I don't know how you do it."

Gladys laughed. "No I don't know how she does it either. But I don't even try to bake, I just haven't got the knack. Luckily my mum can bake, so I don't need to. Between her and your mother I am well supplied with home baking. So your brother is well looked after." She sipped her tea contentedly.

"How is Arthur? I haven't seen him for a couple of weeks." Dorothy asked.

"He's busy with the ARP at the moment, and he keeps getting worked up about this new law the government is going to introduce about conscription and six months military training." Gladys replied.

"But that's for men aged twenty and twenty one isn't it? Arthur is twenty three. The same age as Fred more or less." Louisa said.

"That's what dad said. He is worried about it too, though he knows he himself is too old for service." Dorothy frowned trying to remember what else her father had said.

"Yes that's true, but I know Fred is worrying about what might happen." Louisa said. A frown crossed her face. She was worried too. "He reckons that eventually the government will look for older men and it won't matter if they are married or not."

"That's what Arthur said, which is why he is trying to do his bit by volunteering to do things locally. He's also been volunteering with fire fighting duties too. He's really very busy and I'm frightened he will make himself too tired. I just hope we don't have a war. I can't bear the thought of him going away and leaving me with little Brian and another baby on the way." She looked as if she was about to cry, and Louisa patted her arm to soothe her. But Louisa too shared her anxiety. She had two months to go before her baby was born, and was frightened of being left alone to look after it.

"Let's try not to think about it. We've had some good news today for Dorothy, let's think about that. I will make us some more tea." Louisa got up to go to the kitchen to put on the kettle. Dorothy followed her with the tea tray. "I don't suppose I will be able to come and see you on Saturdays after next week, because I will be working. The store is closed on Sundays, and I get a half day off in the week too. So it's not too bad, and I forgot to tell you the pay is double than at the farm so it will more than cover my train fares to work." She grinned and Louisa hugged her sister. "Well done, I'm so pleased for you."

Dorothy smiled. "Strangely enough so are mum and dad." They took the tea things back to the sitting room where Gladys was reading a magazine. She looked up as the girls entered and asked Dorothy, "How long are you going to stay this afternoon? The reason I ask is that Arthur is at the football match with Fred, and he is coming here to pick me up on the way home." She glanced at Louisa for confirmation, and Louisa nodded. "So you will be able to see your brother if you stay a bit longer."

"I was going to ask if they had gone to the match. Who are Wrexham playing?

"Oldham something." Gladys said frowning trying to remember.

"Oldham Athletic." Louisa amended. She looked at the clock on the mantelpiece. They should be home in about an hour or so. They will be in to the second half by now. It might be on the wireless if you want to hear it?"

"No thanks." They both chorused.

"We will hear enough about it when they get here." Gladys laughed.

Very soon both men came through the front door with broad smiles on their faces. When Arthur saw Dorothy he swung her off her feet. "Hello little sister, I haven't seen you for a while." He put her down and stared at her incredulously when she told him that she had a new job. He patted her on the shoulder. "Well done you. Good luck. He looked across at Louisa. So I won't have to come and rescue you like I did with your sister."

"Did you enjoy the football?" Dorothy asked. She looked from her brother to her brother in law. Both men nodded.

244

"Who won?" Louisa asked.

"Wrexham did. The score was 4.1. There wasn't a huge crowd though." Fred said. He sat down and put his hands around the teapot. "Is this tea fresh?"

Louisa got up immediately. "No but I will make some more."

Eventually Arthur got up to take Gladys home. "I will take you too Dorothy if you like. I can see mum and dad for five minutes."

When they had gone, Louisa related to Fred the conversation she had had with Gladys about conscription. This wasn't the first time they had discussed it, and as always Fred tried to calm Louisa down.

"I don't believe it will happen. If Hitler has got any sense he will back off Poland and we will have some peace and no more nonsensical talk about a war."

Secretly Fred was worried. He didn't want to upset Louisa with her being seven months pregnant, but deep down he feared he would be called up to go to war. Already young men on the construction site where he was working had been told to register for duty. So far all they had to do was register their names, but it would only be a matter of time before they were summoned to go on six months training. The fields in Borras adjacent to where he had been working had recently been bought by the Air Ministry. The huge area was flat and would be a good place for a makeshift air strip. It was well known locally that both RAF Sealand and Hawarden airports would not be able to sustain heavy planes if they were needed for war. Both areas suffered from flooding because both airstrips had been created on reclaimed land from the

River Dee marshes. Any heavy storm would render those air strips into useless mud baths. Some of the men he worked with knew the area well. They had told him that the ground could only withstand lighter planes such as the Tiger Moth and Lysanders.

He realised that the government were well aware that the Borras site was perfect for a landing strip and more reliable than the ones in Hawarden and Sealand.

Fred had other chilling information that he had chosen to keep to himself. Some of his work colleagues had also worked with him previously whilst helping seal the shaft at Gresford pit. From there, many of them had subsequently gone to Chester to help build shelters underground. They told him that it was supposed to be hush hush. He had never said anything about this to Louisa because he knew she would worry. Rumours got back to him that as each shelter had been completed, some army officials had started to move in to set up secret offices.

On the building site, additional snippets of information filtered through to Fred and his colleagues from the various tradesmen who visited the building site. During conversations with them they passed on their views about the work they had carried out for the government. Some had installed air conditioning and others had installed plumbing systems in the underground offices. Fred's mates told him that the government were preparing big time for war. All of it was supposed to be secret, but it was obvious to them that the government expected to be bombed.

Fred sighed. Everything seemed to be threatening their peace. He took off his shoes and sat down on his favourite arm chair by the fire. Louisa handed him a letter which had arrived in the morning's post. "It's from Liverpool." Louisa said enthusiastically. She had been wondering all day what was inside but managed to stop herself from opening the letter. Fred opened the letter and began to read it. Then sighed again before telling Louisa the contents.

"Our John is going to register for six months military training. I suppose he hasn't got much choice now the government has made it compulsory for men of his age."

"I suppose he falls into the category of young single men between twenty and twenty one." Louisa responded gloomily. "And your Tom is already in the army. "At least Edward is too young at seventeen."

"Yes, that's one good thing."

Louisa sat in the chair opposite him. "Fred do you think the government will ask for more men, such as those over the age of twenty one?" She looked into his worried face. He didn't need to say anything, she saw confirmation of her fears in his eyes. "But surely not married men?" she said helplessly.

"If the government want more men they will take anyone, except the infirm." Fred replied ominously. "Let's try not to dwell on it, and try to be cheerful. Maybe Hitler will have the good sense to back off Poland." He picked up the *Wrexham Leader* to look at the times of wireless broadcasts. "Let's see what we can listen to on the wireless to cheer ourselves up." Whilst he was talking he switched on the instrument. "We should just hear the end of the news." He was right. The presenter mentioned that Albert Lebrun had just been elected president of France. He then gave a summary of the weather. Fred looked over his shoulder at Louisa, "Would you rather listen to some music?"

"Yes I think I would."

A few weeks later one Saturday afternoon, Harry and Dot came around to see how Louisa was feeling. "You haven't got long to go now, about six weeks isn't it?" Dot smiled as she asked Louisa.

"Yes it's due about 18th June. I can still get around quite well though and I feel well."

"She's still going around sniffing soap though." Fred laughed. "No bar of soap is safe when she is around. I always thought pregnant women craved food."

"Well at least I don't eat it." Louisa laughed too.

"I remember craving for your mother's treacle tarts when I was expecting Gordon." Said Dot.

"Fortunately my mother was only too happy to bake them for you." Harry said. He put down his half empty tea cup. We've got some more news for you. We have bought a house."

"Where?" Both Louisa and Fred said simultaneously.

Harry grinned. "In the same street where we are now – the other end. It was going for a song." He looked at Fred. "The thing is it does need some work. Do you think you could help out with the brick work renovations?"

Fred looked at his wife and she nodded. "Certainly I will, but this is an awkward time, with Louisa expecting. Can we start soon?"

"Well, next week if you like. We don't want to move in just yet, but I would appreciate you giving me an assessment of the work. However, even with my little knowledge, I don't think it's a big job Fred, but I just thought I would ask as I know I can trust you to do a good job."

"Ok. I will come around tomorrow and have a look."

The following morning Fred rode his motorbike to Rhosrobin to assess the work that Harry wanted to be done. The building seemed to be in good condition, and most of the work that needed to be done was cosmetic. Fred said that a couple of Saturday afternoons and Sunday mornings would be all the time he needed to do the work.

"I was expecting major brick work when you told me you needed help." He told Harry. "It just needs pointing. I will have to get rid of the old mortar first. It's not a big job, but it is essential work."

"Well I wasn't sure how to describe it, so I feel relieved too." Harry returned. "If you tell me what materials you need, I will get them for you for next week end." He leaned against the window in the small kitchen. "I just hope we will all be able to enjoy living here."

"What do you mean?"

"In a word – Hitler. Did you hear that he has signed a pact with Benito Mussolini? It doesn't augor well. And despite Hitler promising the Prime Minister in that treaty he signed where he promised not to invade Poland, Chamberlain is evidently preparing for war."

Fred nodded his head and breathed deeply. "Yes I did hear that. Its obvious Chamberlain doesn't believe Hitler. If you look around everywhere even in Wrexham we have Air Raid Patrol groups forming and other voluntary services. Arthur has joined one of them. I don't like to think what will happen especially with Louisa expecting our baby soon. I would have joined the ARP with Arthur too but if I do, Louisa will be even more upset."

"And Dot." Harry added.

Over the next few week ends Fred and Harry worked on improving Harry and Dot's new home. Occasionally Arthur helped, though he was often working on a Saturday afternoon. Clarks Garage, Arthur's employer, offered taxi services for weddings, and Arthur helped out with the taxi service as he got extra money. During the spells when Fred was away working in Rhosrobin, Louisa accompanied him on the bus into Wrexham. It was too uncomfortable for her on the motorbike. He would make sure she got on to another bus safely to Pandy where she could spend some time with her parents. Satisfied that she was comfortable in Pandy, Fred would continue on to Rhosrobin cycling there on Louisa's old bicycle.

It was one of these late Saturday afternoons in Pandy on the fourth of June that Louisa began to have terrible pains in her stomach. She rushed to the lavatory at the end of the garden groaning in pain, then realised her waters had broken. She began to call for her mother, who hastily ran outside to the lavatory and helped her daughter back into the house. With a great deal of effort from both women, they managed to get Louisa upstairs to the back bedroom. "Stay there, and I will go and get the midwife." Mary Ellen said catching her breath. She put her hands on her hips as she observed her daughter writhe in pain.

"Can someone tell Fred?" moaned Louisa.

"Never mind Fred." Her mother said. "He will be no use." She ran downstairs again and left Louisa to continue to writhe on the bed. She stared helplessly at the familiar ceiling in the bedroom. It was the same room she had shared with Dorothy. Her sister had moved into the room next door now which was bigger. Her two brothers had previously occupied that one. She screamed in pain as another spasm hit her.

Miraculously her mother arrived half an hour later, with Mrs. Penson who was experienced in bringing babies into the world. She was cheaper than the midwife who charged four pennies.

"It's her first one." Mary Ellen told Mrs. Penson.

"And the last!" Louisa cried.

Deep into the night Louisa suffered terrible labour pains and soon after midnight she gave birth to a healthy baby. Very soon she was cradling her new born child, whilst her mother was wiping the sweat from Louisa's brow.

"A big baby that. Nine pounds and 10 ounces. No wonder you were in such pain." Her mother smiled. Congratulations. You have a baby girl."

"Has someone gone for Fred?" Louisa whispered. Her voice was hoarse. She was tired and had lost all track of time.

"He's downstairs. In fact I think I can hear him coming up the stairs now. We had to turn him away from the door several times. He's been up and down these stairs worrying about your cries." Mary Ellen went to the door with her face beaming. "Come in Fred and meet your baby daughter." She went out and closed the door, leaving the new parents and baby together.

Fred took Louisa's hand and smiled down at his wife. "You gave me a fright."

"I was frightened too. But it was worth it." She weakly smiled at the sleeping baby in her arms. "Do you want to hold her?" Carefully she handed the baby to her husband.

Fred cradled the baby and looked into her face. "Hello Christine."

Louisa managed to laugh. "So you like Christine?"

"Christine Mary. How about that, your second name and your mother's."

Louisa smiled. "Yes that sounds nice." She closed her eyes and went to sleep. Fred looked at his sleeping wife and then the sleeping baby and thought how lucky he was. He hoped that he would never have to leave them. Oddly, he began to think of Harry and Dot and was pleased that he had finished the job on their new house. Harry was going to start painting and decorating next week so that they could move in the week after. At least Dot would be settled before she had her second baby which was due in October.

Chapter Seventeen

After a couple of weeks Louisa settled into a routine with the baby during the day. She managed to keep on top of the extra washing and still cook and bake Fred's favourite meals. Meanwhile she organised her day to find time to read books in the afternoons and looked forward to listening to the wireless. Her mother was impressed with her household efficiency and praise from her was praise indeed.

"I don't know how you do it." Gladys said to her one Saturday afternoon. You can not only cook, bake, knit and sew, but you do them exceptionally well. And you look after the baby well too."

Louisa smiled. "I enjoy doing those things. I had a responsible job at the dairy and had to be organised. I suppose managing a household and a baby is just an extension of that. At one point in my life, I thought of training to be a nurse. I'm sure that would have demanded good organisational skills too."

Gladys grunted. "I know some rotten nurses. That mid wife was horrible with me when I had Brian." She patted her swelling stomach. I hope we can get a better one next time."

Louisa poured her some more tea and offered her some sponge cake. "Have you heard that the government is planning to evacuate children from the major cities in case they are bombed in an air raid?"

"Yes I read it in the *Wrexham Leader.* The government have been planning this for months. The newspaper said that there are going to be special evacuee centres, some of them will be in Wales."

Louisa nodded her head in agreement and slowly sipped her tea. "Well I suppose we will be safe in this part of Wales. We haven't got any huge cities like Liverpool. I worry about Fred's family though."

"I don't think Hitler is just going to bomb cities though, do you? He's probably going to target the ports. That's what I would do if I was him." Gladys said.

"Oh don't talk like that please." Louisa said. "It's unthinkable that bombs will drop on innocent people."

"Don't get me wrong, I know it's terrible. Let's hope it doesn't happen."

"Everybody keeps saying that. Then they say if it starts, it will all be over in six months. I just can't stand this uncertainty."

"Arthur said, that when people say that it may not happen, it is just wishful thinking."

Louisa was about to say something when she heard the baby cry and she went to pick her up out of the cot.

"You spoil that baby." Gladys said. "She might be crying in her sleep. I would leave her cry it out."

"Well if she's having a nightmare I want her to be soothed." Louisa retorted. "I don't believe a child should be left to cry."

Gladys laughed. "Have it your way. I'm going to have another piece of this lovely cake."

"Would you take in an evacuee family?" Louisa asked her sister in law. Christine had stopped crying now and Louisa was standing with the baby in her arms rocking her to and fro.

"It depends how many of them I suppose. But we haven't got much room in our two bedroomed house. It would be a bit of a squeeze what with Brian only two years old as well. If this one is a girl we will have to think of moving house in a few years to a bigger one. Arthur is saving like mad to make sure we have enough money."

"There's talk of Jewish children being evacuated from Germany without their parents. That seems so cruel. The poor things must be terrified."

"I know. It's terrible. They don't understand that it is for their own safety. It must be hard for the parents too, having to send their children away."

Later when Gladys had gone, Louisa put the wireless on and listened to the serial she had been following. '*The jewel thief strikes again.*' Fred wouldn't be home until late that night. He had finished work at lunch time and then went to catch the train to Liverpool He was worried about his older brother Alf who wasn't very well. He had hoped also to call on his other two brothers Bob and Jim. When her programme finished, Louisa switched off the wireless and settled down to read her book *Miss Pettigrew lives for a day.* Christine was still sleeping and so she knew she would have a few hours before she needed feeding again. The book was pure escapism for Louisa. When she was reading she was able to forget her worries. Fred eventually arrived home at eleven o clock, and Louisa was still in an armchair now feeding the baby. Her book was balanced on the edge of the chair and Fred picked it up as he bent to kiss Louisa and then the baby.

He put the book on the coffee table before hanging up his coat and hat, then went into the kitchen to find his supper ready on the table. After filling a saucepan with water he placed the plate on top of the saucepan. Carefully turning another plate upside down he covered the cold meal with the plate to allow the steam from the saucepan to warm it up.

"How are your brothers?" Louisa called.

"Bob and Jim are ok. Alf is still feeling weak after that bad bout of flu." He came and sat down opposite her and Louisa could see that he was worried about a lot of things.

"We've been talking about the possibility of war." He caught her anguished look. "I know we said we wouldn't talk about it, but in Liverpool, things are changing. People are preparing for evacuation, and in the pubs men are talking about whether they prefer the army or the navy." He took a deep breath. "So I think we should have a holiday before things get too nasty."

Louisa looked up in surprise. "I thought you were going to say you were going to join the army. It would be good to have a holiday. Do you mean in a caravan somewhere?

"Yes. I thought the second week of August. We could go to Rhyl or Prestatyn." He pulled out a newspaper from his coat pocket. "I've been looking at the adverts when I was coming back on the train. I've ringed a few possible places with a pencil. I will write to them tomorrow." He held the *Liverpool Echo* in front of Louisa to see whilst she put Christine over her shoulder to wind her. She nodded in agreement. "They all sound good."

Five weeks later they boarded the train to Chester and then changed for another train again to Rhyl. They needed to get a taxi to the caravan site as it wasn't within walking distance of the train station. The weather the previous week had been terrible, with heavy rain and thunder storms, but on that Saturday in the middle of August the sun was shining and the temperature was warm. They spent some happy days taking the baby in the pram for walks along the promenade, and then sitting on the beach with ice creams. As Fred often said months later "it was a glorious time." He had saved up for a camera and took photos of Louisa and the baby. He then explained to Louisa how to work it and she took some photographs of Fred with Christine.

When they returned to Wrexham the following Saturday, the weather began to break and once more there were heavy thunderstorms and rain. It wasn't just the weather that was changing, the mood was shifting too amongst the people everywhere in the country. Despite the cheerful faces, there seemed to be undercurrents of worry and despair. Everyone was depressed and worrying about what may happen in the near future.

A few days after they had returned from Rhyl, Arthur called to see them. He was on his way to see Harry. Arthur was very agitated. He had read in the newspaper that Hitler had signed a non-aggression treaty with the Soviet Union.

"This is just a couple of days ago." Arthur said. "You know what this means don't you Fred? The blasted Fuhrer can invade Poland knowing full well the Russians will do nothing to stop him."

Fred nodded. He was too aghast to speak. In any case he couldn't get a word in edgeways as Arthur was furious and continued with his tirade against Hitler. "And now

Chamberlain has reiterated that we will defend Poland. Britain and Poland have signed a Mutual Assistance Treaty. This can only mean that he knows that war is coming, and coming for us very soon." He sat down trembling with rage.

Louisa had never seen her brother so enraged, and she looked at her husband who she could see was also extremely worried. She sat down to calm herself. "I wonder what Hitler has offered Stalin." She said nervously.

"Good question." Fred answered.

Abruptly Arthur got up. I'm going to see Harry." At the doorway, he turned towards them. "The British government must have known something like this was going to happen. They've been manufacturing weapons for the last year, building aeroplanes and the like. Look how Hitler has been building up his armed forces. Look what happened in Spain. Why didn't the government do something to stop him then? It was obvious when Hitler started taking possession of territory in Austria and Czechoslovakia that he wouldn't be satisfied. So what do we do – we make damn tanks and aeroplanes!"

Louisa looked at Fred who seemed stunned. Suddenly he got up. "I think I should go with him." He got his coat and ran after Arthur. Helplessly Louisa watched him run down the street to catch Arthur. He managed to stop him half way down and got in the car besides him.

It was several hours later when Fred returned. As soon as she heard the car pull up outside the house, Louisa went to the door to greet Fred. She fell into his arms weeping. He smoothed her hair and tried to calm her down. "Harry reckons it will all blow over."

"Arthur doesn't though, and I bet Father doesn't either." Louisa managed to control her tears." Father and Arthur have been saying for months that war was coming. Even after the Spanish civil war ended in March. Franco is an ally of Hitler's and now apparently is Stalin."

As the last few days of August progressed, it seemed to Louisa that when she went shopping or visiting her family the topic of conversation was always Germany. She felt that everyone was holding their breath each time they read a newspaper or listened to the wireless. Towards the end of the week news came that evacuations from London had begun. Then on Friday 1st September, the news everyone had been dreading was reported via the wireless. Hitler had invaded Poland.

It was obvious to Louisa that Hitler had deceived Britain. He had tried to convince Britain that Poland were the aggressors and not Germany.

Louisa's family all agreed that they felt Adolf Hitler was making excuses. He claimed Poland had started firing on Germany and so they had had to retaliate. Hitler's so called retaliation was to give orders for his army to invade Poland.

"So it was just a coincidence that Hitler had strategically positioned his tanks at various points along Poland's border?" William said sarcastically when Louisa went to visit them on 1st September. "All they had to do was wait for the order and over they go. As easy as that."

The German army had carried out such orders during the early hours of that morning. Louisa had been terrified when she had discovered the news and had hurriedly pushed Christine in her pram to Pandy. Meanwhile the British Prime

Minister Neville Chamberlain discussed tactics with Eduard Daladier the Prime Minister of France who agreed they needed to take immediate action.

Louisa's family and the rest of Britain held their breath whilst representatives from both countries met with the German Foreign Minister Ribbentrop. They warned the German minister that if Germany did not withdraw from Poland, then Britain and France would declare war on Germany. However Hitler refused to back down.

On Sunday morning 3rd September Fred turned on the wireless and hugging Louisa close to him they listened intently to the broadcast from Neville Chamberlain that Britain and France were at war with Germany. Stunned, both Louisa and Fred sat down in silence.

"So what do we do now?" Louisa whispered.

"I honestly don't know. We will just have to wait to see what the government does and what the Prime Minister wants. If I have to go, it won't be straight away. Give it six months and it might be all over."

"But if it isn't, what then?"

Fred hugged her. "I don't know. We must listen carefully to find out what is going on."

Later they heard that New Zealand and Australia had also declared war on Germany. As the week unfolded they learned that Canada had also declared war on Germany and that the United States of America were not going to get involved.

The following Sunday afternoon Arthur called to say that he was taking Gladys and Brian to Pandy to Gladys's parents. He said they would spend half an hour with his in-laws, then take his small family to his own parents. He offered to come back later to give Louisa and Fred a lift to Pandy and they would all get together at William and Mary Ellen's to discuss their future. When they all arrived Harry was already seated with Gordon on his knee and Dot heavily pregnant next to him. They were ready for a family conference. Gladys as well as Dot was also heavily pregnant and both women were agitated at the thought of their husbands leaving them at such a crucial time.

It was a squeeze with so many people and young children seated in the back parlour, but no-one minded. They all felt better when they were together. Mary Ellen and Dorothy made pots of tea and offered slices of blackberry and apple jam tart.

"This war is going to be different from the Great War." William said. "There were not many fighter aircrafts dropping bombs then. We will have to build a shelter in the garden. I have had my instructions from the ARP, I know what to do."

"So do I." Arthur said. Fred nodded too. He was thinking about all the sheets of corrugated iron at the back of the house which he had stored away. Louisa grimaced at the thought of them. "We have barely enough room in our back garden."

"Well you could put it in the house and use it as a table of some kind, but I wouldn't advise it, it would be no use if the house is hit." William said sternly. "You must be sensible and think about the baby as well as yourself. Fred might not be there with you."

Fred put a hand on Louisa's shoulder. "It's alright. There is a bit of space where to dig, I have already had a look. I will do it after work tomorrow."

"If you need a hand I can come and help you." Harry said. "I've set up ours."

"Mrs. Cooper down the road said she is going to take in some evacuee children." Dorothy said. "She said she is going to move her bed downstairs, and they can use the two bedrooms upstairs."

"Those poor children." Dot said. "It's ridiculous sending children without their parents to complete strangers." She nervously glanced at Gordon who was sitting under the table playing with his cousin Brian. They were setting up a domino set that Mary Ellen had given them. Gordon had set it up on top of a hard backed picture book of farm animals.

"Mrs. Cooper said she doesn't want very young children, and would prefer some of them come with their mothers."

"Well that makes sense. Surely the parents wouldn't want to send away very young children." Mary Ellen said.

"Most of them will go to special camps specially built for them, I expect. There won't be any under five years of age." Said Fred. "This is what we talked about when I went to Liverpool to see James and Robert.

"It's still very young for those over five though. Poor little things." Dot said.

"Maybe they have no option." Harry suggested gently. "If their parents have to work, they need to know their children are safe."

"How will we know when to go in to the shelter Father?" Louisa asked.

"There will be a siren warning us, and another for the all clear."

"What if I am in work?" Dorothy asked anxiously.

"There will be air raid shelters in Chester." Fred said. "They have been building shelters in Chester and all the cities for the last year at least."

"They are likely to be at night time. So we will have to black out the windows so the German bombers can't see us. The shops will have to do the same." William tried to reassure Dorothy.

"If we are supposed to be at war with Germany, why are we sending British bombers to Germany shipyards instead of Poland where Hitler's troops are?" Arthur said suddenly.

"God knows. Presumably the Prime Minister knows what he is doing?" Harry ventured.

"If we bomb Germany won't Hitler retaliate and bomb us?" Louisa said fearfully. No-one answered. Louisa had put into words what the others feared.

"How are we going to make the windows black?" Gladys asked frowning. She had been very quiet and looked very uncomfortable sitting on the arm chair. She kept moving around and Louisa wondered if she was due to have the baby.

"Special curtains or you could use cardboard. Anything to keep out the light." William said.

"Where will we get curtains or material to make them?" Louisa asked.

"I will have to let you know." William replied scratching his head. He looked at Gladys squirming, and then at Arthur. "I think you had better get Gladys home, she doesn't look too good. And you need to go before it starts to get dusk. You

263

won't be able to use your lights on the car. Too many risks."
He began to shake his head. The enormity of the war was beginning to have its effect on all of them. "And you had better get used to only making necessary journeys in the car, because petrol will be rationed."

"And don't forget to take your gas masks with you everywhere." Mary Ellen said. She seized hers off the sideboard and shuddered. "Hideous things. Let's hope we won't need them."

Arthur lifted up Brian from the floor and then helped his wife stand up. "Come on I will take you home." He turned towards his brother in law. "If you and Louisa want to stay a bit longer I can come back for you later."

Harry got up. "There's no need to do that. We can take Louisa and Fred. There's plenty of room with Gordon in the back. We didn't bring the pushchair. I don't think you should leave Gladys alone. And besides you need to save petrol."

Gladys smiled weakly. Louisa cast an anxious glance at Gladys and could see that her sister-in-law looked exceedingly uncomfortable.

The next morning just as light was dawning, Arthur came rushing round for Louisa to say Gladys had gone into labour. The mid wife was with her, and so was her mother, but she was asking for Louisa. So hastily getting things together for herself and Christine she got into Arthur's car and waved goodbye to Fred who was on his way to work.

Later that morning Gladys gave birth to a baby girl and they called her Maureen. And for once the family did not talk about the war. However as the weeks slipped away towards the end of September the talk of war was the main topic of conversation. Whilst in the baker's queueing up for bread, Louisa heard someone mention that the Russians had invaded Poland from the Eastern side of the country. The customers idly standing in line in the shop readily exchanged their views on this snippet of information, and Louisa always alert for news, listened intently. She managed to glean from the various conversations in the shop that this meant that Poland was fighting a war on two fronts. The Germans on one side and the Russians on the other. By the end of September Warsaw had surrendered and Hitler and Stalin divided up Poland between them.

"So that is what the deal was between Stalin and Hitler." Louisa said to Fred when they heard the news about the destruction of Poland.

"I find that hard to believe that Hitler has given away half of Poland to Stalin." Fred said as he sat at the table eating his supper. "Given that Hitler was making such a fuss about getting Sudetenland and the Anshluss in Austria, I would have thought he would want to amass as much territory as possible."

Louisa agreed. "Something doesn't seem right. Maybe there is more to this than we know. Maybe Stalin has a plan that doesn't involve Hitler."

After their meal, Fred reluctantly got out their gas masks. "We really ought to start carrying these around with us. We could be fined you know. The lads in work have started to take theirs with them. You will have to learn to put one on to Christine."

Louisa sighed. "I know." She got the boxes out and together they read the instructions. Fred held one of the respirators by the straps and helped Louisa put her chin to rest into the face piece. He then drew the straps over her head. "Is that tight enough?" She nodded her head. "Can you hear me properly?" She nodded again. "Just about."

"You have to take it off by undoing the straps at the back. Can you do it?" He sat in front of her and watched her put her arms behind her to undo the straps. She breathed a sigh of relief. "Yuk they smell disgusting. Now you try." She watched him as he went through the same exercise. After he had removed it, he asked her if she could manage to put one on the baby.

"Yes, it's slightly different, but I think I can manage. She's asleep now I will try tomorrow when she is more alert."

"Right. Now let's look at the instructions for replacing it in the box. We have to make sure the eye piece doesn't get damaged and we have to make sure the heavy end is down flat in the box."

"I don't know how I am going to manage to take that around with me when I am shopping." Louisa commented darkly.

"Maybe it could hang from the handlebars on the pram." He went to have a look at the pram. "I think we could do that or just carry it on your back?"

"I'll just have to experiment." Louisa said. "So will you. How can you manage when you are on a building site"?

"Hopefully we will have enough warning from the sirens to come down and get them. There is an air raid shelter on the site now."

"The only other thing we will have to worry about is I.D. cards. We have to carry them around with us." He produced his own from his wallet.

"I've got mine in my handbag and the baby's." Louisa said.

As the evenings began to close in and darkness came earlier, the impact of the war began to take more effect on their lives. They were unable to go to the cinema in the evenings as the government had ordered them to close after six o clock. However one Saturday afternoon when it rained all day, Fred and Louisa managed to get out and see a film. Mary Ellen had agreed to babysit, and afterwards they got a bus back to Pandy to collect little Christine. It was already beginning to go dark, and Mary Ellen urged them to go home. Carefully, they put the baby in the pram and began the two mile walk back to their own home.

"We will just have to depend on reading books in the evenings, if we can't go out at night." Louisa said.

"Good idea. I just hope that the library have got enough books. Everybody will be borrowing books. I heard too that young children from Merseyside have started to come in huge amounts now, they will need something to occupy themselves during the evenings. Poor souls."

"I know. They were talking about it in the corner shop. Agatha Mason said she had seen a large group get off the train at Wrexham Central. They had labels around their wrists with the name of Wrexham on as their destination. Agatha said that some of them had obviously come from poor families judging by the state they were dressed. They had all been told to bring a pillow case with their belongings in. They also had bits of food and their gas masks. I can't imagine how awful it must have been for the parents to send their children away like that."

"After seeing all those films in the cinema about the war in Spain, I should imagine many parents would have been persuaded that it is the right thing to do." Fred said. "When I went up to Liverpool recently, James and Robert told me that they had seen horrific newsreels about war in the cinemas, and some of their neighbours had been given information at children's schools. Some churches too have been persuading parents to send their children away." He sighed. "They will find it different here. I wonder where they are all going to stay."

"I don't know. I suppose the government would have sorted out homes for them before they were allowed to be evacuated?" Louisa said thoughtfully. "I suppose they will have to find schools for them too." "I hope James and Anne aren't thinking of sending little Louise away. She could come here."

"No, she is only a year older than Christine. She's too young."

"But she would still be in danger." All of them are. What about your brothers and sisters?"

"I know. But they won't leave Liverpool. James and Anne won't let go of Louise, and our Robert and Maggie won't let go of their two little ones. So what can I do? Thomas has already signed up for the army, John is doing military service, and Alfred is not in good health. As well as that, Cissy won't let Neville nor Michael out of her sight. I just hope Edward and our Mary don't do anything rash."

Some weeks later Louisa read in the local paper that 9,600 children had arrived in Wrexham. All of them had been evacuated from Merseyside. Whilst she was concerned about the welfare of the poor children, one item of news cheered her up. She read to her delight, that Wrexham Library had received a large consignment of extra books. Many of them would be for children, though a sizeable proportion would be for adults. She decided to go and exchange her library books for herself and Fred. When she arrived there with Christine in the pram she discovered that a section of the library had been partitioned off and was now an Information Bureau run by the government Food Office. A crowd had formed outside reading the posters on the door explaining that residents needed to collect their ration books and that they would need to register at the regular shops they used for their food.

Later when she told Fred, they discussed whether they would need to register with the farm where Louisa's father worked for their meat and vegetables, or whether they should use the grocer down the road from their house.

"I'll have to ask father." Louisa said. "And I suppose I could make our own bread."

"If you can get the flour." Fred said. "That might be on ration too. Besides, they might not ration bread. We'll need to find out more. No doubt we will be informed by the Ministry of Food. Let's have a look at these books you brought home. At least we are now heading into winter so even without those blackout curtains you have made, we would still have to put the light on." He picked up some of the books and read the titles. "I see you have brought a lot of detective books." He smiled. "Good choice." He then pulled a copy of one of the National newspapers out of his pocket. "Look at this, the paper wants to send dartboards to the troops. They are encouraging us to put this picture of a dartboard up and throw things at it to make us feel better."

"The only thing that will make me feel better, is for the war to stop."

One early morning on the twenty fifth of October just as Fred was about to go to work, Harry came knocking on their door. "Dot's had our baby. Another boy." Harry was beaming with joy and excitement. "We're going to call him Malcolm."

"Well done mate." Fred shook hands with Harry. "That's good news, I have to get to work now." He kissed Louisa and then hurried on to his motorbike. Louisa and Harry watched him go down the road before going inside the house.

"Have you got time for a cup of tea?"

He nodded and helped her to draw back the blackout curtains to let in some light. Harry then followed her into the tiny kitchen. "I can't stay long. I need to let Arthur and Glad know. I expect Arthur is probably in work now. I couldn't come earlier because of this wretched black out business. You can't see a blasted thing out there when everyone has blacked out their houses and no street lights."

Louisa poured out the tea and they sat at the small kitchen table. "How is Dot?"

"She's fine. It all happened so quickly. I hardly had time to get her mother. It was a good job they only live a few houses away!" He laughed. "She was very good about it. Got her coat on straight away and stayed with Dot whilst I ran to get

270

Matilda Penson. It's a good job there was hardly any traffic on the road near her house. Anyway, we walked back most of the way over the fields to avoid the traffic." He looked down at his muddy shoes. "Matilda was better prepared than me. She had some boots on. She keeps her boots in a box by the back door so that they are ready. Apparently this is the fourth baby she has delivered since the black outs, and she has prepared herself with good footwear so that she can use the fields instead of the roads. She said that most of the time she can take a short cut across the fields to get to her expectant mothers. The last thing they want is for her to get knocked down by a car or a bus because there are no lights for her to see her way."

Louisa nodded. "It must be terrifying. And just as bad walking through the woods." She sipped her tea. "I wonder why babies are born during the night."

Harry laughed. "Search me." He put down his tea cup, then got up and stretched his arms. "I must go. Thanks for the tea." He bent to kiss his sister on the cheek. "Come and see us soon."

"I will. Probably tomorrow." She closed the door and smiled broadly that she now had another nephew. She went to feed her own baby, and then propped her up with cushions on the sofa, so that she could not fall off. Christine was only four months old but already she was trying to sit up. Louisa sat on the opposite chair to keep her eye on her, then settled herself with her knitting needles to finish the coat she had been making for little Maureen. Idly she wondered if knitting wool would go on ration, and she determined to buy some more ready to knit for her new nephew and for her own baby. She knew that both Dot and Gladys had kept the clothes they had used for Gordon and Brian, so if the worst came to the worst, the new babies would at least have some hand me downs. She began to think about the future and just how they would be able to keep the growing children fed and clothed.

Just as she feared, a week later Louisa and Fred received information about clothing rations. This news arrived at the same time as they heard the horrific news that Hitler was using euthanasia on the sick and disabled in Germany.

When Fred read this out to Louisa from the newspaper he threw it down in disgust. "They call it 'mercy killing'. He got up and paced the room. "It's downright murder. Who is he to say someone is unworthy of life."

Aghast and fearful, Louisa picked up the newspaper that Fred had thrown to the floor. A cold shiver went down Louisa's spine and she felt sick as she read about the euthanasia warrant. "The wicked man. I agree with you. This is murder."

She folded the newspaper and crossed the floor to Fred who was leaning against the fireplace. He pulled her to him and they held each other close to try to comfort each other.

Fred kissed Louisa before saying. "You know I will have to register for service soon. The government now want men between the age of twenty and twenty three."

"But you are a married man."

"I know, but I still have to register for service. If the war continues and there are not enough men, they will call me up anyway. They might make life difficult if I do not show willing." He wiped a tear from her eye. "Don't cry it might not happen."

However things seemed to get worse. Soon after hearing the harrowing news about the use of euthanasia on young children, they were informed that HMS Royal Oak had been sunk and soon after that the navy in Scapa Flow had been attacked from the air.

A month later they were hopeful that despite the alleged assassination attempt on Hitler had failed, that eventually someone would soon succeed in preventing him carrying out any more inhuman acts of violence. Meanwhile on Fred's twenty fourth birthday at the end of November, they heard that the Soviet Union had attacked Finland.

Despite the bad news, Louisa had made a birthday cake for Fred and had invited her two brothers, their wives and children to help celebrate his birthday. Secretly Louisa had thought that if this was Fred's last birthday she wanted it to be a good one. His birthday had fallen on a Thursday, so they agreed to have a little tea party on Saturday afternoon at the beginning of December. This meant avoiding travelling in the dark. Dorothy was working but was going to visit them the next day. Everyone settled down and complimented Louisa on her baking. She had made some sausage rolls too and had made the flaky pastry herself.

"Well I learned something when I was in service besides making beds and black leading grates." Louisa smiled. "I used to watch them in the kitchen making pastry and cakes."

Harry produced a bottle of whisky. "Let's have a toast to Fred." Louisa got some glasses and a jug of water to add to the whisky. She didn't like it much and preferred a drop of it

273

in her tea. Both Dot and Gladys added large quantities of water to their whisky. Arthur laughed when he saw them. "Well if whisky goes on ration, the girls will be able to eke it out for a long time."

Fred picked up what was left of the bottle. "This should come in handy for Christmas. I will look after it. Thanks very much Harry old mate."

Chapter Eighteen

As soon as it was light during the cold November mornings Louisa pushed Christine in her pram to Pandy and back home again in the early afternoons. This daily routine enabled Louisa to help her mother make Christmas puddings, and Christmas cakes. They had been warned by the government that there would be food rationing as from January 1940 so they had made a decision to make sure that this Christmas would be a good one. Nobody knew how long the war would last. Britain hadn't been attacked and many people thought that the war would soon be over. It was upsetting though for those families who had already lost their young men to the war at sea. She and Fred had been listening to the ongoing reports over the wireless about the plight of the three British cruisers HMS Exeter, HMS Achilles and HMS Ajax.

Mary Ellen commented to Louisa that she had heard from Stan Jones her neighbour that his cousin's son had been killed in the South Atlantic. "He was involved with the battle of the River Plate." Ellen shook her head sadly. "What a waste of young life."

"That's very sad." Louisa commented as she tied string around the muslin of one of the three puddings her mother had put ready for steaming. "That German battleship Graf Spee was responsible for starting the battle. The captain scuttled it in the end. I bet that didn't please Mr. Hitler. Fred said that if it hadn't been for the fact that Uruguay was neutral and that our British ambassador had urged the Uruguayan Prime Minister to tell the Graf Spee to leave port, then there could have been even more bloodshed." She pulled a piece of string from the many cut lengths hanging over the back of the chair, and began to tie up the muslin over another plum pudding. She pulled the string tightly and wound it round the pudding basin several times before cutting the string. "Have you heard anything from Cyril Davies?"

Mary Ellen shook her head. "Lizzie Davies had a letter from France a month ago but nothing else since. Let's hope he is safe. By the way there is a letter here for you. It's from Cardiff. I suppose it's from that friend of yours Olive?"

Louisa opened the letter excitedly and quickly read the contents. "Yes, it is from Olive. It seems that she and Sidney have got married and that Sidney is doing military service 'somewhere in France' with the British Expeditionary Force. Olive has left working in service and is working in a munitions factory in Bridgend. She can't tell me where because it is all hush hush! And she can't tell me exactly what she is doing either, but she said she is being paid well and she has her independence. She has to get a bus to Bridgend every day. She has rented a tiny flat on the outskirts of Cardiff. She has sent me her address. It's in Pearl Street. That's a funny name for a street."

"Well good luck to her. And let's hope her Sidney is kept safe." Mary Ellen said. "I think the baby is crying, you had better go and see what she wants. I will finish these two puddings off then we can have something to eat."

At half past three, Louisa got ready to walk back home. It was a cold afternoon and was beginning to go dark already. It seemed strange not to see any evidence of Christmas outside. The village shop usually had Christmas decorations and lights on in the window at this time of year, but there was nothing to see. Everything was in total blackness. Even in daylight the window's dressing was obscured by sticky tape. It was the same type of tape she herself and other people had put on the windows to prevent glass shattering if bombs were to be dropped on the buildings. She knew it would be the same gloomy aspect across the country. It would be the first Christmas that she and Fred would not be able to visit Liverpool to see all the lights in the city. The government were urging people not to travel unless it was necessary. In any case Fred needed his petrol ration to get to work, so if they went to Liverpool to see his family on the motorbike it would consume too much. They were also discouraged from travelling by train. So they had to content themselves with sending Christmas cards and small gifts in the post.

A few days before Christmas Louisa's next door neighbour Nora knocked on her door and asked Louisa if she would help bake some cakes for the party that the local community was organising for the evacuee children. Nora was one of the few women in Wrexham who had volunteered to help with the evacuees.

"A lot of them have gone back to Liverpool, since nothing seems to be happening." Nora said. "But there are still quite a few here. I think some of them are quite settled living here now. Besides, their fathers and some of their mothers have joined up so there is no-one to look after them if they do go back. Quite a lot of those who have gone back are the ones who came with their mothers. In many ways it's just as well because it was difficult finding them places to stay. I heard

some stories of families being cramped because they wanted to stay together. But we managed all the same." She shrugged. "I know it was hard for some of the families to be separated, quite a few couldn't adjust to living here. They missed the hustle bustle of the city and their husbands and older children. It's not as if we have seen any action is it?"
From her doorstep Louisa looked up to the sky. "Except of course seeing planes fly over on training exercises." She was learning to spot the Tiger Moths; Lysanders and Dragons that flew over from the airbase at Shotwick on training exercises. "Of course I will help."
The next day she made three batches of fairy cakes. She piled the cakes on a tray and balanced it on top of Christine's pram then wheeled everything to town. Nora walked alongside her with two shopping bags full of cakes and sandwiches. On the way to Wrexham town hall where the party was to be held, Nora told her that a lot of money had been raised to be able to provide this party for the children. When they got there, Louisa was pleased to see that Dot had arrived with Gordon and Malcolm and she was setting tables with party hats and crackers. The room had been decorated with tinsel and there was a Christmas tree in the corner. Gordon was running around playing with two other toddlers whilst Malcolm was asleep in his pram. Christine was also asleep and Louisa parked Christine's pram at the side of her baby cousin then went to help her sister in law.
"It's wonderful that we can do this for these children." Dot said. The WVS have been really good. I've been trying to help when I can but I can't commit the same as these women because my children are much younger. Most of the WVS

278

seem to have older children so they can help with the activities."

Louisa nodded. "I feel the same. But I will help as much as I can. I want to do my bit."

"I can see which cakes you have made Louisa." Dot commented smiling. "They are lovely as usual."

Louisa shrugged but was pleased to get the compliment and just as pleased to be able to do something positive for the children.

Nora came across with another WVS volunteer whose name was Agatha and she showed them the presents that had been bought for the children. There were tiny Red Cross uniforms and sailor outfits as well as card games and books. Dot picked up one of the books and wrinkled her nose. "What's this? 'Evenings in and a Blackout' and these card games 'Let's evacuate.' For goodness sake who bought these?"

The women shrugged. "Well it's topical and the children have to understand that this is not a game, the war is real," said Agatha.

"I suppose so. But still I would rather have something more cheerful." Dot said. Louisa agreed.

When all the children had been collected and returned to their temporary homes, and dishes washed and put away, Agatha approached Louisa. "Do you think you could help us again with the children? They seem to like you and you have a natural flair with them." She laughed. "You are also a good cook too. Those cakes you made were the first thing to go."

Louisa hesitated. "I am happy to help out, I'm not sure how much time I could give you though. I have a baby of my own to look after."

"Anything you can manage will help us. If you like I will call to see you after Christmas and perhaps we can arrange a rota?" Agatha pressed. She turned towards Dot where she was helping Gordon to put on his coat. "Your sister in law is helping too. She brings her little ones with her. The oldest likes playing football with some of the children and they do appreciate it." She smiled at Christine asleep in her pram. "She's a beautiful baby. I'm sure we could work something out if you are willing."

Louisa nodded. "Alright. I will talk it over with my husband and my sister in law. Come and see me after Christmas."

On Christmas Eve Fred came home looking very pleased with himself. At first Louisa thought it was because he had the next day off work but he got hold of her hand and pulled her towards the back door. It was cold outside and she shivered when he opened the door and told her to look outside. Puzzled she peered around the door and saw to her surprise a side car attached to his motorcycle.

"Now we can go for Christmas dinner to Pandy in style. Arthur nor Harry need not waste their petrol ration to pick us up, we can use our own!" He said proudly. Louisa didn't know whether to laugh or cry. In the end she decided to laugh. "Oh Fred, you are full of surprises." She kissed him and they went in to their supper both of them determined to be happy no matter what.

So on Christmas day they were all smiles as Louisa got into the side car with Christine on her knee. Fred kicked the bike into action and they arrived at Pandy to see Dorothy coming out of the garden where she had been picking sprouts and digging up parsnips for their dinner. As she held up the basin of bright green vegetables, it seemed to Louisa that the colour contrasted with the vivid red lipstick that she wore. Louisa suddenly realised how much her sister had grown up. Her new job working in Greene and Madisons in Chester certainly suited her. "Merry Christmas." Dorothy called to them and stepped around the side of the house to admire Fred's new purchase. "Well, now you will be able to get out and about more. Wait until Arthur sees this."

Fred laughed. "He's seen it. He sold it to me yesterday."

Dorothy laughed. "Did you get a discount?"

Fred nodded.

"Would you be able to get a discount in Greene and Madisons?" Louisa asked grinning.

Dorothy shrugged. "I doubt it. But you never know. Come on in. Mother's all of a dither over the dinner, and father hasn't come home yet, though he should be here soon." She pushed the bucket of sprouts into Louisa's hands and the parsnips into Fred's then rubbed the excess soil off her hands, before picking up the baby. "Come on beautiful baby Christine Mary, let's see what Santa Claus brought for you."

Louisa laughed. "I've brought her Christmas presents with us they are in the side car. Fred made her a wooden ship and I made a rag doll."

"So does the doll sit in the ship?" Dorothy asked.

"Well it would probably fit. It's big enough. He modelled it on HMS Exeter, the cruise ship that was hit during the battle of the River Plate." Louisa smiled at her sister and winked at Fred. She then hugged her mother and followed her in to the narrow back kitchen to help her with Christmas dinner. She doubted very much that her mother was dithering, as she was

281

a very accomplished cook, but she knew she would like to get it perfect. Leaving Christine with Dorothy and Fred she peeled potatoes and the sprouts, then went into the dining room to set the table for five. Harry and Arthur were going to have Christmas dinners with their wives' families, and would be coming around later for tea. On the stone slab in the pantry there was already a trifle waiting for the guests later. Louisa had made some sausage rolls the night before and she put them in the pantry along with her mother's home made chutney, pickled onions and pickled red cabbage.

When they were all seated, Mary Ellen brought in the roasted chicken. Before William carved it, Mary Ellen served out bits of crispy bacon that had been roasted on top of the chicken. "Make the most of it, because it will be rationed next month. Bacon and butter!"

They ate heartily and there was no other reference to the war and rationing until later that day when Arthur and Harry arrived with their wives and children.

Fred had brought his left over bottle of whisky from his birthday with him, and he gave it to William to share out amongst the men as Mary Ellen had produced a bottle of port for the women. She poured out a small amount in each glass and Dorothy topped up the drinks with lemonade.

"I shouldn't think whisky will be rationed." Harry said as he sipped his appreciatively. "Especially the price it is now. It's nearly six shillings a bottle."

"I wouldn't be surprised if there are some hidden bottles somewhere in Scotland and Ireland." Fred grinned. "The chances are the distilleries will close if everyone goes to fight. And there won't be enough produced to ration."

"The price that tobacco is these days they might have to ration that." Arthur said as he lit his cigarette. "Well much though I like a cigarette and a glass of whisky, I can do without them. The annoying thing to me is the petrol rationing and the fact that the prices are rising. It's one shilling and eight pence now a gallon." He looked at Dorothy. "At least you can get to work on the train from here. How are you managing to get to the station in Chester from work during the blackout? It's a fair step from Greene and Madisons."

"We are usually allowed to leave work just before dark so that we can get home safely. But by the time I get to the station it's very dark because it is only dimly lit by candles. It was frightening at first, but there is a group of us that walk together, and we sing as we walk. And we swing our gas masks too." She caught Mary Ellen's eye who smiled at her youngest daughter. "Mother knitted me a pair of white gloves and a scarf so that people can see me and don't bump into me on the platform. A man fell off the platform once and would have been killed but he managed to scramble back up before the train came. They have painted some white strips on the edges now. It helps a little bit." She sipped her port. "I've got used to the route now. I learned it before the blackout, so as long as I do the same route I'm fine. And when I get off the train here in Pandy, I could get home blindfolded."

"It's probably safer for you to travel by train than it is by bus." Arthur said. "You don't have any oncoming traffic or pedestrians on the track."

Dorothy nodded. "Some of the workers use the railway tracks as a guide to walk home."

"I could knit some white gloves and scarves for the evacuees." Louisa said thoughtfully. "Agatha has asked me to help her look after them. It must be awful shepherding them to and fro from the church hall to their homes in the dark."

"That's a good idea. I can help you if you like. We ought to buy up a lot of wool before that goes on ration too." Mary Ellen smiled encouragingly at her daughter.

"They sell wool in Greene and Madisons. It might be cheaper than that shop you go to in Wrexham. I could get some for you." Dorothy offered.

"Get some for me too." Dot said. "I can have a go. I'm not as good with knitting needles as Louie and mother but my knitting isn't too bad."

"Don't look at me." Gladys said. "But I'm sure my mother would help."

Mary Ellen laughed. "We could be depriving any new babies of white clothes. They will have to make do with blue or pink." She got up and went to bring in some mince pies. "I've warmed these up in the oven. It will keep you warm as you walk home in the cold and the dark. There was a groan from everyone. They had all enjoyed being with their families on Christmas day but it wasn't a good prospect to walk home in the dark.

"Damn Hitler." Arthur muttered.

"And Stalin." Said Fred.

"I read that the Soviet Union has been expelled from the League of Nations." Harry said as he helped Gordon into his coat. He picked him up as the little boy clung on to his box of Draughts and Ludo.

"A lot of good that will do." Arthur said. "Stalin and Hitler are sharing what's left of Poland and now it looks like Stalin has set his sights on Finland."

Fred sighed. "Who said it will all be over by Christmas?"

Arthur picked up Brian and followed his brother and Dot out of the door. Gladys trailed behind carrying a plate of food that Mary Ellen had given her, and balanced it on to Maureen's pram. Louisa wrapped Christine up warmly with a blanket, Fred stuffed another mince pie into his mouth and picked up his daughter to carry her on the walk home. The men had agreed they would leave their vehicles in Pandy and would return early the next day to collect them.

Once at home, Louisa bathed Christine and put her to bed, then she looked for the scraps of white wool she knew she had in her work box. Meanwhile Fred opened up a copy of the 'Wrexham Leader' to see what show they could listen to. "I think we've missed the King's speech. Radio Luxemburg has had to stop broadcasting, so we will have to try to find something else to listen to." Fred put the brochure down and started to fiddle with the knobs on the wireless and tried to find something to listen to. Eventually he managed to tune into a special Christmas show and they were able to listen to Christmas carols whilst Fred began to read through the car brochures that Arthur had given him. Whilst he browsed through the magazine, Louisa started to knit her first pair of white gloves.

"Are you thinking of buying a car?" she asked as she looked up from her knitting.

"At these prices I don't think we could afford it. But it would be nice wouldn't it?"

"How much are they?

Fred grinned. "A brand new car to suit our needs would be about £135.00."

"Well you have just bought the side car for the motorbike, so that will have to do for now until Christine grows up a bit."

"There's no harm in looking though is there?" Fred said. "Harry's car is quite old but is going well though." He looked at her over the top of the brochure. "Arthur could get us a discount."

"Let's wait a bit. Maybe next year." Louisa said.

"Or I could have a go on the football pools." Fred chuckled, then put the brochure down. His gaze fell on the white knitting, and remembering what it was for, his expression changed. He sighed. "Let's see what the New Year brings."

New Year's Eve celebrations were as subdued as Christmas day. The family ate well and saw each other during the day time, but because of the blackout and the danger of being knocked down by drunken drivers late in the evening, Louisa and Fred decided to celebrate on their own.

"There won't be any sirens or church bells ringing tonight in case people think it is an air raid." Fred said.

"God help those people in Finland. Especially Helsinki." Louisa said.

Chapter Nineteen

1940

After queuing to get her ration of bacon, sausage and sugar Louisa went home and looked in contempt at the amount she had been given. When Fred arrived home she showed him the meagre amount. "This has to last us all week."

Fred took off his working jacket and stared down at the brown paper bag his wife held up for him to see. "It can't be helped. We will just have to pull in our belts. It's a shame we had to register with the butcher when we know we could probably get more from Stansty farm. Still it wouldn't be right for us to get more than our fair share."

"How am I supposed to make cakes without sugar? That's what I want to know. It will be eggs next you mark my words."

"Well we will just have to have cakes on special occasions and save the sugar. Why not make some scones, then we can have jam on them to make them sweet?"

"Actually that's not a bad idea. I don't need much sugar for the scones. And I could get some honey though it's more expensive. I'm glad my mother and I made all that blackberry and apple jam last autumn. We've still got lots of jars of it."

The reduced sugar scones were put to the test on a Sunday afternoon, a few weeks later. Dorothy came to visit them on Louisa's old bicycle. "I've brought you some extra slices of bacon. Stansty farm gave some to Father for all the extra work he did with the Shire horses. You know he is so good with them. So Mother has shared it out. She thought you might like a bit more. She gave Arthur and Harry the same. You may as well accept it. You never know if you will ever get another opportunity."

Louisa thanked her for it gratefully. "Well I am going to bake some scones now that you are here. You can try them out when they come out of the oven."

Christine who was sitting up in her pram began to cry when she saw Dorothy and she lifted her out of the pram to cuddle her. The child began to smile again as Dorothy played with her.

"That child is spoilt. She only has to make one sound and Fred picks her up. Now you are doing it."

Dorothy kissed the baby's head. "I know you adore her yourself." She followed her smiling sister into the kitchen and watched her weigh out the ingredients she needed. When the scones were in the oven Louisa filled the kettle and put it on the gas cooker. Then she set a tray with three cups and saucers. "I've given up sugar in my tea, I'm saving it for special occasions."

"So have I. We all have at home. Mother wants to save it for baking. We have fruit pies now instead of cakes. She puts a spoonful of jam on the fruit instead of sugar. And she's found an old recipe for carrot cake."

"Carrot cake?" Louisa said perplexed.

"Yes, mother is going to try it soon. Seeing as we usually grow our own carrots we have plenty."

"How is Mother managing with queuing for her rations?" Louisa asked.

Dorothy tickled Christine with her little rag doll before answering. "Not too bad. She's getting used to it. I've started buying lunch at work in the canteen so that saves a bit on food. I manage to get a sausage sandwich or a bacon sandwich sometimes."

When the scones were ready Louisa put them on the tray with the butter dish and jam. She then opened the back door that led from the kitchen to the small yard where Fred was working on his motorbike. "Fred I've made tea and some scones. Dorothy is here." Fred came into wash his hands and after he had greeted Dorothy they sat down around the small coffee table where Louisa poured tea. She handed them a plate each with a lightly buttered scone and a small dollop of jam.

"I've halved the amount of sugar I normally put in, but they taste quite good actually."

Both Fred and Dorothy agreed.

"Any more?" Fred asked.

Louisa laughed. "He always likes to have two."

"And you always take two chocolates from a box." Fred retorted. He put down his book and switched on the wireless. "Let's find out what's happening in the world.

"It's very depressing in Finland. All because they won't let Stalin use their naval bases, the people are being attacked." Dorothy said.

Fred and Louisa exchanged worried glances.

"I don't think the Finns can resist much longer. They have done well so far, but the way things are going, I think they will eventually be outnumbered by Stalin's army. That wicked man is bombing them from the air." Fred said as he sipped his second cup of tea.

"What do you think will happen if they do?" Dorothy asked. She tickled Christine who was happily sitting on her knee as she asked and the little infant chuckled.

Fred scratched his head as he tried to analyse the situation. "I suppose they would collude with Hitler and try to invade Denmark or Norway."

"I hope Finland win. Arthur has said if they lose he will join the army and go and fight Hitler. And if he goes I suppose Harry will go too. You won't go will you Fred?"

Fred sighed. "There might not be a choice."

By the end of February it was becoming more and more unlikely that Finland would be able to survive the attacks from the Soviet Union. News reports regarding the situation were grim and Louisa feared it would worsen. One cold Saturday afternoon Arthur and Harry came to visit Louisa and Fred to talk about the war and what they could do.

"It's very likely Norway and Denmark will be next." Arthur said. "I don't know if the British and French army can hold out against Stalin and Hitler."

"Do you think Churchill will decide to call up married men?" Louisa asked anxiously.

Fred held her hand. "It looks like he will. I think we had better join up before we are forced to and then forced to go to areas where we don't want to go." In his heart he doubted it would make any difference where he would be sent, but he wanted to play his part. However, it was still a difficult decision to leave his wife and daughter, but he knew it had to be done.

Tears came in to Louisa's eyes. Harry looked at his sister. "We have no choice Louie. Someone has to stop Hitler."

A few days later Fred received a letter from his sister Cecelia. He looked upset when he read it. "Cissy and Jack have split up. Or more to the point he has disappeared. He went to see his family in Ireland and she hasn't heard from him since. Apparently he's been missing since August last year. Why she didn't say before I don't know. That's almost six months ago. He's been sending her money but now it has stopped. She is trying to say he has left her, but I think there is more to it than that, and she is worried."

"Poor Cissy. What are we going to do?"

"I will have to go and see her and see what she needs." Fred answered. I will go on Saturday afternoon after work. I will get the train because it will be dark when I get back. I can walk back from the railway station easily in the dark."

Louisa was uneasy all that day and gave a sigh of relief when late on Saturday night Fred returned.

"So what happened??

Fred shook his head. "It's difficult to know properly. She is in a bit of a state, but when I got there she said she had managed to get a job in a meat pie factory. She is to be the caretaker and she can live on the premises in a one bedroom flat with her two kiddies."

"But what if Jack comes back?" Louisa said. "How will he know where she is?"

Fred was tired and sank into the armchair by the fireplace. The fire was dying now and he poked at the embers to get some warmth. "She's left word with the neighbours. She managed to settle the rent for the week and she is going to

291

start work tomorrow. I gave her some money to help her. To tell you the truth I don't think she will see him again."

"Do you think he's joined up?" Louisa asked.

Fred nodded. "Probably. Cissy said that he had told her that he had to go to Belfast to sort something out, but he wouldn't tell her what it was. He promised to be back within a week. He had mentioned something about a job but was very vague. I think he has joined up and didn't want to tell her."

He watched the last of the embers of the fire burn away then got up. He put his arms around her shoulders. "Come on let's go to bed. There's nothing much I can do, at least her two little boys Neville and Michael are alright and she will be fine. Mary will keep an eye on her. I looked in on Bob and Jim and they will keep an eye on her too. But they have both had their papers and will be going to war soon. Bob is going in the Royal Artillery and will be leaving soon for military training, and Jimmy is going to train in Ballymena in Northern Ireland. He won't be sent abroad though, because he's forty one." He sighed. "As for Alf, he isn't well and has failed the health test, so I expect he will help out in the ARP."

The following evening it was announced on the wireless that the so called *winter war* between Russia and Finland was coming to an end and that it looked as if Finland would fall. The same day Fred received papers to report to HMS Royal Arthur the naval training ship in Skegness on the twelfth of March.

Louisa was devastated and Fred was resigned to his fate. Arthur and Harry had enlisted in the army and were due to go to Newtown for military training within a week of Fred's departure. So a farewell party for all of them was held in Pandy.

The day Fred had to leave Louisa held on to him tightly and promised to write to him and pray for him. He kissed her and Christine goodbye and he made his way by train to Skegness in Lincolnshire. When he had gone Louisa cradled her baby and stared out of the window at his motorcycle in the back yard covered in a sheet of tarpaulin. She gazed despondently at the tarpaulin as it fluttered around the tyres each time a gust of wind got hold of it, but Fred had tightly secured it and it remained in place.

Nearby was the Anderson shelter semi concealed in the dugout that Fred had made for their safety. He had gone to great lengths to make sure everything was as safe and as secure as he could leave it until he returned. In an effort to overcome her melancholy Louisa held Christine to her tightly and whispered to her nine month old child, that her daddy would come home soon. Only that morning, the baby had hauled herself off the floor and clutching on to a chair had tried to stand up. Louisa hoped that her beloved husband would return to see his daughter grow up.

Two days later she had word from him that he had arrived safely and all his details had been recorded. He had managed to settle in to the chalets with other recruits. His lodgings were to be the chalets on Butlin's holiday camp which had been commandeered by the government. He wasn't allowed to tell her where he would be going because there was fear of information falling into the wrong hands. He had been told that it would be a few months before he would get any leave.

To help overcome her loneliness and worry, Louisa spent large amounts of daylight at her mother's in Pandy or she walked through Borras to see Gladys who lived close to the Borras fields that backed on to Holt Road. Together they listened feverishly to the wireless while Louisa knitted or sewed. Many of the evacuees had gone back to Liverpool despite government warnings to stay put, so she wasn't needed so much to help the Women's Voluntary Service. Then in April they were informed that Germany had invaded Denmark and Norway.

"That's just what Fred said they would do before he went away!" Louisa cried one afternoon in Pandy. Her mother looked at her gravely. "Your father said the same to me!"

She shook her head as if to clear away the worry she had for her two sons and Fred. "Have you heard from Harry or Arthur?" she asked her daughter.

Louisa shook her head. "No, but tomorrow I will go and see Dot to see if she has heard anything."

"She was here two days ago with the two little boys, and she told me that Harry was still training in Newtown. There was little information other than he may be posted somewhere next month but he couldn't tell her where."

"Maybe he doesn't know." Louisa said. She took Christine out of the pram and put her on the floor. She held her hands as she tried to stand up by herself and watched her daughter walk a few hesitant steps before lunging towards the sideboard. Her little fingers grasped the handle of the sideboard doors for support. "Fred's missing all this. He and so many other men are denied watching their children growing up."

Mary Ellen leaned forward to pick Christine up. "I know, it's a dreadful thing this war. Tearing families apart. As if we didn't have enough in the last war." She looked at Louisa who seemed to be very thin. "Are you eating enough?"

Louisa nodded her head. "Yes we are alright."

"Talking of families, Mr. and Mrs. Cooper have got their hands full with those evacuees in the house."

"Why. What's happened?"

"Well the four of them are not used to living here in a quiet village, they are running up and down and yelling all the time. They bang the lavatory door in the garden with their football and make quite a racket. And they have trodden on his potatoes running up and down his drills."

Louisa laughed, glad to get some relief from the war. "How old are they?"

The two boys are eleven and thirteen. The girls are younger about seven and eight I think."

"I expect they are missing their parents in Liverpool." Louisa suggested.

"Maybe. I don't know. Their father is in the army, I don't know what their mother is doing. She might be working on the war effort." Mary Ellen handed Christine back to her mother and she got up to make some tea before Louisa walked back home again.

The next day Louisa set off early to walk to her sister-in-law Dot's house. It was a bright sunny day in April and it was hard to believe that in other parts of Europe innocent people were being bombed. Dot looked pleased to see her and Gordon ran out to greet her. "I haven't got any news other than Harry is still in Newport. Is there any word from Arthur or Fred?"

"No nothing other than they are both still training. We are all in the dark. They are not allowed to tell us anything."

Dot's mother stood behind her. "Well no news is good news. That's what they usually say." Louisa took small comfort from that.

"I see that Denmark has surrendered to the Germans. Do you think the Norwegians will survive this battle? Dot said.

"It depends whether we and the French can hold them back. Let's hope so." Louisa said.

However early in May, Louisa heard in dismay that Germany had occupied Norway and that Hitler had launched attacks on France, and was gaining territory in the neighbouring countries of Belgium, Holland and Luxemburg. It seemed to Louisa that as these countries were only just across the English Channel, that Hitler would soon try to invade Britain. She hoped that Hitler would not have a big enough navy or army to do it. Then amidst all the fear and uncertainty it was announced very suddenly that the British Prime Minister had resigned. Anxious for news Louisa walked to the corner shop to buy a newspaper. She read that Winston Churchill was now the new Prime Minister.

The following Sunday afternoon she sat in Pandy having dinner with her family. Her Father commented that the new Prime Minister had a lot to do to keep Britain safe from the hands of Hitler.

"But surely he hasn't got enough troops to invade us if his army is occupying France and invading Belgium, Holland and Luxemburg." Louisa protested. She was really worried now. She had heard nothing from Fred nor her two brothers where they were to be sent. They were all coming to the end of their training and events in Europe were worsening. Her parents were also worried and both were her sisters in law.

Louisa began to weep and her father put his arms around her shoulders. "Try not to worry. We have to stay strong."

Miraculously the next day Louisa received a letter from Fred to say that he had been sent to Chatham but was not allowed to tell her where he would be sent next. He hoped to see her soon and that he missed her. She had to take some comfort from that. She sent him letters telling him her news, not that she had much to tell, but most importantly that she loved him and missed him and that Christine was growing and trying to take her first few steps. Indeed by the end of May, Christine was able to walk unaided and was happily running around the kitchen in Pandy when Louisa and her parents heard horrific news about Dunkirk. Belgium had fallen to the Germans, though the British army had managed to escape from capture. Attempts were now being made to bring the troops back to Britain.

"Well Hitler may have got his hands on Belgium but he hasn't got his hands on our army." Louisa said to her mother. "I do worry about Fred's brothers Tommy and John, I have no idea where they were sent. I have a feeling that John was with the British Expeditionary force but Tommy I couldn't say. He joined the army long before the war started." A chilling thought suddenly struck her. "Surely our Arthur and Harry aren't in Belgium?" She looked up at her mother's anxious face and saw the same worry she was feeling mirrored there.

Louisa's heart felt heavy with dread.

To help overcome their anxiety both women kept busy with their knitting. Over the months they had produced several pairs of the promised white gloves and scarves for the evacuees and anyone else who required them. Nora and Agatha had been delighted when Louisa had taken them to the evacuee centre. They were soon distributed amongst those who needed them.

One day at the end of May, Louisa again wheeled her daughter to her mother's house in Pandy and was about to sit down to a cup of weak tea, when the back door opened and a man whose face was covered in mud and oil, his uniform filthy with one leg ripped to the knee, stood in the doorway. His blue eyes glinted as he caught sight of first Louisa and then Mary Ellen who had turned around to see who was at the door. Suddenly Mary Ellen dropped the kettle on to the stove that clattered with the heavy weight as she screamed "Arthur! It's Arthur!" She ran to him and he first embraced her and then Louisa who had jumped to her feet immediately when she realised her brother had come home.

He was exhausted and they helped him to a chair at the table. Mary Ellen went for a towel and bathed his face and hair, whilst Louisa made him a cup of tea and rustled up a sandwich for him. "Use that bit of cheese for now." Mary Ellen ordered. "And I will fry this sausage for him."

Between bites of sandwich, Arthur told them that he had been in Dunkirk. His unit had been in the woodland and having suffered heavy losses, had received orders to retreat. But the scraggly line of soldiers had become disjointed throughout the woods. Fragmented groups of men had tried to keep together but even they had separated into small patchy bands of disorientated soldiers. They were all trying to get back to base but got lost amongst the trees. He and a small group of his comrades managed to find their way back to the beaches. Between them they managed to drag back some of their wounded comrades. Arthur paused and took another sip of tea.

"So how did you find your way to the beach?" Mary Ellen asked kindly. She gazed gently at her fatigued son.

"We found another straggly group like ours all trudging along trying to get away from the Germans. Many of them were locals, and some of them were our comrades who had got lost just like us trying to escape from the bombardment of German troops. They were all as bedraggled as I am. A few of the locals could speak a bit of English and said they would show us the way to the beach." He looked down at his clothes and grimaced. "Our comrades were heading for the beaches in the hope of finding our unit and a ship to get us home. So we tagged on to follow them. When we got there we managed to make contact with what was left of our unit and we were re-grouped and told to wait for a rescue ship. But there were so many of us and a lot wounded and not so many ships. Some of the rescue ships got bombed."

He munched on his sandwich hungrily whilst his mother and sister with horrified expressions on their faces had to wait a bit longer for him to tell them the rest of his story. Eventually they learned that he had been picked up by a small rescue ship and taken to South Wales. Once there, volunteers and complete strangers very kindly had offered temporary accommodation. He had been taken with three other soldiers to a house somewhere in Cardiff. The house was a private house owned by a widow and her elderly mother who wanted to help the local WVS. They had been fed and given shelter for the night though they had to make do with sleeping on the arm chairs or on the floor. After that, he made contact with the local army unit who arranged for him to get a lift in various jeeps going from location to location through Wales. When he got to Newtown he reported to his old unit where he was given immediate leave and told to get new clothing. But he was anxious not to lose precious time queuing up for clothes, he needed to sort out some transport to get home and decided to get new clothing on his return. From Newtown he had managed to get as far as Hightown Barracks in Wrexham and from there, he had hitched a ride with a truck that was on its way up the Chester Road.

"We drove past your house Louie, but I thought you might be here. I don't have a great deal of leave so I decided to walk from the Smithy pond to Pandy to see Mother first before going home to Gladys." He sipped his tea. "I hope the rest got back. There were still men further up the coast waiting for rescue ships to come home." He held his head down as he whispered the next sentence. "Many won't come home, they are lying dead or half dead on the beach." He spoke these words so quietly, and a huge wave of emotion seemed to make his body shiver as he finished relating his story. "Some will be floating in the English channel."

Mary Ellen and Louisa just gazed at him greatly concerned about his state of being. If this is what he is like after his first posting, what will he be like next time, Louisa gazed at him worriedly.

"Are you fit to walk to your own home?" Mary Ellen asked. She knew it was another three miles for her weary son.

"I thought I would borrow that old bike of Louie's to get home." He said between mouthfuls of food.

"Of course. I will go and check the tyres. They probably need pumping up."

Louisa went out to the shed with Christine running behind her and the little girl watched her mother check the tyres before she wheeled out the bicycle. Arthur watched the little girl wistfully as she hung on to Louisa. She stared distrustfully at her uncle.

When he was ready, Louisa walked with him to the end of the row of houses and watched him mount the bike on the lane. She managed a grin. "It's been a while since you rode that."

He nodded. She noticed how much older he looked since the last few months she had seen him. "What do you think will happen next?" She asked him nervously. He put his arm on her shoulder and she gazed into his battle fatigued face. His skin was lined with sweat and grime from traveling in jeeps or standing up wearily in over crowded trains and from the long stretches of walking in the countryside.

"It doesn't look good. Winston Churchill will have to think of something fast. It's very likely the French navy will be commandeered by Hitler. I have heard a rumour that the British have already sunk one of the French ships to stop Hitler using it. It would mean we are in greater risk of invasion here. They can use France and Belgium air bases

301

and start bombing us from the air." He grunted. "We must take care of ourselves. Have you heard from Fred and Harry? They have probably been posted by now." He sighed heavily.

She told him all she knew which was very little. He cycled off then and promised to call to see her again before he reported back for duty. She stood and watched him cycle down the road, a tall figure on a small bike, with his torn military trouser leg flapping in the breeze.

Chapter Twenty

It seemed Arthur was right about France, because two weeks later soon after Arthur had re-joined his unit, they heard that Germany had occupied Paris and again British troops had to retreat quickly. She hoped that neither Arthur nor Harry would be amongst the wounded or dead in Paris. Meanwhile Fred had written to her to say his ship had gone on "trials" and he now had his first posting. He couldn't tell her where he was going or even the name of the ship but he could tell her he was not in the same port he had received his training. He sent her all his love and to take care of herself. He was sorry to have missed Christine's first birthday and to see her take her first steps. Louisa sighed. It was such a shame that he couldn't see his little girl run up and down the house.

As the summer progressed, Louisa now an avid listener to the wireless learned that convoys of ships were escorting merchant ships in the South Atlantic. She looked at the atlas that Fred had bought and noted the names of some of the coastal towns in that area. She knew that Sierra Leone was an important trading route for Britain because it was a major supplier of Britain's food and other goods. She hoped that Fred would not be going that way. It was a large expanse of water and who knew what mines would be lurking in the seas. Everywhere she went Louisa listened for information from wirelesses or newspapers and gossip from the people she met from the WVS. Whilst she learned that Operation Dynamo meant that British, French and Belgian troops had been evacuated, she was also aware of the terrifying news that Germany was now dropping bombs on London as well as Paris.

More evacuees were returning to Wrexham, and Louisa helped her neighbour to help to calm down the frightened children who had arrived each day from the special trains bringing them from Liverpool. The Majestic theatre where she and Fred had visited so often was now used as a reception base for the children. The harsh reality of war was dawning on those people living in Wrexham who so far had managed to escape nightly bombings.

As the days and evenings got lighter during the summer, it was easy to see the Luftwaffe flying over Wrexham to Liverpool, Birmingham and Manchester dropping their bombs. It was a terrible sight and Louisa's heart went out to the little ones gathered in the cinema clutching their bags and gas masks.

Many children were split up from their siblings and had to cope with being in a completely different environment without familiar faces around them. A family of four children were singled out to go and live with a Mr. and Mrs. Simpson who lived in Bersham on a small holding so at least they would have each other for company. Another group of four had to be split into two, and the two older ones tried to soothe the younger ones that they would keep in touch. Both hosts agreed that they would see each other at their new schools and week-ends at the community halls and on Sundays at church. On the way home Louisa had to wipe her own tears away. She couldn't stop thinking about the little ones and how they were suffering. She also couldn't stop thinking about Fred.

As the month of June continued, the news seemed to get worse and worse. Britain seemed to have no strong European allies and was fighting Germany with very little aid. France being almost completely Nazi occupied made it difficult for them to aid Britain. To make matters worse, Italy – an ally of Hitler declared war on both France and the United Kingdom. When Louisa and her family heard news that Norway had finally surrendered they became even more distraught. Meanwhile the Norwegian King Haakon had managed to flee Norway and was now seeking protection in Britain.

"It seems they are all coming to this country, but who is coming to our aid?" William said one late afternoon mid June. "Now President De Gaulle is on the run."

They were all sitting in the front parlour. Dot was also there too with Gordon and Malcolm. It gave her some small comfort to be with Harry's family when he was away.

Louisa agreed. She was leaning against the sideboard with her hands folded indignantly. "How can President De Gaulle run France from here? The Germans have occupied most of France and the Vichy government is just a paper government. If you ask me for my opinion, this Vichy government is no better than the Nazis. They are persecuting people who have been living peacefully in France for many years."

Dot sipped her tea thoughtfully. "Life in France for ordinary people must be very difficult these days."

"Why is no-one helping us?" Louisa said wringing her hands. "What chance has Britain got against Hitler now he has occupied a huge amount of Western Europe?" She turned towards her mother who had been sitting in the back parlour fiddling with the knobs of the wireless. Mary Ellen looked bemused and Louisa and Dot frowned as they caught her expression.

"I have just turned off the wireless as there seems to be a lot of interference. But it seems that Operation Ariel is going very well. They are still bringing the troops back from France, some of them were further North from Dunkirk." Mary Ellen told them. Her expression had brightened at this snippet of news and Louisa could see her mother was hopeful of good news. She watched her as she poured herself a cup of weak tea from the teapot on the table.

I wonder if Fred will be on the rescue ships. And maybe Harry will be rescued, if he is there." Mary Ellen speculated. Dot looked up at the sound of her husband's name but said nothing. Her face remained expressionless, but Louisa knew she was worried.

"It's good news about the rescue I agree, but we don't even know if Harry is there." Louisa said. She picked up Christine who was clamouring for attention and cradled her on her hip as she sipped her tea. Inwardly Louisa wondered about the cost of life the rescue operation had suffered. For her mother's sake she tried to remain cheerful.

Her mother nodded. "The bad news is that the French government are seeking an armistice with Mussolini."

"But that isn't De Gaulle's government though is it?" Louisa observed. "It's the Vichy government." She cried indignantly. "And now joining forces with Italy! France is supposed to be our ally."

306

Mary Ellen sighed. "It must be difficult for the French people if they are occupied by Nazis and have a Vichy government that is almost as bad." She stopped speaking because she could hear the back door being opened and all three women stared at the door expectantly.

"Let's hope this country is not occupied by Nazis." Nancy said. She entered the room smiling. Behind her Little Pat trailed in leaving the door wide open.

"Nancy! What are you doing here? Why didn't you tell me you were coming?" Mary Ellen jumped up to embrace her youngest sister. Dot got up to close the door then she lifted Malcolm in to his pram as he had fallen asleep. Gordon and Pat ran into the parlour to play with Christine. Louisa hastily put the kettle back on to the range to make some more tea. The surprise visit helped them to take their minds off things. Nancy was a vivacious and energetic person who loved life and Louisa and Dorothy adored her. Dot was fond of her too. Nancy explained that her husband Alf who was considerably older than her, had travelled to Wrexham to see his solicitor to sort out his mother's will. So she had accompanied him to the General Station and then caught a train to Pandy to come and surprise them.

"Alf's dear mother was eighty two when she died. A good age really and she died peacefully. Now he has to deal with the sale of her house in Penley." She sighed. "Never mind that for now. I only have an hour. So fill me in with all the news."

The hour was scarcely enough to update Nancy with all the family news. When it was time for her to go, Louisa walked with her to the station. She hugged her aunt and promised to

307

visit her as soon as she could. It was nearly five o clock by this time and she needed to get home to see her neighbour Nora. She wanted to find out what she had organised for the returning evacuees and how she would be able to help.

By the end of June, France had officially surrendered to Germany. It was reported too that De Gaulle was recognised by the British as leader of the Free French. Louisa couldn't understand how De Gaulle could administer a French government when he was hiding in Great Britain. She tried hard to keep up with what was happening in Europe. She continued to listen keenly to the wireless and bought and read newspapers whenever she could. She learned that the Soviet Union had occupied Bessarabia and the Northern section of Bukovina. Louisa had no idea where these places were but later discovered that they had been territories of Romania.

It seemed that Romania had refused to relinquish these two areas to fulfil the demands of the Soviet Union, and so the Soviet Union had invaded Romania and had taken them anyway. However Louisa was more devastated when very soon afterwards she learned that Germany had invaded the Channel Islands. She felt that Hitler was getting closer to Britain. And still there was no news of Fred.

After the success of Operation Ariel both Mary Ellen and Dot received letters from Harry to say that he had been rescued from France and was safely returned to Britain but would almost certainly be given fresh orders again very soon. He couldn't give them much more detail but at least he was safe. Gladys had also received a letter from Arthur and had brought it for Mary Ellen to see. They were all sitting in

Mary Ellen's kitchen towards the end of June exclaiming over these letters.

Eventually Gladys rose from her chair and rounded up Brian and Maureen. "I am going to my mother's now. We are going to stay the night there, so I will see you all again next week." She bent down to kiss Louisa on the cheek. "Try not to worry about Fred. Maybe he has written and the letters have got lost. Keep smiling."

But Louisa was worried. She knew she couldn't do anything about it so kept silent. She didn't trust herself to speak. It didn't help when the next day they all heard the chilling news that the Luftwaffe had dropped bombs on Southampton. She imagined all sorts of horrible things that may have happened to Fred. She worried that his ship may have docked in Southampton and had been hit by a bomb. She knew that after the German bombers had dropped bombs on their target – usually the docks - they would drop other bombs randomly before flying back. The Luftwaffe knew that they risked being gunned down from the gunners below but they still did it. On one such particularly bad air attack, the planes heading back over the English channel dropped their surplus bombs and one had hit a Greene and Madisons store killing many people mostly women and children.

"They hit their target then drop any remaining bombs anywhere making the plane lighter for a faster getaway. As if they haven't caused enough devastation!" William said to his neighbour. He puffed on his pipe agitatedly and they stared at the sky. They were outside in the garden discussing the latest raid. William was waiting for Louisa to get ready to return home. He liked to watch her walk down the lane until she was out of sight. Christine was fast asleep in her pram and William gazed at the sleeping baby. "Take care going home." He said gruffly and waved her goodbye.

For the next few weeks Louisa busied herself with helping the Women's voluntary service to look after the evacuees. She helped organise trips to the cinema and parties on Saturday afternoons, as well as walks and picnics through the woodland. Her organisational skills proved to be very efficient and were very much appreciated by the other women. By the beginning of July she had got into a familiar pattern, and Christine went with her everywhere she went. She missed Fred dreadfully, and wouldn't let Christine out of her sight. Then in July a new horror befell Britain. Hitler had started targeting more bombs on the south coast of England.

"He's trying to get our ports to make us surrender. Just like he tried in Southampton." William said darkly one summer evening. As the summer evenings were lighter now, Louisa was spending more and more time with her parents in Pandy in between helping out in Wrexham town centre with the evacuee children. She had spent a pleasant afternoon talking to an old school friend who had taken in two young girl evacuees into her home. She had no children of her own and was looking after two sisters aged six and seven in the nearby village of Summerhill. William's comment made her depressed again.

"I hope they don't bomb Fred's ship." Louisa said quietly.

"Our air force will see them off, don't you worry." William said trying to cheer up his daughter. Inwardly he was worried about Hitler's attempt to invade Britain. He switched on the wireless and heard a reporter describe an air attack by British Hurricanes and Spitfires. Apparently they had fought off the German Stukas and Messerschmitts close to the English Channel. But more bad news was to follow as Coventry was bombed and then Bradford and other parts of the United Kingdom. They heard that Cardiff and Newport had also been hit and Louisa wondered about her friend Olive's safety. It became evidently clear that Hitler was targeting not just Britain's sea defences but also major factories and iron works.

Meanwhile the random bombs were causing havoc in the towns and cities killing innocent civilians. Hearing air raid sirens during the daytime seemed to be the order of the day throughout July. Towards the end of that month, Louisa was beginning to wonder whether she should not risk walking to Pandy every day, but on the other hand she felt if she was going to be killed she would rather be doing something. She didn't want to stay at home and wait for a random bomb to drop on her. Besides she had received a letter from Fred. It was a week old, and the date and the place he had written from had been censored with thick black lines. There was hardly anything in it that she could read other than he missed her and hoped to see her soon. But at least she told herself he was safe a week ago. His letter gave her strength to try to carry on as normal.

Gladys was sitting at the table with Louisa's parents when she arrived the following afternoon and so was Dot. She shared her news with her mother and sisters in law.

"Where do you think he was when he wrote this?" Gladys asked. She took the letter from Louisa's hands and held it to the light from the window as if trying to see through the black marks. However she couldn't see anything.

"I really haven't a clue. He could be anywhere in the world." Louisa said.

"He could be in a convoy somewhere in the Atlantic." Dot suggested and instantly regretted her statement when she saw Louisa frown. She got Malcolm out of his pram and put him down on the floor next to Christine. Both children ran off into the back parlour to find Gordon, Brian and Maureen who were playing with toy soldiers under the table. They were hidden from view by a huge table cloth that hung over the sides. The children liked playing there as it was like a den where they pretended to hide from their mothers. Dot and Louisa sat knitting clothes for their children, whilst Gladys paced up and down impatiently. Just lately she had begun to smoke heavily and she pulled out a cigarette from her bag and lit it. Eventually she said "I'm going round to my mother's now. I think I will stay there tonight. I can't settle." She quickly gathered up Brian and Maureen, said her goodbyes and left.

An hour after Gladys had gone they heard the siren of an air raid and they all hastily dived for cover to the Anderson shelter in the garden. Louisa couldn't help thinking that if a stray bomb fell on top of the shelter, they wouldn't stand a chance. She hastily put her gas mask on and helped Christine into hers. Several hours later they heard the all clear. When they climbed out of the shelter they were surprised that despite the time of night the sky was lit up.

"And when they looked up they saw a blazing light coming from the direction of Liverpool.

"Oh my god" Louisa cried. They all looked in the distance their faces grim with disbelief. None of them could speak. The sight was horrific.

"Those poor souls." Dot whispered. Mary Ellen suggested that her daughter and daughter in law should stay the night rather than walk home late at night.

"But there's no room for all of us." Louisa protested and Dot agreed. Mary Ellen shrugged. She was worried about her other daughter. "Dorothy won't be home tonight. She is probably in the air raid shelter in Chester. There won't be any trains back now. And your father is probably staying in Stansty so there is plenty of space. Besides I would like your company." Reluctantly Louisa and Dot agreed to stay.

Eventually when they got back into the house again, Dot and Louisa got the little boys comfortable in the small bedroom that used to be Dorothy's. She shared her sister's slightly bigger bed with Christine and Dot slept downstairs on the sofa. Louisa couldn't sleep at first, she was too horrified about what they had seen. Eventually she became too tired to think and she dropped off. When she saw Dot's face the next day she could see by the haunted expression on her face that she too had scarcely slept.

Meanwhile, the children totally oblivious of the previous night's destruction were up chattering and eating dry toast and jam when Louisa finally got downstairs. She felt worn-out through lack of sleep and worry. Christine ran to her and she picked up her little girl who put sticky fingers on her mother's face. Mary Ellen gave her a cup of tea. "Your father called early this morning and has now gone back to work. Dot is still sleeping."

313

Louisa sat down numbly. "Fred will be devastated when he hears about those bombs in Liverpool." She said.

Mary Ellen said nothing. She was too upset. She cut some more bread to make toast then bent to wipe the sticky faces and hands of the two younger children. An hour later Dot came in to the kitchen and after a hasty breakfast she got ready to go home. "They will be worrying about me at home, though they'll know that no bombs fell here. Poor old Liverpool. You can still see the smoke from the window."

When Louisa got home later that morning she found a letter on her doorstep from Fred. Eagerly she tore it open and smiled when she read that his ship had docked in Birkenhead and that he had been granted two weeks leave. The letter was dated the day before, and she was suddenly seized with alarm. Birkenhead was very close to Liverpool. Surely he hadn't been caught in the attack. Frantically she switched on the wireless to get some news and couldn't get a signal. To try to keep busy, she spent an hour washing and cleaning. Then began to worry about food. She had only rations for herself and Christine. Fortunately her mother had given her some extra bacon and eggs. She also had some potatoes. As she was well off for eggs she decided to be lavish and bake a cake for her husband. She would use her sugar ration that she had been saving to make jam. She and her mother had planned to pick the blackberries in the bluebell wood to make bramble jam. It was too early in the year yet so she knew she could spare some for a cake for her husband. She had just taken the cake out of the oven when there was a knock on the door. Her heart missed a beat. She dreaded getting a telegram.

Hesitantly she opened the door and saw a very dirty man with a beard in a sailor's uniform. "Hello Lou." He said and Louisa fell into his arms. "Oh Fred, Fred."

When he finally let her go, he rubbed a smudge off her face which had smeared itself from his skin to hers. "I will go and get a shave. I am looking forward to a bath and a change of clothes. But first of all where is the baby?"

Louisa smiled. "She's asleep, and hardly a baby now. She is getting into all sort of mischief." Fred climbed upstairs and went to see his baby daughter sleeping in her cot. He touched her tiny hand and smiled as she rolled over totally unaware of his presence. Later clean shaven and dressed in fresh clothes he joined his wife to eat a plate of mashed potatoes, bacon and egg. When he had sampled some cake with a cup of tea Fred sat back with a satisfied sigh. "That was the best meal I have had for months. I've missed your home cooking. But most of all I have missed you love." He kissed her and she contentedly put her arms around him. They sat close together on the sofa for hours as they talked until eventually Christine began to cry and Louisa went upstairs to fetch her. "Come and see who has come home. It's your daddy."

Christine rubbed her eyes wearily and stared at Fred. She didn't recognise him and Fred looked at her sadly. She wouldn't look at him and kept clinging to her mother. "She's just woken up, she'll be ok when she's settled down. I will give her something to eat first." Louisa sat Christine down on an arm chair whilst she went to the kitchen to prepare her something to eat, but the little girl got up and followed her.

"Leave her for now, give her time to let her get used to me again." Fred said, as Louisa tried to disentangle her daughter from clinging to her legs. "At least I can see her." Louisa sensed the disappointment in his voice but knew that after a couple of hours, Christine would be more sociable. This seemed to be the case because by tea time the little girl was sitting on her father's lap. However this cosy scene was soon destroyed by the sound of the air raid siren and they dashed outside to the Anderson shelter. With her husband's arm around her Louisa didn't feel so scared, but the deafening sound of the machine guns from the nearby barracks trying to shoot down the planes was horrendous. In the distance they could also distinguish the sounds of the firing from the night fighters trying to bring down the Luftwaffe. When the all clear siren was heard they clambered back into the house and Louisa put up the black outs on the window.

Fred switched on the wireless whilst Louisa got Christine ready for bed. "Let's hope the Luftwaffe missed their target." He said. "There won't be much left of Merseyside if they haven't." He looked angry and distressed and Louisa went to put her arm around him. "Damn Hitler." She said. "Do you think it will be reported yet?"

Fred shrugged. "Probably not. And Churchill never gives us all the facts anyway in case spies are listening."

Louisa shuddered. "Is anywhere safe?"

Fred took her in his arms. "We have to be vigilant and take care who we talk to. I will tell you about the ships I have been on and the one I am due to report to, but you mustn't tell a soul. I think we could make up our own code so that the code breakers won't know what we are talking about. It's worth a try anyhow."

Louisa nodded.

The next morning the three of them sat at the small kitchen table and whilst Christine sipped some milk Fred and Louisa tried to make a plan. Fred told Louisa that after he had left HMS Royal Arthur in Skegness he had been transferred to Chatham to HMS Pembroke another training ship. After that he was assigned to HMS Mooltan as part of a convoy escorting merchant ships back and to from Sierra Leone to Stranraer.

"Stranraer is sometimes known as Wig Bay." Fred explained. "It's very important for us because the ships come back and to from Freetown."

"So you have been on the North and South Atlantic." Louisa said in astonishment.

Fred shrugged. "It wasn't pleasant. Let's not dwell on it." He started to write down the names of the places he had been and was probably going to go to again.

"We have to be very careful about this. It needn't be an elaborate plan, it's just to let you know that I am safe so it has to be something general. How about if I want to talk about Christine I write 'the baby.' If I write her name Christine it means I am in Sierra Leone. And if I mention a barber or needing a haircut it means I'm in Scotland. I will have to be careful how I mention it though."

"Alright." Louisa sipped her weak tea and grimaced at the taste. She was trying to stretch her tea ration. This was another commodity which had recently been added to the list of rations. Tea and margarine. "If you don't go to those

317

places how will I know? We can't write a code for all the countries in the world. It would be impossible."

"It's more than likely I will be doing this route indefinitely. I don't know when I will see you again." Tenderly he wiped a tear from her eye with his finger. "If for some reason I am elsewhere then I will just say "I don't know where I am." If even that gets censored, you will know that I am not in Sierra Leone. When I report back I have to go to Chatham."

"Will you be on HMS Pembroke again?"

Fred nodded. "Yes then I will transfer to another ship – probably HMS Edinburgh Castle, and back to Freetown, but that is not confirmed. I will more than likely be spending a lot of time crossing the Atlantic as part of the Freetown Escort force. So I will be on and off the Edinburgh Castle, because it is an accommodation ship."

"How will I know?"

Fred shook his head sadly. "I can't tell you because I don't know myself."

They stared into each other's eyes with love and fear. Both wanting to protect each other from the horrible blow that the war had dealt them. Yet they both knew they were lucky to be alive. Fred held her tightly and Louisa tried to smile.

"I know what will cheer you up. How about some whisky in your tea!" Louisa cried. There is still some left from your birthday last year." She fetched the bottle from the kitchen cupboard and poured small amounts into their teacups.

Fred laughed as he watched her pouring the alcohol. "Good idea first thing in the morning. And I will have some of that tonight. There's not much left now I may as well finish it." He finished writing down their little code and showed it to

318

her to memorise. Once they both remembered it he set light to it with a match and then threw the burning paper into the sink and watched it turn to ash. He then got up and lifted Christine on to the table. She started to do a little dance and smiled up at his adoring face. "Come on. Let's walk over to Pandy. It's a nice day."

Chapter Twenty One

Mary Ellen was excited to see Fred home and hugged him tightly. "Thank God you are safe." They didn't stay long, just long enough to answer all Mary Ellen's questions about where Fred had been. She understood that he was restricted in what he could tell her. However she was satisfied with his answers and just glad that he was alive. Afterwards they walked across to Rhosrobin to see Dot. Before they left they promised Mary Ellen that they would return later to see William and Dorothy. Once again Fred got another warm welcome and hug, this time from Dot and they settled down to drink yet another cup of tea. Dot had been saving her tea rations for such a special occasion and she made them a good strong pot of tea.

"You are spoiling us." Louisa laughed. Whilst they were chatting Dot decided to rustle up some homemade scones that used very little margarine and plenty of dried fruit. "As dried fruit isn't on ration yet, I put plenty in to compensate for less sugar. And instead of spreading butter, I do the same as you, Louie and spread some jam instead. I've still got some left over from last year's jam making."

Very soon their conversation turned to Liverpool. "The bombers are trying to get the ports and munitions factories aren't they?" Dot suggested. "Do you think they met their targets last night?"

Fred shook his head. "I think a lot of the Luftwaffe were brought down by the gunners in Birkenhead, and those Stuka planes escaping tried to get Monsanto chemicals on the way back but they missed fortunately. The explosions seemed very close last night. They might be trying to get the munitions factory in Wrexham too. It's not that far away. I hope it's well concealed." He sipped his tea appreciatively. He loved strong tea.

Louisa shuddered. I know someone working at the Royal Ordinance Factory in Marchwiel. Her name is Phyllis. She used to be in school with me. It seems terribly dangerous. They have to handle 'gun cotton' whatever that is and then press it into nitro glycerine. I saw her the other day with her sister Janet. It seems to have turned their skin a funny yellow colour."

"Yes I've heard stories about women's skin turning yellow." Fred said. "If a bomb was to drop on that nitro glycerine it would cause one hell of an explosion. Let's hope the Luftwaffe don't find it. Has the government finished upgrading the airfield at Borras yet? There was talk of having a night fighter squadron based there so that they could defend the area from an air attack. They need to hurry up and get it finished, then they can provide some protection for North Wales and the North East. It could be too late for Liverpool."

"Do you know where the ROF is?" Louisa asked surprised.

Fred shook his head. "No. It's top secret isn't it? I know it's in Marchwiel somewhere though."

"Phyllis was very secretive too. She kept touching her nose and saying "careless talk costs lives."

"I don't know how Germany found out about the munitions factory. How can they know when I don't even know where it is?" Dot said.

Fred shrugged. "Intelligence from either pilots taking photographs or someone infiltrating into our society. You have to be careful what you say to people, especially people you don't know." He took another sip of his tea.

"There could be spies everywhere." Dot said. She looked over her shoulder as if there was someone listening. Only her elderly grandfather was in the house. He hardly got up these days and stayed in his bed downstairs.

"People do talk though. There is always a rumour and it has to be started somewhere. My neighbour Liz Phillips told me that a man had been found dead, somewhere near the river Alyn. People are saying he was a spy and she reckons he was Italian. Nobody seems to know who he was or where he was going. If he was near the river Alyn he could have been going to Bradley or Gwersyllt or Summerhill, or even coming here. And every time I ask questions most people look at me suspiciously as if I were a spy!"

"So what happened?" Fred asked incredulously. "Just two miles away from here, that's worrying. I wonder what the man was looking for and where he had been living."

"I don't know any more details I am afraid. There wasn't anything in the local paper, it's all just hearsay. For all I know he could have been the victim of a personal dispute and somebody may have murdered him. I don't know how he died. Like as if there isn't enough murder going on in the world."

Fred turned towards Louisa. "We could ask your father, maybe he knows something." She nodded her head in agreement.

Dot sighed. "I don't know what to think. There are so many rumours flying around. The information I got from Liz was already third hand. She got the rumour off the milk man and she likes to embellish everything! It could even have been an accident. I worry that it may have been an escaped intern. There were a few Italians living in that area however I thought they had all been transferred to a camp. Still there's no smoke without fire."

Catching Fred and Louisa's worried expressions, she changed the subject. "I don't suppose you have seen anything of Harry or Arthur?" She looked hopefully at Fred and he sadly shook his head.

"No I have only had contact with my little brother Edward. He's joined the Navy. He's gone into submarines."

"Didn't you warn him not to join the navy?" Louisa asked.

"Yes, but apparently he's got himself engaged and thought the money would be better in the submarines." Louisa smiled as she recalled the fresh faced youth who had attended their wedding just two years earlier.

"Are you going to stay for some lunch? Dot asked. I've got plenty of potatoes and a tin of spam." She took the scones out of the oven. And we can have one of these too."

Later that evening, they walked back to Pandy so that they could see William and Dorothy. The first one to arrive home was Dorothy. As soon as she came through the door and saw Fred she flung herself at him and started to kiss him all over his face. "I'm so glad to see you." she said excitedly when she had calmed down. We've all been worried about you. Especially poor Louie and little Christine." She took off her jacket and hung it on the back of the chair to sit down at the

kitchen table. She then picked up Christine who had run to her when she heard her voice and had stared in wonder as she saw her hug Fred. When William arrived it was a joy to see the pleasure in his eyes as they fell upon Fred. He shook his hand affectionately. "Glad to see you lad." He said gruffly.
Presently Mary Ellen put some sliced bread, ham and cheese on the table and made a pot of weak tea. Guiltily Louisa said she would bring some tea for her mother the next day as she didn't want to use up her rations.
Her mother smiled. "Thank you. I do miss a good cup of tea. She stared at the dry bread. "And butter, but there are people worse off than us."
"Have you heard from your brothers Fred? I hear they are all in the army." William asked.
"None of them recently except Edward. He's joined the navy. He's in a submarine somewhere. I have no idea where Tommy is. Jimmy was in Ballymena but I think he is based somewhere in Lincoln now near the aerodrome; Bobby is a gunner in the Royal Artillery somewhere in the Anti-Tank Regiment. I believe it is the 161st Battalion. I don't know where John is either, all I know is he is in the Guards. The Coldstream ones I think."
"What about your sisters?" Dorothy asked.
"I've heard nothing from them either. I must admit after the bombing in Liverpool the other night, I'm concerned about Cissy and her little ones. Our Mary joined the ATS and was learning to drive trucks. I think I might have heard something by now, if it was bad news."

"Let's think positive." Mary Ellen said. "Tell us again Fred, where have you been and how long have you got before you go back?"

Fred glanced at Louisa. "I can't tell you too much other than I have been on the Atlantic Ocean. And I will probably be going back to the Atlantic."

William looked up sharply. "That's a dangerous place to go. We hear so much of the ships being sunk and submarines lurking in the area."

Fred shrugged. "It's dangerous everywhere. I have to do my bit like everyone else."

"Let's hope Hitler doesn't get Liverpool docks!" William said. He patted Fred on the shoulder.

"If the war is still on in November, after my birthday, I am going to do my bit too. I will be old enough then." Dorothy announced suddenly. Everyone stared at her.

"What do you mean?" her father asked.

"I'm going to apply for work in the ammunitions factory." Dorothy announced.

"What?" Both Mary Ellen and William stared at their daughter.

"It's very dangerous to work with that nitro glycerine." Louisa said gently. "Do you know what it can do?"

Dorothy was defiant. My friend Clarissa at work said her sister works in one in Wolverhampton and she gets good money. They use cordite there."

"But that is just as dangerous." Fred said. "And how would you get to Wolverhampton?"

"I would have to stay in digs. It's good money," she repeated. "Anyway the war might be over by then."

Fred sighed. "I wish it would be, but somehow the way things are going it could be next year."

No more was said about the munitions factory. Everyone was secretly thinking that Dorothy wouldn't give up her job in Greene and Madisons. She loved working in Chester. In any case just then the air raid siren warned them of an attack and hastily they all crammed into the shelter.

The next morning Fred went outside in their small back garden and took the tarpaulin off his motorcycle. He tried to start it but the engine wouldn't fire. Louisa stood in the doorway watching him. She bit her lip as she saw her husband give up and then went searching in their small coal shed to find his tools. After a couple of hours she heard the engine fire up and she came back to the doorway to see Fred grinning. His face was spattered with oil. "Shall we go for a run? There's enough petrol to get us to Acton Park and back with a bit to spare."

Louisa laughed. "We can't go there. It's full of Nissen huts and soldiers. Don't you remember?"

Fred shrugged. "I'd forgotten. How about Farndon then? We could stop by the bridge and walk along the river bank for a while."

It felt good to be in the side car again with Christine sitting on her knee. Both of them were in need of a break from the depressing news of the war. The news that morning had told them of evacuees trying to flee Gibraltar as Churchill had warned them of a possible invasion by the Germans just as they had invaded the Channel Islands.

Besides the threat about Gibraltar, they had both been upset, Fred particularly, when they exchanged their views regarding the destruction of the French vessels in Mers-el-Kebir off the coast of Algeria early in July.

"So many lives have been lost because of this war. Surely there could have been another way. To destroy much needed vessels and kill innocent men caught up in a war we don't want."

He had looked across their tiny breakfast table at Louisa, the anguish covering his face matching her own. "This war is slaughtering men women and children every day."

Louisa sympathised with him, she knew he was loyal to his fellow seamen and felt deeply for the loss of life. They were both keenly aware that every time he went aboard a ship that it could be his last time alive.

"You know what will happen next? Fred said. The Germans will commandeer the Vichy French air force to increase their attack on Britain."

"Do you think all the Vichy government ministers support the Nazis?" Louisa asked Fred as they walked slowly along the river bank. Christine was in the middle and each of them held one of her hands as she toddled along blissfully unaware of the tragic consequences of war.

"I doubt it. When your country is occupied by Nazis, you have little option to either obey orders, or be shot. I have heard stories of a strong and brave resistance in France though. Life must be really tough if you don't support them." Just then he looked up and to his dismay saw a low flying aeroplane. It was so low Fred was easily able to make out the bright yellow markings on the fuselage and the tail plane as well as the French tri colour that denoted Vichy French. "Look out. Get over here." He dragged Louisa and

Christine behind some bushes. But after a few seconds the plane flew back up in the air again. "What were you saying about the French?" Fred said, trying a lop sided grin.

"What was it doing here flying so low?" Louisa gasped. "Do you think it was lost?"

"Probably, or it might be damaged and fortunately for us has already discharged its ammunition on some other unlucky people. They seem to have started spasmodic bombing during the daytime now. Maybe it's using the river Dee to get its bearings. Or it could be a German taking photographs for the enemy." He sighed, and Louisa felt a cold shiver trickle down her back. Neither of them wanted to discuss any other possibilities. Fred's expression and his gaze conveyed to Louisa the same mixed up emotions. Gazing into his eyes they both seemed to give mutual consent to try to not let the incident spoil their day.

On their way home they called to see Gladys and she hugged Fred. "So glad to see you home safely." She said. "I've had a letter from Arthur this morning." She went to fetch it and held it up to them laughing. "It's covered in black marks. He must have tried hard to tell me where he is."

"Well at least he is safe and his letter got through." Louisa said. "The date is two weeks ago."

Fred grinned. "Maybe he's having a rant about the generals, or explaining how he could do things better."

Gladys smiled. "You could be right about both."

When they finally arrived home, they heard the air raid siren. "Come on quick into the air raid shelter." They grabbed a jug of water and dashed outside. After an hour the all clear sounded. "Must have been a false alarm. It's risky bombing us in the daylight. They must have a lot of planes to spare, in case they are shot down. That's bad news for us." Fred said. Later they discovered that there had been a bombing raid in Croydon and a low flying aeroplane had dropped a bomb on a Greene and Madisons store in nearby Lewisham.

When Dorothy heard the news she was outraged as indeed were all her colleagues at Greene and Madisons store in Chester. The attack made them feel more vulnerable. "There were mostly women and children in that store. Why are they killing civilians?" She cried.

The day before Fred was due to return to his ship, they arranged to go dancing at the church hall in Garden Village. It was a charity event for the Red Cross. Dorothy had agreed to look after Christine and they left her in Pandy with the agreement that they would collect her on the way home. The entertainment was to be provided by a local brass band and a pianist. The members of the band comprised of volunteers from the now officially named "Home Guard" and some younger people who had been declared medically unfit to serve. They had put together a collection of pieces from some well known popular jazz singers.

Luckily that night there was no air raid warning and happily Fred and Louisa enjoyed a pleasant evening. When the music stopped they made their way to the cloakroom to get their coats to go home. At the doorway someone shouted Fred's name and a young man leaning heavily on a walking stick carefully moved towards Fred. It was an old colleague from work. "Hello Archie old mate. I had a feeling that was you playing the piano." Fred shook hands with him and saw that Archie had lost half a leg.

"It's good to see you Fred." He turned towards Louisa. "Is this your beautiful wife?"

Louisa smiled and held on to Fred's arm whilst he continued to talk to Archie. "I'm sorry about your leg," he said. "What happened?"

Archie grimaced. "I was left for dead in Dunkirk. But some kind soul carried me off the beach. I owe my life to him and the Red Cross." The two men held each other's gaze for a few seconds, neither of them speaking, both of them recalling scenes of unspeakable horror. Eventually Archie broke the silence. "Did you enjoy the music?"

Both Louisa and Fred nodded that they did. "So what will you do now?" Fred asked kindly.

"Oh don't worry about me. I'm still doing my bit. I'm working in the Royal Ordnance Factory as a wages clerk. I had to do an intelligence test first and then they put me in with some other wages clerks. Fortunately I was always good at arithmetic in school, so I had no problem with the test. As well as doing the wages, I also have to keep records of anyone coming to the factory." He leaned back against the wall to let people go through the door. "And in my spare time I practice on the piano. I've been teaching myself to play with some help from my Gran. It's my Gran's piano really. I'm living with her now. We must be a musical family because my dad was in the colliery band. Dad died at Gresford pit as you know, and most of the band players were wiped out in the explosion." He shrugged. Mam spends all her time in the WVS, so I keep my gran company."

Fred stared at his old work colleague. His eyes misted over and Louisa squeezed his hand to comfort him. "How do you get to work Archie? Is there a special bus?"

Archie grinned. "Better than that. I get a lift with four others, all girls! They come for me in an old banged out convertible." He shook hands with Fred and then Louisa. "Take care. I'll be seeing you."

The next day Louisa went to the railway station with Fred to wave him goodbye. As the train pulled out Louisa ran along the platform with Christine in her arms. The platform was crowded with other wives and sweethearts waving goodbye, and many a tear was spilt as the train was lost in the distance. Sadly she blew her nose and tried to smile for Christine's sake, then began the two mile walk back home with her daughter. She wondered if she would ever see her husband again.

Just a few days later there were more day time raids on Britain. The docks and major ports were the obvious targets of the Luftwaffe. Then towards the end of August a bomb dropped in the city of London killing nine civilians. The attacks, chiefly on London continued relentlessly day and night, killing and maiming innocent people right through to the end of August. The whole country lived in terror and feared for their lives and loved ones. Louisa and her family felt despair and helplessness when they witnessed the planes flying overhead destined to drop more and more bombs on harmless unarmed city folk. By the end of the month it was reported that the Luftwaffe had been responsible for the death of over 1,000 civilians.

Outraged that Hitler could attack innocent citizens, it became evident that Prime Minister Churchill's War Cabinet had made a decision to retaliate by bombing Berlin. During a wireless report the nation was informed that seventy planes had flown from Britain to attack Berlin.

"God help them". William said. "They are as innocent as those civilians in our country."

Meanwhile the raids on Britain intensified during September. On the afternoon of the seventh day of that month Louisa looked skywards and could barely see the sky for the black dots which were German aircraft. She knew with a sinking feeling of dismay that those black specks were the outlines of bombers and fighter aircrafts as they crossed the English Channel to raid yet again Liverpool. She realised that it would not be just Liverpool where bombs would rain down, but also all the cities along the East coast towards London.

The sight and sound was deafening as well as frightening. Louisa spent most of her daytime sitting in the Anderson shelter terrified that a random bomb may drop on her and Christine. To calm herself she would take her knitting and read stories to Christine by candle light. Every night there were raids, and standing in the garden with Christine in her arms after each attack, Louisa could see the distant fires and black smoke coming from the direction of Liverpool. The smoke and fires increased as Manchester and Birmingham were also incessantly bombed. The news on the wireless praised the British air pilots who put up huge and long dogfights in the sky especially over London and over the Thames Estuary. Louisa found it odd that there was no mention of Liverpool or the other big cities that must have suffered heavy losses.

During the months leading up to winter, church bells rang out perpetually to warn people of raids, almost every night. The only reprieve was when the bad weather prevented the Luftwaffe to fly. When the weather improved, the raids resumed, leaving behind a trail of dead and injured people and destroyed buildings.

A few days before Christmas, Louisa received a letter from Cissy telling her that she was safe but that Liverpool was blazing. She said it was a miracle she was still alive. Many of the places bombed and ruined were places she had previously rented, and so at the end of July she had moved to Ormskirk and was living in a small flat, she shared with a woman friend called Eve who was a nurse working on the ambulances. Cissy managed to survive by working as a cleaner in a nearby stately home that had been commandeered by the army. She and Eve managed between them to get the children to school (Eve had a little girl called Anne aged seven) and still do their jobs. She hoped that everyone was alright in Wrexham. She hadn't heard from Bob's wife Margaret. She knew she was working at the old Meccano factory that was now producing war materials, but as far as she knew it hadn't been bombed. She also said that she had lost two good old school friends in an explosion in Durning road. She told Louisa that a parachute mine had caused the collapse of a college and had killed many of the college workers. Cissy finished off the letter by saying that her step father John Barton had died in hospital on the twelfth of December. She had written to all her siblings including Freddy and to Edward to tell them. Mary was overseas driving ambulances and as far as she knew she was safe. She didn't write so she assumed she was in a safe place. "Thank God she's alive and well.|" Louisa said. She took the letter to Pandy with her to show her parents. It was the Sunday before Christmas the twenty second of December.

"I don't think Fred will be too broken hearted about John Barton." Louisa said sadly.

"I've got some news too." Dorothy said after she had read the letter. "I'm going to work in munitions in Wolverhampton."

Louisa stared at first her sister and then her mother who nodded her head acknowledging that it was true.

"Single women are being called up Louie, I would rather choose now what I prefer to do. I want to do my bit."

"So when do you go?" Louisa asked. She would miss her sister.

"After Christmas. Thursday – boxing day to be exact."

"So soon."

Dorothy hugged her sister. "Let's enjoy Christmas and make the most of it."

"This will be different to last Christmas, now we are being rationed." Mary Ellen said ruefully. "But let's see what we can do. If we pool resources with Louie's we won't do too badly. It seems Gladys is pooling her rations with her mother and Dot is doing the same with hers, so it will be just us."

"They are coming on boxing day though aren't they? Louisa asked anxiously.

Dorothy nodded. "Yes they are coming early so that we can have lunch before I go. I have to catch a special bus at two o clock from King Street in Wrexham."

"Well at least the government have doubled the tea ration and the sugar ration for Christmas." Louisa said.

"That reminds me, Dorothy said. "I know fruit is so scarce and even when you can get it, it is so expensive, but would you like me to get some for Christine as a gift instead of toys? Not that toys are in big supply."

Louisa smiled. "Yes that would be a nice idea. Do you know where you can get some in Chester?"

Dorothy winked.

The next few days before Christmas Louisa helped Nora and Agatha and the rest of the women in the WVS to organise the Christmas party in St. Mary's church hall in Wrexham for the evacuee children. Since the increased bombing of Liverpool, more and more evacuees had returned, some with their mothers as most of them were now homeless. She helped make Christmas decorations out of old newspapers and got the smaller children to paint them in different colours. Whilst they were occupied doing that, one of the volunteers sat at the piano and began to play some Christmas carols and encouraged the children to sing. Meanwhile Louisa and the other volunteers unpacked all the donated knitted clothes, as well as the ones she and her mother and Dot had made for the children. Together they distributed them to all the children. It was heartbreaking to see so many desperate yet grateful mothers. She knew that some of them had to spend their nights sleeping on floors in the church halls around

Wrexham. For those poor souls, she and the WVS had managed to get donated blankets to help keep them warm.

On the afternoon of Christmas Eve she hurried home from the evacuee centre with Christine and packed a few things to take with her the next day to Pandy. She didn't bother hanging up a stocking for Christine as she didn't think she would understand. In any case she had very little to fill it other than the new rag doll she had managed to make for her. Toys were hard to come by as so many factories were now making armaments for the war effort.

As it turned out, Dorothy presented everyone with an orange on Christmas day as well as scented soap for Louisa and Mary, and some vegetable seeds for her father. She also produced a bottle of port.

The women laughed when they opened each other's gifts because all of them had bought practical gifts – soap!

For once there were no air raids and later that morning on the wireless William was able to listen to a football match between Everton and Liverpool. After lunch he was surprised to hear that Tommy Lawton who had played that morning for Everton had also agreed to play for Tranmere in the afternoon match against Crewe!

"Well I wonder what Fred would think of that!" William exclaimed. "You had better write and tell him Lou." Louisa smiled contentedly. She was with her family and she sat by the fire playing with her daughter. They were going to stay the night in Pandy so that they would all be together when Dot and Gladys arrived.

There was a changed atmosphere at breakfast on Boxing Day. As usual William got ready for work. He tried to hide his heavy heart from his daughter as he hugged Dorothy and wished her good luck in her new job. Some neighbours popped in also to say goodbye to Dorothy and all too soon it was time for her to leave. Mary Ellen and Louisa waved goodbye to her from the doorstep. Mary Ellen was tearful and Louisa put her arm around her mother to comfort her.

Chapter Twenty Two

1941

The air raids continued soon after Christmas. And each day when they thought it couldn't get any worse, it seemed to intensify. The sirens increased, and the sky appeared to be forever littered with menacing flying blobs of metal destined to destroy and maim. London and Liverpool were bombed night after night. Other cities across the United Kingdom too were getting heavily bombed, Coventry, Birmingham, Manchester. The South Wales cities were also targeted. Every day Louisa heard of bombings in Swansea, Cardiff and Newport. They knew that it would only be a matter of time before Pembroke docks would be hit and very soon they heard that it too had not escaped a cruel attack that left the area burning for days and nights on end.

In March, Louisa heard more distressing news from Cissy about Liverpool. In a letter, she told her about her flat mate the ambulance driver Eve who every day carried a haunted look of grief on her face as she had witnessed first hand the most shocking sights she hoped she would never see again. Yet each raid brought more fear and horrific casualties. The ambulances seemed to be on constant call, yet Eve and her colleagues as well as the Home Guard worked tirelessly every day to try to rescue people from blazing buildings, searching through rubble for signs of life.

Cissy feared for her friend's sanity. Very often the ambulances couldn't get through the rubble and so Eve and her colleagues had to search, by removing the rubble with their hands. The task was impeded by having very poor light because of the black outs. As well as getting cuts and abrasions from searching the rubble, the rescuers themselves were also in further danger. They could easily inadvertently stand on an unexploded bomb and cause another explosion. There was also the risk of loose timbers falling on top of them or rubble giving way underneath them. Eve had told Cissy that sometimes the stench of blood and dying bodies was so over powering that they had to cover their mouths to stop themselves from vomiting.

Cissy's explicitly vivid writing told Louisa that the gallant rescuers only had very small torches to carry and it took them a long time to find people. And as if that wasn't bad enough Eve had told her of the cries for help and of children crying but they couldn't reach them. 'It's heart breaking. Eve is a trained nurse and sometimes has to treat the injured there and then where they have been found. The hospitals are bursting at the seams with injured and dying people, and the government has had to set up emergency hospitals for the wounded. As fast as they rescue one person another one is dying.'

Cissy was worrying about the effect of it all was having on Eve, but she accepted that somebody has to do it. For her own part she looked after Eve's daughter so that Eve could continue with her aid work. Eve scarcely got any rest but she like many others continued to help to rescue people. Cissy finished the letter by hoping everyone was well and asked Louisa to pass on her regards to Fred and to anyone from whom she had news.

"Oh God." Louisa said. Tears ran down her face as she finished reading the letter. She had heard similar stories from the women who had been evacuated. There was one family whose story had remained in her head for days and she had decided she was going to do something positive to help. When she told her mother she was surprised that she supported her decision so quickly.

"I think that is a very kind gesture Lou." She said. "When are you going to do it?"

"There's no time like the present. Today I will suggest it to the committee members at the church hall and see what the reaction is."

The reaction was as Louisa guessed it would be. They all approved and applauded Louisa. She had decided to let out her whole house to the mother who had arrived from Liverpool with four children. She felt sorry for that poor woman whose baby had been killed when bricks and plaster from the gable end of the house had dropped on the shelter where they had been sheltering. Miraculously the rest of the family had all been spared except for sustaining a few scratches and being covered in dust. She had crawled out of the badly damaged Anderson shelter with her children, and the dead baby in her arms to see just the front of the house remaining, the windows smashed and the door flat on top of a pile of rubble. The baby had been asleep in the corner of the shelter where it had received the worst damage. Her husband was in the navy just like Fred.

When the mother who was called Joan, was told of Louisa's decision she was rewarded by a rare smile. "But where will you and Christine go?" she asked.

"I will move in with my parents. It's not far away. If you can wait a few days, I will move the things I need and will get the house ready. It's a two bedroomed house but it will be much better for you than sleeping on the floor in the church hall." Joan gripped Louisa's hands tightly in gratitude. So, very soon all was complete and the family moved in to Louisa's home and she and Christine moved in with her parents. Immediately Louisa wrote letters to Fred, Cissy, and Dorothy to tell them what she had done. Still the raids continued and still Liverpool and London took a blasting. Meanwhile the government introduced more rationing. This time jam and then in May it was cheese. During May another letter from Cissy told her that the bombing in Liverpool had practically raised the city to the ground. Bootle had also suffered under the Luftwaffe. She said that the main streets in the centre of Liverpool had been hit so hard the city was practically unrecognisable. Those roads leading from the Pier Head were the worst. Well they would be Louisa reflected, since they are closer to the targeted ports. Miraculously the Power station escaped the bombing.

Helplessly Louisa read on as Cissy described the chaos, 'there is so much disruption that transport has practically come to a standstill. Some people try to take their motor cars into the centre, even though they are not allowed to. They cause more chaos with their cars, especially when they have to try to turn around to return from where they came from. There's so much rubble it's bad enough trying to clear the roads for the ambulances to pass through. There is a lack of clean water, and scarcely any water to put out the fires. The fire fighters are doing their best with the fires but their equipment can't cope with the scale of the damage.

I'm so worried about the homeless people especially the children. I thought the government would find them alternative accommodation but when so many people are homeless I suppose it must be a difficult task. They don't want to stay in church halls in case they get bombed again, and in any case most of them are too frightened to sleep in the city, they say it is safer out on the outskirts. Some are even camping out in the fields though quite honestly they have little shelter from the weather and no protection from random bombs. There is destruction everywhere, yet the strange thing is that the statue of 'Auntie Lizzie' that Fred so lovingly has dubbed Queen Victoria is still upstanding! Ha ha!'

She ended the letter as usual with God bless and love to all. Louisa handed the letter to her mother to read. Later her father read it and commented that "It's strange that we haven't heard much about Liverpool on the news. We know that Coventry has been raised to the ground, and London is taking a pasting, but why doesn't Churchill tell us about Liverpool? Anyone living in Wrexham and the surrounding areas can see for themselves what is happening in that city."

"Probably Churchill doesn't want to give the nation more bad news. But what's the point of hiding it when the people of Liverpool are suffering?" Louisa blurted out. "Why aren't we stopping this massacre and destruction?"

"Well the spitfires have been doing a good job fighting in the air. And the squadron at Borras airfield are working hard now that they have made concrete runways. I heard that

342

some of them have come from RAF Cranage. Most of them are night fighters now that the daytime raids are fewer. They have managed to bring down a lot of planes. Those Boulton Paul Defiants are proving to be good night fighters. They have been fitted with some kind of radar too." William said. He tried hard to cheer up his daughter.

"Those fires that the home guard have been lighting on Minera Mountain and Esclusham have helped to disorientate the Luftwaffe, some of the bombs intended for Monsanto chemical works and Liverpool have been dropped on the mountain."

"It's not enough." Louisa retorted weakly. "We need to stop them before they even reach our coast line."

William sighed. "I know that love."

It was true that the day time raids were now less frequent. It was reported that the Germans had lost a lot of planes as they had been either shot down by machine guns from the ground or by the Spitfires which could fly low. A great deal of the Hurricanes too also participated in the dogfights. William had been told that Borras airfield was more superior to RAF Sealand because the land in Borras was dry and could sustain the weight of heavier machinery, whereas Sealand had been built on reclaimed land from the river Dee.

Right from the start of the war the locals in the outlying villages of Wrexham had got used to seeing the familiar sights of the uniformed men of the Flying Training school based in Borras. It had gained a good reputation except that initially it had no air traffic control. Sometimes on her way home from Pandy, Louisa would spot various aircraft such as Bristol Blenheims, Lockheed Hudsons and Westland

Lysanders. She learned to recognise them in the sky, telling herself that the information might be useful one day.

They were all cheerful much later towards the end of May when a letter from Dorothy arrived. Her mother opened the letter and smiled when she saw the blacked out lines. "It looks like our Dor has said too much in this letter. We will have to wait until she gets home." She passed it to her daughter to read. "Well at least she seems happy and she seems to be having a good time going to dances. I'm glad to see that she has more money to spend. She's bemoaning the fact that there is hardly anything in the shops to buy these days." Mary Ellen smiled. "It won't do her harm to save her money or put it into National Savings bonds." She sighed. "All the manufacturers are making materials for the war effort." Louisa stirred her weak tea thoughtfully. "I wonder what next will go on ration." Louisa was soon to find out. Eggs were also put on ration.

Meanwhile, Christine was growing fast and Louisa was worried that she may not be able to find the clothes she needed for her. Ironically, the answer came from the Germans. One morning, Louisa looked out across the field from her bedroom window and saw a huge swathe of material spread across the grass. The home guard and her father were removing the dead body of a German airman. There were bits of metal everywhere. Louisa's heart went out to the poor young airman even though he was the enemy. She contemplated for a few minutes then snatched up Christine and passed her to her mother who was in the kitchen. "Quick can you watch her, I am going to get some silk." She took the scissors from the drawer in the sideboard and dashed across the road. Before she could climb over the fence she was joined by her neighbours Ethel and Beryl who were both holding pairs of scissors. They both grinned at her. "Come to share the silk? There's plenty there to make petticoats and knickers for the little ones."

Before they could do anything though, they were sternly told to stay away until the dead body had been removed from the site. Patiently they waited by the fence and each woman hung their head in pity for the young man who had lost his life. Finally they were given the all clear by William and the women climbed into the field to cut at the much coveted parachute silk. Meanwhile William and the ARP began to search for any bits of metal or other equipment that may have been strewn on the ground.

Louisa efficiently cut away two large sheaves of silk. As she walked home with her bounty, two more neighbours started to climb the fence into the field. "Leave some for us they cried."

"There's plenty left." Louisa smiled at them, as she returned to the house. As she crossed the road she heard one of the ARP men tell them to take care not to trip on any pieces of metal that might be still on the grass.

Mary Ellen lifted Christine down off the chair where they had been sitting and got up to examine the material and together they spent the day washing and sewing. They managed to make several pairs of knickers and two petticoats for Christine and with what was left, Mary Ellen and Louisa each had a new camisole. Louisa kept some to make one for Dorothy. When William returned to the house his face wore a doleful expression. "That pilot was such a young man. What

345

a waste of life. So many of our men just like him have fallen too." He said sadly.

The following week end Dorothy came home. She had managed to get 48 hours leave. She swept in one Saturday afternoon and brought with her some butter and jam and tea. Mary Ellen pounced on them with glee. When William arrived home later she told them all about her work in Wolverhampton.

Louisa was surprised when Dorothy pulled out a packet of cigarettes. "Are you smoking now?"

Dorothy laughed. "Yes, but we dare not smoke at the factory, it could cause an explosion. Onc girl was caught smoking just outside the entrance and was put on a warning. They are very strict with us. We can't have hairclips in our hair either and we have to wear horrible hats to cover up every scrap of our hair."

Later when Mary Ellen and William had gone to bed, Dorothy confided in her sister that she had met a wonderful man. "His name is Frank and he is gorgeous looking."

"How come he hasn't joined up?" Louisa asked.

"He failed the medical test. Apparently he has a weak chest. He's not allowed to work with the cordite with us either. He works in the office next door. Mind you the smell is not much better in there."

"Do you mean to say that the cordite is toxic?

Dorothy nodded. "Everything we do is either toxic or highly inflammable. You have to be very careful. But I am careful Louie, so don't worry."

Before Dorothy left she gave Louisa two parcels to look after. There was one for Christine whose birthday would be in a few days' time on the fifth of June and another for their mother whose birthday was four days after Christine's.

So, on Christine's second birthday she opened a parcel to find a colouring book and some coloured pencils. Four days later Mary Ellen was surprised on her birthday to find a lace collar to put on her dress or jumper.

Throughout the summer, the government started calling up more men to the war including coal miners. Even though miners had been exempt from war, it seemed there was now a shortage of men and so skeleton shifts was formed in the collieries. As a result coal was to be rationed.

Louisa sighed. "In other words Hitler is killing all our men so now we have to get more from the coal mines."

"Let's hope we have warm weather and won't need coal." William said lightly. He had just finished his breakfast and was putting on his coat to go to work when there was a knock on the door. He turned around to open it and then stood staring at the telegram he had been handed by the telegraph man. Louisa came to stand behind him and saw it was addressed to her. It was edged in black. "Oh no, no it can't be Fred." She moaned. She tore open the telegram her eyes misting over so that the words were blurred. But she saw the words she knew would be there. 'Frederick Cartlidge lost at sea.' presumed dead."

Her father tried to console her though he knew that there were no words to compensate for loss of life. Mary Ellen came to hug her daughter, and William took Christine outside. The little girl was oblivious to everything. Louisa didn't know how to get through the rest of the day. She went upstairs and lay on the bed sobbing. Every now and again her mother went to check on her.

The next day Louisa got up early and went downstairs. She felt dreadful. Her parents looked at her anxiously but said nothing. They knew there was nothing they could do or say to bring Fred back. When a knock came to the door they all froze. Surely not another telegram. Their immediate thoughts were for Arthur or Harry. Steeling himself, William got up to go to the door, but the door opened and a bedraggled sailor stood in the doorway. He shook William's hand as he stared at him bewildered, then the sailor's gaze caught sight of Louisa sitting with her head in her hands. "Lou?" He called. She looked up at the sound of his voice, and then flew out of the chair, her face wreathed in smiles. "Fred, Fred. I thought you were dead."

It was now Fred's turn to look bewildered. He looked from Mary Ellen to William and to Louisa again who were now all smiling. The gloom had been lifted from their faces. Quickly they explained. Louisa showed him the telegram and he then understood the confusion. He stared at it for a long time and his eyes glimmered wet with emotion before saying "So many men were lost from that ship and I have two weeks survivors leave."

Louisa hugged him as if she would never let him go again. Gently he dried her eyes with the back of his hand then presently when Louisa was comforted, he went to get washed, shaved and changed. Feeling happier by the minute both Louisa and Mary Ellen rustled up a meal of sausages and dried bread for Fred and William. Later, William went to work muttering about a tractor that Mr. Lawrence his employer had bought for the farm. He loved his shire horses and didn't want to learn how to handle a tractor. Now that his son-in-law had returned unharmed he could now start worrying again about the new-fangled machinery on the farm.

After William had gone, Fred now washed and shaved, suggested he and Louisa take Christine for a walk to the Bluebell wood. They examined the blackberry bushes and were able to pick one or two early ones, though most of them were unripe. "We'll be able to make jam with these next month. We have been saving our sugar ration." Louisa said. "The government have started encouraging people to go on cookery classes to learn how to cook with our rations, but we reckon we can manage to invent our own recipes."

"Have you tried that dried egg and dried milk yet?" Fred asked. "It's horrible. The food isn't too bad in Freetown, but when we transfer to other ships it isn't so good."

"The dried stuff is alright for baking and making sauces. Our fruit and vegetable patch has done well this year, so we aren't doing too badly. Father brings us stuff from Stansty too. We get a lot of potatoes and sometimes a bit of extra bacon. I'm not sure if he is supposed to but I am not asking questions."

On the way back to Pandy they saw Ethel one of the neighbours who remembered Fred. "Good to see you home Fred. Are you coming to the charity event next week in Garden village? It's War Weapons week. We lost a lot in Dunkirk you know. The government wants money to build Spitfires and Hurricanes now, since the Americans are sending us ships." Fred gazed at Ethel slightly amused. She was a very small young woman with light wispy hair that always seemed to look blown about even when there was no wind. Just then she had a look of fierce determination on her face. He transferred his glance from her to check with his wife, who was nodding her head, then said "I'm sure we would want to support that." And for confirmation Louisa smiled. "Yes Ethel we will be there." For the rest of the day Louisa could not stop smiling. It was a dramatic change in her emotions. The day before she could not stop crying. She realised how lucky she was to get her husband back in one piece.

On the day of the charity event, they set off after their midday meal. It was only a mile and a half to Garden Village and a pleasant walk across the fields from Pandy. It was nice to see the bunting, and everyone determined to have a good time and raise money for the war effort. Hitler's attempt to invade Britain had been thwarted and everyone was grateful to the armed services. The only regret was that now Russia was Hitler's target. As a result of Stalin's change of sides, Russia was now being bombed mercilessly by Hitler's Luftwaffe. There hadn't been any day time raids passing over North Wales for a while, and when two aeroplanes flew low down as they circled the village hall no-one panicked. Though all those people standing outside of the hall, looked on with pride at the pair of spitfires. "They are trainee pilots I expect." Louisa said. They are either from Borras or the RAF place near Oswestry. I think it's called RAF Rednal."

Fred nodded. "Yes I have heard of it. The planes have to practice in pairs and get as low as possible so that they can bomb the enemy from varying heights. It's quite a skill. The trouble is when they are at a low altitude the visibility is impaired." They looked up to the sky to watch the Spitfires come down again flying just about six feet to clear the hedges. Fred looked impressed. "That is known as hedge hopping."

"Hedge hopping." Christine repeated. She laughed and repeated it again. They made their way to the refreshments stall and bought some home-made lemonade. It was very weak and not very sweet. "Well at least it is wet." Fred grimaced.

"I think I will stick to water." Louisa replied grinning.

Before the end of Fred's leave, they went to their own home to see the family who were living in their house. Fred was keen to meet the occupants of his house and he also wanted to check on his motorbike too. They chatted for a while to Joan about Liverpool and both of them looked sad to talk about the devastation of their home town. Previously Louisa had shown Fred the letters she had received from Cissy and he had been shocked to hear of how badly the city had been bombed. He knew that Liverpool docks would be a target for the Luftwaffe but had not been prepared to hear about the devastation and merciless killing of civilians.

Meanwhile, Louisa was pleased to see that at least Joan's children looked happier than the last time she saw them. Despite her grief over the loss of her baby and her home, Joan was looking after them properly and she was obviously keeping the house clean too. Before they left they made arrangements for Fred to visit again so that he could have a bath before he returned to his ship.

351

Eventually the two weeks survivor's leave soon ended and again Louisa waved goodbye to Fred from the railway station. She and Christine waved and waved and ran down the platform until the train was out of sight.

The rest of that summer seemed to get gloomier as news of the war seemed to get more and more terrible. As summer turned to autumn, Louisa, Dot and her mother planned on making use of all the fruit growing wild in the countryside. They and several of their neighbours went blackberry picking together with the intention of making as much jam as they could. William brought a bag of windfall apples from Stansty farm and they peeled the best of them to help make the jam go further and in any case they needed the pectin to make it set.

At the end of September Harry came home. He had only forty eight hours leave and as soon as he came home it was almost time for him to go away again. Looking beyond his tired war weary face, Louisa saw reflected, the same expression she had witnessed in both Arthur's and Fred's faces. Each of those men wore a countenance that exhibited relief and gladness to be home, yet tinged with a fear and dread that soon they would have to return to unimaginably distressing scenes of warfare. She guessed that both her husband and her brothers had kept back from the family information too terrible to talk about.

Harry was able to tell them all that he would be posted to the Pacific islands but could say nothing else. And so all too soon he had to go away again. A month later Arthur came home and he too had just forty eight hours. He managed to take Gladys to the cinema before he returned to his unit.

They went to see *"Pride and Prejudice."* He had grumbled that it wasn't his type of film but Gladys wanted to see it. Louisa had laughed. "You never know you might enjoy it. Some of your favourite actresses are in it." Arthur had shrugged.

Louisa had no opportunity to ask him how he enjoyed the film. The next day he called for just five minutes to say goodbye as he had to get back to his unit. He hinted that he too, just like Harry would be going to the South Pacific.

As the days became shorter they began to think of Christmas. Mary Ellen was thinking of ideas to make plum pudding using the jam they had made if they couldn't get enough dried fruit. Louisa decided to give up tea drinking for two days. Eventually she made a strong pot of tea and poured the water from the tea leaves over the meagre amount of dried fruit they got to plump it up. Rationing was getting tighter. Together they planned how to spend their points to make the most of their resources. They decided to buy mincemeat so that they could make mince pies and also planned to indulge in some cheese and canned salmon in case they had no meat for Christmas dinner. Though they were fairly certain William would be given a chicken for Christmas they made sure they had something in the larder just in case. And as a standby they had sausages or could make a rabbit pie.

One Sunday evening on seventh December they heard on the wireless the horrific news that Japan had attacked Pearl Harbour in the United States. There had been no warning. Four of America's battleships had been destroyed with men aboard and four more had been badly damaged. It was reported that over two thousand Americans had been killed.

The Japanese had also bombed the USA's aircraft destroying almost two hundred planes.

"Good God!" William shouted in dismay. Both Mary Ellen and Louisa just looked at each other in rising fear. The next day they were informed that President Roosevelt had declared that America was at war with Japan. The day after that, the Japanese sank two of Britain's biggest warships the HMS Repulse and HMS Prince of Wales.

Soon after this horrific news, Britain was informed that the United States of America had become fully engaged in the war as Britain's ally. Everyone in Britain thought that now the USA was on their side, the war would be over by Christmas.

Louisa wanted to get some kind of a toy for Christine for Christmas, but there was hardly anything in the shops, as no-one was manufacturing them. What was available was too expensive or badly made. In the end William went into the garden and dismantled the old mangle that he had been thinking of chopping up for firewood. After several days of chopping, sawing and shaping and drilling pieces of wood from the old mangle rollers he managed to make a puppet. He screwed some hooks into the wood and then threaded string through the hooks and managed to make moving limbs. These could be drawn up and down by pulling the string from the top of the puppet's head. Stepping back to admire his handiwork he then painted a roguish mouth and eyes on it with some black paint. A thin ring of paint around one eye became a patch. When he had finished both he and his wife grinned at the wooden pirate. Mary Ellen knitted a striped jumper to dress it with and made a paper hat out of newspapers. Satisfied with her father's creation, Louisa decided on buying a practical gift. She took Christine to the shoe shop and spent her clothes coupons on buying the little girl a pair of shoes. Dorothy had thoughtfully sent her a National Savings book with some saving stamps.

It was a sombre Christmas. Gladys called with Brian and Maureen before going to her mother's house in the next street. Dot called with Gordon and Malcolm and they were treated to a mince pie each to eat on the way home. When they had gone they indulged themselves in a strong cup of tea before they went to bed.

Chapter Twenty Three

1942

The year didn't start very well, especially for Dot. She had received a letter in January from Harry which she presumed was from somewhere in the Pacific. Despite the letter with holes in it, she guessed where he might be from how he had worded the letter using their private code. This plus information on the wireless and the newspapers gave her an inkling that Malaysia would be his location. However the letter she received at the end of February left her brokenhearted. Harry had been taken a prisoner of war by the Japanese.

When Dot came to Pandy to tell them the bad news Mary Ellen and Louisa sat still in stunned silence. They did not know what to say or what to think. After they had shed their tears, the three of them strengthened their resolve to do what ever they could to help the war effort.

Upon hearing the news about his son that evening, William went outside into the garden and stayed there a long time in the dark before returning into the house to prepare for bed. Mary Ellen went out to him and together they came back into the house, their eyes downcast. William's face was hard and he looked very sad.

Rumours began to fly that the government had mishandled the affair in Malaysia, and that the army had been left with no air cover from the RAF whilst the Japanese had overwhelmingly outnumbered the allies. The family began to fear for Arthur too. However a letter to Gladys a few days later re-assured them he was safe. Trying hard to read through the black lines and make sense of the holes and Arthur's style of writing, they managed to work out that he too had been in Malaysia, but they assumed in a different part. The fact that he was safe and able to write led the family to believe that somehow he and some of his comrades had managed to escape being taken prisoner.

"Well thank God for that." Mary Ellen said when Gladys showed her the letter. "But where is he now?"

Gladys shook her head. "I don't know. But at least he and Harry are alive!"

Early in the spring the Women's Voluntary Service received a special consignment of wool from the government. They had been asked to knit sea boot socks for the Navy. Having a special interest in the Navy because of Fred away at sea, Louisa and her mother and Dot set about eagerly to do some knitting. Together they studied the pattern, which they had to follow exactly in order to be passed by a vigilant committee on the WVS.

"It isn't an easy pattern to follow." Mary Ellen commented. Her daughter and daughter in law nodded their head in agreement. They daren't speak as each had to concentrate very hard especially when they had to turn the heel on the socks.

"I would like to make a special pair for Fred but I don't suppose I can keep any if all the wool is accounted for." Louisa said.

"It's a very special type of wool. I doubt we would be able to buy it anywhere. It's difficult to get wool anyway these days." Mary Ellen remarked.

"Make do and mend." Dot sighed. She put her hand out to feel the yarn. "I've got an old jumper that is made of something like this yarn. Maybe if we unravelled it we could knit it in to socks for Fred." She offered kindly.

"But won't you need the jumper?" Louisa asked.

Dot shrugged. "I tore one of the sleeves when I was walking down bluebell lane in the black out, it got caught on the brambles. I stepped back too far when I heard a truck coming back and got tangled in the hedge. I meant to mend it, but haven't got round to it. I don't wear it much." It's warm, but I can easily spare it. Fortunately I have knitted plenty of jumpers over the years and there is still plenty of wear in them. I can easily spare it. I will bring it next time I visit."

Knitting seemed to be the main occupation for Louisa, Dot and Mary Ellen during the coming months. All three were competent knitters, and it turned out that the WVS valued their efforts.

"Martha at the WVS told me that we three are amongst the best knitters in Wrexham." Louisa told her mother and sister in law proudly one spring afternoon.

"When did she tell you that?" Mary Ellen looked up with a pleased smile at the compliment.

"Yesterday at the *Warships Week* committee meeting."

"Have they decided which warship we are adopting?" Dot asked. "Or does all the money raised go to the same kitty?"

Louisa sighed. "I don't know. I think we will be supporting the adopted ships that Liverpool, Birkenhead and Wallasey have agreed upon. I don't suppose it matters, if it is all for the war effort."

Mary Ellen snorted. "Don't say that to the WVS. They are very competitive you know. Some areas have raised more than others." She began to knit faster as she spoke, as if that would make the coffers fill with money for ammunition.

"That reminds me. Martha asked me if you have any old aluminium saucepans you don't want." Louisa smiled at her mother. "Apparently they are going to melt them down to make aeroplanes."

Mary Ellen stared at her daughter as if she had gone out of her mind. "They will need a lot of saucepans to do that." She chuckled. "I suppose I can spare one. I've got one that's getting quite thin. Whatever will they think of next?"

"Garden railings are needed too. So I have heard." Dot said.

A few days later it was decided that Wrexham would adopt HMS Veteran for War Ships week.

"It's a destroyer." Louisa told her mother. Mary Ellen shrugged and carried on knitting.

At the end of May, Louisa received two letters. One was from Fred to say that his ship had docked in Chatham a few days earlier and was in UK on sick leave. He had been injured and needed surgery on his ears at Gillingham hospital so would be in hospital for a few days. Louisa didn't know whether to laugh or cry.

"Look on the bright side, he's alive and able to write to you." Her father said when she told him that evening. "Send him a telegram to say you will visit him at the hospital. I trust you are going to see him."

"Of course. I am going tomorrow." She sighed. "I have some bad news to give him about his brother Alf. It seems he is dying of bowel cancer. Cissy told me in the letter I got this morning along with the one from Fred."

The next day, Louisa sent a telegram to Fred to say she was on her way and then got a train to Chatham. It was a long journey and as usual the train was packed with military men and women. When she changed at Crewe she managed to get a seat as far as London. She lost some valuable time in London trying to find the right platform and almost missed the connection, but a young woman in uniform managed to help her and together they sat in the luggage room on some crates. The young woman was also headed for Chatham and she helped Louisa find a bus stop to get to Gillingham hospital.

Tears ran down her face when she eventually found Fred. She hugged him as if she would never let him go. He had already received surgery and his head was bandaged. Despite being slightly groggy he managed to sit up and smile at his wife. She decided not to tell him about Alf until the next day. Upon the advice of the hospital staff she managed to find a bed and breakfast place to spend the night. When she went to see Fred the next day he was much more cheerful and she hated having to tell him the news about Alf. However, it seemed he already knew. He had received a letter from Jimmy a few days earlier telling him about Alf's health problems.

"I know he hasn't been well for a while." Fred said quietly.

A few days later Fred was allowed to travel home to Wrexham, but was to rest and not to allow water to get in his ears. On the way Fred told Louie how he had spent the last twelve months on various ships on the Atlantic. Louisa knew

360

that Fred had frequently been assigned to various convoys. He had left Freetown in Sierra Leone several times to escort ships to Stranraer protecting the important supply route for the allies of all kinds of goods. She also learned that his ships had to escort other ships and troops from Australia, India and South Africa onwards to Gibraltar as well as the United Kingdom. Louisa was immensely proud of him but also very worried. They held hands tightly on the train. They had been lucky to get two seats together as far as London. They had to whisper as the train was packed with service men and women, some of them swayed and fell on them every so often as those standing up lost balance on the moving train.

Fred whispered to her that many ships had been torpedoed in the waters off West Africa—and off Freetown in particular—by German and Italian submarines lying in wait for passing convoys. "Our ship was hit, but we were lucky it didn't sink. The Ship's surgeon saved my ears. I was close to the main blast and that is how it burst my ear drums."

Tears welled in Louisa's eyes and she squeezed her husband's hand tightly. When they got to London they were not so lucky with seats and they found themselves propped up against crates and baggage in the luggage carriage all the way to Crewe. As before, the train was crowded and service men and women stood around engaging in chat and generally they were all in good humour. Some shared their cigarettes and Fred gratefully took one. He refused at first but the young soldier was in earnest and kept waving the box of cigarettes at Fred. "I've got plenty. I lost my mate just a couple of days ago and before he died he handed me his ciggies. It only seems right to share them."

At Crewe they bought cups of tea and sandwiches from the WVS mobile canteen and managed to find a quiet corner whilst waiting for their connection. Fred looked tired, and Louisa knew that he was worrying about his brother. He perked up again when they eventually reached Pandy station. They had managed to get the last train before the station closed, as not all the trains stopped in Pandy after six o clock. When they arrived home, Fred livened up a bit when he saw Mary Ellen but was disappointed that once again Christine had forgotten who he was. However her curiosity overcame her and after an hour she started chattering to Fred. She was now approaching her third birthday, and Fred was pleased to be able to participate in the meagre celebrations they could make for her. Using some old newspapers he managed to make a collection of paper hats plus an aeroplane and a ship for his daughter to play with. He showed her how to fold the paper and rip pieces off to make a ring of dancing men and women. It was a very cheap way of making playthings, but these pleased Christine and the gifts marked her birthday. Louisa and Mary Ellen had saved their sugar rations to make cakes and had used up their last stock of white flour.

"We can cut up the sausages into cocktail size and we'll just have to use a mixture of white bread and the wheat bread for our sandwiches." Louisa said. "It's not so bad once you get used to it. Apparently it has a lot of fibre. Very soon we won't be able to have as much white bread, so we may as well get used to it. The Government have introduced the National Loaf."

Fred nodded. "Yes the import of wheat plus other food stuff from abroad is one of the reasons I am sailing back and to across the Atlantic. Protecting the merchant ships."

Gladys brought Brian and Maureen to the birthday tea party and Dot brought Malcolm and Gordon. So whilst the children ran around outside in the garden, wearing their paper hats, the adults sat on the wooden bench at the top of the garden to watch them. It was a beautiful summer day and for the first time in almost two weeks Fred seemed to be able to relax. He still woke up in the night muttering things, and Louisa knew he was reliving some dreadful memory. He had told her that prior to the ship explosion which had caused his injury, he had been two months earlier in another ship which had been torpedoed and blasted to bits. He was one of the lucky survivors. She could only imagine how horrendous it would have been for him to be on a ship so badly torpedoed that it had torn the vessel apart. She knew he was devastated that some of his mates had drowned when the blast had thrown them all into the sea. She sighed. In a few days' time he would have to return to Gillingham hospital for a check up and then he would rejoin another ship to go back overseas.

As they sat watching the children play, Gladys rummaged in her handbag and produced a letter which she handed to Fred. "There's a message in there for you from Arthur. She pointed to the penultimate paragraph of the letter. I hope you can make it out, the letter got crumpled in my bag. Fred took the letter and read it out. "*Tell Fred to go to blank and pick up my blank. It's ready for you, they are expecting you.*" Fred grinned.

"Do you know what he is talking about?" Gladys smiled. "It's not his suit is it?"

"No, I don't think a suit would be censored. He grinned. "It's a very nice offer of the use of his car. Has he left it at Clark's Garage?"

Gladys nodded. "Yes he registered his ration book with them being an ex employee so he has probably managed to get some fuel for you to use."

Louisa laughed. "That's generous of him. Good old Arthur."

"Perhaps he wants me to take you all out for a run." Fred said.

"That would be nice!" Louisa and Gladys said together.

"Where shall we go?" Fred asked. He smiled at his wife's excitement, then made a suggestion.

"I know where we can go. Let's go and see Nancy in Ellesmere. We can take the children to the mere. I will have to be careful not to get water in my ears though."

"What about mother? Do you think we can squeeze her in too?"

"We can but try." Fred grinned. He looked happier today than he had been for a while and Louisa was grateful to her brother for this gift that meant so much to them all.

The next day the sun was shining and they set off to Ellesmere. Nancy and Alf's farm cottage was surrounded by woodland and just a mile away from the Mere. The cottage was capacious and so it was no surprise to see two American soldiers billeted there. Fred was in his naval uniform and they shook hands. Both soldiers were on their way out when the little group arrived, so the door was already open with

364

Nancy standing on the doorstep. Her face beamed in smiles as she saw her sister and several members of the family in front of her. "Come in, come in, let me put the kettle on."

They all trooped in behind her and the children, having slept in the car happily ran out into the garden to play. Very soon they were helping themselves to the peas growing on rows upon rows of canes.

"It's good to see you Fred. I have been worrying about you and of course Arthur and poor Harry. Is there any news of him?"

They all shook their head sadly, then stared in wonder at the array of cakes and biscuits that Nancy put in front of them with a tray of tea. She caught their glances and laughed. "I'm not short of food. The Americans keep me well supplied. I don't know what I would have done without them."

"How long have they been staying with you?" Mary Ellen asked. She helped herself with glee to a chocolate biscuit and bit into it with great pleasure.

"About three months. Those two you saw just now are new, the others left - they don't stay long because they get posted away." She sighed. "I've had up to five here at a time during the last few months, some of them injured and convalescing. The hospital at Oteley gets overcrowded, and as soon as they are able to, we need to move them on to make their beds ready for others badly wounded. In fact today is the day when I stay at home to catch up with things here, normally I am helping at the hospital and you would not have found me at home." She took a sip of her tea, "though Pat would have been here. She helps out too during the school holidays, but I don't like her spending all her time there."

Just then the three children ran into the house and Nancy gave them a glass of milk and a biscuit. They each stared at their biscuit and turned it over in their hands before they ate it. Their parents looked on indulgently. Once they finished their snack they ran outside again.

"And how are you Gladys?" Nancy asked. "Do you know what regiment Arthur is with?"

"He is not in the original battalion from Wales, and I think he said he was being transferred to another regiment, but I'm not sure. Things change and you have to be so careful what you say." She lowered her voice and looked around her guiltily.

Fred nodded. "Careless talk costs lives. It's best not to say anything even if you do know especially in front of the little ones. They repeat things without realizing what they are saying."

"Talking of the children, shall we walk them down to the mere? It's such a beautiful day?" Louisa said.

"You three go and take the children, I will stay here and chat to Nancy." Mary Ellen said. "It's not very often I get the chance to see her."

On their way down the narrow lane towards the mere, an open truck full of G.I.'s passed them. Upon seeing Fred in his uniform they saluted him and promptly threw out oranges, apples, tinned peanuts and jam. They laughed and drove off leaving the three adults ecstatically gathering up the gifts of food.

"That was kind." Louisa said. "I haven't seen oranges for a very long time. She held up three in her arms. "We will have to share these things out with mother." Gladys nodded. She had four apples, whilst Fred had picked up the nuts and jam.

"History repeats itself." Fred said. "When I was little and out walking with my two eldest brothers towards the end of the Great War, a similar thing happened. American soldiers went past and from the centre of their column a large box of chocolates was thrown out to land at my feet, followed by a Jaffa orange and a few coins."

"What a coincidence." Louisa said. "And what a lucky thing to happen to you twice."

When they got to the mere they found a quiet spot and hid their American gifts under a cardigan. Then they encouraged the children to take their socks and shoes off and all of them holding hands they formed a line to paddle in the water. Fred and Louisa smiled at each other enjoying the simplicity of an impromptu family outing. Louisa thought how good it was to hear them laugh and shriek as the cold water rippled over their toes.

Later when they arrived back at Nancy's they found that Pat and Alf had returned and Alf shook Fred's hand warmly. "Good to see you Fred." He said to him gruffly. Mary Ellen was bemused by the American food gifts and wanted to share them with Nancy, but she wouldn't hear of it. "We have plenty. We even have fizzy drinks. I don't like it but Pat drinks it." She winked at her sister, "don't worry about us, we don't go short of anything." She bustled into the large kitchen to make them some more tea before they left. And they all exclaimed how nice and strong it tasted. Nancy laughed. "Enjoy it whilst you can I say."

Alf took Fred's arm before they left. "Take care of yourself," he said. The others hugged each other goodbye before piling themselves back into the car to drive home. The children soon fell asleep on the way home and they had a peaceful journey arriving home before dusk.

Three days before he was about to leave for Chatham, Fred and Louisa sat with her parents around the wireless at nine o clock to hear of news about the battle in the Pacific. Apparently the Americans had managed to destroy four Japanese carriers and a cruiser. This was later referred to as the Battle of the Midway. The next day they heard that British forces had gained ground in North Africa.

"I wonder if Arthur is there." William said. "We've heard nothing from him for a long time." He looked at Fred. "Have you heard anything from your brothers lately?"

"I haven't heard from Tom nor Edward, but I know Bob is in the Royal Artillery somewhere in Africa. That's all I know. I have his address and have written to him but I don't know how easy it is for him to get his mail."

William shook his head sadly and poked the fire with his stick. His action was so vicious, they all looked at him surprised. He caught their stare and grimaced. "Damn Hitler."

Just as they started to put the black out boards up, the door opened and Dorothy rushed into the room. "Fred. It's you. It's really you." She rushed into his arms saying "it's so good to see you."

Over her head which was covered up in a head scarf, Fred met the eyes of a complete stranger. Dorothy turned around to pull the man closer into the room and then closed the door. "This is Frank. Mother do you think he could sleep on the couch please? We have to go back to work tomorrow. I just wanted to see Fred before he goes back."

All this came out in a jumble of excited sentences, but Mary Ellen though taken aback, managed to keep her composure upon seeing a strange man in her kitchen. She agreed to find some blankets for the young man and went upstairs to get them. William and Fred shook the young man's hand and tried to make him welcome. Louisa went in to the small washroom cum kitchen to put on the kettle to make some tea. Dorothy squeezed in behind her sister and closed the door. "What do you think of him Louie? Isn't he handsome?" she whispered.

Louisa laughed. "Yes he is very handsome. He is very blonde and blue eyed isn't he? Though he looks terribly thin. Is he hungry? We could make some sausage sandwiches."

Dorothy shook her head. "We got something at the station. We were lucky to get here. I thought it might be much later than this. We managed to get a lift with the munitions workers bus as far as Chester, then we walked a bit and then managed to get a bus as far as the smithy pond. We walked from there."

Louisa took the tray of tea back into the scullery and they sat down to discuss the latest news. Frank produced a whisky bottle which was three quarters of the way full. He shared it out with everyone.

"So how did you manage to get this whisky?" William asked. He looked at the young man suspiciously.

Frank laughed. "My father won it in a raffle for 'War weapons week.' He gave it to me for my 21st birthday a month ago. As you can see it is not full, because I opened it to share it with him and my mother to celebrate. I've been saving it for another special occasion." He gazed adoringly at Dorothy, and Louisa wondered if Frank and her sister were in love. She was right, because after the first sip Dorothy couldn't hold back any longer and announced. "Frank and I are engaged."

"What?" Mary Ellen cried. William looked stunned. He drank back his whisky as if to give him time to think, then coughed. Before her parents could say any more Louisa congratulated them. Fred stood up and shook Frank's hand. William, still bewildered also shook his hand.

"This is very sudden." Mary Ellen said. She glared at her daughter.

"I know, but I hope you will give us your blessing mother." Dorothy hugged her mother before she could say anything else.

"We are going to wait until after the war is over." Frank assured William and Mary Ellen.

"The war. This wretched war." Fred said.

"Let's hope it is over soon." Mary Ellen said. The couple looked so happy she didn't want to spoil things. So she took it upon herself to find out about his background. He was good humoured about it and whilst William and Mary Ellen plied him with questions, Louisa and Fred listened and sipped whisky. It appeared that Frank's family were from

370

Wolverhampton, his father was a sergeant in the local police, and his mother volunteered in the WVS. Frank's sister Polly also worked in munitions alongside Dorothy. After several hours Mary Ellen and William appeared satisfied with their future son-in-law and Mary Ellen went to make up a bed in the back parlour. Meanwhile Dorothy snuggled down with Christine in the bedroom she had previously occupied.

All of them got up early the next day as Dorothy and Frank had to organize transport to get back to Wolverhampton. Louisa and Fred walked with them to Pandy railway station. Fred carried Christine in his arms.

"This line is very busy these days taking troops to various places. We've seen a lot of locomotives up and down too." Louisa said as they walked down the steps to the platform.

"I expect that will be a treat for the train spotters." Frank grinned.

Fortunately there wasn't a block on the line and Dorothy and Frank squeezed themselves on to the train and waved goodbye.

On the way home, Fred suggested that they go and see a film at the cinema. "The government is actually encouraging cinema going now. They want us to watch all their propaganda."

"Are you sure your ears will be alright and you will be able to cope with the noise?"

He kissed her. "Of course. It won't be too loud. And if it is, well we will just have to leave. Do you think your mother will look after Christine for us?"

"I'm sure she will."

Whilst Fred looked in the *Wrexham Leader* to see what was on, Louisa checked with Mary Ellen that she would babysit. Once settled they set off for the early evening showing so that they would be home before the blackout. They arrived home from the cinema just as William was getting the black out boards ready for the windows. "Did you have a good time?" he asked them. "What film did you see?

"It was a thriller called *Suspicion*, plus the usual propaganda newsreel from the Ministry of Information." Louisa answered. She yawned as she watched her husband help William put the boards up.

"I've been meaning to ask you, why are you using boards and not the black out curtains?" Fred said.

William laughed. "Two reasons. It's easier than pinning the blackouts to the other curtains, and secondly your wife has found uses for the black material for sewing various garments. It's not on ration you see."

Louisa grinned. "For example this blouse. I embroidered the collar and put white buttons on it to brighten it up." She removed her cardigan to parade her short sleeved blouse.

"Very resourceful." Fred agreed. He smiled at his wife.

"As resourceful as borrowing that suit of Arthur's from the Fifty shilling shop." She grinned again at him as she stared at Fred's clothes.

"It's a good arrangement. As long as he is not on leave when I am." He answered her good humouredly.

The next day they were not as jovial as they said goodbye on Wrexham railway station. The platform was heaving with people in uniform and Fred knew it would be difficult to get a seat on the train. Louisa had wanted to go with him to Chatham, but he wouldn't hear of it.

"It will be too crowded. Better to let those people who need to be on the train get a chance to sit down, or lean on something."

"Don't forget to write and tell me what the doctor says about your ears." She said. He kissed her one last time and then got on the train, and she waved goodbye like many other tearful wives and sweethearts on the platform.

A few days later Louisa received a letter from Fred to say that the doctor at Gillingham hospital was pleased with his progress but he had been pronounced unfit enough yet to go overseas. He was to report for duty on HMS Pembroke at the Royal Naval Base for shore duties. Meanwhile he was being billeted in Staines as he would be based for a while in Chatham. It meant travelling every day to get to work but at least he had a proper bed! He had more appointments at the hospital before he would be at sea again. This would be temporary until he was fit to serve abroad. He didn't know what ship he would be on but guessed he would continue to be on a battle ship or destroyer that formed part of a convoy. Louisa realised he meant Sierra Leone and her stomach lurched at the thought of him returning to the Atlantic. He advised Louisa not to try to travel down to see him as he would not be able to see her, and the travelling to and fro from Staines took up a lot of time.

Louisa was frustrated at learning this news. She felt she could at least travel down to stay the night with him before he was posted away again.

Her mother advised her against it too. "You would only be a distraction to him and he would not be able to give you his full attention!

Louisa sighed. She knew her mother was right. A month later she wrote to tell her husband that she was pregnant with their second child.

Fred was ecstatic upon hearing the news that he was to be a father again. He wrote back promptly sending his love and to look after herself. Then unexpectedly in August he wrote to her again to say he was entitled to another seven days sick leave and that he was coming home to Wrexham. "It looks like I will be borrowing Arthur's suit again." He joked.

Louisa was overjoyed to see her husband again and that he appeared to be a little healthier than the last time she saw him. He was still having problems with his ears though.

"Yes I feel a lot better, though always hungry. Like everybody else I suppose. At least these berries aren't rationed." He reached out for another blackberry. They had gone for a walk along bluebell lane for the very purpose of picking blackberries.

"The good thing about these blackberries, is that there seems to be enough to supply the whole village, because they seem to ripen different days at a time, so if you plan it properly there is always enough." Louisa said stretching out to get some larger ones she had seen. She put them in to the little basket that Christine was carrying. Her face was covered in juice and her hands were sticky too.

"So will you make a pie as well as jam?" Fred asked. "I suppose it will be difficult to get white flour for the pastry."

"It will be easier to make a summer pudding with the National loaf, or I could make a bread and butter pudding with that dried egg stuff, it isn't too bad in cooking." She straightened her back and he stood behind her with his arm around her waist. They both gazed at the masses of blackberry brambles covering the hedgerows.

"It's hard to imagine that all this covers the coal mines where people lost their lives." Louisa said.

"Yes and some of those who survived have been unlucky to have been killed in this awful war."

Later that day they walked across to their own house to see Joan and to use the bathroom facilities. Louisa took a change of clothing for Christine so she could be bathed too. Since Joan had been living in Louisa and Fred's house she had helped where she could with the WVS as she was so grateful of their support when she had been bombed out of Liverpool. She told them she would be helping out at the Salvation Army fundraising ball the following Friday. She was going to play the piano.

"I used to play a lot." She said, but of course the piano and most of everything I owned was lost during the bombing," She choked back some tears before continuing. "But the children's school in Acton have kindly let me practice on the one in their hall, so I go there during meal times and play a few melodies. When it is raining the children enjoy listening, and the volunteers from the ARP sometimes call in to have a sing song. They use it as a meeting place when the children are on holiday. I don't know what I would have done without the kind people of Wrexham and the WVS as well as the Salvation Army. And you Louisa have been especially kind."

Fred squeezed Louisa's hand and she smiled at him before saying. "We have to help each other. It's the only way we can get through these terrible times." She searched in her shopping bag for some clothes that Christine had grown out of. "I think these will fit your little one. I should really take them to the WVS but I know you need them too." She caught sight of the threadbare clothes that three year old Brenda was wearing. The little girl was playing with Christine who only a few months older, was confidently leading the younger girl by the hand as they walked around the room. Louisa wasn't sure how to tell Joan that she was pregnant, but knew that eventually she would have to know so she tried to break the news to her gently. "And very soon I will be needing baby clothes again."

Joan glanced at Louisa's stomach. "You mean you are pregnant?" She smiled at Louisa. "Congratulations." Her brave smile diminished as a cloud of sorrow veiled her face. Louisa put her arm around her to comfort her. She knew Joan was still grieving for her lost baby. Tactfully Fred slipped upstairs to use the bathroom. Later they went outside to look at Fred's motorbike and miraculously it roared into life. He looked at the fuel gauge and sighed wistfully. "Well we won't be going anywhere now that petrol is scarce, but at least it fires up".

Very soon Fred's leave came to an end and Louisa found herself again waving goodbye to Fred on the railway station. Two days letter she got a letter to say that he had reported to HMS Pembroke and was told he would still be based on shore at Staines, as he was still not medically fit to serve at sea.

At the end of September the WVS were upset to hear that their adopted war ship HMS Veteran had been sunk.

"Well that means we will have to raise funds to build another ship." Mary Ellen said determinedly. She got out her knitting and picked up her needles and worked them so ferociously Louisa thought that the needles would catch fire.

Early in October Fred wrote to say that he would be leaving Chatham soon to go to sea again. She guessed from their secret code that he was on his way to Sierra Leone. Fred had been away a few weeks away at sea when Louisa received a letter from Cissy to say that her brother Alf had died. Cissy had already written to tell Fred. A few days later Fred wrote to say he was now back in Chatham and would be leaving the next day to go to Liverpool to Alf's funeral. He would be staying with Jim's wife Anne in Wallasey. The word's Liverpool and Wallasey had been blacked out but Louisa got the gist of the message. She contemplated going to the funeral as well even though Cissy and Fred had advised her not to go. She was desperate to show her support and she wanted to see Fred again. She knew she was luckier than most about seeing her husband again so soon, whilst so many wives had not heard from theirs for years on end but that didn't help her heartache. Some women she knew had not seen their husbands since the beginning of the war. She decided she would get the train to Liverpool and make her own way to Ford cemetery.

Mary Ellen was shocked when she heard Louisa's intentions. "But you are four months pregnant! Have you taken leave of your senses?"

"I've made my mind up. God knows when I will see him again." She sent a telegram to Cissy and then set off for Liverpool. She was quite used to seeing aircraft flying overhead but was unprepared to see German bombers trying, she suspected, to bomb Crewe. They flew low over the train and she had to admit to herself she was frightened but she remained determined.

However her resolve was shaken when she reached her destination. Despite having read about the destruction described in Cissy's letters, she was unprepared to witness for herself the devastation in Liverpool when she got off the train at Liverpool Exchange. So many streets were reduced to rubble she became disorientated and not sure which way to go. Nothing seemed to resemble anything familiar. Fortunately both Fred, Cissy and John came running towards her and saved her from walking in the wrong direction. Fred hugged her and then scolded her for coming. Before she could answer Cissy had taken hold of her too. "Hello my darling, long time no see." She stepped back to look at Louisa's slightly swollen stomach, "and beginning to show again I see." Fred and Louisa walked arm in arm through the rubble followed by Cissy and John. It seemed Anne was heavily pregnant and was unable to attend. They walked for almost a mile before they were clear of most of the bomb stricken streets. They then boarded a crowded bus and then another one until finally they were outside Ford cemetery.

After the funeral they said goodbye to Alf's widow Ellen. She went away with her own family. Then Cissy, Mary, Fred and his younger brother John escorted Louisa back to the railway station. Louisa wanted to stay the night, but Fred insisted she went home where it would be safer. Reluctantly she agreed. They managed a few snatched minutes to talk alone at the railway station. They found a quiet corner so Fred could explain to her where he was likely to be working. He lowered his voice and she leaned closer to him to catch what he said. "The navy are finding all kinds of jobs for me ashore, and I have been spending it mostly in Staines, but there is a chance I may be sent to help out in Lowestoft."

"Is Lowestoft far from Staines? I don't know that coast line very well, I know it is in Suffolk though."

Fred nodded. "There will be transport available for me but no doubt I will have to get up early. It will be interesting to work with the men at Lowestoft. I've heard a lot of good things about them. I don't know what job it is they have for me and I suppose I couldn't tell you even if I knew." He longed to whisper in her ear "Gibraltar." But knew it was too risky to tell her.

All too soon it was time to go and on this occasion it was she who hung out of the train window waving goodbye. She was satisfied that at least she had seen her husband. It had been good to catch up with Cissy, Anne and John too despite it being an unhappy event. She was upset that she couldn't stay longer but deep down she knew that she would be a burden to her husband and his siblings. It was difficult enough for them all to cope with the death of their brother and what had happened to their home city. She knew they would find it heartbreaking to find their way back through the forlorn city to their lodgings. John had to report back to his unit the next day, and Fred had to report back to the Royal Naval Base. Mary too had to get back to work. She refused to tell anyone where she was going so they accepted that she couldn't tell them. Jim had been unable to get leave for the funeral and neither had Tommy or Bob.

So two weeks later Louisa wasn't surprised to receive a letter from Fred to say that he had completed the job that he had been asked to do, and that soon he would be ready to go back to sea. Just a couple of more days working ashore then he was leaving Chatham. She guessed from his wording in the letter despite a few black lines on the paper that he was about to leave again for Sierra Leone.

At the end of October she had some cheerful news from Wallasey. Fred's oldest brother Jim and his wife Anne now had a baby boy. They were going to call him Alfred. "I will write to Fred to tell him the good news, though I expect Jim will have written to him too! Still belt and braces as they say! She had little contact with Fred over the next few months and was unsure if her letters had reached him at all. Communications seemed to get more erratic and sometimes Louisa would go months without a letter and other times she would get three in the same day.

The day after Christmas day she and her family listened to the wireless to hear that a submarine had been sunk by an Italian torpedo boat. Little did she know until much later that the submarine was the P48 and that Fred's youngest brother Edward had been killed.

Chapter Twenty Four

1943

A telegram from Cissy during the middle of January confirmed that Edward had been killed at sea. He had been serving on board a submarine that had been due to report at another location on fifth January but had failed to make contact. The Navy believed the vessel to be the P48 that had gone missing on Christmas day. An Italian torpedo boat 'the Ardente' was responsible for destroying the P48 and it was itself destroyed after a collision with one of its own Italian destroyers called 'Grecale'. Cissy had informed her brothers and Mary of the news but was unsure if Mary had received her letter as she had not heard from her sister for quite a while.

Devastated to hear the news Louisa wrote to Fred to commiserate and also to Cissy, Anne and Ellen. She hoped and prayed that no more bad news would come her way. The war was having a terrible effect on everyone and life was grim. Even though she knew that living in Pandy was much safer than other parts of the country, she and many others longed for the safe return of their loved ones.

A glimmer of hope that the war may end soon came to their attention in February. They heard excitedly that one of Hitler's greatest armies had been defeated in Stalingrad. Louisa was listening to the news with her mother and father when they heard about the Soviet Government's announcement that the German 6th Army at the port of Stalingrad, in southern Russia had fallen.

"Well that victory is probably due to Joe Stalin's command." Said William. "Let's hope this is a turning point. Hitler is not going to like the fact he has lost so many men. My only regret is that so many men have lost their lives due to that idiot's wickedness."

The next day it was revealed that the Russians had taken thousands of German soldiers as prisoners. It was also reported that many of them were so weak as a result of lack of food and warmth that they were likely to have been unfit to fight.

"Probably suffering from malnutrition." William commented. "You can't expect any man to fight in sub-zero temperatures with hardly anything to eat. Hitler should have taken heed to what happened to Napoleon's army in Russia during the 1815 revolution. His army starved to death from cold and hunger, and I daresay frostbite too." He shook his head sadly. "What a waste of life. So many men sacrificed on both sides."

"The fact that they surrendered and didn't fight to the death suggests that perhaps the Germans are fed up of the war too," observed Louisa.

"You could be right." William stared at his daughter thoughtfully.

Meanwhile Louisa's pregnancy was advancing and on the twenty fifth of March she gave birth to another little girl. They had agreed earlier on a name and so Louisa wrote to Fred to say that 'Susan had arrived safe and well.' It was well into May before she got a reply and it was very brief. He sent his love and hoped to see her soon. He was unable to say much more and Louisa knew why.

Reports on the wireless continued to comment upon the battles on the Atlantic. She shuddered when she heard that twenty seven merchant ships had been sunk by German U boats. She began to wonder that if the merchant ships had been lost, then how many escort ships in the convoy would be lost too. Both her mother and father told her not to worry but she knew that they too were worrying.

They took some comfort from the news on the wireless that Germany had lost high numbers of their U-boats in the Atlantic. So when Admiral Karl Donitz finally withdrew what was left of the German fleet from the Atlantic, Louisa and her family were ecstatic. This information was met with great joy in Britain and Louisa hoped that maybe Fred would be due some leave.

However Louisa's hopes of seeing her husband soon, were dashed when she received a letter from him to say that he was now on a different ship elsewhere in the world and didn't know when he would be home.

"Well at least he is safe." She told her mother. Mary Ellen nodded her agreement. "I wish we had news of Harry and Arthur." She sighed as she got on with her knitting. Louisa wrote to Fred to say that Susan and Christine were growing fast. She also informed him that the vegetable patch was doing well and they were managing to eat enough food, even though sausages were now on ration.

Before the month of May was over they heard an announcement on the wireless that German and Italian forces in North Africa had surrendered to the Allies. As the summer progressed the nation were informed that the combined forces of the British and the American armies had also managed to gain the upper hand in Sicily. It was reported that the allies were making encouraging progress across Italy forcing the German tanks to retreat. This news helped Louisa and her family to be more hopeful that the war would end soon.

However at the end of July there was a mixture of both heartening and disheartening developments. It was reported that Mussolini had escaped capture and had fled to Northern Italy. Meanwhile the Italian and German armies in the south of Italy had surrendered. It was hoped that soon the rest of Italy would capitulate and they would recapture Mussolini.

"Maybe the tide is turning now." William said. "And not before time."

At the beginning of August Gladys called to see them with her two children and reached into her shopping bag to show them two bars of chocolate and two oranges. "Look what the Americans have just given me," she said delightedly. "I've just been in town and as I walked past the butter market a few American soldiers came out and bumped into the children. They apologised and gave these to me. The butter market has been requisitioned you know. They use it as their canteen."

They shared out the chocolate and oranges between them. "I will take some of this chocolate for my mum. What a nice change."

"Which part of America are they from? Do you know?" Louisa asked as she sucked on an orange segment.

Gladys laughed. "I didn't think of asking, but they have got funny accents. They kept calling me Mam."

"They must be the ones billeted at Acton Park. I heard Nora say that they were from a variety of States. I think she said Ohio and West Virginia." Louisa said.

"There are also some from Kentucky and Indiana." Mary Ellen added. "I saw all their tanks and stuff in Smithfield when I went with your father last week to the beast market. Ethel Roberts was there too and she told me she had been to one of the parties at Acton school and had danced with some of the soldiers. She was quite excited about it. Apparently the soldiers are from two different battalions. There is the American 33rd Signals Construction Battalion and the other one is the 400th Armoured Field Artillery." Mary Ellen looked pleased with herself that she could impart this information.

"Do they have parties all the time then?" Gladys said excitedly.

"The WVS have organised a few for them to welcome them to Wrexham. I have helped them with the food but I haven't actually attended the parties." Louisa said. "I don't think Fred would like it if he knew I was dancing with the American soldiers."

Gladys nodded her head ruefully. "I don't think Arthur would either."

In September, Arthur himself arrived for a much needed rest. He had a week's leave. He slept almost solidly at home for two days before he visited his parents and sister in Pandy. Both Mary Ellen and Louisa fell upon him as he came through the door and cried tears of joy. Gladys stood behind him in the doorway smiling whilst Brian and Maureen ran around with Christine. Eventually they let him go and Arthur sank into a chair.

Over a cup of tea Arthur related to them where he had been over the last few months. It turned out that he had been in Sicily fighting with the Americans to try to force back the Italians and Germans.

"Dear God." Mary Ellen said wiping the tears from her eyes. "We heard some of the reports on the wireless. Somehow I knew you were there."

Arthur grimaced. "It wasn't pleasant. The Americans were terrific, they came from one direction and we came from the other. A lot of German troops got away though, and took Mussolini with them." He slurped his tea. "There's still a lot to do before we win this war."

"Will you have to go back to Italy?" Louisa asked.

"I don't know, but I can't tell you anyway." He looked into Louisa's eyes. "How's Fred? He was on the Atlantic last I heard."

Louisa stared at her brother incredulously. "How did you know?

Arthur shrugged. "You know I can't tell you that. Besides the bits of information I pick up is usually second hand and so I can't always rely on it."

It was Louisa's turn to shrug before she continued speaking. "Now that things are quieter on the Atlantic I thought he would be home for a bit. He hasn't seen Susan yet."

Arthur studied his sister kindly. He didn't want to worry her, but he knew that despite things being a bit safer on the Atlantic there was no place for complacency. For all he knew Fred could still be in danger of being hit by a mine.

He decided to play safe and be non-committal. "They could be patrolling the channel looking out for mines and shooting down planes. We've a lot of convoys patrolling the English Channel searching and attacking. He's probably on one of those new destroyers in a convoy. Sometimes you get no time to write and when you do it's hard to know what to write to get past the censors. I suppose you and Fred have some kind of code?"

Louisa nodded and smiled ruefully. "Such as it is."

Gladys who had been quiet for some time now and was looking as if she had some secret suddenly couldn't hold back any more. "Arthur's a Sergeant now!"

Arthur grinned and caught his sister's and mother's astonished expressions. "I wondered when you would blurt that out Gladys!" He turned towards his mother grinning. "I'm wearing Fred's suit today so you can't see my stripes."

"Is it your suit or Fred's?" Mary Ellen asked beaming proudly at her son.

He laughed. "It's mine when he's wearing it and it's Fred's when I'm wearing it. I hear he took you all to see Aunt Nancy last summer. Maybe we can all go again tomorrow if you like. I've got fuel."

"That would be nice but I think she is spending more and more time at the military hospital in Oteley. I suppose you could call at the hospital on the way to Ellesmere to find out. Perhaps you and Gladys could take Dot and the two boys, to cheer her up. We haven't heard anything from Harry."

"That's a good idea. With a bit of luck we will overcome the Japanese soon." He said darkly. An angry expression fell over his face and it remained smouldering there for the next

387

few days. Just before he left to return to his unit he managed to pull Louisa aside to talk to her. He wanted to warn her that some prisoner of war camps were known for brutality. "But we must be strong for Mother and Father's sake as well as Dot's." He hugged her and Louisa held back the tears she longed to shed for her husband and two brothers.

Towards the end of October Louisa received a letter from Fred who said he was thinking of learning another language but the language he had chosen had been blacked out so she was none the wiser! He also complained of mail being delayed and black holes in it when he got it! She wrote back and told him she was getting black holes in her letters from him too and that they were often out of sync! She gauged from his letters that he was no longer escorting ships to Sierra Leone so she guessed that Arthur's suggestion that he was engaged in patrolling the seas closer to home was probably correct.

Another letter from Anne in Wallasey practically confirmed that he was patrolling the Channel and the North Sea as well as the Mediterranean. Apparently Fred had stayed with Anne in Wallasey when his ship had docked for a refit and he had been given twenty four hours leave. Reading between the lines of Anne's carefully worded letter Louisa was able to fathom that Fred was engaged in work closer to British shores, and had managed to get a twenty four hour leave twice over the last few months where he had stayed with her in Wallasey. He had told her how he had been pleased to see little Alf and that he longed to see his own new baby Susan as well as Christine and Louisa.

"Well at least he is safe." Mary Ellen said when she read the letter that Louisa passed to her. "Do you think she is trying to hint that he is patrolling the seas as far as the Mediterranean? It might be that Fred is learning Spanish."

"It might be, but don't they speak Spanish in Sierra Leone?" Louisa frowned. She wasn't sure.

"I don't suppose he will be home for Christmas." Mary Ellen sighed.

Louisa shook her head sadly. "I don't think so. It would be nice for him to be here for Susan's first Christmas. Not that there is much Christmas food and drink to be had."

"We have been promised a chicken for our dinner, and we have plenty of potatoes, parsnips and carrots in the garden. Your father has worked hard to give us vegetables. I think he said there were a few sprouts too. He's promised some to Dot and Gladys. And we can have some jam tarts and custard." Mary Ellen said to cheer her up. "We are quite lucky here actually living in the country, when there are so many food shortages in the cities. Some poor souls don't even have proper homes let alone any gardens. Are you helping with the evacuees Christmas party again this year?"

Louisa agreed. "Yes we are lucky, and yes I am helping with the children's party. If you can look after Christine and Susan next Saturday, I will go down to the church hall and take what I can to help feed them. I will also cut down some holly and take that to decorate the place."

"Are you going to do what the Ministry of Food suggested on the wireless and paint some pinecones with white paint or whitewash?"

Louisa laughed. "I suppose I could try it, and didn't they suggest Epsom salts to dip the holly in? Apparently it makes it sparkle when it dries. Ha. Ha. I'll take Christine with me to the bluebell wood to see if I can find some cones. They might not dry out in time though. That reminds me. I must take that pile of old newspapers with me so the children can help with making paper chains. At least it looks festive with the chains hung up in the church hall. We can make some paper hats too."

The day of the children's party was two days before Christmas. Louisa joined Dot with her two little boys Gordon and Malcolm and they ran about the hall playing together. Christine joined in with their fun and soon many of the younger evacuees were playing with them. Susan had been left at home with Mary Ellen which was just as well as one of the women evacuees went prematurely into labour. Louisa assisted Nora and Agatha to get the frantic young woman to a side room to help her with the birth. Neither Nora nor Agatha had been trained in mid-wifery. They knew a few basic principles, but just like Louisa all three of them had given birth. Louisa asked Dot to go for Matilda the midwife.

"I hope it's not too late for that Louie." Nora said. "Look at her, I think she is going to give birth any minute now."

Agatha was trying to calm the young woman Eileen down. She was crying out with pain and the sweat was running down her cheeks. Louisa and Nora held her legs on to a blanket on the floor and tried to make her comfortable. Eventually the head of the baby emerged just as Matilda arrived and she calmly took over the situation. Louisa hunted for towels and brought them back for Matilda just in time to see her deliver a healthy little boy. She laid him on the clean towels and after wiping him down handed him to his mother.

Eileen smiled weakly at her son and smiled her thanks to Matilda then looking up caught Louisa's eye. "Thank you." She whispered. "Thank you." She whispered again acknowledging Nora and Agatha. Tears ran down her face and all of them felt emotional as they looked down at the healthy little boy.

"What are you going to call him?" Matilda asked.

"Bernard after his father and James after mine. I hope we will see them both soon."

She gazed at her son whilst the small group of women inwardly held the same longing for their menfolk away at war. Presently Matilda suggested that the three women return to the children's party as she would attend to Eileen and organise getting her and the baby home. So when the trio reappeared in the main hall, all the children were being called to sit down at the two lines of trestle tables. Each table had been laid out with homemade Christmas crackers alongside the food donated by various people. Louisa noticed that quite a few American GI's were present and they good naturedly mingled at the tables with the children. When the meal was over each GI produced large bags of boiled sweets and handed out a few sweets to each of the excited children. Christine had two sweets in each hand and showed her mother her booty in delight. Louisa marvelled at how her daughter knew instantly that it was something nice to eat. There were more edible surprises for the WVS. The

Americans had brought butter and tins of fruit as well as bars of chocolate.

"It's a small token of our gratitude for giving us such a welcome. It means a lot to have a bit of Christmas when we are so far away from home." One of the GI's commented. The others agreed wholeheartedly. In total there were eight GI's. They had contacted Agatha at the refugee centre in Hill Street when she was sorting out crockery and decorations for the Christmas party. They had donated the much sought after sugar and butter to make cakes for the party and Agatha had invited them along not thinking that they would accept. However only four were of the original eight she had spoken to, she realised that they couldn't get leave. The Americans made excuses for their comrades and kept saying they were rehearsing but wouldn't say any more about what they were rehearsing for nor what they were actually doing.

"We must give some to Dot and Gladys." Mary Ellen said beaming as she saw the tins of peaches and pears that Louisa had brought home.

"Well Dot was already there and has had her share, but we can give some to Gladys. She was unable to come because Brian has a cold and she didn't want to leave him with her mother and Maureen. Actually Christine, Malcolm and Gordon shouldn't really have been there, but Dot and I were needed to help. As it turned out I helped someone to give birth to a little boy."

Ellen looked up from examining the chocolate and butter with surprise. Louisa explained to her mother what had happened.

"A fine time to have a baby." Ellen commented wryly. She laughed. "Was it her first?"

"No her second. The other one is six years old and was running around playing when his brother made an appearance into the world." Louisa laughed. "Matilda organised some transport to take them all home. The house where they are staying is on Ruabon Road so it wasn't far to go. There are two other mothers and their young children living there so she won't be short of someone to look after her. The two other women work at the ROF but they work shifts. And from what I can gather Eileen has been helping look after their children as well as her own little boy."

"That's good. So she won't be alone over Christmas."

"Speaking of Christmas, mother, some of the WVS women have invited one or two GI's to their homes for Christmas dinner. They seemed so excited at spending Christmas day with a family, I was wondering whether we could do the same? What do you think?"

Mary Ellen looked at her daughter's earnest expression and felt it was the least thing they could do to show their gratitude to the Americans so far away from home.

"I suppose we could manage, we will just have to roast more potatoes to make the meal go round. And we have this tinned fruit and butter and chocolate with which I'm sure we could make something nice." She hesitated. "You don't think Fred would mind?"

Louisa shook her head. "Of course not. I'm sure he would think it was the right thing to do. Dot is going to invite some too, and I'm sure Harry wouldn't mind. She will be spending it with her grandfather and her parents."

In the end Louisa invited two of the GI's to their family Christmas meal. When they arrived early on Christmas day, the American GI's brought even more food to the table. Mary Ellen, Louisa and William were overwhelmed by their generosity. Yet the Americans said that they were honoured to have been invited. Louisa's family and the soldiers as well as the children enjoyed their Christmas meal especially with the contributions of chocolate. Afterwards the appreciative American soldiers played with Christine and Susan. Both soldiers had small children of their own in America, and after they had gone Louisa was glad that she had invited them to share her family at Christmas.

They left just as it was getting dark so that they could find their way back to camp without fear of being lost or knocked over by passing vehicles. No sooner had they gone when Dorothy arrived with Frank. They too brought foodstuffs and their table was heaving with traditional food. "This really is like Christmas." Louisa said as she hugged her sister and got a slight whiff of a pungent smell emanating from Dorothy's coat that she assumed would be cordite. She looked at her sister who though she was smiling looked very tired. Frank looked even more exhausted. Dorothy lifted Christine up and gave her a hug. "We only have twenty four hours and then we have to get back. We will have to get up early because we don't know what the transport will be like. We may end up hitching and walking." She laughed as she put Christine down and then picked up Susan who was crawling around trying to pull herself to her feet as she stretched her little hands out to various chairs to hang on to. Frank sat in a chair and warmed his hands on the fire. He looked as if he was about to fall asleep. William gave him a small glass of whisky. "I kept you a drop of your own booze and I've just shared some with the Americans." He said to him quietly. He poured the last of the bottle into four small glasses and handed them to his daughters and his wife. Mary Ellen poured a little water on to hers and gaining consent from a nod from her two daughters added water to their glasses. William picked up his own glass and said "Merry Christmas."

"Merry Christmas." They all repeated.

"You can sleep with me." Louisa said to Dorothy. "Then Frank can have your old room. He looks done in."

Frank opened his half closed eyes and smiled sheepishly. "I'm sorry. I'm not much company."

Dorothy put down her glass. "Come on, I will show you the way upstairs."

The next morning they all got up early to wave goodbye to Dorothy and Frank. Mary Ellen wiped tears from her eyes as they set off towards the small railway station in Pandy. Louisa accompanied them to the platform and waited for their train to take them to Chester. As she waved goodbye she wondered when she would see them again. Little did she know that it would be the last time she saw Frank.

Chapter Twenty Five

1944

Just two months after waving goodbye to her sister and her fiancé at Pandy railway station, Dorothy arrived home late one night in a forlorn state just as her family were about to retire to bed. She sank in her mother's arms with unchecked tears as she told her parents and sister that Frank had died of pneumonia.

They all stared at her in stunned silence. Then Mary Ellen hugged her daughter to her as she sobbed out how it had all happened so quickly.

"He had been coughing for a while for several weeks, and I had got so used to hearing him coughing that I took no notice. Then a fortnight ago he had some chest pains and was finding it difficult to breath. He had always been susceptible to chest infections which is why he failed the medical tests when he tried to join up." She paused, speaking between sobs, gasping for breath as she choked back her tears. Listening sadly to her sister struggling to breathe and talk, Louisa mused it was as if Dorothy herself was living Frank's condition. "But the pains got worse and though he valiantly made the effort to get to work every day, he finally collapsed at his desk. He was taken to hospital and he died the next day." She burst into fresh tears and the sound of her sobbing brought tears to both Louisa's and Mary Ellen's eyes.

Dorothy had been so distraught she had been unable to concentrate on her job and had been given forty eight hours compassionate leave. Louisa and Mary Ellen tried to comfort her, but she was heartbroken. Dot called to see her and then Gladys arrived. Both were shocked to see her in such a listless state. Eventually when all her little nephews and nieces innocently pulled her hand to play with them, a spark began to fuse some life into her. She knew she had to pull herself together because production of bombs had intensified and she knew she was needed. The war wasn't going to end because Frank had died. With an effort that was admirable she went back to work. Louisa walked with her to the station and with some misgivings, waved goodbye to her sister returning to make bombs. This time her send-off was to a sad figure in contrast to the happy woman Dorothy had been, the last time Louisa had waved goodbye from Pandy station.

As she strolled thoughtfully over the railway bridge and down the lane back home Louisa saw huge squadrons of the allies' planes passing over and she wondered where they were all going. It was the first of many squadrons she saw flying overhead that she saw every day during the next few days. She was unsure if it were the same planes returning and flying out again or whether they were different planes. At first she thought they may be training, but then as the days went by she saw tanks and trucks filled with soldiers passing the house on their way to the Chester Road. She never saw any one of them returning. It was as if everyone was leaving. Louisa tried to make sense of everything, and was beginning to feel uneasy.

At the end of March, Louisa walked through the town on her way to the evacuee centre. She noticed that everywhere seemed much quieter than usual and there was an absence of uniformed people on the pavements. She assumed the American troops had left. This made Louisa feel even more apprehensive. Over the preceding weeks, those GI's who occasionally came to help had seemed to dwindle in numbers and no-one seemed to be able to tell them why. The GI's had organised a dance at Acton school hall a few weeks earlier and two of the young WVS volunteers had gone along. One of those who had attended the dance was Irene, and when Louisa saw her busy sorting out donated clothes at the evacuee centre, she walked over to her to ask if she knew where all the soldiers had gone. Irene told her that she had been very fond of one of them called Nigel, and was upset that she might not see him again. He had told her at the dance that they were all going on a big campaign but couldn't tell her where.

"Rumours are flying around that we are going to win the war soon." Irene told them all one afternoon a few days later.

"How many times have I heard that?" Louisa said shrugging. "I just wish it were true."

In April Louisa got two letters from Fred both of them dated mid-February. As usual there were black lines on the pages though she got the gist of the letter that he was missing her and looking forward to seeing his two daughters.

He hoped that Anne had been able to tell her he was safe and that he was thinking about her every day. He also said that though he has always liked the sea and ships ever since he was a child he didn't like the reason he was on a ship. He had seen a lot of battles and was lucky to be still alive. This information filled Louisa with dread. It was as if he was telling her that his days were numbered. She didn't even know the name of the ship. He must have told Anne the name of the ship and she had tried to tell her in a previous letter, but Louisa recalled that there had been a hole in the letter where the name of the ship should be. In her head she muttered the words that so many people uttered each day, and there were posters everywhere saying "Careless talk costs lives."

In the second letter he wrote that a Mr somebody from somewhere had admiration for the British Navy and that all free men can bow their head in thanks. She knew that Fred had a lot of respect for the Americans but he was not so keen on the hierarchy of any of the services amongst the allies. Louisa assumed it was probably an American Commodore or such like to whom Fred was referring. Fred had written underneath that whilst he gave thanks for his own life, he was not proud that so many people had died. In his opinion it was murder.

When she showed the letter to her father when he had returned from fire watching duty, he sighed. "Poor Fred's seen far too many deaths on both sides. So many lives of brave young men have been sacrificed to the war effort. It's probably on his conscience. This war has gone on too long and too much has been lost on both sides. That man Hitler and his cronies are too blame. Let's hope it ends soon. From what I can gather the tide is turning. There seems to be a lot of activity in the sky just lately, squadrons of planes flying back and to almost as if they are rehearsing for something big."

Her mother nodded hopefully. "Let's hope you are right."

Throughout the month of May the activity intensified, and in June they soon realised why. On fifth June it was Christine's fifth birthday, and Louisa decided to take her and Susan to see Joan. It wasn't a particularly sunny day, but in any case Louisa wanted to talk to Nora about WVS matters. As she lived next door to Joan she thought she would be able to see both women. She pushed the pram slowly with Susan tucked inside it. Christine walked beside her, along the familiar lane.

It was unusual not to see any trucks or tanks passing by which she had become accustomed to seeing each time she walked that way towards Acton Park. The nearer she reached the camp, there was normally some sound of life coming from the Nissen huts but everything seemed very still. She decided to take a closer look to see what was going on and was shocked to see the fields completely empty.

There was nothing left, save for a few full bottles of fizzy drinks and quite a lot of bottles of beer that someone had left

400

behind. It looked as if they had been stacked ready for packing and then forgotten. Either that or there was no room for them on the trucks Louisa mused. There was also a small trail of stray packets of chewing gum. It looked as if the chewing gum had fallen out of someone's pocket as there wasn't much. She picked them up and stared at the small wrappers somewhat bewildered. What on earth is going on she thought. Anyway the drinks would be useful for Christine's birthday she smiled wryly to herself. Her father would enjoy the beer, so she helped herself to a few bottles, and as for the chewing gum she would put it in the bin. She looked around hoping to find some food but didn't see anything else.

Louisa and Mary listened intently to the wireless the following morning. They thought they may hear something that would explain why the troops had deserted Wrexham. At nine thirty am they heard a report on the wireless that went in some way to explain the departure of the Americans from Acton. They were informed that the allies had landed on the northern coast of France. Not only the allied naval forces but also the air force were involved. It seemed that this was under the command of General Eisenhower

"So what does that mean?" Louisa asked her mother. Mary Ellen shook her head. "I can only think that the Americans are trying to liberate France."

That evening things became clearer and Louisa began to realise what had happened. As she and her parents gathered around the wireless they heard the Prime Minister confirm that the allies had successfully landed behind enemy lines in France. Both by air and by sea, troops had been landed on the

Normandy beaches with the aid of thousands of ships crossing the channel. The intention was to liberate France from the Germans.

"Well it seems the tide is certainly turning now. The war will soon be over." William said. Yet even though he believed this, he despaired when within hours, allied ships were bringing back the wounded and transferring them to ambulances to take them to the military hospitals. They later discovered that some of the hospitals were newly built in anticipation of the wounded in what the press was referring to as the D day landings. News came to Louisa that hundreds of American and British troops badly wounded had been transferred to nearby Penley and Ellesmere. Louisa wondered if any of them would be soldiers who had been based in Wrexham or if Nancy knew any of them who arrived for treatment at Oteley.

As they listened every night to the wireless the War reports informed them that the allies were gaining ground supported by the destroyers and troop ships in the channel. One of the ships had essential radar that was able to signal to the allies' air force their position as well as blast the German snipers and tanks.

"Maybe Fred is on one of those destroyers." Mary Ellen suggested to Louisa. Her daughter merely shrugged hopelessly. Wherever he was she just hoped he was safe. On Monday the twelfth of June she bought one of the national newspapers and read about the battle that appeared to be happening all along the coastline of Normandy which apparently spanned thirty miles. The newspaper referred to the type of various tanks and aeroplanes as well as nineteen cruise ships converted into war ships and Louisa wondered if Fred had been on one of them. She didn't know the names of any of them so she knew it was no good speculating.

"I see they are bringing prisoners of war over here now as well as the wounded." William commented later. "I wonder where they will take them."

Mary Ellen shuddered. "Nowhere near here I hope." She glanced at the back door where William had a box of long nails and a hammer. He started to nail two extra bolts on the door. He caught her glance and said. "Those bolts will keep the Germans out." He wanted to reassure his wife though he knew very well if a group of armed men attempted to break into the house, a few extra bolts wasn't going to stop them. Both Mary Ellen and Louisa knew that too but the extra bolts gave them some small sense of security.

"There are so many tanks in France now maybe Arthur is there too." Mary Ellen said one evening a few days later. Louisa agreed. "He might be. So might one or two of Fred's brothers. Fred has been writing to them but I don't know how often he gets mail from them."

By the end of June, they were exhilarated by the news that the allies had liberated Cherbourg in Normandy and that the army were now forcing back the Nazis as they valiantly thrust through towards liberating Paris.

Meanwhile at home, Mary Ellen received a letter from Nancy telling her that some German prisoners of war had been billeted in a camp not far from her. Mary Ellen looked up in surprise from her letter to tell Louisa that, "It seems the prisoners have been made to work on the farms. Is that such a good idea? I thought they would try to escape."

403

Her daughter glanced up from her darning to ask "Where would they go? Besides I expect the home guard would be watching them to make sure they don't escape. If they don't speak English it will make it difficult for them to understand what is going on." Louisa sighed and then said "ow" as she accidentally stabbed herself with her darning needle. Her mother continued to read the letter and then said in astonishment, "Nancy reckons the German prisoners are so exhausted that they seem to be almost glad to be captured now that they are being fed and looked after properly."

"I daresay." Louisa replied. "I just hope the Japanese are looking after our Harry." She regretted her outburst when she saw the grief on her mother's face, but before she could say anything to soften her remark, her mother offered her more information from Nancy's letter. "Apparently some of the Germans speak very good English. There are a few Italian prisoners of war too, but the ones Nancy has nursed don't speak very good English at all."

"So Nancy has nursed the enemy's wounded too?" She realised it would be a humanitarian deed to treat the prisoners as well as they could.

Mary Ellen nodded. "Nancy won't differentiate between helping the wounded prisoners of war at Oteley hospital as well as our own wounded. She's spending more and more time at the hospital now."

Frequent news reports on the wireless told them that the allies were gaining ground in France, yet just as everyone was thinking the war would soon be over, Hitler launched another air attack on Britain. Everyone said that Hitler was obviously outraged that the allied forces were gaining ground

404

in France. The new attack was in the form of randomly dropped incendiaries that appeared without warning and caused havoc wherever they fell. Later they discovered that they were called V1's and V2's. William scratched his head in bewilderment and horror when he heard about these lethal bombs which made a searing noise just as they fell – too late for anyone to take cover. "They're calling them doodlebugs" he called to his wife and daughter as he listened to the wireless in the parlour. "It looks like Hitler is aiming for the Northern coastline, where our shipping ports are based. Like as if they haven't done enough damage to Liverpool."

Louisa shuddered. She worried about Fred's family in Liverpool, and she worried about the ports, and she worried about his ships. She had received no word from him for well over a year. Furthermore she hadn't seen him for nearly two years. She was fed up of people saying "no news is good news."

On the last Saturday at the end of August Louisa received three letters in the post all of them from Fred. Delivery of their letters had been so erratic that they had started to put a number on the back of the envelope so they each knew which ones to read first. It didn't always work though, and they were so overjoyed to get a communication that they read which ever they eagerly picked up first, regardless of the time span. Her mother caught the radiant smile on her face as she rushed into the garden to read them. She sat next to the wooden shed on a thick log that her father used for slaughtering chickens.

It was a sunny day and as she feverishly opened the first letter she sighed in frustration at the thick black lines across most of the two pages. The letter was six months old and the gist of it was that he was not in Freetown and that he was unable to tell her where he was going. He and his mates had been training hard and despite being worried about what was to happen next, he was reasonably comfortable, though always hungry and missed her home cooking.

The second letter was similar, other than he said he had survived the first battle, and that he missed her and Christine. He prayed that he would live to see them both again and to see his new daughter Susan. Exasperated, yet elated Louisa opened the third letter. She almost screamed with joy when she read that he was in Portsmouth. His ship had been hit, not badly but needed to be repaired and had been tugged away. Meanwhile he was on duties ashore. He asked her if she would like to come down to Portsmouth to see him as he would be there for several weeks. He could not get leave just yet but would probably be able to get a twenty four hour pass if she was there. He sent all his love and hoped she would reply soon. She noticed the date of the letter was twenty fourth August. She dashed into the house shouting "mother, mother, Fred is in Portsmouth." She clutched the letters to her and hugged her mother.

Amidst her smiles, her two little daughters ran up to her wondering what was happening. "Daddy is in Portsmouth." She told them, and Mummy is going to see him on his ship." She glanced at her mother as she spoke, to catch her eye. She didn't need to ask her mother to look after her children, because Mary Ellen had already guessed that is what she would do. There was a look of concern in her eye though.

"Are you not afraid of the doodlebugs? The ports seem to be the targets."

Louisa nodded. "I know but they seem to be targeting the Northern ports." She took a deep breath. "Mother, I have to go. I haven't seen him for nearly two years." Mary Ellen gave her daughter a watery smile and said no more.

Straight away Louisa wrote a letter to Fred that she would be getting the train to Portsmouth on the second of September, she would try to find accommodation at the same bed and breakfast place they both stayed in many years ago "The Rope and Anchor guesthouse" and hoped that he would meet her there at 6pm. If she could not get a room she would still wait for him there until 8pm. If he did not appear she would leave a note with the guesthouse owner to tell him where she was staying.

Chapter Twenty Six

The train journey from Wrexham seemed endless. As usual all the carriages were full of servicemen and women either going or coming from the war. Louisa managed to get a seat for most of the way. From Bristol onwards she sat on her overnight bag that soon squashed underneath her weight almost touching the floor in the guards van. She sat with some other wives also going down to Portsmouth. They chatted to each other all the way which helped pass the time. She had chosen the longer route as she didn't want to change trains in London. Despite having reassured her mother that she was unafraid, the truth was she really was frightened that there may be some more doodlebugs dropping. She said as much to her two companions Edna and Winnie.

"I think Hitler is in a panic now, he is aiming for the ports now we have invaded Normandy and pushing back the Germans in Italy. He has seen what we can do with our floating harbours and ships and is retaliating, but those buzz bombs won't stop us." Edna said.

"What do you mean floating harbours?" Louisa asked.

Edna and Winnie lowered their heads so that they could whisper. "Didn't you know that's how we managed to get through to the Normandy beaches?"

Louisa shook her head in wonderment. "I expect Fred will know, I will ask him when I see him."

Both her companions nodded their heads. "Yes your husband will know. If he is a sailor he will know, just like my husband. Maybe they know each other. Ask him if he knows Eric Brown, he's a stoker, but I can't tell you the name of the ship he's on. It's all hush hush." Edna whispered.

"And my husband's name is John Ellis, he's a stoker too" said Winnie. "When was the last time you saw your husband?"

"Two years ago." Louisa said. "I have had my second baby since then and he hasn't seen her. I have brought a photograph of her and the other one for him." She rummaged in her bag to show them and she smiled as they both said how lovely the two little girls were.

"It was nearly two years since we saw our husbands, but this is our second trip to Portsmouth in the last month, that's how we know so much more."

"I didn't know he was in Portsmouth until three days ago." Louisa said. "I got three letters all at the same time."

Winnie shrugged. "I got two letters a month ago on the same day each one written months apart!"

Edna nodded. "So did I. The post is no quicker in Bristol than it is in Wrexham."

Much later Louisa made her way to the *Rope and Anchor* and was pleased that she managed to get a double room on the third floor situated across the landing from the communal bathroom. It was half past five by the time she reached the small guest house so she hastily washed and combed her hair and straightened her pink cotton print dress. It was faded but the best she had. After washing off the gravy browning, which she had used to draw a line down the back of her legs, she took out of her bag a pair of stockings that she had been saving for such an occasion. Gently she put them on and admired herself in the mirror. She hoped that Fred had received her letter and was able to meet her. At six o clock she went down the stairs to the small reception room and bar and held her breath hoping he was there. She looked around over the shoulders of various people and each time she saw a sailor's uniform her heart leaped only to discover it wasn't Fred.

At six fifteen she decided to go outside and wait in the beer garden and just as she walked through the door she spotted him walking up the cobbled road. In the same moment he saw her and they both hurried towards each other with big smiles on their faces. Fred picked Louisa up and swung her round showering her in kisses. "Oh my god I've missed you." He put her down and put his arm around her waist to steady her as they walked back to the guest house. "I've missed you too." Louisa smiled at him. "I was afraid you wouldn't get my letter in time. I should have waited a bit longer, but I'm glad I didn't because it worked out in the end."

He squeezed her tightly and they walked into the bar to get a drink. "Have you had something to eat?" he asked her. She shook her head. "I thought we would find somewhere to eat together locally because I wasn't sure how long you had before you got back to your ship. What is the name of the ship?"

Fred helped Louisa to find a seat in a quiet corner and then whispered to her. "I will tell you everything in a minute, let me get us a drink and we can talk."

Within a few minutes he returned with a port and lemon and a pint of beer. He took several gulps of beer before talking again. Louisa sipped her drink slowly never taking her eyes off her husband's face. He still had the same dark hair and twinkling brown eyes, but his face though tanned looked thin. He looked tired too.

"You may have guessed that I have been in Normandy since early May. The sixth May to be precise." He began.

"I wasn't sure, but I wondered if you might be, Arthur said that you might be there."

Fred's face lit up interested suddenly in his brother in law. "Have you seen Arthur?"

"Not for nine months, but he told us that a lot of things were going on in all the sea ports. Then early May all the troops in Wrexham seemed to disappear so we guessed something big was happening, but we didn't know what."

"It was all top secret. I have been on HMS Goathland for almost two years, we transferred troops to one of the five beaches on the Normandy coastline. We had thousands of ships and troops ready to take Hitler by surprise, and it worked." He took another long drink of his beer, and looked seriously at Louisa, "but not without a lot of casualties, we brought back a lot of wounded, as well as prisoners."

"So did you come back and forth to Britain a few times then?"

He nodded. "Yes, and we would have returned sooner after D day and probably would have been sent elsewhere, however our ship was needed for another purpose. The Goathland was specially equipped with radar and communications equipment. So any hint of an attack from Hitler our equipment was able to send an early warning to our air force. And as the ship is also fitted with ammunition

411

and weapons we could also provide cover for our brave fighters as they flew over the landing beaches." His eyes locked on to Louisa's face and she gazed at her husband with tears in her eyes.

"So will you have to go back to HMS Goathland and to Normandy?" she asked him unable to keep the fear out of her voice.

Fred managed a grin and shook his head. "I doubt I will be going on HMS Goathland again. We were on our way back to Portsmouth when we struck a mine on the twenty fourth of July. Fortunately no-one was injured, but the ship had to be taken out of service, so we were towed back here and now the ship is in Scotland waiting its fate. It's just as well the French coast is not so far away and that there were plenty of ships to help us out. Since we got here, I've been working on HMS Pembroke and then HMS Frobisher on and off for the last six weeks."

He held her hand as she listened to his story. She realised that what Fred had told her was a simplified version of what really happened and she would have to wait until he was ready to fill in the details.

She watched him drain his glass and she shook her head when he asked her if she wanted another drink. He got up to go for another pint, but not before he dropped a kiss on her head and squeezed her hand before letting go. When he returned she showed him pictures of their two little girls and he grinned at his daughters. From his pocket he produced an old photograph of them when Susan was a baby and Christine was then four. "Ever since I received these from you I have carried them around with me, now I have one that is more up to date" and he put them both in his pocket again.

When Louisa finished her drink they both went out again to find somewhere they could eat and settled into a small place that served a variety of fish dishes and vegetable curry sauces. As best she could, Louisa gave him all the news she had from Liverpool and to tell him how sorry she was about Fred losing his youngest brother Edward. His eyes were full of sadness at the mention of his name, and she knew he felt his loss very deeply. "I'd warned him not to join the navy you know, but he insisted."

"Cissy said that he went into the submarines because it was more money. He wanted to save some money to get married. Did you know that he had got engaged?"

"He wrote and told me, but only after he had signed up. This war has taken so many innocent people. It's so frustrating." He shook his head maddened by it all. "Have you heard from Harry?"

"No. We have heard nothing. We have sent food parcels and clothes, but have never received any news. I hope he is ok. Dorothy tries to keep busy, and Gordon and Malcolm don't ask any more because she gets upset when they do."

Fred reached for Louisa's hands. "Let's try to think positive. I've got some news for you which I hope you think will be good. It seems I have the opportunity to be discharged providing…" He stopped talking when Louisa looked at him in excitement.

"Discharged! Are you coming home?" she blurted out, her face flushing with pleasure.

"Shush, I don't want people to know just yet. It's not finalised and anyway I can only come home if I agree to work in one of the reserved occupations."

"You could work on the farm with my father." Louisa said unable to contain her excitement.

Fred shook his head. "It's more or less understood that I will have to go down the coal mines."

"Mining, oh no, that's dangerous! Louisa's smile faded for a second. "But where?

Fred grinned "Gresford!"

"Gresford! Are you joking?" Louisa started to laugh. "It is a lot safer now isn't it? You helped them to seal it up so that it is safe?"

"Yes, much safer. So what do you think? Shall I come home?"

For an answer, Louisa flung her arms around him ecstatically. "Yes please. Come home. Christine is starting school next week, you will miss the first week but you will be there for her most of the time."

Fred's eyes lit up at the thought of seeing his two daughters. "The time is going so quickly, I can't believe she is going to start school. I wish I could be there for her first day." His face was full of emotion, and Louisa kissed him gently, as he took a deep breath and shrugged his shoulders.

"You will be there for her very soon. You may miss the first week, but you will be able to watch her develop and that is something to treasure. So many fathers have been lost already." It was Louisa's turn to get emotional and they hugged each other and took comfort in the knowledge that they were the lucky ones.

Still hugging each other tightly they strolled back to the guest house for the night where they slept in each other's arms. The following morning, though it was hard to say goodbye, Louisa was hopeful that in less than three weeks, she would have her husband home again for good. On the train journey home she couldn't help smiling and started to make plans for their future.

When she reached Pandy station she practically ran all the way home bursting with her news and flung her arms around her mother. "Fred's coming home soon for good!"

Mary Ellen was startled at her daughter's behaviour. She was peeling potatoes and she had to move her hands quickly to avoid stabbing either of them with her knife. Before she could ask any more questions, Christine and Susan who had been playing in the garden ran into the kitchen to see their mother. Louisa gathered them up and kissed each of them. "Daddy is coming home soon." She danced around the floor with them both clinging on to her neck. She set them down presently and Christine ran back to play in the garden. Susan settled on Louisa's knee and listened quietly as her mother related to Mary Ellen, everything that Fred had told her. When her Father came home from work two hours later, she excitedly told him the same story.

William was pleased that his son-in-law was coming home. "Obviously the government think that Hitler is on the run, and we are winning the war. Still it's not over yet which is why he will have to work down the mines. It's fortunate that he will be working so closely in Gresford."

"What are you going to do about your house? Are you going to ask Joan to leave?" Mary Ellen asked.

415

Louisa bit her lip. "I'm not sure what to do. I feel terrible asking her to leave, where would she go? Liverpool has been devastated, she has no family left and four young children to look after. I'm sure Fred won't mind living here for a while until the war is over. It will be better than being at sea." She caught her mother's expression. "Is that alright with you mother?" She glanced quickly at her father for support, but needn't have worried.

"Yes of course, if you think Fred won't mind. I just feel the poor man would like to have his own home back, he worked so hard to get that house and is very proud of it."

"We will get it back when the war is over. And we can pay you rent when Fred gets back. He told me the government have introduced a new payment of War Service Increments that started on the third September this year. You have to have served at least three years, and as he has worked four and a half years on the war effort, he is entitled to extra payment."

William smiled at his daughter's happiness. "Well good luck to both of you."

The next day, Louisa took her two daughters to see Joan and to tell her the good news. She also wanted to arrange with her for Fred to have a bath when he got home and again before he started work. She had begun to worry about Fred being covered in soot when he came home from the pit. She knew from some of the miners that worked there that the washing facilities were not the best.

"This is wonderful news for you Louisa, I'm so pleased for you." A worried expression fell over Joan's face and Louisa rushed to reassure her. "Please don't think that I want you to

416

move out of my house. I know you have no-where to go and the war isn't over yet." She could see the look of relief on her friend's face.

"But won't Fred want to move back here?" Joan asked.

"He will understand. It is only until the end of the war. It should be safe for you to go back to Liverpool then. The government will have to re-house you." Louisa said.

"It will take time to reconstruct that mess." Joan said. "Every part of Liverpool I knew has been affected and what is left standing will probably have to be demolished. It could take months if not years to rebuild the city."

Louisa sighed. "I suppose it will take a long time, and all those men who come home from the war will need somewhere to live too."

"And jobs." Joan said. "Maybe that's why the government have started discharging service men and women now to avoid a mass influx of unemployment." She looked at Louisa. "I think it could be at least another two years before I can think of returning to Liverpool even if the war is over by the end of this year. Maybe I should start looking for alternative accommodation to rent in Wrexham."

Louisa took hold of Joan's hands to reassure her. "Don't distress yourself over this, we have to help each other in times like this. We will manage somehow. Take your time, we will help you find somewhere."

Joan looked as if she was about to cry with gratitude. "I have an idea though. Fred will need a bath when he finishes his shift. How about he comes here first to clean up before going home to see you?" Seeing Louisa's expression of doubt, she rushed on. "It is the least I can do and you know it makes sense. Your parents won't want Fred bringing coal dust to their lovely clean kitchen and demanding pans of hot water every night. Let me do this for you. You have been so kind to me."

Louisa could see that it was a good suggestion and it was a good compromise that she felt sure her husband would welcome. The pit was a two mile walk to their house on Chester road but he could cycle there quite easily and then cycle back to Pandy. And depending on the time of his shifts during the day she could walk across to meet him. Maybe he could get his old motorcycle to work again. She wasn't sure though if he could get fuel.

When she told her mother, Mary Ellen thought it was a good plan and confessed to Louisa that she had been worried about the soot and how Fred would be able to clean himself up. She knew that her neighbours had to boil a lot of water and put it in a bath tub in front of the fire. They also had to close, and in some case lock the doors to give some privacy to the bather. Louisa said she had been anxious about that too and didn't want Fred to feel embarrassed. So that settled, they began to look forward to Fred's arrival.

A few days later Louisa received a letter from her husband. Excitedly she ripped the envelope open and read that The Royal Navy had prepared his documents and he would be travelling home on Friday the fifteenth of September.

"I would like to give Fred a hero's welcome." Louisa confided in her mother after she had finished reading the letter. "Do you think we could manage to put together a party for him?"

"I was thinking the same myself. I could make some sausage rolls if we roll the sausages in thin slices of that National bread then cut them into bite size pieces. If we use up that national dried milk with some water and use our eggs we could make some pies. We've plenty of potatoes and carrots and I'm sure Dot and Gladys will chip in with something. I've made a lot of blackberry and apple jam so we could make some summer pudding with the bread. I will sprinkle it with sugar. I might be able to trade some of our eggs with the neighbours for some extra sugar. I used up most of our sugar ration for the jam."

Louisa smiled. "Yes that would be good. What about beer, do you think we will be able to get some?"

"I will ask your father to get some." Mary Ellen said. She was rewarded with seeing her daughter's face glow. It was nice to see her happy, Mary Ellen thought. They were all war weary now, and though she longed for her two sons to come home safely, it was a joy at least to know that Fred would be coming home safe and well.

"Do you think we should have the party on the day he arrives, or on the next day - Saturday?" Louisa asked anxiously. "Fred might be too tired after the journey, and we don't know what time he will arrive."

"Doesn't he say in his letter?"

Louisa shook her head. "He might have to work on his last day and then travel in the evening. I think we should do it on Saturday. He can have time to get to know the little ones before he meets everybody again. I will tell Dorothy and Gladys to bring their children in the afternoon and we can have a meal as soon as Father gets home at six o clock. I can

419

make an apple pie, he loves apple pies. And we have plenty of apples on the tree this year." Louisa couldn't stop talking she was so excited.

"What about fire watching duties, is it your turn this week end?"

"Yes but Fred can come with me. I'm sure he won't mind. He still wants to do his bit."

All day Friday, Louisa was on edge worrying about times of trains and food and what time Fred would arrive. At half past five she looked through the window in the back parlour for the hundredth time. Her heart skipped a beat when at last she saw a glimpse of a sailor's uniform on the hill by the railway. She flew through the kitchen and called to her mother, "he's coming. I can see him!" She ran down the road, and Christine and Susan who were in the garden ran to the gate to call to their mother. Louisa quickly told them to go into the house and she would be back very soon. Mary Ellen caught hold of the two little girls as they watched their mother run down the side of the house towards the lane. In two minutes she ran into Fred who dropped his bags to pick her up and swing her round smothering her in kisses. Together they walked slowly back to the house.

In the kitchen, Mary Ellen hugged Fred as soon as he got through the door, and despite herself felt tears welling into her eyes. She turned around quickly so that the children didn't see her. Meanwhile the two little girls stared at Fred who had knelt down in front of them. Christine hid behind Mary Ellen but Susan stood her ground. "This is your Daddy," Louisa said smiling. She held her hand out to Christine, "come and say hello."

Reluctantly Christine held her mother's hand but would not go near her father, however Susan smiled at him and said hello. Tenderly Fred picked Susan up and she laughed as his beard tickled her face. He turned to Christine and smiled "Don't you remember me?"

Christine shook her head and Fred looked sad. For a little while he was content to sit down at the table with Susan on his knee. Mary Ellen made him a cup of tea, and eventually William came home and greeted Fred warmly. "I'm so glad to see you back safely. It's a relief to get at least one of you home." A glimmer of sorrow passed swiftly across his face, and Fred put his arm on his father-in-law's shoulder. "Have you not heard from Arthur and Harry?"

William shook his head. "They say no news is good news, don't they?" He put some tobacco in his pipe and began to light it. He looked across at his son-in-law, "let's not dwell on it, we are pleased that you are here."

Mary Ellen and Louisa began to lay the table for their supper, and they managed to keep the conversation light until it was time for the children to go to bed. Fred followed Louisa upstairs and stood in the doorway and watched her help the children into bed. He heard Christine whisper a question to Louisa "is that man really my daddy?" Upon Louisa's nod, she then asked "but what about Grandad, will he have to go away now?"

Louisa laughed and comforted her "no of course not. You go to sleep now." Quietly she closed the door on the two sleepy girls and met Fred on the landing. He looked a bit worried. She hugged him. "Don't worry she will be fine, when she gets used to you again. Remember she was like this last time you were home, and she is two years older now. She's asking all sorts of questions."

"I suppose you are right." He kissed her. "At least Susan seems to accept me!" They both grinned.

The next afternoon Dot arrived with Gordon and Malcolm, and an hour later Gladys arrived with Maureen and Brian. Both women showered Fred with hugs and kisses, and whilst the children ran around in the garden they managed to chat a little while and catch up with the news. They were both anxious to hear about the Normandy landings, and Fred managed to give them answers to some of their questions. In fact Fred was plied with questions all day and well into the night.

Louisa and Mary Ellen needn't have worried about food because neighbours and friends arrived with various plates and dishes of food that they had made especially for Fred's homecoming. So many people arrived that many had to stand and chat in the doorway or walk into the garden to lean against the fence.

It was still a warm sunny day even though it was mid-September. The partying went on until ten o clock and people were still chatting and drinking even as they were putting up the blackout curtains.

Louisa watched her husband proudly, he didn't seem to be tired and answered questions as well as he could. So many people were anxious for news and asked if he had met anyone they knew. When Hilda Parry asked about the troops on the beaches, he held back from telling her about the many dead soldiers that he had witnessed, their lifeless bodies drifting in the water, killed before even making it to shore.

Instead he described the amazing floating mulberry harbours and the tanks that his ship had helped take across to Normandy. He also told of how brave and determined the soldiers were to free France from Hitler's control.

He understood how they were worried about their loved ones still fighting in other parts of the world. He shared their anxieties as he worried about his brothers Robert and Thomas and John as well as his brother-in-law Arthur. There was a very good chance if at least one if not all of them were in Normandy. He had looked for them when his ship had transferred troops from Southampton. However, HMS Goathland was one of three ships carrying British troops to Sword beach. If they had been in Normandy they may have boarded different ships. So when Fred answered the neighbours worried questions, he kept back all the gory details from these kind people who were showering him with food and praise.

"Do you think the war is nearly over now?" Olwen asked Fred anxiously. She had two sons in the army and had heard nothing in two years.

"We are making good progress, it will all be over by Christmas."

Everyone groaned. "That's what we have been saying since 1939." Millicent Walker said.

As it turned out the war was not over by Christmas, however the allies were making such good progress in Western Europe that the British government announced in December that there would be no need for black outs. Furthermore light would be allowed to shine through the churches stained glass windows. The most exciting thing for most was the announcement from the Ministry of Food that for Christmas, extra rations would include extra sugar, extra meat and a half pound of sweets.

In between shifts at work, Fred began to help prepare for Christmas. He collected scraps of wood and cardboard and old cigarette boxes and made aeroplanes and ships for Gordon, Malcolm and Brian. He even managed to make a chess set using scraps of card and oddments from Louisa's and Mary Ellen's sewing and knitting bags. Meanwhile knitted rag dolls, scarfs, slippers and gloves were being constructed in secret for the little girls. By the end of November Fred had also managed to get his old motorcycle working again. He arrived home from work one late afternoon and drove the machine around the side of the house and parked it by the garden gate. He had a look of triumph on his face and was delighted when his two little girls ran out to greet him with surprised expressions on their faces. Louisa came to the door to see what the commotion was about and saw her children excitedly clambering into the side car. Fred winked at Louisa "I will just take them around the block for a ride." He started up the engine again to the delight of the girls and set them down again five minutes later. He entered into the kitchen with his daughters at his heels. Both girls ran into the scullery to tell Mary Ellen about their adventure.

"Well that's a good birthday present. I have my motorcycle working and my oldest daughter recognises me as her father at last."

Louisa smiled at him and kissed him. "And I have made you a birthday cake. Happy birthday."

Since Fred's arrival home, there had been some kind of normality restored to their lives and both Louisa and Fred were able to relax again. There seemed to be an air of excitement and expectancy which lasted to the early part of December. Then the dreadful news was announced that the Germans had launched a counter attack in Southern France. It was heart breaking to hear that thousands of Americans had lost their lives.

"Hitler is aggrieved that the allies are making progress across France." Fred said one evening. "He's retaliating and losing a lot of his own men, as well as killing so many of ours."

As if that tragedy was not bad enough, England suddenly became the target again of further attacks. Early on the morning of Christmas Eve, Hitler launched thirty doodlebugs that bombed randomly on civilian areas that ranged across Cheshire to County Durham.

Fred wasn't working that day and when he turned on the wireless later that morning he was horrified to hear that one of the bombs had exploded in Kelsall.

"There must have been a raid early this morning. Probably one of those Heinkel bombers that can fly almost undetected and drop V2's." He turned the wireless off in disgust and walked outside to the garden and lit a cigarette. Louisa joined him. "Do you think Cissy is ok? We haven't heard from her for a while? Kelsall isn't far from Liverpool is it?"

Fred sighed. "It isn't far, but far away enough for her to be safe if she is still in Ormskirk. But if the Luftwaffe drop any more doodlebugs anything can happen. You can't hear them until it's almost on top of you, and then it could be too late."

He breathed heavily on to his cigarette. "There's not much we can do about it. Have you heard from your Dorothy?"

"Yes, she can't get time off yet, but hopes to come home for New Year's Eve."

Fred put his arm around her and hugged her to him. They stood outside for a few minutes more and then Fred put out his cigarette. "Come on, chin up. Let's enjoy life while we can. At least we won't have to put the blackouts up tonight. Churchill is obviously confident we won't need them. This Christmas could be the last of the war years."

Louisa nodded. "I hope so!"

Chapter Twenty Seven

1945

Early in January Fred received letters within two days of each other from Bob and Tom. They were both safe. Bob was in France still, and Tom was in Italy. Neither had actually said that in their letters, but some of the things they mentioned in their letters gave Fred the clues he needed to know where his brothers were located. The dates of the letters were November. Both had mentioned their wives Margaret and Nancy, and Fred was assured that they had survived the terrible bombings in Liverpool. Bob also mentioned that he had heard from John recently and was well. A week later Gladys came to the house in Pandy waving a letter in front of Louisa and Mary Ellen. "I've got a letter from Arthur. He's safe but he can't tell me where."
Mary Ellen hugged Gladys tightly her eyes welling up with tears. "Thank God." She said.
Later that day when Fred arrived home from work, he and Louisa walked the three miles to see Gladys. Fred asked if he could read Arthur's letter to see if he could pick up a clue of where Arthur might be. After reading it several times he had to say that he wasn't sure but he thought that he might be in France or possibly Belgium. "From what he describes and coupled with what we are hearing on the news, I think he is somewhere on the border of France and Belgium. He keeps saying we are moving forward now after our great breakthrough, and getting close to the border. The letter was

written early January and it's nearly February now, so the Allies will be on the move now. Possibly trying to advance towards Germany." He put the letter down and looked at Gladys, "I wouldn't mind betting that he was in Normandy when I was there."

Louisa shivered. "If they are moving towards the border, do you think they are trying to capture Hitler?"

"Possibly, if they can, the ultimate aim will be to invade Germany and destroy Hitler's army." Fred said. "Let's hope so." He handed the letter back to Gladys.

On March twenty fifth Susan was two and they celebrated her birthday the best they could. Dot brought Malcolm and Gordon, and Gladys brought Maureen and Brian to a little tea party. Everyone contributed to the food and the children ran around playing with Joan's four young children who had also contributed some tiny fairy cakes. She had burst into the kitchen flushed with the effort of balancing a tray of tiny cakes that rested precariously on one arm whilst shepherding her children into the house. The youngest child who was almost the same age as Christine was hanging on her other arm "I hope they have survived the journey, it was a bit of a hazard trying to negotiate the roads and watch the children."

"They look very nice." Mary Ellen had said warmly as the children ran to play with their friends.

A month later Fred received a letter from his eldest brother James in Liverpool, and Fred made a decision to go up and see him and his wife Anne. They both had two children almost the same ages as Christine and Susan. So one afternoon in April he kissed Louisa goodbye and caught the train from Pandy station. Tucked under his arm was a chicken that William had killed so that Fred could take it as a gift. William knew that they did not have the means to grow vegetables and keep chickens where they lived.

The gift of food was well received and Fred had been emotional when he had seen the devastation of his home city. He and Jim lamented the bombing of so many land marks. "Your church St. Francis Xavier is still standing in Salisbury Street." Jim told his younger brother.

Jim grinned when he saw Fred's expression of amazement, "but the sheltering house where you always seemed to find yourself has gone."

Fred managed a rueful smile, he was very fond of his eldest brother who had been more of a father to him since their own father had been killed in Passchendale in 1917. Fred had only been two years of age at the time. As he grew older he often considered it odd that Jim's religion was that of Church of England, and that he himself was a catholic. The Roman Catholic church of St. Francis Xavier was just a stone's throw away from their childhood home so it was a convenient place to go when Fred was a child and he had never questioned it as he grew up and attended services with his older sister and other siblings.

"There's not much left of Shaw Street, nor of some of the large department stores we used to know. John Lewis and the rest are just shells of what they used to be." Jim sighed.

Fred nodded. "I know, I saw a lot of the mess the Luftwaffe made when I got off the train. It all seems pointless, we are doing the same to Germany and the rest of Europe, all because of that mad man."

At the railway station in Liverpool much later that evening Fred bought the local evening paper to read on the train. He discovered that the previous day, the American President Franklin Roosevelt had died. It appeared that he had suffered a brain haemorrhage. The Vice President Harry Truman was to take his place.

"The United States of America will be devastated at that news." Louisa said when she had been informed. "I hope it won't mean that it will hold things back with winning the war."

As it turned out the final battle against Nazi Germany was won very soon after President Roosevelt's death. The allies and the Russians were making major gains across Germany and eventually the Russians broke into Berlin towards the end of April. News of encouraging breakthroughs came in almost daily and everyone Louisa spoke to seemed to be holding their breath desperate to hear the war was finally coming to an end.

When they had heard that Mussolini had at last been captured there was much rejoicing and not much sympathy for the way in which he had met his death. William said that after the atrocities he had committed it was no wonder that Italian partisans had taken the law into their hands and had hung him upside down. The rest of the family agreed, and whilst they all admitted it wasn't a very nice way to die, many people in the war had met worse deaths.

Very soon after this, the nation was informed that Hitler had killed himself. Then on the seventh of May Winston Churchill announced that Germany had surrendered and that the war was over. The very next day was declared Victory in

Europe, and people in the streets in Pandy rejoiced with the news. Flags were waved and the children who had been given a day off school danced and played, whilst singing was heard all over the town.

Louisa and Fred stood at their end of the row of terraced houses and waved with the rest of the residents on their street. Then when a brass band marched past with the neighbours following the band, they tagged on behind with Susan and Christine at their heels. Fred lifted Susan up in to the air and put her on his shoulders. He put his arm around Louisa as she held on to Christine's hand.

"We just need the allies to overcome the Japanese and the rest of the world can get on with their lives. At least we can start thinking of our future now. As soon as I can I will get out of the pit and look for building work. We have to rebuild the country." Fred said. He swung Susan down on to her feet so that he could bend down to kiss his wife. And as she saw the optimism in his eyes and renewed energy surging through his face, Louisa hugged him and allowed her hot emotional tears to run unchecked down her face.

Not far away from her more tears fell as from the doorway of their house Mary Ellen and William watched the procession.

"Let's hope this means Arthur and Harry will be home soon." Mary Ellen said. Her face was puffed and pink with emotion. William hugged his wife to him. "Let's hope so."

Author's note

This book is based on a true story. Most of the people mentioned actually existed with a few exceptions. These are listed below:

All those at Patterson House, Alynsedge Hall, Broughton Hall, except Olive and Megan. Patterson house and Alynsedge Hall are fictitious though a mansion similar to these existed. The events experienced by Louisa in Patterson House actually occurred. Broughton Hall also existed though the people mentioned did not. Again Louisa's experiences there were real. The hall has subsequently been demolished and the land now used as a housing estate. The dairy and the farm existed though the people referred to did not.

The Mining disaster in Gresford which occurred on 22nd September 1934 had a great impact on the mining community in North Wales. The event sent shock waves across the United Kingdom. Any similarity in names of the deceased miners is coincidental. Frederick arrived from Liverpool to help with the rescue. He subsequently stayed to help seal the mine and ironically worked there again towards the end of the war. Ralph Roberts also worked in the rescue team.

The names of those women in the WVS and those mentioned on train journeys with Louisa are also fictitious as well as the names of the GI's. The names of Mary Ellen's neighbours are also fictitious, however some of her neighbours did take in evacuees who found it difficult to settle down in Pandy. Again any similarity in names is coincidental. The cottage guest house in Pandy also existed, the name of the owner is fictitious. The building has now been demolished.

The research for this novel has come from many sources. The war diaries of my father; the information from The Royal Navy concerning his service; Wrexham Leader, Liverpool Echo and stories told by older members of my family both living and deceased and their friends.

Thank you to:
Wrexham Leader
Wrexham Football club
Friends of Gresford Colliery Disaster Memorial
John Lewis Liverpool
Liverpool Echo
Acton hotel, Chester Road, Wrexham
My sisters and cousins for their support

10227971R00256

Printed in Germany
by Amazon Distribution
GmbH, Leipzig